THE AGONY HOUSE

HOUSE

BY CHERIE PRIEST

ILLUSTRATED BY
TARA O'CONNOR

SCHOLASTIC INC.

ISBN 978-1-338-26731-0

10 9 8 7 6 5 4 3 2 1   18 19 20 21 22
Printed in the U.S.A.   23
First printing 2018
Book design by Phil Falco

CONTENTS

Denise Farber stomped up the creaky metal ramp and stood inside the U-Haul, looking around for the lightest possible box. Her mother's handwriting offered loud hints in black marker: POTS AND PANS (no, thank you), BOOKS (forget it), and BATHROOM CABINET SUPPLIES (maybe). She pulled that last one out of a stack and shook it gently. It probably held half-full shampoo bottles, tissue boxes, and rolls of toilet paper.

The ramp squealed and groaned behind her. She looked over her shoulder. "Hey, Mike. Did you get the AC working?"

Her stepdad joined her in the truck's muggy shade. He was a bean-pole of a man, with short black hair and a sunburn that somehow made him look even more unreasonably cheerful than usual. "Almost!" he replied brightly.

Denise set down the box and used the bottom of her shirt to swab her sweaty forehead. "'Almost' isn't going to cut it."

"Yeah, I know. I called a guy, and he ought to be here in an hour or two — so let's see how much of this truck we can empty before he shows up."

"Or . . ." She raised a finger and flashed him her most charming and persuasive smile. "Hear me out . . . we could wait until we have AC, and *then* unload the truck. That way, nobody dies of heatstroke."

"Come on, kiddo. It's still early, and it's not that bad. If we all work together, the job won't take long."

"So where's Mom?"

"Good question. Sally? You coming?"

"I'm right here," she declared from somewhere outside the truck. She leaned around the ramp and waved. Her hair waved too. It was dirty blond, curly as hell, and tied up in a scarf that had no hope of containing it. "Power's still out on the second floor, and I couldn't fix it by fiddling with the breakers, so I don't know what's wrong. We'll have to call a guy."

"We're gonna need a *lot* of guys," Denise observed.

Sally ignored her. "I've opened all the windows, so at least we'll catch the breeze." Her sunglasses melted down her nose, and she pushed them back up with her thumb. "And in that box, over there" — she pointed — "the one marked OUTDOOR MISC, I packed an extension cord. One of y'all two dig it out for me, and I'll go hook up the big square fan. It'll be better than nothing."

Denise shuffled over to the OUTDOOR MISC box and punched the lid until the tape gave way. She fished out a thick orange coil, then dropped it over the truck's back bumper.

Her mother caught it before it hit the ground. "Hang in there, baby. The fun's about to start, I promise."

"Yeah, I just bet." Denise turned away, back toward the boxes. She briefly daydreamed about what would happen if she stole the U-Haul's keys out of her mother's purse and drove the truck right back to Texas, fast as can be, before anyone could catch her. Houston was almost as hot as New Orleans this time of year, and the apartment they'd left wasn't all *that* much better than this new house . . . but Houston was familiar. It had air-conditioning. It had Trish, and Kim, and Bonnie, and everybody else she was supposed to spend her senior year of high school with.

But it didn't have her. Not anymore.

She quit fantasizing and retrieved the lightweight box she'd chosen in the first place — the one that was destined for a bathroom. Sighing all the way, she trudged down the ramp and through the overgrown yard, toward the new family homestead.

312 Argonne Street was all theirs. Such as it was.

Built sometime in the late-1800s, the house was three stories tall if you counted the attic, and it wasn't very wide. It was the only building left standing on the block, surrounded by vacant lots that held overgrown grass, discarded tires, and the empty foundations of long-gone homes . . . if they held anything at all. All the flat nothingness nearby added to the impression that it had been crafted high and thin — a jumble of Victorian rooms piled up like blocks, dripping with gingerbread trim that'd gone all crumbly with rot. Once upon a time, the roof was maybe black, and the siding was maybe white. Now they were both more or less the same shade of laundry-water gray. The front porch was a ruin of peeled and bubbling paint, water damage, and missing spindles. The chimney bricks hung as loose as a first grader's teeth.

If it hadn't looked so decrepit and sad, it might've looked angry — but the Storm had washed away everything except the brittle, aching bones.

Denise stared the place down. Its front door was open, like a dare.

She adjusted her grip on the box and marched up the porch steps like she was going to the gallows, but that was an awful thing to think, wasn't it? It was only a house . . . a big, ugly house, and until she could leave for college, it was home.

Eventually, if nobody died of tetanus first, it would become the bed-and-breakfast her mom had always wanted. She was going to call it "Desa Miranda's" after her late mother-in-law, Denise's grandma who'd died when the Storm came. It'd been Grandma's idea in the first place — to take one of the big old houses that nobody loves, and bring it back to life.

Make it a destination. Put people up and feed them right, that was always Grandma Desa's big Someday Plan. Maybe she didn't plan to have it happen in what felt like a half-ruined neighborhood, scrubbed down to the studs by the Storm, but beggars couldn't be choosers. The houses that were still standing were either rugged, half-repaired survivors, or empty shells full of mold.

But this was it. This was home.

Bienvenue New Orleans.

Denise didn't remember the Storm.

She'd been a toddler when it'd hit. She didn't recall the wind or the water, and she didn't know how high the river had come when the levee failed, or how everything had smelled like death and mildew for months after the fact. For years, even. She didn't know how many days had passed before her dad's and grandmother's bodies were found, but it was at least a week. (She'd heard that much, when no one thought she was listening.)

Now at seventeen, Denise was back in the Crescent City.

She stood on the porch in front of a wide-open door, while the house inhaled and exhaled — swamp breath and rot, soaked wood and rust. Maybe somebody had died in there too. The place sure as heck looked haunted by *something*.

One grim foot in front of the other she crossed the threshold, box in arms, and stared around the foyer. Sure, the outside of the house was bad . . . but at least the inside was terrible.

According to Sally, some guy had bought the place in 2015, hoping to make a quick flip. He'd started a bunch of projects, but then ran out of money and ran out of town, leaving the bank to reclaim the property. He'd also left behind a real mess — floors half-warped and half-new, and fixtures removed for rewiring but never replaced. Ceiling medallions hung at precarious angles. The windows were missing their sills, and the remnants of old rugs had decomposed into stains. Some of the walls were open, wiring and mold exposed to the living area. Soggy plaster fell from the studs like wet cake, and strips of wallpaper curled into scrolls.

Denise sniffed and said, "*Gross.*"

"Don't be so judgy." Mike grunted past her, hauling both the box of books, and the box with pots and pans — stacked one atop the other. He set them down with a grunt, then took the kitchenware to the appropriate room, leaving the books behind. "When we get the place cleaned up, it'll look great. You'll see."

"I believe you. Thousands wouldn't." Denise looked around for a bookshelf, or a table, or any reasonably flat surface apart from the conspicuously swollen floorboards.

She peered around the corner. There, she spied a dining room table set that had come with the house. It was right beneath a hole in the ceiling where a chandelier used to be. All six of its original matching chairs were stacked beside it. Beyond them, an arc of three bay windows bowed out over the yard, offering a semi-panoramic view of the empty lot across the street.

The room was a ruin like everything else, but for the moment, the table was uncluttered and dry. It could hold a few books, for now.

She didn't want to lift the whole box, so she pulled out handfuls of paperbacks, two-fisting them all the way to the table. Some of them were her mom's mysteries, and some were Mike's military or science fiction favorites. But most of the books were hers — an odd assortment of true crime and biographies, plus a couple of nonfiction paperbacks about passing the bar exam. Denise was a good decade or so away from being a lawyer, but she'd found the books at a church swap meet for a quarter apiece, so what the hell, right?

Thirty minutes later, the air-conditioning guy showed up. Much to everyone's surprise, the unit was soon running again, as loud and wheezy as the box fan and only marginally more powerful. It blew the smell of mold and dust around the first floor, stirring the abandoned wisps of curtains and taking the edge off the heat. Kind of. A little.

The AC guy said it was the best he could do, because they really needed a whole new unit. He wished them luck as he collected his postdated check that wouldn't clear until Thursday, and then he hit the road.

By two o'clock the truck was empty — and the house contained all the stuff the old owner had left behind, and all the things the new family had brought from Texas. Once it was spread out like that, it didn't look like much. It *wasn't* much, and the house was about five times the size of their old apartment in Houston. Everything they owned would've fit into two of the bedrooms, with space to spare.

"Is that everything?" Mike asked with a wheeze. Sweat beaded up from every inch of his skin, soaking through his red Texans T-shirt and leaving a dark swath of dampness in the creases of his shorts.

"I think so," Sally said. "At this point, if there's anything left in the truck . . . Jesus. I don't care. U-Haul can have it."

Denise pushed the front door shut, sealing in the feeble draft of chilly air. "Yeah, they can have my half-drunk Coke in the cupholder."

Mike waved his hand. "No, I'll toss it out. I need to clean out the cab when I stop to fill up the tank, anyway. Speaking of, we need to return the truck before six, don't we? Why don't we go do that and you can unpack your stuff upstairs, Denise?"

"Can't I just come with? There's *real* air-conditioning in the car and I think I saw a Dairy Queen on the way . . ."

Sally smiled, but it was a tired smile. "I like Mike's idea. Especially since you haven't even picked a bedroom yet, have you? There are five in total: one down here, three on the second floor, and a big attic space that'll be a great room someday — but that one's not built out yet."

Her stepdad added, "The one down here is the master suite, and that's ours. Go pick out something on the second floor."

"So instead of five rooms to choose from, I have three. Got it."

"That's two more rooms than last time we moved. So go on, now. See what suits your fancy."

Denise strongly considered airing a list of things that suited her fancy, including such elements as air-conditioning and Dairy Queen. She could even add her old friends, her old school, and her old bedroom.

But instead of firing off at the mouth, or collapsing into sobs, or taking a plea bargain for a Peanut Buster Parfait . . . she went the dry route. "Fine. Leave me alone, in a sketchy neighborhood. In a house that's basically condemned. I'm sure I won't get murdered, hardly at all."

Sally said, "Atta girl, wiseass. And for the record, I'm less worried about you holding down the fort here, than when you had an encyclopedic knowledge of the METRO and a boyfriend out in Sugar Land. Speaking of sketchy."

"Aw, leave him out of this." Her ex, Kieron, was all right. But he was just all right, and she wouldn't fight for his honor. They'd broken up months ago, and she wasn't about to let him cause drama when he wasn't even there.

"Besides, the neighborhood isn't sketchy," Mike added. "It's . . . up-and-coming."

Denise ran the back of her hand under her nose, and behind her neck. It came back slimy. She wiped it on her shirt. "If you say so," she surrendered. She was too tired and too hot to push back too hard. "It looks run-down and empty to me. Just . . . *please*. I'm begging you: Bring me something cold."

Sally nodded and fished her keys out of her purse. "We'll see what we can find. The AC and the fan are running, and it'll cool off soon. Come on, Mike." Then, to Denise, "We'll be back in twenty minutes."

The door closed behind them with a creak and a scrape, then settled on its hinges with a miserable groan. Denise knew how it felt.

She waited until she heard her mom's car and the U-Haul pull off the two dirt ruts that served as a driveway, and into the road. Then she pulled out her phone and rubbed it on her thigh until only a faint smudge of butt-sweat remained, then unlocked the screen.

No messages, no notifications. Not even one of those stupid animated emoticons from her best friend, Trish.

But everyone knew she was on the road. Everyone knew she'd be busy. They probably just didn't want to bother her. There was no good reason to feel lonely or forgotten. Yet.

Her eyes filled up, anyway.

She put the phone beside the books on the table, and wiped at her face — but that was a dumb thing to do. The salty sweat on her hands only made things worse. Her vision watered and her eyeballs burned. "Screw it," she mumbled, sniffling hard and making for the kitchen.

The kitchen wasn't very big, but Mike said that was normal for a Victorian house. It was probably somewhat *less* normal to find it outfitted with a bunch of Formica and linoleum from the 1960s, but none of that was any uglier than the rest of the place. It was just a different kind of ugly, that's all.

Denise fished a bottle of dishwashing liquid out of a box. She washed her hands and splashed down her face, then rinsed and blotted herself with some paper towels. Briefly, she was pleased to smell the soap's "spring citrus scent" rather than the house's "perma-stink of old plaster and something dead."

She checked her phone again. She still didn't have any new messages. Not so much as a Facebook thumbs-up, or a Snapchat of Annie's cat doing something ridiculous.

She might as well take a look around.

Denise crammed her phone into her back pocket so she'd feel it if it buzzed, and glared at her shabby surroundings. Exploring was usually a good time, but maybe not here, where she was afraid to touch anything or step anywhere. A very bad feeling in the pit of her stomach hinted that nothing would *ever* be fun in the Argonne house.

"The Argonne House . . ." she said to herself, pronouncing the *e* on the end. She knew she wasn't supposed to, because it was French. In French, it was "argh-on." She grinned, but she grinned *grimly*. "More like the *Agony* House." Yes, that was better.

But Argonne or Agony, she needed to pick a bedroom.

She poked her head into the master bedroom out of idle curiosity. It was pretty big, with old-fashioned wallpaper and a door that led to a bathroom. Besides the foyer, parlor, dining room, kitchen, and master bedroom, there was also an empty room on the first floor. Denise thought it must have been an office and not a bedroom; it wasn't very big, and it didn't have a closet. The remnant of a vintage AC unit was stuck in the wall beside the door. A veil of rust-colored water marks drained beneath it, and stained the floor below.

"Yuck," she declared.

She felt the same way about a hall door that opened to a linen closet, or maybe it'd been a place where a washer and dryer went? It was hard to tell, and she didn't want to fight the fortress of spiderwebs to find out, so she shut the rattling bifold doors and tried the knob to a storage spot beneath the staircase. It wouldn't open, no matter how hard she pulled, twisted, or swore like her mother after a date with the box wine.

Giving up, Denise scaled the stairs with one hand skimming along the rail, and one hand trailing along the far wall. Most of the wallpaper had been removed, but patches of roses and vines appeared where the glue had been more stubborn than whoever had tried to get rid of it. She liked the pattern. She wished it was still there, and still bright and pretty like it must've been, once upon a time.

One by one the stairs winced and squeaked, and every few feet the temperature climbed—ignoring the ailing fan that greeted her at the top landing. It hummed along from its spot on the floor at the end of the hall, blowing manky air against Denise's bare legs.

She paused there, letting the fan dry the damp, sticky spot behind her knees.

Here on the second floor, five doors awaited. She nudged them open, one by one.

The first door revealed a long, narrow room with a broken fan dangling overhead, suspended from a frayed tangle of wires. Part of the ceiling had fallen in, and a broad, shiny stain occupied most of the floor. Denise hoped it was just an especially big water mark, but for all she knew, the place was a crime scene.

No thanks.

The next room was larger, with a broken window and a wasp nest the size of a football mounted in the far corner. She slammed the door shut and leaned against it. Her stomach flipped, because holy cow, *wasps*. One or two buzzed angrily against the door, perturbed at the intrusion.

Her heart pounded. Her mouth was dry. Her house was full of wasps.

This was her life now.

She took a deep breath and twisted the knob on the next door down the line, hoping for something less awful than wasps but not counting on it. She pushed the door open. Pleasantly surprised for once, she let the breath out slow. This room was by far the largest — even bigger than the downstairs master — and it had an oversized window like the ones in the dining room, plus an old brown ceiling fan that looked like it might actually work. But when she flipped the switch on the wall, nothing happened.

"Oh yeah, the power's not working up here," she reminded herself.

Up here, the walls were a light sky blue, and most of the paint wasn't even bubbled up with moisture. The floor was beat all to hell, but there weren't any holes or suspicious stains. Sure, the corners were full of dust bunnies, the bottom right windowpane was cracked, and the tiny closet didn't even have a door . . . but there was plenty of space and a window bench to boot.

Window benches were kind of neat, and she'd take dust bunnies over wasps any day of the week.

Back in the hall, the fan rattled away. Denise retrieved it, and hauled it toward her grudgingly chosen base of operations — but the extension cord stopped about three feet outside the door. She dropped the fan beside her foot and aimed it toward her bedroom.

She left it there, and went to check out the floor's lone bathroom.

All things considered, it could've been worse. There was a claw-foot tub, and that was pretty cool. The sink was all right too — a pedestal with old-fashioned hot and cold knobs, so you could have one or the other, but not both at the same time. When she turned the cold knob, it even spit out water that looked like water, and not like chicken soup. The tiles on the walls were minty green with black accents. Hardly any of them were chipped or broken. A bottle of half-empty liquid hand soap was perched on the sink's edge. It smelled like gardenias.

So far, the bathroom was the real highlight of the tour.

One more door to check, and her survey of the house would be complete. This last door was too narrow by half, and too tall by a foot. The knob was small and weird, and the twisty bit of hardware beneath it turned out to be a dead bolt. The screw turned reluctantly, with a grinding protest. The knob turned too, though it moaned like it would have preferred not to.

The door opened.

A dank gust of hot air belched into the hall. It tousled her hair and curled into her ears, wrapped itself about her waist, and felt around her calves. It tickled the sweaty places between her toes.

She sneezed and blinked hard, then sneezed again. She'd turned something loose into the house, and it wasn't just air — it was powder-fine dust, and particles of mold, and the odor of something that once must have been unbearable . . . and now was merely unpleasant.

The dust and the accompanying stench settled down the steps and pooled around her ankles. It slipped away; it dissipated down the hall, into the bedrooms and the bathroom. But it never quite *left*. It lingered and stank.

The grimy air made her face feel dirty, but she squinted through it anyway. Through the gloom, she saw a staircase so thin that she'd nearly have to turn sideways to climb it — and she was on the small side of petite. Always the littlest one in every grade. Always last-picked for kickball . . . but first-picked for gymnastics. You'd practically *have* to be a gymnast to navigate those oddball stairs without breaking your neck. She quietly thanked all those lessons, and all those trips to the top of the pyramid. Maybe they would come in handy after all.

"So . . . this must be the attic." Another sneeze escaped, before she could cover her mouth and nose. She wiped them both on the back of her hand, then wiped her hand on her shorts and stared at the steps.

The attic door moved.

Denise jumped back.

Maybe it had drifted in the breeze, or drooped on its hinges, or performed some other trick of very old hardware in an uneven house — but it had *moved*. All by itself.

Denise smacked the door shut. It rattled in the frame and a couple of rusty old nails rolled loose, away from the threshold.

She stood there in the hall, staring at the door and hoping her heart wouldn't pound right out of her chest. The house settled, and somewhere far away a board stretched, squeaked, and went silent. She held very still and listened, but heard only the dull roar of the box fan a few yards away. She listened harder, and heard another buzz that might've been the wasps in that other bedroom, or it might've been some other big bug brought around by the river mud and the late summer heat.

Firmly, but softly — like she didn't really want an answer — Denise asked: "Is someone inside the house here with me?" But she didn't believe the silence, so she tried again. "Am I really alone in here?"

Behind the attic door something moved, just loud enough to be felt.

Never mind the gymnastics lessons or her spirit of adventure: The attic could wait.

Quickly, she sprinted back down the hall to her bedroom. She stood in the middle and stared at the box fan, which didn't quite reach inside. Its motor turned with a crunch like a coffee grinder, and its blades did that funny thing where they made every noise sound warped and low, like it came from someplace far away. It was an illusion. It *had* to be, the way the fan blades were spitting out vowels, wide and loud. The way they were spitting out words.

Her chest was tight. Her heart stuttered. And she almost jumped out of her skin when she heard her mom's car pull off the road and up next to the house.

She darted to the window and looked down at the "off-street parking" the real estate listing had mentioned. It was only a space beside the house where nothing was built and nothing was growing, but it was big enough for Sally's old light blue Kia to camp with room to spare.

The car doors opened. Sally and Mike stepped out. And Denise could breathe again, even if she hadn't forgotten the attic door, or the smell, or the sound of something moving just out of sight. She couldn't forget any of that, but she could push it out of her head for a few minutes — because Sally was carrying three bags of Dairy Queen take-out and Mike was holding a cardboard beverage tray with three sodas wedged tightly in its grip.

So maybe the house was gross, and maybe it was practically condemned, and real talk? It was *definitely* haunted. Maybe Denise didn't have any friends at all within three hundred miles, and maybe she'd have to start school in September at a place where no one knew her name, and no one had her cell number. The situation was bad. Real bad. Wasps-in-the-bedroom bad. Crying-when-nobody's-looking bad.

But it wasn't the end of the world, because there was ice cream. It was the thinnest of all possible silver linings, but if there was chocolate fudge on it, Denise would take it.

And to hell with whatever was hiding in the attic.

The next day was a whirlwind of housework and unpacking, of breaking down the free liquor store boxes they'd used, and bagging up the newspaper that had wrapped the plates and glasses. By Sunday evening, the place was almost clean . . . for a relative value of clean. A vacuum cleaner and a dustrag couldn't do much about a hole in a wall or missing floorboards, or the wires that hung loose in their frayed cloth wrappings. But they could clear out the cobwebs and the dust bunnies, and make the place feel a little less abandoned.

Still, there was always more work to be done. On Monday morning, Sally said merrily, "If you've got time to lean, you've got time to clean!"

"Kill me now."

"Oh, come on. It isn't that bad," she promised. "We're making real headway, here!"

"On *what*?" Denise asked miserably.

Mike replied, "Getting ready for the big stuff. The electrician and plumber will come around later this week, but nobody's gonna be taking down walls or anything. We're only planning a little bit of demolition, and that'll be fun. Picture it: pulling down cabinets, whacking stuff with a sledgehammer . . . it's always more fun to break things than build things."

"Says you."

"You'll be saying it too, soon enough. I bet you a trip to Dairy Queen."

"*Now* you've got my attention."

He laughed. "Good, because after breakfast . . . you can come with me to the hardware store down the street. We need a few things before we get started."

"All right. Anything that'll get me out of the house, and I've got a shopping list anyway. I think we need some light bulbs."

Mike couldn't have agreed more. "You're not kidding. Last night we were down to two bulbs down here on the first floor, and we had to move them around from room to room. I burned my finger on one."

"Very dignified."

"Don't I know it. Your old man is a real class act."

She was still getting used to hearing Mike talk like that, calling himself her dad — even in a roundabout way. Sometimes he referred to her in passing as his daughter, and that felt strange too. Not bad-strange, just . . . awkward. Even though he tried to make it as not-awkward as he could. Before the wedding, he'd gone out of his way to ask if it was okay and she'd given him the green light. Why not? It made her mother happy, and the more Denise thought about it, the more she didn't honestly care, one way or the other.

The truth was, she didn't remember her real dad. He was just a smiling man in someone else's memory, a grainy figure in other people's photos. Shorter and heavier than Mike, Billy Farber had been pale as a cave fish, with sharp cheekbones and kind eyes. If Sally could be believed, he was a Saints fan and a dog-lover — a fisherman when money was low, and a street market warrior when it wasn't. If the surviving pictures could be trusted, he was a mean cook who hosted the block's best shrimp boils. He was also a middling musician who never quite got the hang of playing bass, but enjoyed it anyway.

Then the Storm came, and the water took him. It wasn't Billy's fault that Denise hardly remembered him, and didn't love him. She just never got a chance to know him.

Now there was Mike Cooper, and Mike was pretty all right. He could call her his daughter if he wanted to, and she hoped her bio-dad — up in heaven, or wherever — wouldn't hold it against either one of them. If he was as nice as everybody always said he was, then he probably thought it was cool.

But it still felt weird.

When the remains of breakfast had been washed up or stored, Sally wished Mike and Denise good luck and said she'd stay there and wait for the city to deliver the dumpster.

"We get our own dumpster?"

"We're going to pull a lot of garbage out of this house, and it won't all fit in the bin that goes to the curb. The guy at the office said they'd bring a big one around between eight and nine, so . . . you two have fun. I'll stick around and sign for it, or whatever they want me to do."

Denise had her doubts about "fun," but she said good-bye and climbed into the Kia's passenger seat.

Mike got behind the wheel. "The hardware place is only a few blocks away. If I wasn't planning to buy stuff, I would've just walked."

She nodded approvingly. "I appreciate your laziness, good sir."

"I'm not that lazy, but it's awful damn hot."

A minute or two later they drove past a two-story building that looked brand spanking new. The sign outside read RUDY LOMBARD HIGH SCHOOL. The parking lot was big and empty, and a cluster of buses were lined up beside it — silent and still.

She didn't remember doing it, but she must've sighed and her step-dad must've heard her, because he said, "Don't be so dramatic. It looks nice. It'll be a good place to spend your senior year."

"Maybe, but I was really looking forward to *not* being the new kid, for once."

Mike shrugged. "That school's only been open for a year or two. Everybody's a new kid."

"But they're all from the same neighborhood. They all know each other already."

He didn't have an answer for that, but Pete's Notions and Hardware appeared around the corner, so he didn't need one. "Hey look. We're here."

"What's a notion?"

He pulled into a space and they both climbed out. "I think it's just another word for 'stuff.'"

It hadn't been five minutes, but Denise was pretty confident that it was already hotter outside than it'd been when they left the house. She wiped her forehead and looked around: Pete's had an empty lot on either side of it, and a gas station across the street. Both the store and the gas station looked like they'd weathered the Storm with only marginally better success than the Agony House, but there were two older black men on the front porch of the store, sipping beers and chatting about the fat old dog that lounged at one man's feet. It looked like a friendly enough spot, and through the glass front door she spied the glowing red light of a Coke machine.

Mike saw it too, and he knew who he was dealing with. He pulled out his wallet and gave Denise a couple of bucks. "Go get yourself a Coke, if you want. I won't be long, because my shopping list ain't."

"Cool, thanks. But you added light bulbs, right?"

"Top of the page, yes ma'am."

The AC inside the store wasn't a whole lot better than the one inside her house, but at least there was shade. The shelves were stacked high, and everything was crowded on top of everything else. It looked like Mike was right about "notions," because from where Denise was standing, it meant "any kind of junk or stuff that doesn't fit the description of hardware." She saw everything from pet food to suncatchers, bug spray to canned beans.

She homed in on the soda machine, a moth drawn to the lit-up logo.

She needed a dollar fifty to get the bottle of her choice. The first bill went into the slot just fine, but the second one was wrinkled. She straightened it on the machine's corner and tried it again. No dice.

"You want to trade?"

She stopped wrestling with the dollar, and turned around. Behind her, a black guy about her own age was holding out a crisper bill than the one that came from Mike's sweat-dampened wallet.

"Um . . . sure. Thanks."

They switched money, and the new bill went into the feeder just fine. Denise pushed the button for a Diet Dr. Pepper, and listened to the internal mechanisms spin up the selection. "Right on," she said. "Seriously, I appreciate it."

"No problem. And I'm Norman, just so you know."

She tried not to frown quizzically at him, but mostly failed. "Norman?" She'd never heard of a guy under the age of eighty named Norman before, but there was a first time for everything. He was beefy, like he probably knew his way around some of Pete's power tools. Maybe he worked construction in the summers. Back in Texas, she'd known a lot of guys who did that. They always came back to school in the fall looking like linebackers. He had buzzed hair and hazel eyes, and dark skin that showed a little tan line around a bead bracelet on his left wrist. "You don't *look* like a Norman."

"I was named after an aunt."

"Aunt Norma?"

He grinned. "Got it in one. And what's a Norman *supposed* to look like?"

She didn't know. "Sorry, that was a dumb thing to say."

"Don't worry about it. I've heard a lot worse. Are you new here? Haven't seen you around before."

"Um . . . I'm *from* here . . . but my mom and I left when the Storm hit. We ended up in Houston, and now . . ." She half shrugged, half gestured around at the store. At the whole neighborhood. "Now we're back."

"Welcome back, then."

"Thanks. It's been an adventure."

He leaned against the Coke machine. She noticed a camera hanging off a strap on his left side. "Good adventure, or bad adventure?"

"Let me put it this way: The house my parents bought is a *total* wreck. It's practically condemned."

He laughed. "We got a lot of wrecks around here. Wrecks, and a few houses that are so nice, nobody can afford them. But mostly wrecks."

She sighed. "Yeah, we can't afford the nice ones, so we've settled for a crappy one. Maybe if we're lucky, someday we'll be able to make it nice. But between you and me, I'm not holding my breath."

"Aw, come on. With a little time and money, you can fix practically anything," he protested. "There's life in the neighborhood yet, you'll see."

"I believe you, but this house is going to take a lot more than a little time and a little money. If we had a dump truck full of both, I'm not sure we could save it." She paused, suddenly afraid that she was being insulting. This guy obviously lived here. She didn't want to dump all over his home turf. She backpedaled a little. "We'll do our best, but I don't know."

Mike came around the corner pushing a rusty half-sized shopping cart. It was loaded up with extension cords, a massive bargain-sized box of trash bags, a roll of plumber's tape, two big bundles of rags, a pair of scrapers, and five or six boxes of light bulbs. "Hey girl, you ready?"

"That was fast." She reached into the bottom tray and picked up her cold bottle of soda.

Mike glanced at Norman, nodded, and turned the cart toward the counter.

"I'm right behind you," she promised him. Then she told Norman, "That's my stepdad."

"He looks . . . ready to light up half of New Orleans. How big is your house, that you need so many bulbs?"

"Kind of big," she admitted. Then she inserted herself into Mike's sad story about the burned finger. "And we only have, like, two bulbs that actually work. We were moving one of them around last night, from room to room."

Norman shook his head sadly. "That is just freakin' tragic."

She snorted a small laugh, right out her nose. "Like I said, we've got a lot of work to do."

"Anyway, it was nice to meet you . . . ?"

"Denise. Sorry. I'm Denise."

"All right, Denise. Catch you around."

"Yeah, it was nice to um . . . to meet you too. You're the first person I've met, actually. Since we got here." Did she sound weird? She thought she sounded weird.

"Cool. Do I win a prize?"

"My undying . . ." She stopped herself. Her undying what? Gratitude? Affection? Nothing sounded right, so she let it go with, ". . . remembrance."

He winked, and reached into his pocket for some change for the machine. "Hey, I'll take it."

Before she could embarrass herself any worse, she fled for the counter and caught Mike as he was checking out. When they were finished paying, she helped him load up the car. All the while, he very studiously avoided asking any questions. Denise couldn't stand it, so when they were inside the Kia and the doors were shut, she broke the ice. "Since I know you're dying to ask, his name is Norman. He swapped me out a decent dollar for one of your crummy dollars."

"Look at you, making friends already."

"Dude, I'll probably never see that guy again."

"He's a cute kid, though."

She rolled her eyes and leaned her head back against the seat. "Please do not ever call any guy cute again. You're making it weird. Weirder. I already made it weird enough."

"Okay, okay. I'll try to keep from making it weirder. You've obviously got that part under control."

The electrician came around later that day. She went on for fifteen minutes about how ancient the house's wiring was, and how many expensive-sounding code violations they would have to fix eventually—but then she flipped some breakers, tested some wires, rearranged some connections, replaced some fuses . . . and restored power to the second story of the Agony House.

Sure, they'd need another week's worth of electrical work before too long, but hey. It was a start.

With AC now wafting weakly through all the rooms, livable and unlivable alike, the small family sat down to another fast-food meal. They'd cleared out the dining room and set up the left-behind chairs, and it almost looked like civilized people lived there. The sun was going down; there was light enough to see by, but when the shadows stretched out long and low, Mike pulled out a lamp and plugged it in.

They all sat around feeling fat and almost happy, leaning back in those spindly seats and licking the last bits of chicken grease from their fingers, until Sally gestured with a french fry and warned, "You two know it won't always be like this, don't you? Enjoy the junk food now, because I'm going shopping tomorrow. We'll have real meals on a regular schedule, like normal."

Denise asked, "Will we ever get the kitchen to . . . I don't know. Work?"

"Oh, come on. It's not that bad in there," her mother scoffed. "For Chrissake, honey—it's no worse than that place on Elgin Street."

Mike frowned quizzically. He'd never seen the Elgin house.

Denise told him, "We only lived there for a year, after Mom lost that job — when the restaurant folded. It was pretty bad."

"When was this?"

She shrugged. "Not long before she met you."

It wasn't the world's most romantic meeting — trapped in a stalled and sweltering METRO light-rail train, waiting for the service crews to let them out. But love grows in the strangest places, like a bluebell on a cow pie. Or so her new Uncle James had declared in the best man's toast, when he'd recalled the story for the sake of the audience.

"No, it was at least a couple of years before Mike," her mother insisted. "Because after Elgin, we ended up a few miles away, on Burkett — and that wasn't much better, but at least it was clean. After that, we lucked into that place in Old Chinatown. That one wasn't so bad."

"What she means to say, Mike, is that we've lived in some real dumps."

Sally and Mike spoke at exactly the same time. She said, "It's not a dump!" and he said, "It won't be a dump forever!" They turned and giggled at each other like they'd done something cute.

Denise rolled her eyes. "But *look* at all this. It can't be healthy . . . ?" she tried, using a straw to point at the holes, the stains, and the dark patches they hadn't gotten to yet, all of them probably made of deathly black mold. She was sure of it.

Sally said, "We'll make it healthy. We'll do the big stuff first — the rewiring and plumbing, and then the roof. The rest of it, we can do ourselves with some elbow grease."

"And money."

Like her mom needed reminding. The loan had come with funds to fix the place up and trick it out as a proper business, ready to host and feed out-of-towners, but the money would come in bits and pieces, gradually doled out as the house was brought up to code. They could only have a chunk of it at a time. It was supposed to protect the bank from a risky investment, but it felt like a dirty trick.

"We have *some* money," Sally insisted.

Denise pushed. "But is it *enough* money?"

"It's always enough, baby. One way or another. It's always enough."

"Technically you're right. I mean, in the sense that we haven't died of starvation or exposure. Yet."

Mike laughed at the pair of them. "Denise, if your mom wanted to whip this house into shape all by herself, I do believe she could. But it's not just her, all by herself with a little girl anymore. Now it's us, all together. Three adults, more or less."

"Um, I'm eight months shy of 'adult,'" Denise pointed out. "I have eight more months to screw up big-time, and still get off as a juvenile."

Sally shook her head with mock exasperation. "What a terrible way to look at a birthday."

"It's a perfectly practical way of looking at it," she argued.

Mike rose from his seat and wadded up his trash, then stuffed it into the takeout bag. "I hope you aren't planning a last-minute crime spree. When college applications ask about your extracurricular activities, they don't mean armed robbery."

"Courts seal juvenile records, you know."

"Yeah, and I wish you *didn't*." Sally gathered her own trash and produced a plastic garbage bag to collect it all. "Here, give me your stuff. We've sat around on our butts long enough."

Together they picked up after supper, and Mike produced a speaker set for his iPhone. That could only mean one thing: a terrible evening of music that quit making the radio rounds before Denise was born. He hunkered over the screen and scrolled through his playlist.

"Mike, I love you, man — but it's been a long day, and I can't handle whatever weird old stuff you're queuing up."

"Aw, you love me?"

"Well, I like you enough to let you stay . . . but I've gotta go work on my room. Y'all have fun down here, doing the fox-trot or peace-ing out, or whatever it is you old folks do when I'm not looking."

Denise headed for the big box of cleaning supplies in the kitchen. She rummaged through it and made her selections, tossing them into the bucket. She snagged the broom too. She tucked it under her arm and stomped up the stairs, flipping light switches as she went.

It was getting good and dark outside, and after twilight, the second floor hallway was practically a tomb. It had nothing to let in natural light except a small window at the far end, so even in the middle of the day with all the doors open, it was pretty bleak. Once the sun went down, you were screwed without a lamp.

The fixture over the stairs worked, or it mostly worked. It was a square glass shade that housed four bulbs, but only one was lit up. Another lamp at the far end of the hall sputtered and warmed, but it mostly just hung out on the ceiling looking sad and yellow.

Downstairs, Mike found his groove and turned it up, sending shouty 1980s white-guy hip-hop drifting up the stairs.

Denise didn't know the group, and she was entirely unprepared to admit that it sounded kind of fun, so she disappeared into her room. The ceiling fan came on when she flipped the switch. The fan had space for three bulbs in three flower-shaped glass shades. Two of the three beat the odds and lit up on cue.

The room looked better by the dim, fuzzy light of the old-fashioned incandescent bulbs — but only a little. It was harder to see the dust bunnies and cobwebs without the sun streaming in, but Denise wasn't fooled. She still knew that it was the best of the worst, and that was all.

She heard a chime and felt a buzzing in her shorts.

She jumped like she'd been shocked, then fumbled her phone out of her back pocket. "Trish!" she yelped. The text message read: NEW DIGS HOT OR NOT LOL? Before she could unlock the phone for a reply, a second one landed on its heels: y so quiet ru ok?

Her thumbs got into gear, and she hastily replied: I'm quiet? Haven't heard from u since I left.

liarpants, quoth Tricia. Oh wait my phone is

Denise sat down on the floor cross-legged, and tapped back: *ur phone is???*

I have like 50 texts dint go thru sry

She smiled down at the screen. *Thought you didn't love me anymore.*

Then she leaned back against the wall and tried not to think of how grimy it was, or how the plaster was soft with water and mold. She settled down instead and thumb-typed at lightning speed — giving Trish a quick rundown on the move, and the heat, and the house she was now forced to call home. Then she mentioned Norman, named for an aunt. Since he was the only person she'd met so far, and she was running out of subjects that didn't sound like whining.

It was a relief to talk to anybody back in familiar old Texas, even if talking was just keyboard swiping, and trying to win a game of Who Can Find the Most Ridiculous Emoji. Poop-coil in a party hat with fireworks usually won, but Trish showed up with a brown beard smoking a cigar and holding a martini glass, and Denise admitted defeat.

How's Kieron? Is he ok or still weird? she asked as an afterthought.

Not as weird as ur super-proper texts but still weird. I hrd he has a new gurl.

Super-proper, but u alwys understand me. She hit SEND before either she or autocorrect caught the typo, and scowled at it, but she refused to be embarrassed about cautious texting. She'd once read about a court case that happened over a comma in a contract. You could never be too careful.

Did u read me? Kieron has a new um-friend. Like this is my, um, friend.

She didn't really care, but she was curious. *ORLY?*

Sophomore. 2 young 2 no better I guess.

Denise laughed. *She'll learn.*

So tell me about this house of yours its haunted as crap, right

Her thumbs hovered over the screen. She thought about mentioning the attic door, but that'd be silly. It hadn't been anything at all. What would she say? "I opened a door and it smelled bad." That wasn't a ghost story, and Trish wanted a ghost story.

Haunted as crap, she typed in return. *Crappy as crap, 4 sure.*

PICS OR GET OUT

She realized she hadn't taken any. She hadn't thought about it, or hadn't wanted to. Maybe in the back of her head, she was too embarrassed at the thought of anybody else seeing this place, and knowing she lived there. But she really ought to take some in the light of day — for the sake of a good before-and-after, if it all worked out someday. Or to show how narrowly she'd escaped death by debris, if it didn't.

Don't have any.

SNAP ME SOME. DOO EET.

Later, she promised. She wasn't sure if she meant it or not. *Busy right now. Unpacking. Getting my bedroom set up.*

OK BUT L8R

I PROMISE

When Trish didn't respond in a few seconds, she put the phone aside. Their chat had run on long enough, and the phone's battery was low — so Denise pulled the charger cord out of the messenger bag she typically used for a purse. Of the three outlets in her room, only one worked, and it took her a few minutes to find it. She chalked it up to one more thing on the list of Things That Suck About the Agony House.

Maybe she really should keep a list . . . or maybe she should make some effort to have a life, because keeping track of all the house's failings could turn into a full-time job. Technically, she could afford a part-time job. Summer had just begun.

But where would she work? Doing what? The house was sure to eat her life for the next couple of months.

Besides, come fall she'd be headed for that school they'd passed earlier today. It was one of New Orleans's new "recovery zone" charter schools, where she wouldn't know a single soul.

She sat down beside the phone and leaned her head back against the wall. She hated the thought of a new school for her senior year. It made all the celebration of her PreACT and PSAT scores feel moot. Her stellar numbers and top-notch grades had brought some great college recruiters sniffing around, but their offers would all depend on good scores on the real thing and a strong finishing GPA. Would this year be a string of easy A grades, or would it be a miserable slog that felt like a personal vendetta?

Nothing was in the bag just yet. Like her old gymnastics coach used to say, she still had to stick the landing.

She was glad to see her mom happy — she truly was, and not even in a bitter way. It felt like it had been Sally and Denise Versus the World since forever, since the Storm. But it also felt like someone had pitched a grenade into her life now, right when she was finally building up some momentum. Now it was time to start all over again.

"This is going to suck," she told the ceiling.

The ceiling didn't argue with her.

She closed her eyes and listened to the bouncy music playing downstairs, dulled by the floorboards but chipper-sounding all the same. Mike said something, but Denise couldn't make it out. Her mother laughed, and the music played on. They were definitely happy, and that was something.

It would've been really, really great if Denise got to be happy too, but she already knew the world didn't work that way. Sometimes, you had to take turns.

She gave up and got up, and used the duster to swab the fourth corner clean of spiderwebs. One spider took offense, and scuttled across the ceiling — disappearing into a crack in the plaster. Then she took the broom for a half-hearted spin around the floor, but she hadn't brought a dustpan with her, so she just turned off the box fan and swept all the dust and junk out into the hall. "Screw it," she said to the puff of debris as it settled on the floor. "Nobody cares, anyway."

The fixture at the top of the stairs rattled as if offended. Denise frowned at it, but it kept jiggling anyway—like someone was jumping up and down on the floor above it. But no one was up there in the attic, or that's what she assured herself because she sure as hell wasn't about to go look.

The glass shade trembled, and the lone illuminated bulb twitched in its socket. It flared, sparked, and went out with an angry poof.

The hallway dimmed. At the other end of the corridor, the lone yellow bulb was so dull that you could hardly tell if it was on or not. The rest of the light filtered up from downstairs or out from Denise's bedroom. She stood in the doorway, holding the broom and casting a narrow shadow onto the dirty carpet runner.

Without the weak light from the fixture, the hall felt close and crowded.

Denise listened hard, focusing on some faint noise that played above Mike's music, or around it: a low-pitched buzzing, like the sound another failing bulb (or a wasp) would make. No, not that. Not exactly. A vague rushing, like water running from a tap.

No, not that, either.

It was both quieter and more deliberate—and when Denise closed her eyes, she thought she heard a woman humming a song. She couldn't make out the tune, not with Mike's music going to town downstairs, and her mother talking and laughing. They were dancing in the parlor, she thought. Their feet were circling, jumping. Playing hopscotch with the holes in the floor.

Maybe that's all it was, rattling the lamp—only the newlyweds, being happy together.

The discordant humming grew louder, and the song came clearer—but she didn't recognize it. Was it her mother, singing along to the wrong track? She didn't think so. Louder and louder, and this wasn't Sally's voice at all. This wasn't what it sounded like when she murmured a lullaby, or the lyrics to something old and dorky.

Denise opened her eyes and the humming stopped. Just like that.

She blinked hard, and rubbed her knuckles against her eyelids. The weird singing was gone, but it'd left something behind: There, on the floor, in the dust she'd cast out of her bedroom . . . a very distinct set of marks had appeared. They marched in delicate pairs — footprints, too small to be a man's, and not small enough to be a child's. They came from the top of the stairs.

No, that wasn't true. They came from the attic door, and they pattered right up to Denise, stopping in front of her — not eight inches away from the tips of her toes.

No, that wasn't true, either. When she turned around she saw that the footprints kept going, the pointed shapes strolling into her bedroom, tracking the dust back from where it'd come.

And then vanishing.

Denise's gaze went wild, back and forth from the attic door to the bedroom — where there wasn't any dust to leave any tracks, and there wasn't anybody standing, singing a song. The room was as empty as before, and there was nowhere to hide. Only a few boxes were stacked, and those were against the wall. The closet was full of hanging clothes, and it still didn't have a door. "A door," she whispered hoarsely. It was a frantic thought, and she held it like a tiny lifeline of rational truth. "I need a door."

She needed a lot of things. She needed a glass of water and a shower. She needed to assemble her bed frame, unless she wanted to keep sleeping on a mattress and box spring flat on the floor — and maybe she *did* want to sleep that way, just for the night. When the bed was on the floor, there was nothing underneath it. When the bed was on the ground, there was nowhere for anybody to hide — even an invisible, softly singing anybody who left behind a funny smell. Not a bad one. Just a funny one.

Denise sniffed for clues and picked up something sharp but sweet. It could've been the scent of cleaning products, perhaps, or the bottle of shower gel she'd left beside the tub. The bathroom door was open, right around the corner.

She sniffed again.

No, it wasn't gardenia soap lingering in the air. It smelled more like roses, mixed with something else. Some kind of perfume, something an old lady would spritz all over herself before heading to church.

So it could've been worse, right? If you were stuck with a ghost, better a nice old church-going lady ghost than a violent murdering poltergeist. I mean, if you got to pick. Did she get to pick?

Denise glared around the room, silently daring any hypothetical spirits — old ladies or otherwise — to show themselves. She didn't really want to see a ghost; but maybe the ghosts didn't really want to see her, either.

The music downstairs played on, and the ceiling fan overhead churned — stirring the warmish air that was only half cooled by the feeble AC that struggled against the sheer volume of hot air. The house held on to it stubbornly. It was holding its breath.

Denise held hers too.

It wasn't late and she wasn't tired. She had boxes to unpack and a bed to make, even if she wasn't going to touch the frame still lying in pieces along the far wall. For one more night, she could sleep on the floor, couldn't she?

Just this one night, she could sleep knowing that nothing lurked beneath her.

The next morning, Denise came downstairs to Sally talking on the phone with one of the contractors, who was asking her a bunch of questions. "I'm not sure . . . ? Where would I look? Is that important? I couldn't tell from the fuse box."

While she nattered on, Denise joined Mike in the dining room, where he was tackling the mold they had seen the night before.

"I don't even know what to do next," she declared. Despite all their cleaning efforts, everything still felt filthy, and everything needed to be removed, replaced, or restored.

"We just have to keep plugging away," he said. "If it's broken or rotted, pull it out. Throw it away. Start yanking wallpaper — that's one of those things that'll take forever, and you might as well get started now. When you're done with that, move on to that bathroom upstairs. We're going to save the tub, but we have to clean the crap out of it first."

"Please let it be figurative crap, and not literal crap."

"I doubt anyone's been crapping in the tub, honey. It's just dirty as hell. We'll get some enamel repair stuff later. I'll put it on the list for our next trip to the store. But those shelves behind the tub are awful. Get a sledgehammer and take them down. While you're at it, let me know when you want to wreck the vanity. None of that stuff is original, and it's all too gross to keep."

"Why do I have to let you know before I sledge the vanity?"

"Because I'll need to turn off the water first. You smash it now, and you'll get a geyser — so please . . . *don't.*"

Resigned, Denise collected the cleaning supplies and grabbed a bucket. "Fine. I'll see what else can be done about my room, and then I'll move on to the bathroom."

"Thanks, trooper."

She felt more like a hostage than a trooper, but if she was going to be trapped in this place, she might as well clean it up. The only thing worse than being stuck in a craphole was being stuck in a dirty craphole.

She still didn't know where to start. She needed a plan of attack. Maybe there was more to be done on her bedroom? She could check the closet, which was full of . . . she wrinkled her nose. Spiderwebs, mostly. She'd gotten all four corners with the broom, but not the closet.

Back downstairs she went, and found the Shop-Vac, which would probably work better than a broom. Loudly she announced, "This Shop-Vac is coming with me!" because she didn't know where either of her parents were.

From the kitchen, her mom yelled, "Good to know!" Then she went back to her phone call.

Mike was outside. She saw him through the sidelight windows that flanked the front door. He was directing a truck that was hauling the dumpster, which should've arrived yesterday, but at least it'd arrived eventually.

There was no one else to protest, so the Shop-Vac was officially hers. For now.

It was a pain to get it upstairs, but it was 100 percent worth the trouble. The tall nozzle end reached up into the corners to get the very last of the dust bunnies and cobwebs, and she used the wide head attachment to do a proper job of vacuuming — probably the first one the room had gotten in years.

When she was done, the floor felt less like sandpaper and more like wood, and the last of the creepy footprints were completely gone. Like they'd never been there at all.

(It was easy to pretend they'd never been there at all.)

She was just thinking that the wallpaper was too daunting, and it might be time to move on to the bathroom, when Sally knocked on the doorframe. "Heads up," she called. "You have a visitor."

She frowned and put her hands on her hips. "I have a what-now?"

"You heard me." Over her shoulder, she added, "Come on in, honey. Denise, this is Terry Jones. He's our neighbor, down the street."

Her visitor was a freckled white boy with a glorious red 'fro. He was a little shorter than her, and a little heavy. "Hi, Denise!" he said perkily. "I'm Terry. Terry Jones. Your neighbor."

"I . . . yeah. I remember. From just now. When my mom said it."

Terry was wearing a sweaty yellow T-shirt and cargo shorts with sagging pockets. "I wanted to introduce myself, that's all. Since we're neighbors and everything."

"It's um . . . it's nice to meet you," she told him.

"Likewise." He was angling to get a good look at her room, and being none too discreet about it.

She sighed. "You can come on in, if you want."

Sally made a quiet exit, and Terry strolled inside, his flip-flops slapping loudly on the floor. Over his shoulder, he lugged a large backpack that bowed his posture with the weight of its contents.

"Man, would you look at this place!" he announced, or exclaimed, or maybe he just said everything like it thrilled him.

"Yeah, check out my five-star accommodations." She didn't get up from her spot on the mattress "Behold the peeling paint, and the plaster falling off the ceiling. You ought to see the Yelp reviews."

"Oh, please. My room is just like this, without the tall ceiling and the big fan. You're lucky," he told her. "This is the neatest house on the block."

"It's the *only* house on the block."

"Okay, then it's the neatest house in the neighborhood."

"Have you seen the whole neighborhood?" she asked.

"Most of it." Terry roamed her room like a robot vacuum, bumping off boxes and furniture. "Some of the houses are like this one." He paused to look out over the driveway where Sally's car was parked. He looked back at Denise. "But some of them have been restored, and not *good* restored. I like them better like this."

"What do you mean, 'good restored'?"

He admired the window seat covered in boxes with a hearty, "Mm, nice." Then he said, "Most flippers gut them, and put in whatever shiny junk is popular right now. They don't pay any attention to what the house wants, or what looks nice inside it. My friend Dominique calls them 'Things White People Like' houses. But you guys aren't going to do that, are you?"

"We definitely don't have the money for shiny junk, but eventually my mom wants to open up for business. Maybe we'll go shabby chic out of necessity."

"Good, good." He nodded, and dragged his fingers across the windowsill. Denise was glad it wasn't covered in dust and spiderwebs anymore. "My dad says it's a tragedy, every time they gut a place like this. He says it's a crime against history."

Denise wanted to offer him some hand sanitizer, but she didn't have any. "So . . . did you just come over here to look around inside the house?"

"Yep," he admitted frankly. "I've wanted to see inside for ages, but it was boarded up pretty good. I couldn't find a crowbar big enough to pry anything loose — not by myself."

"I'm sorry, are you saying . . . ?"

"I *didn't* break in."

"But you tried. That's what I'm taking away from this conversation."

He thought about it and shrugged. He set his overloaded back-pack on the floor and straightened up, leaning his neck from left to right, and producing a good crack. "What do you care? It wasn't your house. Now that it belongs to somebody again, I knocked. No crow-bars, see?"

"I don't know. Your backpack is looking kind of fat—you could have a crowbar in there for all I know."

"It's just schoolbooks, mostly."

She frowned at him, puzzled but not upset. "Are you in summer school?"

"No, but some of the teachers offer summer tutoring, over at the trailer lot. I stay late on Tuesdays and Thursdays, and help the PE lady load up her stuff. She brings soccer kits and basketballs, that kind of thing. For the kids whose homes haven't come back yet."

"Haven't come back . . . ?"

"They took the FEMA trailers out of the park and put the baseball field back in it, but that don't mean everybody's got a real roof over their heads yet. So anyway, I was walking home, and I have to go right past your place, and I thought I'd see if anyone was here. And if anyone would let me in. And if I could look around. Your mom asked if I was here to see you, so I just rolled with it."

"You're a weird one, Terry."

"I wear it as a badge of honor."

"You might as well. You um . . . you mentioned a dad. Do your parents know where you are right now?"

He sat down on the floor and unzipped his bag, then started poking through it. "I have a dad, and no mom anymore. Dad's an EMT, and he works third shift. Unless somebody tells him otherwise, he assumes I'm home safe."

"Maybe someone should have a word with him. What are you . . . Terry, what are you doing?"

"Looking for my digital recorder."

"Because . . . ?"

"Because this place is haunted like crazy. Everybody says so," he solemnly assured her. He located an old recorder and brandished it like the key to the city. Its battery compartment was held together with a strip of medical tape, wound around it twice and going gray from all the lint it'd picked up in his bag.

Denise swallowed. She'd almost forgotten the stink from the attic and the door that moved by itself (except that she hadn't), and she'd almost forgotten the old lady perfume, and the humming and the footsteps that went right through her (except she hadn't forgotten those things, either). "What makes everybody think it's haunted?"

"Because somebody famous *died* here."

She sat forward on the bed, idly wishing she could offer him a real seat someplace — but there was no place but the floor for now, or one of the dozen boxes that held her clothes, shoes, and bags that hadn't yet been unpacked. "Oh God, seriously?" She wasn't surprised, but she was definitely horrified. "Who?"

"Some writer, that's what I heard. Can't remember his name."

"Then he must not have been that famous." She flopped backwards, sprawling her arms across the blanket. "Where did he die? How did he die?" For no good reason except a grossed-out suspicion, she flashed a glance toward the hall and the creepy attic door.

Terry continued, fiddling with his gadget. "Don't know. It's just a rumor. Have you seen anything ghostly since you've been here?"

"Of course not." She didn't want to encourage him.

"Then you'll be totally fine giving me a tour of your ghost-free home, while I run my recorder and ask questions."

"Now you want to interview me?"

"Not *you*. You don't know anything. I'm going to ask the ghosts, and see if they're willing to communicate."

"With an old digital recorder?"

"So what if it's old?" He pressed the power button, and a tiny green light came on. "Old things are great. They're built to last. And things like this . . ." he wiggled it in her direction, ". . . can record things we can't hear."

"Like ghosts. Talking ghosts." *Or humming ghosts,* she did not say.

"Yep." He climbed to his feet and flashed her that undaunted, unrelenting grin of his. "I don't care if you believe me. Heck, it's probably better if you don't. That way, you won't unconsciously interfere with my results."

"You do this kind of thing a lot?"

He vigorously bobbed his head. "Every chance I get. Are you going to show me around, or what?"

"You're going to keep asking until I give up and say yes, aren't you?"

"'Never give up,' that's my motto."

"It ought to be, 'Wear 'em down until they admit defeat.'"

On that note, Denise grudgingly ran Terry through the house — pointing out such highlights as the broken windows, the duct tape repairs of yesteryear, the fixtures that didn't work, and the wasp nest that they still hadn't knocked down yet. Against her will, she started to enjoy herself. After all, here was somebody with an honest interest in the house, somebody who wasn't utterly repulsed by it. If anything, the happy little nerd was enthralled.

All around the second floor, Terry stopped and held up his recorder, asking silly questions. "Are we alone in this house?" "Are you a man or a woman?" "How did you die?"

Denise never heard anything in response, but supposedly, that's what the recorder was for.

She wrapped up the tour back at her bedroom, since they'd gotten a little warm just hiking around from floor to floor. They took a minute and cooled off under the ceiling fan while Terry went through his voice recordings — revealing nothing new as far as Denise could tell. Just awkward pauses and fuzzy static.

"Get anything good?" she asked, for the sake of being polite.

"I can't tell yet. Hey, what about that skinny door, on the far side of the staircase?"

It should've been easy for Denise to say, "Oh, it's just the attic. No big deal." Instead, she froze.

He crinkled both his lips and eyebrows. "What? Did you see something? Did I say something wrong?"

"No. It's just the door to the attic — on the other side, there's a little corridor with some stairs."

"Have you been up there?"

She sniffed with derision. "No. It's too gross. Nothing but bugs and dust and the corpses of rats or possums or raccoons."

"If you've never been there, how would you know?"

She cooked up a fib on the fly. "My mom and Mike checked it out. They said I shouldn't go up there, because it isn't safe. They're going to pay someone to clean it out, and get rid of all the nasty stuff."

Terry's eyes narrowed down to tiny, skeptical slits. He leaned out into the hall. "Hey, Mrs. Cooper!" he called at the top of his lungs. "Is it okay if me and Denise go see what's up in the attic?"

A reply wafted up from downstairs. "Knock yourselves out. Be careful, though. Okay? It's not super safe. Holler if you need help!"

"Yes ma'am!"

It was Denise's turn to dole out the ol' squint-eye. "Terry?"

"Uh-huh?"

"You're a jerk."

"Yeah, but I'm a jerk who's going upstairs. Are you coming with me, or are you chicken?"

"That is a logical fallacy, because those are *not* my only two options," she insisted, but all the same, she followed him out.

He went directly to the too-tall, too-narrow door and yanked it open.

She waited for a cloud of dust and doom and terrible smells to roll out into the hallway, but it didn't. Not this time. This time, she saw nothing but grimy stairs, and smelled nothing but mildew and staleness.

"I don't see what the big deal is," he fussed.

"Me either," she countered. "I can't imagine why you want to go up there."

"Does this light work?" He flipped the switch on the wall, back and forth, and on the third try a light bulb somewhere in the distant beyond fizzled to life. It didn't do much to brighten the stairwell, but Terry was determined to take it as encouragement. (As far as Denise could tell, he took *everything* as encouragement.) He thrust his recorder ahead, and before he climbed onto the first step, he asked, "Are there any spirits in this house?"

Without waiting for an answer he started up the stairs — leaving Denise to trail behind him. Hey, at least he was going first.

She let him take a pretty big lead — *not* because she was chicken, but because she didn't want his butt jiggling around in her face. She also didn't want him falling down backwards and taking her out like a bowling pin. The stairs were narrow and steep, and they were only meant for one person at a time.

She didn't know much about Terry yet, but she was pretty darn sure he didn't have her gymnastics background.

When Terry was near enough to the top that she couldn't see his feet anymore, Denise took a deep breath and brought up the rear. She stretched out her arms and put one hand on each wall, using it to support herself as she climbed.

Up she went, counting the steps . . . one, two, three . . . and listening to Terry articulate his questions with the speed and precision of a kindergarten teacher explaining vowels to five-year-olds. "Can you tell me your name?" Four . . . five . . . six . . . "Did you die in this house?" Seven . . . eight . . . nine. "Man, I wish I had the money for an EMF meter."

Denise passed the struggling light bulb and reached the top of the stairs. It should've been a relief; it should've come with a sense of accomplishment. But it only came with a muggy, hot cloud of mold-speckled air. "What's an EMF meter?" she asked him.

"It's a tool that measures electromagnetic activity. Sometimes you can detect spikes, when there are spirits present." Then, more to himself than to her, he added, "While I'm wishing for toys, I'd love a laser thermometer too. That's a —"

"I can figure that one out on my own, thanks."

The afternoon sun was orange and sharp through the attic's two round windows. Denise shielded her eyes from the dying westward glow, and Terry waved about in an odd little dance. At first she thought he'd walked through a spiderweb, but it turned out he was only fishing for the string to a light bulb that hung from the center of the tallest vault in the ceiling.

He finally caught the string and pulled it. The bulb clicked on.

The attic was a lumpy and angular space, unfinished and unfit for habitation by man or beast. A scaffold of roof supports crisscrossed above, supporting sheets of plywood — some of which were new, but most of which were a dark, swollen brown that said they'd been soaked down one time too many. The house had five gables, and all five were evident in the swoops and peaks of this impressive overhead space. In some spots, it was easy to stand upright — and you couldn't touch the ceiling, not even if you jumped — but in others, you'd have to crawl.

The floor was not so much a floor as another layer of more plywood, dropped across the ceiling beams of the next level down. It creaked and bent with every step they took.

The air smelled gray and green, sharp and soupy. The attic was at least thirty degrees warmer and much, much moister than Denise's room. She was already sweating through her clothes when she said, "Well, here you go. This is all there is to see. Let's go, please? You could steam rice up here, I swear to God."

He ignored her. "Are we alone in this attic?" he asked the empty space.

As her eyes adjusted to the uneven light, Denise stared around, noting the four chimneys that shot from the floor and went up past the ceiling. Their mortar was crumbled, and their bricks were sagging. A good sneeze would send them scattering, and if it did, maybe the roof would come down too.

She didn't like the thought.

She also didn't like the squishiness of the plywood under her sandals, or the grimy feeling on every inch of her skin, even between her toes. She didn't like the fluffy, rotten look of the insulation between the gaps where the plywood didn't reach. It was a gross shade of yellow, eaten up with what looked like soot or mold. And she *really* didn't like the old hatchet she saw lying under one of the tiny attic windows.

"Um . . . Terry?" She pointed at it.

"So?"

"There's an ax. In the attic."

He gave her a look that said he thought she was an idiot. "How do you think all those people got up on the roofs, when the Storm came? They didn't *all* climb out a window and swim."

"They hacked their way out? Why would so many people have axes in their attics?"

"It wasn't exactly the first hurricane the city ever saw, or the first flooding. Naw." He shook his head. "People learn. They remember. And then they put an ax up in the attic, for next time the water comes around."

She shuddered, feeling worse about the fact that the old bit of hardware wasn't a potential murder weapon. Somehow, its true purpose was even more horrible. "Look, man. It's probably not healthy up here," she warned. "Come on, let's go back downstairs."

Terry ignored her, and asked the attic, "Can you tell us your name?"

A faint puff, just the barest whiff of roses drifted up Denise's nostrils. She flinched, tensed, and looked around — but saw nothing. No footprints. No ghosts. Just Terry, holding up his recorder like the Statue of Liberty's torch.

He fired a hard look at her. "Did you hear that? I heard something, over there, behind you."

"Oh God, do *not* try to creep me out. I will *not* appreciate it."

He stumbled past her, his foot sticking in a seam between two pieces of plywood. He yanked it out and went to the nearest chimney column — the largest of the four. It was almost twice the size of the rest; Denise couldn't be certain which fireplace it served, but she thought it must go down to the big one in the parlor.

He asked, "Do you have a flashlight?"

"Sure," she told him. "Let me just pull one out of my butt."

"I don't want your butt-light, and I don't think . . ." He peered into a corner full of shadows. "I don't think I need it. I see something. There's something back here."

"Please tell me it's not alive. Please tell me it's never *been* alive."

"Not since it was a tree."

She came up behind him, and looked over his shoulder. "What? Oh," she said, intensely thankful to see something so harmless and ordinary stuffed behind the bricks. "It looks like . . . a book?"

He reached in slowly, in case of bugs or bats or anything else that might bite, and pulled out a rectangular brown shape wrapped in layers and layers of crinkly plastic-looking stuff. He unwound the film to reveal a package that was heavier than it appeared.

Something with a multitude of legs scuttled out from between the wrappings, and Terry shrieked. He dropped the book. It landed with a thud, and stirred up a mighty puff of dust that left both kids coughing and wiping at their eyes. When the debris cleared, they could see that the book was wrapped in a final layer that once might've been a garbage bag, or a grocery bag.

They crouched beside it, unwilling to touch anything until they were certain that all resident insects were gone.

Denise extended a finger and picked at the sack until the book slipped loose — a thick, dirty volume, tied up with two loops of twine.

She rubbed a place where she figured a title ought to be, but turned up nothing but a gritty film. Then she tugged at the strings. They came undone easily, and fell aside.

"It's a photo album, or . . . or something." Terry poked at the spine, but it wasn't really a spine. The album wasn't a properly bound book, but a collection of pages that were held together with three rusty metal rings.

Denise slipped her thumb under the front cover and flipped it open.

The topmost page was faded, and the edges were crinkled with age — but the text and illustrations were as bold as if it'd been printed there yesterday.

THEM!
A HORROR HORDE
OF CRAWL-AND-CRUSH
GIANTS

THAT WAS JUST AWFUL. I'LL NEVER UNDERSTAND WHY YOU GET SUCH A KICK OUT OF SCARY MOVIES.

OH, BUT THEY'RE SO MUCH FUN! NEXT TIME, LET'S CATCH A DOUBLE FEATURE.

OF COURSE, MY DEAR! ANYTHING, IF YOU'LL TAKE A BREAK FROM CRIME FIGHTING.

HE IS NOT
YOURS,
AND YOU
CANNOT
KEEP HIM!

"What. In the hell. Is this?" Terry asked, pausing between the words like he might need an inhaler.

"It's . . . a comic book. Not a real published one, I mean . . ." Denise fiddled with the pages, pushing them forward and backward. "The art doesn't look printed. It looks like . . ." She held it up to her face, breathing in old paper and mildew. "It looks like it's drawn right onto these pages. I'm pretty sure."

Terry leaned past her and flipped back to the title page. "Here it is: J. Vaughn. It's right there. That's who wrote this, and . . . there's nothing about an artist, so I guess he drew it too. I've never heard of Lucida Might."

"Me either." A plump bead of sweat rolled down off her nose and splatted right on the sheet, beneath the *V* in "Vaughn."

"Gross."

"Well, it's hot up here. And it's dark too," she added, glancing toward one of the windows and seeing the last seam of sunset slipping through the glass. "Let's take this downstairs and get a better look at it."

"And maybe clean it up a little."

"Totally." She reached up to the light bulb string, and yanked it until the bulb turned off.

Back downstairs in Denise's bedroom, beneath the ceiling fan light, she pulled a couple of socks and a pajama top out of her dirty clothes pile. Terry made a face about it, but she told him, "They're cleaner than the book, aren't they?"

"They're clothes."

"They're not *underpants*. Get a grip." She tossed him the pajama top, and shoved the socks one over each hand, like gloves. "Now hold up the book while I wipe it down."

With a little patience and a whole lot of "ew" noises from Terry, they got the peculiar album as clean as it was going to get. When they were finished, it looked like it'd only been stuck in a box for twenty years — rather than stuffed in an attic for a hundred.

"It *can't* have been up there for a hundred years," Denise argued when Terry suggested it. "They didn't even *have* comics a hundred years ago."

"Are you sure?"

Upon reflection, she wasn't sure at all. She didn't know much about comics beyond the holy trinity of Batman, Superman, and Wonder Woman — plus whoever Marvel was building up for a summer blockbuster. And if she was honest with herself, or with Terry either, she'd only read a small handful of *actual* comic books, mostly at the library. Her knowledge of comics came almost exclusively from TV and movies.

She cleaned up her objection. "I don't *think* they had comics a hundred years ago, but even if they did, they wouldn't look like this. Look at the clothes Lucida and Doug are wearing. Look at the movie theater behind them, and the cars on the street. This isn't *that* old."

Terry squinted down at the page with the shadowy man, evaporating into bats and spiders. "I bet you're right. This wouldn't survive a hundred years up there. Not even wrapped in plastic. Not even sealed in Tupperware."

From downstairs, a loud shout rose up — followed by an even louder, "*Yikes!*"

Denise and Terry sat upright. "Mom?" Denise called out, but when no one answered, she scrambled to her feet. Terry followed suit, leaving the book on the floor behind them.

Denise was out in the hall, and at the top of the stairs in a heartbeat. "Mom, are you okay?"

"Fine," came the answer, but it came from Mike. "She's fine."

"Yeah, I'm fine," Sally groused, as the kids rumbled down the steps and into the living room. "It's that stupid . . ." She gestured at the nearest window. "The window. I was going to clean out all the old paint and rethread the rope, so we could open and close it again." She cradled her right hand in her left, and hissed and breathed and stomped around to take the edge off the pain. "Stupid old single-panes. Stupid old ropes."

Mike took her injured hand and checked it out himself. "It's not that bad. Nothing broken, all right? You'll just have a great big bruise, in the morning."

Sally reclaimed her hand and squeezed it some more, wringing out the dull throb of an injury that was already starting to swell.

"Windows like this, they're on a rope-and-pulley system," Mike explained. "Half of ours are painted shut, and the other half are missing their ropes and weights. But this one." He indicated the problem child in question. "We wrestled it open and the line snapped, and the window dropped shut on your mom. It could've been a lot worse — nothing broken, nothing bent. Only a bruise," he said again, in case saying so could make it true.

"All the work it took, all the paint stripping and sanding just to get it open . . . I never would've thought it could fall shut so fast," Sally mused, still massaging her right hand with the left. "It was strange. It shouldn't have happened."

"Those old nails must've been holding it up and they . . . rusted out, or . . . something," Mike said, gesturing at a few loose, round-headed nails rolling around on the ground. "We'll have to be more careful, that's all."

Denise let out a long, tense sigh, and sat down on the fireplace's brick-lined bottom. "We're going to need better health insurance."

Terry checked his phone. "And I'm going to need to get home. Dad won't be back for a while, but I should get supper started."

Sally knitted her brows in his general direction. "Seriously?"

"I'm an excellent cook," Terry said proudly. "He's pretty tired when he gets off work, so . . . I try to have something ready for him."

He was politely excusing himself, so Denise helped him out. "I'll get your bag. You left it in my room." A moment later she returned, with his backpack, which felt like it was full of rocks. "Here you go. I'll um . . . I'll catch you later."

"Let me know what you find out about that comic. Here, actually . . ." He reached into his bag and pulled a pencil stub that was only an inch or two long, with an eraser nub that was chewed down to nothing. He spied a napkin on the dining room table, and he wrote on it. "Here's my phone number. Give me yours."

She tore the napkin in half and obliged him. "Okay, here you go."

"What comic?" Mike wanted to know.

"It's . . . kind of weird. I'll tell you later."

Denise really *did* mean to tell Mike later, but later, it was time to sit around with Sally and an ice pack, and time for him to fret over his wife like she was a baby bunny. He forgot all about the passing reference to comics, and Denise forgot to fill him in.

Later, it was alone time upstairs in her bedroom with her phone.

She had no other Internet access, not yet, and maybe not for a long time. Getting the power working and the plumbing un-leaky was more important than getting Wi-Fi set up. Mike could leech Wi-Fi from a coffeehouse when it was time for him to go back to work, that's what he said — and Denise could do the same. She had a laughably old laptop and a printer for schoolwork, both of them propped up on a couple of milk crates beside her closet, gathering dust at the moment. But for connection to the outside world that wasn't reliant on borrowed Wi-Fi . . . all she had was this out-of-date iPhone that her mom had found on Craigslist. It'd been her sixteenth birthday present.

It was better than nothing.

Denise sat cross-legged on her bed, phone held longwise between her fingers. She used her thumbnail to turn off the sound so she wouldn't hear the text clicks, and went searching for "lucida might and the house of horrors" or anything related to "j. vaughn."

Down the Internet rabbit hole she went, and an hour later she'd learned a great deal about Lucida Might and her enigmatic creator.

For starters, he was allegedly "one of the great golden age masters of comics," according to Wikipedia. The article had been edited a handful of times, as a couple of guys had gone arguing back and forth over whether he was now "largely forgotten" or merely "little known," because apparently some people cared a lot about that kind of thing; but the meat of the page appeared to be generally agreed upon.

JOSEPH P. VAUGHN (born circa 1910? — d. sometime in March, 1955) was an American author and artist, widely considered to have been one of the great golden age masters of comics. Best known for the *Lucida Might* comics.

BIOGRAPHY

Little is known about Vaughn's personal life, including his exact date of birth. According to some sources, he was a talented finish carpenter who took up the visual arts in the wake of a back injury, and found success in the precode publishing industry. He was active from the late 1930s through the mid-1950s, when the **Comics Code Authority** regulations effectively ended his career. The remains of his estate were represented by Marty Robbins at **All Hands Literary Agency** up through 1996, when the agency folded.

CAREER

Although Vaughn produced over a dozen short-run comics during his prolific career, he is best known for creating *Lucida Might*. In the *Lucida Might* stories, the titular girl hero has many adventures—often in order to rescue her boyfriend, the hapless Doug Finch. With her wits and her fast-talking, fast-shooting skills, she fights everything from mummies in an Egyptian tomb[1] and Eastern Bloc terrorists with nuclear aspirations[2] to mafia dons[3] and corrupt police departments[4].

Vaughn was a regular guest of science fiction and comic book conventions around the country, although these events were not (at that time) as large and media-centric as they have become in more recent years. By all reports, he was an enthusiastic panelist who enjoyed talking about his best-known heroine to fan audiences.[5]

LUCIDA MIGHT

The comic's tagline, progressive for its time, was "When no man can save the day . . . when no man can answer the call . . . when no man can solve the mystery—Lucida *Might*!" Sometimes described as noir or pulp, the Lucida Might comics were marketed alongside such staples as **Weird Worlds**, **Detective Comics**, and **Amazing Stories**. Initially published by the now-defunct **Future Age** press, Lucida Might was in print for thirteen years. It was syndicated nationally in dozens of newspapers, and collected into countless digests. It even spawned a short-lived television show (**Lucida Might: Girl Adventurer**—1951-1952). But when the **Comics Code Authority** seized control of the industry in 1954, Vaughn disappeared—leaving behind a vast pop culture legacy and many unanswered questions.

COMICS CODE AFTERMATH

Some said Vaughn quit writing because of the CCA's strict regulations, which effectively prohibited not only gore and violence, but people of color and women in nontraditional roles. Therefore, Lucida Might's feisty, rule-breaking heroine was no longer welcome on newsstands or in comic shops. [Needs citation] Her rueful refrain of, "Doug won't save himself!" did not align with the new standards.

ARCHIVE

Some of Joe Vaughn's papers are archived at Tulane University, in New Orleans, where he lived and died. The special collections library lists a collection that includes letters, drafts of comics both published and unpublished, and limited edition digests.

The article continued, mostly with a list of known Lucida Might comics and a bunch of footnotes, but Denise didn't see any mention of a "House of Horrors" on the list. The closest thing to a vampire comic was one where Lucida fights a "monstrous cave beast" . . . and the cave beast in question was only vaguely batlike. There was no *Lucida Might vs. Dracula* on the list, or anything like that, either.

Not that the list was guaranteed to be all-inclusive.

Denise'd had enough teachers yelling at her about citing Wikipedia to think for one hot minute that it was the end-all and be-all of research, but she always considered it a safe place to start—and it *did* mention the archives at Tulane.

She left the list and scrolled back up, to the last biographical bit.

CIRCUMSTANCES OF DEATH

In 1955 Joe Vaughn was found dead in New Orleans. He'd fallen down a set of attic stairs and broken his neck. Police investigation suggested that the home's owner had gone missing sometime before, and although Vaughn was found on March 5, he might have been dead for several days by then. The home's owner was never found.

A terrible sensation filled the pit of her stomach. The math was just terrible: Terry said somebody famous had died here, and Joe Vaughn had died in a house in New Orleans. What were the odds that it was *this* house, where she'd found *his* manuscript? Better than zero.

She looked toward her bedroom door, but couldn't see too far into the hall; she didn't get a peek at the attic door, too tall and too thin, with its stairs inside that only a gymnast could navigate in one piece.

"I guess Joe wasn't much of a gymnast," she said out loud, trying to make it sound ironic, or funny, or anything but completely horrified. Was there a spot on the hall carpet runner? A man-shaped stain that never quite went away?

Dead for several days, the article said. Lying there in the Louisiana heat. Even in March, it would've almost certainly been warm.

She could imagine the smell, even though she didn't want to. Or was it her imagination at all? She'd smelled the perfume before, and something foul from the attic corridor . . . was that the stink of death, left too long in a place that was too warm, and too wet?

Denise shuddered. "It might not be true," she whispered. "He might not've died *here*, in the Agony House." But she didn't believe herself, not even a little bit.

Denise's phone's battery was deceptively low; it had a bad habit of saying she had more time remaining than it was prepared to give her. It was getting late anyway, so she plugged it in to the socket beside her closet and went downstairs to tell Mike and Sally good night.

She found them sacked out together on the couch, Sally's hand cradled by a melted ice pack that used to be a bag of frozen corn.

"Cute," she whispered with a smile, and she left them where they were.

Mike had taken a few weeks off from his job with the digital map management company, and therefore, he wouldn't get up in the morning until he good and felt like it. His boss had offered him a month without pestering him for contract work, as a wedding present.

Must be nice, she thought. Sally had never had any time off in her life, not that Denise knew of. Man, having a gainfully employed stepdad was a whole new world. Even if he was minimally, contractually employed.

She crawled into bed and kicked the thin velour blanket down to the foot—then whipped the cotton sheet open like a sail. It settled down slow across her body starting at her feet, catching the peaks and valleys of her knees, ribs, belly, and toes. Last of all, it draped over her boobs, then she took the top hem and tucked it up under her chin. She blinked over at the tiny lamp that was sitting on a box beside the bed, since she didn't have a nightstand. It didn't make much light. She might as well leave it on.

Not that she was afraid of the dark. And not that she needed to see anything, but she gazed around the room anyway, secure in her cotton sheet cocoon.

The fan above the bed spun just too fast for her to watch an individual blade go full circle, and the cracks in the walls and on the ceiling looked just like they always had. They did not seem to wobble into weird stick figure pictures when she stared too long. Along the floor at the far end of the room, something crawled . . . but it was probably a palmetto bug, and nothing more sinister than that.

The peculiar manuscript was sitting on the floor where she and Terry had left it. Its cover was open, revealing that title page and the big black letters that'd gone watery from old age and damp.

"Lucida Might and the House of Horrors," Denise breathed.

Her eyes drooped shut. In the end, she dreamed of spiders and bats, and shadowy men, and old ladies in musty perfume.

Denise's bedroom was sparkling. Or not exactly sparkling . . . but low-key respectable.

It was the next day and sure, the closet didn't have a door and she had no furniture that wasn't a box, and she still had a mattress and box spring on the floor for a bed, but it was tidy *and* now it was scrubbed. She'd even taken soapy rags to all the baseboards. Sometimes it felt like she was just redistributing spiderwebs, but hey. Effort had been made, and the room felt like it was properly *hers*.

The bathroom felt like it was nobody's yet. Denise had smashed out the weird shelves behind the tub with the sledgehammer — and she'd done it to her mother's wild cheers, and a great sense of satisfaction. She'd never gone out of her way to break anything before, and it felt good. She knew she was helping the house, in the long run, and it was nice to have a good outlet for her frustration.

Wallpaper was good for frustration too. Good for creating it, anyway. Now that the shelves were down, the wallpaper was supposed to come down too — but that was easier said than done.

Denise shoved the scraper along the wall and dragged it up and down. The paper she slowly, laboriously peeled was once red with white pinstripes. Now it was a feeble shade of mauve, with pale lines running up and down — disappearing into the wainscoting. It came loose a single scrap at a time, slowly and none too steadily. It was the kind of job that could eat your whole life, if you let it.

She knew she'd lost track of time when Sally came upstairs to ask, "Pizza?"

"Yes?" Denise pushed her hair out of her face.

"I'm too tired to cook. It takes too much going up and down the stairs for another damn lasagna." The microwave was plugged in upstairs, in the wasps' bedroom, which was a decidedly inconvenient location when you wanted to cook a meal. That cursed room had one of only three-prong outlets in the house that worked, and the refrigerator was using the other one. If you tried to make it share, it'd throw a tantrum and flip the breakers. They'd learned this the hard way.

Rather than point out that her mother had been wrong about the kitchen mostly working, Denise caved to convenience. "Yeah, I'd eat some pizza. Hook it up."

"Usual toppings?"

"Y'all two fight it out. I don't really care."

Thirty minutes later, there was a knock at the door. Denise dropped the scraper beside the pile of old wallpaper scraps and headed down the stairs, where Mike was trying to figure out where he'd seen the delivery guy before.

"Swear to God, I've seen you someplace." He looked up and winked when Denise hit the bottom stair. "Maybe Denise can refresh my memory."

Lo and behold, it was one of the only two people in the neighborhood she'd actually met. "Norman?"

"Oh, hey. Wait, *this* is your place?" He looked back and forth between Sally, Mike, and Denise. He settled on Denise. "Holy cow, I am *not* stalking you. I had no idea."

She laughed and almost blushed, but didn't quite. "I believe you. I think."

"I've just got your large pizza, that's all." He pushed it forward to Mike, who put it on the table.

Mike felt for his wallet, realized it was missing from his pocket, and held up a finger. "Let me get some cash; hang on." Then he turned away. With a short, shuffling hop, he limped off towards the master.

"Hey, Mike," Denise called after him. "What's wrong with your leg?"

He stopped short, and leaned against the doorframe. "It's not my leg. It's my foot."

"Fine. What's wrong with your foot?"

Her mother jumped in. "A brick fell on it. He was lucky, really. It could've hit his head."

"Never fear, though. The brick is fine. My foot broke its fall."

"That's why we call you Mike. It's Greek for 'graceful,'" Denise joked. "Next time you get a case of the dropsies, stay away from the power tools, why don't you."

Sally sighed. "I told him not to work in sandals. They make steel-toed boots for a reason."

"Maybe he should go to a doctor?" she tried.

"Trust me, I'll live. Contrary to all the evidence so far, the house isn't actually trying to kill us. I don't think . . ."

Norman took this opportunity to clear his throat. It was the kind of throat-clearing that's asking for an audience. "Um, sir?"

"Call me Mike, son."

"All right, if you want. I was just going to say . . . you guys have a lot of work to do, here. It's gonna feel like even *more* work, if you've got a bum foot."

"It's not *that* bummy," Mike protested.

"But if you want to take it easy, or easier . . . I could help out. I work for cheap, and I know my way around power tools. Pete's my uncle."

"Pete?" Sally asked.

"The hardware store. It's called Pete's," Denise filled her in. "But you've already got a job . . ." She gestured at the pizza box.

"I've got a couple of jobs. I also do cleanup in the cafeteria at Tulane, a few days a week. School's out, and I've got to hustle. I'll take minimum wage. How about eight bucks an hour?" He looked around the demolition in progress, no doubt realizing they couldn't afford any more than that.

Denise felt embarrassed by the house, but encouraged by the idea of having Norman around. He was all right, and her social life wasn't exactly on fire. "It'll take me another week to bring down the second floor wallpaper all by myself," she hinted. "Oh, hey — Norman, are you afraid of wasps?"

"Wasps?"

"We've got a wasp nest. Or a beehive, or something. In one of the bedrooms." She set aside her embarrassment in the name of practicality. He wasn't blind; he could see for himself that the place was a dump. Why not bring him all the way up to speed on the situation? "So far, nobody's bothered to knock it down. We just leave the door shut, unless we need to microwave something."

He opened his mouth slowly and closed it again, like he was about to ask about the microwave, but then he didn't. "I might charge a little extra for the beehive."

"That settles it," Sally declared for everyone. "When are you available, between your other two gigs?"

He thought about it. "Tuesday and Thursday, from noon until suppertime. Then I've got to get home to my mom."

Soon it was agreed that they'd see him from noon to four o'clock, twice a week.

"Let me leave you my number," he said, pulling a coupon out of his pocket and using the pen he kept on hand for credit card signatures. While he scribbled across the back, he said, "Call me if you need to. If you change your mind, or anything." Then Norman took Mike's cash and said, "Good-bye, Coopers. I'll see you Tuesday. Unless . . ." He looked at Denise. "Do you ever go down to the po'boy place, a couple blocks past Pete's? They've got Wi-Fi and the beignets are cheap. That's where everyone kind of . . . kicks around, when school's out. It's called 'Crispy's.' It's got AC."

"That's . . . good to know. Thanks. Maybe I'll see you there."

After he left, Denise cocked her thumb awkwardly back up the stairs and said, "Sooooo . . . Trish finally messaged me. I need to text her back. I could use a break from the wallpaper, anyway. I'll take my pizza upstairs with me."

"Shouldn't you start studying those prep books, for your ACT and SAT?" Sally said. It sounded like a question, but it wasn't. "You're still taking both of them. The real versions, not the 'pre' versions."

"I'm sure I'll do great on the real thing. *Anyway*," Denise stressed. "At this time, I'm going upstairs to text until my fingers fall off. When I'm done, if I still have the energy, I'll open those stupid books to see how much studying I really need to do."

"All of it. You need to do it all, whatever it takes."

"*Mom*. I know. Have a little faith. Please?"

Sally tensed up tight, squeezing the back of her chair and loudly not saying anything she'd said a thousand times before. Unspoken keywords included: "scholarships," "amazing opportunity," "exorbitant college costs," "broke-ass family," "so much potential," and "don't screw this up."

But all she said in her outside voice was, "I have all the faith in the world. And you only have another year to go. Then you're free to go have a first day of college somewhere else, on someone else's dime, and I will be the proudest mom on earth. I know it's hard now, but—"

"*Mom*. I'll be fine. I'm tired, and I have some trashy food, and I have my phone and books. Holler if you need me," she concluded.

It wasn't quite a masterful exit, but it worked well enough. She picked up her backpack and messenger bag, grabbed a couple slices and some napkins, and lugged everything up the stairs to keep her word about the texting and the studying.

She had to.

The next day, Denise decided she could use some Wi-Fi. Her beat-up, secondhand laptop was slower than Christmas, but it had an antenna — and it was easier to type on the keyboard than on her phone. She had some more questions for the Internet, mostly about the writer named Joe Vaughn.

Sally was stuck on the phone with the plumbers, so Denise asked Mike if he'd give her a ride to the po'boy place. "I've got the directions on my phone. It's not very far past Pete's."

"What you're saying is, you could easily walk there."

"But it's *hot* . . ." she whined. "Come on. It'll only take you a minute."

"As opposed to the *five* minutes it'd take you by foot. We gotta get you a bicycle or something." But he reached for his keys. "Come on, now. I'll tell Sally where you're off to when she finally pries that phone off her ear."

Crispy's looked like a chain restaurant — which was to say, it wasn't very sketchy, and once Mike saw it, he felt a little better about dropping her off there for an hour or two of nonmanual labor. "Call or text when you want a pickup, okay?"

"I will," she promised. She heaved herself out of the car, slung her messenger bag around her chest, and stepped into the parking lot — then shut the door with her butt.

Mike waved and drove off.

Denise stood there, looking up at the big light-up sign. She'd never heard of Crispy's before, but the place was bright and shiny, with a sign on the door that said WI-FI FOR PAYING CUSTOMERS ONLY. She had three dollars in her pocket, plus the change from her soda the other day. Mike hadn't asked for it back, so she'd kept it.

She might not be able to afford a po'boy, but she could get a drink and some fries or something. They'd let her use the Internet for that much, right?

The glass door chimed when she pushed it open and came inside. There were a dozen other customers. Many of them were about her own age, but none of them were Norman or Terry, so she didn't know anyone. She went to the register and ordered a Coke and some beignets, because those sounded better than fries right that moment and you could get an order for ninety-nine cents. When she got her food, she picked a seat and tried not to feel weird about being the only white person who wasn't working behind the counter.

She opened her laptop. It would only last for ninety minutes without the cord, but she didn't see a place to plug it in. She pulled up a browser window, and started to type.

Before she could check the first round of results for Joe Vaughn that weren't on Wikipedia, several girls sidled into the table right behind her.

One of them started talking, loud enough and pointed enough that Denise knew it was intended for her ears. She ignored it until the girl got more direct about it. "Hey. Hey, you. I heard somebody bought the old nail house on Argonne. Was that you?"

Denise looked up from the laptop and turned around to make eye contact with a black girl about her own age, lean and tall, with short, natural hair. "Nail house?" she asked her. "What's a nail house?"

"A house that sticks up, like a nail on a board. And there's . . ." She sat back. "There's nothing else on the block. Just the one house. A nail house, get it?"

She must be meeting more of the neighbors. "Yeah, that's us. My mom and stepdad bought it."

"Aw, man . . ." A guy sitting alone at the next table over turned to look at her. "The Argonne place? I know that house. You're lucky."

"Lucky?"

"*Everybody* knows that house," said the girl who'd originally asked the question. "And now you've bought it, and I guess you're gonna fix it up."

"My mom wants to make it a bed-and-breakfast. Like . . . a little hotel, kind of."

The girl rolled her eyes. "I know what a bed-and-breakfast is, and now I know you're a carpetbagger. You gonna wind up at Rudy Lombard this fall, or what? I know y'all usually get homeschool, or you go some-place private."

Denise swiveled on the seat to face the girl head-on. She wasn't alone, and Denise was, but that didn't stop her from responding. "Excuse me? How am I gonna *carpetbag* out of Houston?"

"You can carpetbag from anyplace," the girl said offhandedly, like it was something everybody knew. "Y'all come in from Florida, from California, New York. Wherever. It's always the same: You kick people out of their houses, and make them so much better, nobody here can afford them." She returned her attention to her lunch, and to her friends. "I seen plenty of her kind, coming and going. They look better going."

Denise closed her laptop. "Come on, now. The house my mom bought was abandoned — we didn't take it from anybody. And for real: Do I *look* like money to you?"

"Hell no, you don't," offered the guy who'd almost been nice, a min-ute before. Maybe he was still being nice. It was hard to tell.

Most of the girls at the other table still had their backs to her, but she told them anyway: "I got a laptop that's old enough to go to pre-school, and a bedroom without a bed, for Chrissake. We didn't come here to flip. We came back *home*."

"Back?" Another girl drew up her knees and stretched out one leg, taking up two seats beside her. "How come you left in the first place?"

"The Storm chased us to Texas. Couldn't afford to come back, not until now."

"Yeah, you sound like Texas."

"Well, that's where I been."

"But now you're back? In a house?" asked the guy.

Denise didn't quite shrug, and didn't quite roll her eyes. But she kind of did both. "If it makes you feel any better, the nail house is a total craphole."

The first girl was unconvinced. "Maybe you started out here, and maybe you didn't — I don't always know a liar when I see one — but I *know* when I see another damn gentrifier." She gestured with a spoon, and announced to the restaurant at large, "My aunt and cousins lost their place to people like this. My grandma did too. Landlords sell out fast; they take that flipper money and *run*. Then new folks push out folks who belong here, and let in folks who don't."

"I told you, I was *born* here."

"In St. Roch?"

"No . . ." She hesitated. "We were out in St. Bernard, I think. I was real little. But my daddy *died* in this city." She played her only ace, wondering if it'd matter. "The Storm took him, and my grandma too. That's why we couldn't come back any sooner."

"Should I feel sorry for you?" the long-legged girl with two chairs underneath her asked.

"I didn't say you should. I was just explaining." Denise heard mumbling all around her, and behind her. She mumbled too. "I didn't hardly know them, anyhow." This was pointless. She swiveled her legs back over the seat, and returned to her food. "Forget it. Y'all don't want me here, and I don't want to be here — so there's something we agree on. But look, I only got a little bit of time before my battery dies. Leave me alone, or keep giving me grief, I don't care. I've got headphones."

They were only earbuds, turned gray from being bounced around in her messenger bag for a couple of years, but she pulled them out and plugged them in. She opened the laptop again and pretended to give the screen her full and undivided attention.

Slowly, the curious onlookers who had started watching turned back to their tables.

"Come on, Dominique," the guy said, just loud enough for Denise to hear him around the earbuds. "You and Val don't have to be like that."

"She can take it," Dominique said. Then she turned and to another girl sitting at the table, she asked, "Why aren't you eating?"

"Fries are ninety-nine cents, and all I've got's a dollar."

"What's tax? Anybody got a dime? Something like that?" she asked the room. "Come on, get her a handful of pennies or something. Between us, we've got it." All around the restaurant, hands fished in pockets, scaring up change. "Y'all need one of them jars, where you can take a penny and leave a penny," she hollered at the front counter. The guy at the register shrugged.

So Dominique wasn't always awful to everybody, mostly just gentrifiers. Didn't Terry say he had a friend with that name? Maybe this was her. Denise sighed down at her computer, and pulled up Google.

It was much easier to search around on the computer's big keyboard than on her phone's tiny one. She found several links she'd missed the first time, two of which were about Joe's reaction to the CCA. She'd seen mention of it on the Wikipedia page, but didn't really understand what it was about. An article written by someone at the Comic Book Legal Defense Fund looked like a promising place to start. Besides, she needed to get used to reading things by lawyers — if she ever planned to become one.

But the article was also really, really long. She might have skimmed, even though she very much wanted to hear what it had to say.

She felt a little out of her depth, so she kept clicking around and picked up the gist.

Apparently, the Comics Code Authority happened when the government wanted to start censoring comics for being too obscene. To avoid being squashed by federal regulation, the industry formed the CCA to regulate itself. People who wrote and drew comics agreed to submit them to the CCA, and the CCA would decide if they were clean enough to be published.

Lots of people had lots of opinions about that. Lots of people thought it was really stupid and bad.

For one thing, the new code meant that you couldn't write stories about vampires or werewolves anymore — and for another, there were lots of regulations about *how* you could tell stories, and who could be in them. Denise got the very distinct impression from some of the code's wording that stories about kick-ass girl detectives and boyfriends who needed rescuing would have been a no-go. Something about the whole "value of the home and sanctity of marriage" lines, along with all the bits about "honorable behavior" and respect for the order of society.

Yeah, she could read between the lines.

A bunch of comic book producers went out of business when the CCA went into effect. People left the industry, or were pushed out of it.

Denise tried to understand why it'd ever happened in the first place. Supposedly, librarians and teachers and cops were burning comics and banning them, because of all the filthy and gruesome content, so that must've been part of it. Maybe the CCA was trying to save the industry from itself, but it sure sounded to Denise like the comics code did more harm than good.

After an hour, her screen started to flicker. She was never going to make it to ninety minutes, not today. The laptop beast was cranky, so she texted Mike for a rescue.

Could you come get me? Laptop is dying.

She packed everything back up, finished her beignets, and refilled her soda. By then, the girls who'd bothered her had left. The guy who had halfway tried to stay out of the fray studiously avoided eye contact.

And Mike was pulling into the parking lot.

He was singing along to some weird bro-country song on the radio — she could tell before she was even close enough to hear it. His head was back, and his eyes were closed, and it was like he couldn't care less that anybody could see him.

Denise grabbed the door handle and let herself inside to a wave of crooning about barefoot girls and pickup trucks. "Jeez, Mike. You know these windows aren't tinted, right?"

"Yes, madam, I *do*," he said with all due solemnity. Then he turned down the radio before she had a chance to demand it, or do it herself. "Not that it's ever stopped me once. And how was your time with proper Internet?"

She shrugged. "It was cool."

"Make any new friends?" he asked, a note of optimism rounding out the question.

"God, no. I only had time to make a couple of enemies."

He hesitated, not sure how serious she might be. "Are you being funny?"

"Just calling it like I see it."

"All right, fine. Today you're the strong, silent type. But when we get home, I have a surprise for you — and I damn well want to hear a squeal of joy."

"Temper your expectations," she warned. "I'm not much of a joyful squealer."

"Not usually, I know. But give me a chance."

She gave him a curious side-eye. "Mike? What did you do?"

"You'll see!"

Denise hoped she wouldn't have to disappoint him. "Okay, I guess I will. So how about your foot? Is it getting better, or should you *really* go find a doc-in-a-box?"

"Much better." He wiggled it around on the gas pedal for emphasis, and the car surged forward.

She rustled up a weak laugh. "Very nice. I'm glad you're so improved that you feel comfortable risking our lives."

"Oh, there's nobody out here — and we're almost home. Hell, kid . . . you're almost home when you're sitting on the restaurant's stoop. I was serious about that bicycle."

"You want me to ride a bike in this heat? Through this neighborhood?"

"The heat, I'll give you. But don't crap on the neighborhood. Don't be one of those white kids who's weird about being around black kids."

"I'm not. I'm trying not to, and . . . that's not what I meant. I've . . . I've got black friends in Houston. Kim's black." She knew it sounded dumb even before it left her mouth, but there it was. "But that's not the problem, I don't think. Well, I don't know, maybe that's part of it. The point is, I don't have any new friends."

He glanced back at Crispy's and continued, "Well, you've met Norman, and he seems like an all right guy. You've met that Terry kid too. That's two friends you'll have at Rudy Lombard, in a couple of months. It's a start."

She sighed and nodded. "I think 'friends' is a little premature, but yeah. At least I'll know *somebody*." As Mike pulled into the two ruts that worked for a driveway at the Agony House, Denise changed the subject. "Hey, what's Mom doing? Did she sort things out with the plumber?"

"Yeah, but now she's meeting with an electrician about the knob-and-tube wiring. There's no sense in throwing up drywall and new fixtures if we're only going to have to yank it all down again. Tomorrow the plumber's coming by, and then we'll know how expensive that's going to be too."

"Mike?"

"Yeah?

It took her a few seconds to figure out the question she really meant to ask. Then she asked it, like she hoped and prayed he'd tell her the truth. "Mike, are we going to be okay?"

He put the car in park, set the brake, and turned off the engine. "The loan is supposed to cover repairs because we're contributing to the community and opening a new business; but I'm not going to lie to you — the money will barely get this house up to code, and that's if we all pitch in for labor. Sally and me, we knew when we bought it that the house was . . . you know . . ."

"A craphole?"

"Fine, it's a craphole. But the sheer *scope* of the crapholeyness is bigger than we thought, and it's going to get expensive. Electrical and plumbing . . . I can repair that stuff in a pinch, but I can't replace their entire systems. We *have* to suck it up and hire some professionals."

"So you're saying . . ."

"I'm saying, the next few weeks are going to be noisy and they're going to be tight, but we'll make it." It was already getting warm in the car without the engine and AC running, so Mike opened his door and stepped out onto the gravel driveway. "Don't be surprised if you find some random dudes hanging around when you get home."

She followed his lead, and shut the car door behind herself. "In my room?"

"In every room. But we'll give you a heads-up so you can hide the bodies, or whatever, before work gets started in your space."

"Thanks. I appreciate it. So . . . where's this joyful squeal-worthy surprise I've been promised?"

"Inside!" He led the way, meeting Sally at the door. She gave him a kiss, and he asked, "Where's the electrician?"

"He'll be back on Thursday, with people and equipment."

"And the estimate was . . . ?"

She lowered her voice, like Denise couldn't hear her anyway. "Don't worry, we can swing it." Then, louder, she said, "Get inside, young lady. Mike picked up a surprise for you."

"Should I be afraid?" she asked, stepping past her mother and into the foyer. "I don't see anything . . . ?"

"Upstairs," Mike told her. "Go check out Fort Denise."

It probably wasn't a trick, but it probably wasn't the grand event that Sally and Mike implied. Or so Denise assumed . . . until she reached her bedroom and heard the steady hum of something that wasn't the rickety ceiling fan. She put her hand through the doorway, and a trickle of ice-cold air weaved between her fingers.

"Shut. *Up.*" In the window that opened the easiest — maybe the only window that opened at all — an AC unit was mounted and running, chugging away and leaving a faint fog of chill around its vents. "Y'all got me a window unit?"

Behind her, Sally and Mike reached the top of the stairs. "It's all yours, baby! It's secondhand — pulled out of a house that was getting central heat and air installed, but it still works fine and it didn't hardly cost a thing. Mike saw it beside the road and gave a guy ten bucks for it."

"Aw, don't tell her that."

"I don't care where you found it, or what it cost. I seriously *don't.*" Into the room Denise strolled, hands out, eyes closed, doing a little twirlie in the empty space that was now as frosty as a fridge. "This . . . is the greatest of gifts," she said dreamily. "I might sleep tonight. I might not wake up with my hair melted to the pillow."

Sally joined her in the room, flexing her elbows and airing out the damp patches under her arms. "Now I want to be clear," she warned. "This thing costs a lot of money to run, so I don't want to find it cranked up to eleven, day in and day out. This is for evenings —"

Mike jumped in. "And for daytime breaks, when us manual laborers need some decent climate control."

She quit twirling happily, and flashed him an honest smile. "Thanks, Pops. This was a real score."

Mike cheesed back, from ear to ear.

Supper was all right too. Sally had gone grocery shopping after all, and she'd been cooking a big home-style tray of frozen manicotti upstairs in Wasp Central because the oven still didn't work worth a damn — or that's how she put it. At Denise's invitation, everyone took their plates upstairs, and sat on the floor of her room with a chilled two-liter of Coke to pass around, campfire-style. Especially if the food was hot, it helped if the room was cool.

Sally took a swig of soda, and wiped the mouth off with her sleeve. "I bet dorm life will look something like this," she advised. "I hope you get lucky, and get good roommates."

"Trish will be a great roommate."

Her mom ignored that declaration. "Those college applications, honey — you need to fill them out and send them off, sooner rather than later, so I hope you're doing some research *now*." Her mom had paid her way through two years of college before running out of money. There had never been any scholarships or grants. Just loans that piled up until she cried uncle and dropped out.

"I'll figure it out later." Denise sighed, and accepted the Coke when it came her way. "Let me deal with one problem at a time, please."

Mike asked, "Have you given any thought to anyplace other than Houston?" Then he scooped a forkful of ricotta into his mouth.

She knew what they wanted to hear. They wanted her to pick Tulane, even though a school like that would be on the lower end of the offers she might (emphasis on *might*) get — part of her tuition, and none of the living expenses. The university was right there in the city, though. Close enough to home that she wouldn't even need to live in the dorm. She could live here, where renovations would be ongoing forever, and ever, and ever. She could spend the next five years studying to the sound of power tools and the smell of dead stuff in the attic.

Or, she could go back to Texas and become a Cougar on a full ride (hopefully), and share a room with Trish and maybe even Kim.

"I'm still thinking about it," she said diplomatically. "Just give me some breathing room. Let's get this house livable, and then I'll worry about whether or not I want to live somewhere else. First things first. Right?"

Sally nodded reluctantly. "First things first."

"You trust me?"

"It's the world I don't trust. Or luck, or fate, or what have you." For a moment, Sally looked like she'd love to have something stronger than a Coke in hand. "We've been close to good before, haven't we? But things fall apart, last minute. Things go to hell."

"Mike, you gonna let her talk about you like that?"

He shrugged, undaunted and unteased. "She's only saying, she doesn't want you to struggle."

"Not like I did. Not like *we* did, when you were little. You can do better, that's all."

When supper was finished, they carried all the plates and cutlery back downstairs, and Denise grabbed a tumbler full of ice to finish off the last of the soda. "I'm going back upstairs to the civilized part of the house, okay? I've got some messages to reply to."

No one argued, and before she took the stairs, Denise saw Sally pull a box of wine out from the fridge. *Good for her,* she thought. *Have at, you crazy kids. You've earned it.*

It wasn't late—it wasn't even dark—but she turned on the lamp and settled in with her headphones and her cell phone. The phone was blessedly full of text messages . . . even a couple from Annie, who she hadn't been super-close with. She responded politely and briefly.

After exchanging a few tired texts with Trish, she reached into her pocket and pulled out a pizza coupon that had a different phone number written on it. She thought about using it.

But she was getting sleepy, and she chickened out.

The next day, Denise spent half the morning poking around links related to Joe Vaughn when she should've been working on the hallway wallpaper with the scraper. She hadn't read any further on the comic book, but she couldn't shake the thought of Joe Vaughn, dead comic writer, lying on the floor just outside her bedroom — so she spent some time combing that all-too-brief web listing for clues that might suggest that somehow, he'd lived or died someplace else.

After all, there were too many loose ends to call it a done deal. For one thing, all she knew about the house where Joe died . . . was that it didn't belong to him. That's all the Internet had told her so far. It was in New Orleans, and it wasn't his.

If the Agony House was really his, then he couldn't have died here. That said, if he never lived here, why was his old manuscript stashed in the attic? This house could've belonged to anybody — a fan, a friend . . . She considered the perfume and the humming.

"A lady friend?" she mused.

At any rate, there were holes in her horrified suspicions, and she clung to them. She had more questions than she had answers, and maybe she wouldn't like the answers when she got them — but she had to keep looking.

She settled on the All Hands Literary Agency as a possible source of info. She googled the company eight ways from Sunday, along with the name "Marty Robbins," and mostly turned up unrelated garbage. Here and there, she caught his name or the agency's name in reference to an old trade paperback deal. But she found nothing any newer than the mid-1990s.

Then she idly clicked back four or five pages in the search results, and a related name turned up: Eugenie Robbins, a partner at a firm called the Kessler and Robbins Literary Agency.

It couldn't be a coincidence. Could it?

Another few clicks revealed that Eugenie Robbins was accepting new clients, and was particularly interested in science fiction, fantasy, and romance. She accepted queries by email. She expected to see the first three chapters and a synopsis of any book you wanted to show her.

She probably didn't expect a message from someone like Denise Farber, but that didn't stop Denise from pounding out a quick letter with her thumbs.

> Hello Ms. Robbins,
>
> My name is Denise Farber, and I'm hoping that you're some relation to an agent named Marty Robbins. Marty Robbins used to represent a man named Joe Vaughn who wrote comic books a long time ago, and I think he might have died in my house. My parents bought this place in New Orleans (a neighborhood called St. Roch, if that helps) and I found a manuscript hidden in the attic. It's not a printed comic book, but more like a script for one. It's called Lucida Might and the House of Horrors.

She paused, and scrambled off her bed to where the comic was still sitting. She flipped it open and carefully snapped some pictures of the first few pages. Then she went back to the email and attached the pictures to it.

> Anyway, I've included some shots so you can see what I mean. Can you write me back, and tell me if you know Marty Robbins? Do you know where Joe died? Whose house was

it? Why would he leave this manuscript hidden upstairs in mine?

Also, do you know if this comic was ever published? It would be cool if I could see it all finished.

Thank you for your time, and I look forward to hearing from you.

It was a formal sign-off, but she'd read it someplace and liked the sound of it. Very professional. Very confident. It totally stuck the landing.

She hit SEND and her phone immediately chimed in response. It was Terry, texting to say he was on his way over. Not asking if he could come over . . . just giving her a heads-up.

"Typical," she sighed, even though he'd never done it before. She had a feeling that he did it all the time. Give him an inch, and he'd take a mile. Well, he already had an inch, and there was no stopping him now.

From downstairs, her mom called out: "Honey, we're going to grab breakfast. Shall we bring you the usual?"

"Yeah, that's fine!" she called back.

But just before they could leave, Denise heard Terry arrive. Her mom greeted him at the door with a question, "Oh! Hello, Terry — are you here to help Denise scrape wallpaper?"

He floundered, and said something like, "Um . . . whatever she needs me for, I guess!" and scurried up the steps with Mrs. Cooper following behind him. "Hey Denise," he greeted her, then moved aside for Sally to lean into the bedroom.

She scanned the scene for signs of productivity. "I see a lot of ratty wallpaper on the walls up here, and not on the floor."

"I'm *working* on it," Denise said with an eye-roll. "I'm just taking a break. It's hot, okay? It's miserable in every single room except this one. I'll get back to the bathroom in a little bit."

"I hope we don't regret getting you that AC unit."

"You won't, Mom." And after she'd left, Denise admitted under her breath, "Not until the power bill comes."

"Have you *actually* scraped any wallpaper today?" Terry asked, looking around her room. She hadn't started in there yet. Or out in the hallway, where she kept picturing a corpse lying, decomposing, leaking body-juices down into the floor.

"No, but I've thought about it real hard. What brings you over today? You want to read the comic some more? Because I'm pretty sure my mom would frown upon such leisure activities, when there's so much wallpaper intact."

"I would love to read more of the comic, but that's not actually why I'm here." Then he asked if he could show her something.

"Sure, hit me."

He whipped his backpack around his shoulder, unzipped it, and pulled out his voice recorder. He sat down on the edge of her bed, and motioned for her to come closer. "I'm going to turn this up real loud, okay? You have to listen hard. It's kind of tricky to hear, but I've got the good stuff all queued up."

She humored him by leaning forward and cocking one ear toward the handheld device. "All right. Go for it."

He pressed PLAY. At first, Denise heard only full-volume static blasting from the tiny speaker. It was loud and rough, a noise so big that it took up the whole room. She listened because she was supposed to, not because she thought there was anything to hear — but then, very softly, she caught something else buried within it — a whisper of rushed words, harsh and low.

I keep what's mine.

She jerked her head away from the recorder like it might bite her. "Is that . . . was that . . . ?"

He beamed from ear to ear. "It was a *ghost*."

She shook her head, not really believing him, but not arguing with him, either. "How do I know you even recorded that here? You could've done it at home, when nobody was looking. You could've . . . you could've gotten your dad to say it."

His broad smile went sly, like something was funny. He pressed PLAY again, and Denise's own voice blew out of the speaker, louder than life — since he hadn't turned down the volume. "You're wasting your time," she heard herself say. "This is completely stupid."

"I think I got this one out in the hallway, right in front of the attic door." He didn't turn down the volume, but he rewound the tape to play that first bit again. "What does it sound like he's saying, to you? To me, it sounds like "I want more time.""

"Don't play that again —" she started to command him, but he'd already hit the button and the gravelly, angry-sounding words rushed out again.

I keep what's mine.

It scared her, because she knew good and well that it wasn't Terry or his dad, and it didn't sound like anybody she'd ever heard speak. It didn't sound like anybody who was alive. Before she could stop Terry, he played the damn thing once more.

I keep what's mine.

She snatched the recorder out of his hand. "It's not *time*," she said, clutching it to her chest. Her heart banged against her hand. "I think . . ." She tried to compose herself. Slow breaths. Stay cool. "I think he's saying '*mine*.'"

He wiggled his fingers at the recorder. "Give it back. Let me play it again."

"I don't *want* you to play it again!"

Terry grabbed for it anyway, and got just enough of a grip to wrench it back into his own grasp. "It's not awful — it's evidence of the afterlife!"

She held up her hands, not surrendering, but calling for a halt to all this nonsense. "Maybe you used an old tape, and some other recording bled through . . . or my parents had the radio on downstairs and we didn't notice, or somebody was outside the window, or out on the street. Anybody could've said that, Terry. It doesn't have to be a ghost."

"But it *was*, and you know it. If you thought it was anything else, you wouldn't be so scared right now."

"I'm not scared!" she yelled at him.

"Do you always holler when you're not scared?"

She quieted her voice. "It's not a ghost, it's just somebody, somewhere, saying 'I keep what's mine.' I think that's what it says."

He considered this. "Hmm. Maybe." He whirled away from her, rewound the tape against her wishes, and hit PLAY even as she danced around him in a circle, trying to take the recorder away again.

I keep what's mine.

"Yeah, I think that's it. 'I keep what's mine.'"

"Put that thing away. I don't ever want to hear that voice again. It's gross, and weird, and it sounds mean."

"No, not yet," he protested. "I got several other pieces too, when I was walking around the house, asking questions. I want you to hear them."

"Oh God, no . . ."

"They're not all from that same guy, I promise! I got one that sounded like it came from a lady."

She could've chosen that moment to tell him about the humming and the perfume, and the tiny footprints that came and went.

But she didn't. "Jesus, Terry. How many people do you think died in this house?"

"I don't know. It's really old. Probably lots of people haunt it. At least two, I know that much for sure. The mean guy, and the nice lady."

Denise clenched her fists, and unclenched them again. "I've had enough of this, and enough of your stupid recorder."

"That doesn't mean your house is any less haunted."

"Stop talking like that!"

"Maybe I'll ask your mom . . ." Terry ignored her like he always did, except that he paused to look around. He went to the window and asked, "Hey, where are your parents going?"

The blue Kia was sliding out of the parking pad and reversing into the street. "They've gone to pick up breakfast," she told him. "The electrical breakers are off, down on the first floor — so we can't use the kitchen."

"What are *you* going to eat?"

"They're bringing something back for me."

"Do your parents believe in ghosts?"

"I don't know."

"I bet they do, and I bet they'll find this interesting." He had his stubborn face on. She wanted to smack it clean off. "I bet they'd be interested in hearing from Mean Guy and Nice Lady."

"You're completely wrong."

"Why are you being such a jerk about this? Most people would be excited to find proof of ghosts."

"You're wrong about that too. God, Terry. It's like you don't know anybody in real life."

The stubborn face hardened. "I know lots of people. *Lots* of people like ghosts."

Denise folded her arms and opened her mouth to evict him, but he changed his approach, going from demanding to pleading.

"Come on, don't you at least want to *hear* the lady? If you're going to be scared of the man, you should at least—"

"I'm *not* scared."

"— Fine, but wouldn't it be great to know that there's someone nice, looking out for you?"

She frowned. "Looking out for me?"

"Just let me play you the other messages. Come *on*."

Denise sighed with great, unhappy drama. She could either force Terry to leave, or listen to him play a couple of clips from his voice recorder. It'd probably be faster and easier to let him play the voices and *then* kick him out.

She relented. "Okay, *fine*. Play them, and then get lost before Mom and Mike get back."

"Great!" He sat back down and waved her over, and she reluctantly obeyed, sitting cross-legged, to match her crossed arms.

"Let's get this over with."

He was way ahead of her, thumbing his way toward something else on the little cassette. "Okay, but listen to this, and listen close. She's quieter than the mean guy." The tape queued up. Terry's thumb squished the button, and static poured out again. Then a whisper, a woman's voice that was low and soft, but firm.

. . . you lousy greaser . . .

Denise laughed, then clapped her hands over her mouth to catch it, and hide it—but it was too late.

"See?" Terry pressed. "This lady ghost has moxie!"

"What the hell is *moxie*?"

"Attitude," he informed her. "I looked it up online. I found a whole list of old-fashioned slang when I looked up what a 'greaser' was."

"Is that what she says?" She reached for the recorder again. This time, he let her take it. She rewound, and listened again. Just three words, clear as day: . . . you lousy greaser.

Terry explained, "A 'greaser' is basically a loser. One of those guys who wears too much hair stuff and thinks he's hot, but he's really just stupid-looking. It's just one of those words they used to use, sixty or seventy years ago."

"Like 'moxie.'"

"Uh-huh. Your nice lady ghost talks like a character from an old detective movie. Here, I've got another one." He reclaimed the device, urged the tape along, and pulled up his next find.

. . . mine . . .

That was the only word she could make out. But the tape kept rolling, and the woman's voice said: . . . never yours. When they find me . . .

. . . they won't . . .

"Wow," she said. She didn't mean to be impressed. She meant to toss Terry out, and eagerly await her glorious fast-food breakfast. "It's like they're arguing about something."

Her phone picked that moment to ring, startling the crap out of her. She flailed wildly and pulled it out of her back pocket, where she wasn't quite sitting on it. It was Mike. "Mike! Where are you, man? I need me some breakfast burritos, stat!"

"The McDonald's was closed—something about a plumbing problem."

Her mom called from the background. "So how about chicken biscuits instead?"

Denise sighed into the phone. "Chicken biscuits sound fine."

Terry swallowed wetly. He didn't say anything—not with his mouth. His eyes, on the other hand . . . he might've been one of those sad-faced dogs in a humane society commercial.

She closed her eyes and slumped down against the mattress, her butt settling on the floor. Surrendering to the inevitable she said, "Mike?"

"Yuh-huh?"

"Any chance you could pick up a couple of extras? Terry's still here, and I was going to send him home, but . . ."

"Two more biscuits, added to the order. Yes ma'am."

When the call was over, Denise put her phone on the table. "Happy now?" she asked Terry, who was vibrating in his seat.

"I completely forgive you for being a jerk about the ghost recordings."

She almost objected, but shrugged instead. "Fine. I was a jerk about those. You're right, and they're kind of cool. Did you catch anything else?"

"So you believe me now?"

"I believe . . ." She hesitated, hard. "I definitely believe there's something strange about this house."

"Close enough. And no, that's all I found—and I listened to this tape backwards and forwards, with the speakers at top volume, for hours, man. *Hours.*"

"Do you think the mean guy is Joe Vaughn?" she asked. "I mean, I kind of hope not. He wrote a comic about a kick-ass girl detective. I'd rather not think he's a jerk."

"Or a lousy greaser."

"Or that, either."

"Have you finished reading the comic yet?" Terry asked, with a greedy gleam in his eyes.

"No, I've been busy."

"Can I read it?"

"You can't take it home with you, if that's what you're asking. It's mine."

"No it isn't."

She unfolded her legs and stretched them out, then put her feet on the floor. "We found it in my house, and possession is nine-tenths of the law."

"Who told you that?"

"Lawyers," she informed him. It was generally true. Lawyers probably wrote the books about passing the bar exam. "It's mine, but you can read it if you want. While it's here. With me."

"It might belong to somebody else, though."

"Like who?"

"Like . . . if Joe Vaughn is our ghost, and he's dead . . . he might have kids who aren't."

She drummed her fingers on the table beside her phone, considering the implications of this. The *Lucida Might* manuscript might be worth some money to the right person, and she could definitely use some money. Maybe somebody would give her a finder's fee. Even the best scholarships couldn't cover everything. "You know what we should do?"

"What?" Terry asked, but it probably didn't matter. He sounded like he was game for anything.

"We should put it on the Internet. Not all of it," she added quickly. "Just some teaser pages, to see if anybody knows anything about it. Maybe someone will come forward. Maybe we can give it back. Or sell it."

"Do I get a finder's fee?" he asked immediately, because apparently they were more alike than Denise wanted to think.

"How about a couple of chicken biscuits?"

"For a down payment," he suggested shrewdly.

"All right, we'll talk about it later — if anybody actually, you know, recognizes the thing . . . much less wants it badly enough to buy it. Come on," she said, smacking him on the arm. She rose from the chair and collected her phone. "Let's open that bad boy up. I need to take some pictures."

"'I keep what's mine' . . . that *can't* be a coincidence!" Terry declared triumphantly.

Denise was flustered. She tapped at the word balloon and rubbed it with her fingers like she could erase it. "*Anything* can be a coincidence."

"It's probably not, though. And I hate to tell you this, but I'm kind of getting into it," Terry informed Denise.

"Why would you hate to tell me that?"

"Because now I'm going to be over here all the time, until I'm finished reading it." He reached for the corner, to turn the page — but she smacked his hand away. "Your hands are dirty."

"Then *you* do it."

"Fine."

THERE WERE PLENTY OF WITNESSES, AND THEY ALL SAW THE SAME THING...

...A MAN-SHAPED MONSTER WHO VANISHED BEFORE THEIR EYES.

98

BUT THAT MONSTER HAS A NAME.

IT HAS A LAIR.
AND NOW IT HAS AN ENEMY.

Denise and Terry sat stunned, the manuscript splayed out on the floor before them, open to the page with the big panel about the big house. Denise slowly dropped a finger down onto the artwork, feeling the faint press of pen strokes on the paper. "Are you seeing this?" she asked aloud. "This is . . . this is *obviously* my house, isn't it?"

"Obviously," he echoed with a nod. "Back before it got . . . before it was . . . back when it was, um, newer."

"Back before it was a dump. You can say that, if you want. I give you permission."

"Okay, back before it was a dump."

"I wonder if there are any pictures of this house, from all the way back then. At the library, or someplace."

"Have you tried the Internet?" Terry suggested helpfully.

"Not yet. It only just occurred to me to look. Hang on." She'd stopped taking photos of the manuscript several pages back, because she was getting caught up in the story — but now she retrieved her phone and called up a browser. She plugged in 312 Argonne Street, and found a bunch of real estate listings, property tax records, assessments, and other pointless things she didn't care about. Next, she tried an image search, and got a little closer to the mark.

"Is that it? Let me see . . ."

"Hang on, Terry. Jeez." She dragged her thumbs around the screen, enlarging a promising black-and-white shot of a Victorian neighborhood that could've been St. Roch. "Is . . . is this it? Do you think? It's kind of grainy; I can't tell."

He squinted at the screen. "Maybe. See if you can find a better picture."

"This is the clearest one I can find. Everything else is just . . . some neighborhood pics, from some survey. Looks like the 1930s? Something about a streetcar line." The caption was fuzzy, and hard to read. "I'd be better off with a real photo and a magnifying glass."

"Or a laptop screen. You need more pixels."

"We don't have any Internet in the house, so it's this or nothing. Unless you want to go down to the po'boy place."

"Crispy's? I don't have any money."

"Me neither."

Outside, the sound of tires on gravel said that the battered blue Kia had returned, bearing her mom, Mike, and extra chicken biscuits for her self-invited guest. Both of them heard it. Terry sat upright like Jesus called his name, and scrambled to his feet.

"That's them," Denise said without even looking out the window. Terry was already halfway into the hallway.

"Wait up, man. You're not allowed to eat my parents' food without me." She hauled herself to her feet and followed along behind him, catching up at the top of the stairs. She could hear them outside, talking and laughing. Well, Sally was groaning — but Mike was laughing. He had no doubt shared some truly terrible joke, and Denise was blessed to have missed it.

She grinned anyway, and took the stair rail, pushing past Terry — then tripped down the steps in a hasty, greedy fashion. Terry was hot on her heels, showing more speed than she would've expected from him, but hey. Biscuits.

Up the front porch steps the food-bringers clomped, and down into the living room the kids descended. They would meet in the middle, at the dining room. There would be biscuits stuffed with fried chicken, and fast-food hash brown patties, and at least a fistful of ketchup packets, because Mike had learned the hard way that when Denise said "a fistful" she meant "preferably more than that, so use both hands when you raid the bin."

Except they didn't come inside. They didn't open the door with their elbows and knees, their arms full of bags.

Denise heard a crash instead — on the other side of the door, out on the porch. Immediately, she thought of the comic up in her room — but that was crazy, wasn't it?

Through the door's sidelights, Denise saw white paper bags go flying, and one of Mike's arms go flailing, and she heard her mother shriek in time with the sound of shattering wood.

Mike yelped in pain, then shouted, "It's okay, I'm okay!"

But when Denise whipped the front door open, her stepdad was chest-deep in splintered beams and jagged edges. He'd stepped right through the porch floor. It'd eaten him whole. He was still holding one bag, but he set it down beside himself and gasped. "I'm fine. No, no." He waved Sally's hand away. "I'm fine, look. I'm freaked out, that's all."

"Um . . . Mike?" Denise gazed in horror at the front of his shirt, just inside the hole.

He looked down and saw the streak of red oozing through the tee. He touched the wet spot and winced, but nodded. "It's a scratch. No big deal."

"You're bleeding!" Sally cried, only a little late to the party.

"It's just a scratch!" he repeated. "My leg's a little scraped up too, but that's the worst of it." He put his hands on the edge and tried to pull himself up, but succeeded mostly in pulling down more wood. He withdrew his hands, and looked around for something more solid.

Terry leaped into action. "Here," he offered, picking up a couple of pieces of plywood and dragging them over. "Use this."

"Not a bad idea," Mike agreed, reaching for it. "Put it down over here, and someone give me a hand, hold it steady. I don't know what I'm standing in, but it's squishing through my shoes."

"And you're bleeding," his wife reminded him.

"I'm more worried about the shoes." He might've been kidding, or he might've only been trying to make her feel better.

If that was the idea, it didn't work. Sally scooted to the edge of the plywood and sat on it, then urged Denise and Terry to get Mike's arms. Between them, and with a little cooperation, they got him up and out, and onto sturdier turf. He flopped down and panted, staring up at the underside of the flaking blue porch roof while the stain on his shirt spread ominously.

Sally yanked up the shirt and paused. "It's . . . it's not that bad, you're not going to die."

"Nope," he agreed, still catching his breath.

"But you need stitches."

He looked down, scrunching up his chin against his throat. "Oh yeah. I guess I do." He sounded more disappointed than traumatized. He swore, then apologized for his language when he remembered he was using it in front of somebody else's kid. Terry shrugged it off with a look on his face that said he'd heard far worse.

"What happened?" Denise wanted to know, as she stared down into the dark, wet, dirty hole.

Mike sat up, and used the hem of his shirt to dab at a scrape on his chest. "The floor is old. I am heavy. You do the math."

"We need to get you to an urgent care, and knit you back together. And maybe shoot you up for tetanus," Sally fussed, still patting him down for any further tears, scrapes, breaks, or bruises.

"I know, I know." He struggled to his feet, and checked out his left leg while he was at it.

Denise asked, "Did you cut up that one too?"

He shook his head. "Not cut up—just bruised up. Might be a little raw, in a place or two."

Sally directed her attention to Denise and Terry. "You two, stay here—and stay off this porch! I'm going to get him help, at the first place I can find on my phone."

"I'm going to tell the doctors you beat me up, because I dropped the chicken biscuits," Mike teased.

"I'm going to beat you up for real if you don't get your ass into the car." She hoisted him up and positioned herself under his armpit, for support. He didn't really seem to need it. He was only a little wobbly. "You kids, you heard me? Stay off this porch."

"Yes ma'am," Terry assured her.

"Good. Don't touch anything. Don't *do* anything," she ordered. "I'll be back as soon as I can."

"I'm not dying. You're overreacting," Mike protested, as she ushered him toward the car.

"Our house just tried to kill you." Sally stuffed him into the passenger's side, and opened the driver's door. One last time, she pointed her finger at Denise and Terry—who still stood in front of the open door. "Get inside, and stay inside. We'll be back." She closed herself inside the car, flung the gearshift into reverse, and peeled out of the gravel drive, back into the street.

"Oh God," Denise whispered.

"That was *crazy*," Terry agreed.

He looked around, and spotted the scattered, still-sealed bags of breakfast food. Slowly, carefully, he reached for the nearest sack and collected it under his arm. He wasn't exactly being sneaky, but you could see it from there.

"Terry . . . what are you doing?"

"The food's getting cold."

"You want to eat? At a time like this?"

He grabbed another crinkly bag and adjusted the top, rolling it up tighter. "You heard your stepdad: He's fine. He'll get some stitches and call it a day. We can't let this perfectly good food go to waste."

She was hungry enough that she kind of agreed with him—but she agreed with her mother, more. "I think Mom's right. This house is trying to kill us."

He hesitated, then collected bag number three. "I hope not. I mean, it wouldn't be the house, but maybe the ghosts . . . ?"

"Oh, knock it off," she said grouchily. She turned to go back inside. "It's an old building that creaks, and moans, and shakes, and falls apart — every chance it gets! It's not a conspiracy."

He bobbed his head toward the hole in the floor. "*That* didn't just fall apart. Look, would you? Look over there, and over there . . ."

At first, she didn't know what he was talking about. She didn't see anything except broken boards, loose nails, and the ragged edges of the plywood. They'd collected the plywood because they were going to use it to cover the floor holes inside, so the workmen could walk around without falling through the floor, like Mike had done.

"What are you talking about?" she asked.

He nudged the nails with his foot. "These nails. They're all over the place, like someone pulled them out. The mean guy really does want to kill you! Or kill *somebody* . . ."

She tiptoed to the edge, and craned her neck over the side. He was right, but she couldn't bring herself to agree out loud. She backed away from the edge, and returned to the doorway. It felt safer there, though maybe it shouldn't have. She didn't know what to say, or how to undermine the fact that yes — someone must've done it, no matter what she said to herself, or Terry. "They must've been like that already."

"That's not true, and you know it. The ghost did it. I bet you anything."

Denise headed inside, and paused in the foyer to let Terry catch up. He was the one bringing the food, and like it or not, she was starving. She thought about telling him to beat it, and leave her alone with the biscuits. She didn't want to hear his theories about ghosts, or bad mythical somebodies, or yanked-out nails. But she wasn't quite that mean, not even when she was quivering from low blood sugar and the leftover fright from seeing Mike halfway buried in the front porch, like it'd tried to eat him.

Terry swung inside behind her, balancing the bags with less skill than Mike had done; but everything made it to the dining room table, and Denise went to the kitchen to grab some paper towels because there were never enough napkins. She pulled the bottle of ketchup out of the fridge while she was at it, in case Mike had failed her on that front.

She threw the ketchup onto the table so hard that the bottle fell over, and her hands fluttered as she tossed the paper towels down too. She grabbed for the nearest bag, and unrolled the top to take a big sniff. The aroma of fried batter and salted potatoes wafted up and out.

Terry opened the next bag. He shoved his face in, and frowned. "There's nothing in this bag but ketchup packets."

"Really?" Denise asked, suddenly cheerful. She swiped the bag and dumped the packets onto the table. They tumbled out, along with two sleeves of hash browns. "Naw, see. You're a liar."

"It's *mostly* ketchup. Who even needs that much?"

"I do. If Mike was here, I'd give him a big hug. I never should've doubted him."

The third bag held everything else of note, and soon the table was covered with food for them, and food set aside for the adults upon their return. Mike and Sally could reheat theirs in the microwave upstairs when they got back.

They *would* be back, and everything *would* be fine.

Denise believed it with all her heart. But she ate her chicken biscuit with a mouth that was a little dry, and with an imagination running wild. What if Mike was hurt worse than it looked, and he didn't want to say so in front of her? What if he had some weird internal injuries — what if he was dying and no one noticed? They had health insurance, but it was bare-minimum stuff; Sally said it was just liability coverage on their bodies. What if he wound up in the hospital and it cost thousands and thousands of dollars, and they couldn't afford to do any more work on the house?

What if they had to keep living in it, just like it was?

What if they lost it, and had nowhere to live at all?

"You okay?" Terry asked.

Around a mouthful of food, she said, "What?"

"You're eating weird. You stopped chewing, like, a minute ago."

She swallowed, barely working the big lump down. She looked around for a soda, or a glass of water or something, and saw none. She also saw no reason to answer his question. "I need a Coke. You want one?" She shoved her chair back and went to the fridge without waiting for an answer.

"Sure."

The fridge was still kind of cool, even though the breaker was off. She pulled out two sodas and returned, rolling one past the wads of discarded wrappers and into Terry's hand. They cracked their respective cans at the same time.

The soda barely helped anything at all, but it did wash down the lump.

Terry took a sip and said, "Seriously, though: Are you okay?"

"I'm fine."

"You don't act fine."

"I'm worried about my stepdad."

"Is that all?" he asked, honest curiosity on his face. "You're not worried about the ghosts?"

"Say 'ghost' one more time, and I will throw you headfirst out the damn door."

Carefully, he corrected himself. "You're not worried about anything *else*?"

"*No.*"

Terry seemed to understand that he was on dangerous ground. "Do you . . . do you want to read some more of the comic? Might take your mind off the porch, and your stepdad."

"You mean the comic that's obviously about my house, which isn't creepy at *all*?"

He took a second or two to answer. "Yeah, that one."

Denise sighed. They had both finished eating, and they didn't have a TV or anything. "Fine, let's do it."

Terry hopped up out of his seat. "Right on!"

"You are *way* more invested in this comic than I am."

"No, I'm not. I'm just willing to admit that it's hella-cool. I don't know why you're pretending it isn't. Somebody famous used to live here."

"Joe Vaughn didn't live here. Some lady did. I think . . ." She looked over her shoulder, back up the stairs. "Terry, I think Joe Vaughn *died* here." It was the first time she'd said it out loud to anybody, and it felt gross. But it also felt a little good, to have it out in the open.

"You do?"

"Look, the Internet doesn't know that much about what happened to him — just that he was found dead at the bottom of some attic stairs, in a house that didn't belong to him. It belonged to some lady. She disappeared before he died."

"Maybe she's the lady ghost! The one with moxie."

Denise couldn't rule it out. "That's my guess. Except . . ." She started back up the stairs.

The stair rail rattled when Terry grabbed it too, and came along behind her. "Except what?"

"Except, if Joe died here . . . why was his manuscript up in the attic of somebody else's house? Did the lady steal it? Was she . . ." Denise wracked her brain. "Some kind of deranged fan? She could've been a stalker, maybe."

"Or a girlfriend."

"Also possible. Maybe Joe gave it to her. Maybe it was a gift, and she hid it in the attic to protect it."

Terry shrugged. "We can ask the ghosts, next time we try a little EVP. Hey, did you post those sample pages yet?"

"No. Haven't really had the time, man."

"*Somebody* will know *something*."

"But *somebody* might not be surfing the internet. Somebody might be dead and gone."

"Or just dead."

She stopped at the top of the stairs, and rubbed her eyes, and glanced at the attic door without meaning to. "Yeah. Probably just dead."

Denise sat up and smacked the book shut.

"What?" Terry asked, trying to grab it back. "Come on, man! It's getting good!"

"It's getting even creepier!" she squeaked. Exasperated, she climbed to her feet and carried the book away from Terry's greedy little mitts. "Come on, my stepdad fell down through the porch—just like Lucida and Doug did!"

Terry shook his head, motioning for her to give the book back. He gave her such an earnest, hopeful look that she had a hard time refusing him. Reluctantly, she passed it back. He opened it to the last page they'd seen, and pointed at the drawing. "No, it's not the same. Lucida Might went through a trapdoor. Your stepdad went through . . . well, he made his own hole."

"Or somebody else did, you said it yourself!"

"I say a lot of things."

Denise almost wanted to cry. "I don't understand why the house—or anybody in it—would want to hurt us."

"Me, either . . . and it's pretty weird that Doug, Lucida, *and* your stepdad got eaten up by a hole in the porch."

"Dammit, Terry." Gently, she took the book back from him. She looked briefly at its blank cover, and squeezed it against her chest. "This is extremely weird and creepy, that's all I know for sure."

"I am all about the weird and creepy!"

She almost smiled at him, but just then she caught a whiff of something sweet. Not candy-sweet, but flower-sweet. Not roses, or not *just* roses. Some other flower, with a sharp note of alcohol on top.

Her nostrils flared, and Terry perked up too. "I smell something. Do you?"

It wouldn't do any good to deny it. She said, "I think it's perfume."

"More like cologne."

"But for ladies, not for dudes."

He agreed with a nod, then looked around Denise's bedroom. "Is it yours?"

"No, it's not mine." She put the book down on her bed, which still hadn't been assembled yet — but she was totally going to get to it, one of these days. So really, she left the book on top of a mattress and box spring.

"Then where's it coming from?"

Denise swallowed, and crossed her arms under her boobs. "The hallway."

"Is there a ghost in the hallway?"

She gave up, and crossed her arms over her stomach. "You're the expert. You tell *me*."

Terry scrambled out the door like a cartoon character. He got two steps away before he remembered his equipment was in his bag, and his bag was on the floor — so he skidded back, unzipped the bag, and whipped out his recorder. He tossed the bag aside and made it all the way to the hall this time, brandishing the recorder like a torch. "Are there any spirits present with us today?" he asked with ridiculous speed and gravity. He sounded like somebody making hasty legal disclaimers at the end of a drug commercial. "Would you like to communicate with the living? Is there a message you'd like to pass along?"

Denise followed out the door more slowly. The perfume smell grew stronger, and she heard a soft, melodious hum. She looked down at the carpet to see if there were any footprints this time — but Terry was in the way, blocking her view. She couldn't see the carpet runner or the attic door.

She froze in the entrance to her bedroom and let him keep walking, holding up the recorder and staring off into space.

"Do you hear anything?" he asked Denise, not the spirit world. "I hear someone singing, but not quite."

Denise whispered, "It's someone humming. I heard it once before, but it doesn't sound the same. This sounds like . . . like a man, I think. I don't like this. It feels like a trick."

"It's going downstairs!" Without a second thought, he adjusted course to follow the unearthly music that wasn't quite music, because they couldn't quite hear it. They could only sense that it was there, somewhere at the edge of their hearing.

"Terry, don't. Be careful."

"Don't be careful. Great advice. I'll take it." He descended the stairs in quick staccato footsteps, and Denise wasn't sure if he was joking or if he'd actually misheard her.

She went down after him. She *had* to. It was her house and these were her ghosts. These were her stairs, and that was her room full of ladders and extension cords at the bottom; those were her boxes of fasteners and bins of tools; that was her stair rail's graceful swirl at the bottom, stuck through with rusty nails, just waiting for someone to grab on and bleed.

The nails on the porch, scattered like jacks.

Nails in the rail, pounded through so the points stuck out, and stuck up.

"Terry! Nails!"

He wasn't paying a lick of attention. He was too wrapped up in the chase, following his nose like a cartoon bird on a cereal box.

She tumbled down the stairs after him, trying to head him off. Her feet tripped over one another, but she stayed upright and she pushed past him as he reached down for support. The nails were plenty big enough and dangerous enough that Denise and Terry should've noticed them on the way upstairs, shouldn't they? She should've seen them before. Someone should've pointed them out, and removed them. Mike would've done it. Sally would've done it. Denise would've done it, if she'd seen them.

No, those nails had never been there before. Someone had put them there, quietly and deliberately. Unnaturally.

"Denise, I'm losing the trail . . ."

She swore at him, and bodychecked him out of the way before he could low-five the mystery pincushion. He spun around with confusion, smacking face-first against the wall and ricocheting back at Denise in the narrow, sharply angled space. It wasn't graceful. It wasn't fun. But Terry didn't get hurt, so . . . mission accomplished.

Denise put up one hand to catch him. She put back one hand to catch herself.

She felt the nail before she saw it, and before she felt it go clean through the web between her thumb and first finger. The violence was finished before she could announce it with a shriek, and a fling of her wrist that sent a thin spurt of blood across Terry's face, up the wall, and across the rickety steps themselves.

Staggering backward, down, off the steps and into the living area where the parlor had holes in the floors and there wasn't any air-conditioning to speak of, Denise clutched her hand to her chest and squeezed at the dirty, bleeding puncture.

Terry leaped to her aid, or at least he leaped to her personal space. "What happened? What are you doing? Why did you push me?"

She held up her hand and let it bleed in front of him, answering enough questions that he turned white. "Oh. My. God." He wiped a smudge of blood off his forehead, looked at the smear on the back of his wrist, and went even paler.

Her eyes scanned the scenery and spied the napkins on the dining room table. She darted over there and seized a fistful, pinching them against the wound. She breathed in and out through her mouth, making whooshing noises all the way — breathing like she was having a baby, because that was supposed to make pain easier to take. "I have to stop the bleeding. I have to keep it from getting infected. I need a first aid kit."

"Do you have one?"

"Under the kitchen sink." She flapped her other hand to show him the general direction she meant, and he went to retrieve it. A dribble of blood oozed down her wrist and trickled down her forearm.

He produced the kit quickly and cracked open the white plastic case.

Denise said, "I need some antibacterial ointment, and some alcohol." She winced as she said the word, knowing how bad it was likely to hurt. "And a couple of Band-Aids."

"I don't know if a couple of Band-Aids are going to cut it."

She left him for the kitchen sink. She put the bloody fast-food napkins beside it, ran the water until it was a little cool, and forced herself to wash her unwanted piercing with some soap. It wasn't really bleeding that bad, all things considered. It was only a little stab, and that was a good thing too. The nail had gone straight through, palm to back, and it didn't hit anything bony.

"It's only a flesh wound," she decided.

"We should call your parents."

She smacked the lever to turn off the water, retrieved the least bloody and most uncrumpled napkins, and applied pressure to the injury. "Absolutely not."

"But you're bleeding."

"Not very bad."

"You screamed."

She rolled her eyes. "It surprised me. It hurts, but that's okay," she assured him, and herself too. "A lot of things hurt. It's not the end of the world. They've got enough problems without me falling onto sharp things."

"No, but it's a rusty nail," he argued. "When was the last time you had a tetanus shot?"

She honestly couldn't remember. She was too rattled. She knew she'd gotten one at some point. It might've been a couple of years ago, or it might've been a lot longer. "It had to be . . . somewhat recently?

Don't you have to have your shots up to date, before you can go to school?"

"You should get another one, just to be safe. Call your mom, and ask her." He held up the antibiotic ointment and a small bottle of peroxide, which would work as well as alcohol in a pinch. "Please?"

Denise didn't respond other than to nod at the kitchen sink, where he put the supplies. She wadded up all but a couple of napkins, thrust them inside one of the empty takeout bags to hide their bloody nature, and stuffed them deep into the trash can beside the fridge. She wrestled one-handed with the peroxide until Terry took it away from her and pushed the childproof cap loose. He offered to do the honors, so she let him — cleaning the wound and treating it and wrapping it up with the biggest Band-Aid that was left in the mostly empty box.

"Look, I won't tell your parents," he said finally. "But people get hurt less every day, and it turns into a big deal because they didn't take care of themselves," he insisted. "Don't be that guy."

"I've never been that guy."

"Yeah, well. Don't start now."

Outside, they heard a car's engine come low and slow up to the house. Wheels turned and ground on gravel. "Hurry up!" Denise urged, using her free right hand to scoop up the bits of leftover bandage packaging, the ointment, and the first aid kit itself.

While Terry performed the last of his doctoring, she used one hand to cram everything back inside the plastic case and toss the garbage into the trash. When he was finished, she stashed everything where it belonged, running back and forth between the dining room table and the kitchen sink, and the stairway rail — where she used the last of the napkins to swab down the visible blood and wipe down the nails.

But whoever had pulled up to the house was only turning around. The car was large and green, and it didn't stay — it only backed up and headed the other direction.

"Oh thank God," she breathed, watching it leave through the parlor window. "There's still time."

Terry was washing his hands at the sink. Over his shoulder he called out, "Time for what?"

Denise looked around for the tool bins, and selected a sturdy hammer with an oversized head. She quietly thanked God, or heaven, or friendly ghosts, that she'd only hurt her left hand, and the right was still strong enough to pry nails out of the stair rail before they could hurt anyone else. Or before anyone else could see them.

"Like I said, I'm going to fix this mess that Joe made." She tested the hammer's weight in her hand.

"You think it's really him?"

"Yeah, I do. Because of all the nails. There were nails rolling around when the window shut on my mom, and nails on the porch when Mike fell through, and now there are nails on the stair rail." She didn't smell flowers anymore, and there wasn't any more blood on the staircase. Of course, there weren't any more napkins, either, and Mike would probably notice. She'd say she spilled something, and used them to clean it up. It was practically true. She would tell him it was ketchup. He'd believe her.

"What's Joe got to do with nails, though?"

It was a reach, but her gut was giving her the green light so she aired her hunch out loud. "He used to be a carpenter; that's what Wikipedia said. Maybe he thinks he still is one."

Terry nodded thoughtfully, and dried his hands on the dish towel hanging from the stove handle. "Maybe. Or maybe he's just a jerk who likes to play with sharp things. Either way, I'm going to help clean this up."

Denise appreciated the help, but she wasn't sure she should accept it. She half thought about sending him home for his own good. After all, she had a comic book upstairs that was basically a portent of doom; every time she read it, something bad happened.

That was crazy, right? Too crazy to be true, for sure.

She kept her mouth shut while she levered the hammer's head up and down, dragging the nails up and out of the bannister and handing them to Terry, one after another.

Until it was just full of holes.

Denise hid her injured hand in her pocket. When no one was looking, she changed the Band-Aids and squeezed more ointment onto the ragged, round holes that were red and angry-looking, but were they more red and angry-looking than the day before? She couldn't tell. She looked up "blood poisoning" online, because Terry had said she might get it. But no matter how hard she checked, she didn't see any pink lines creeping out from the hole, creeping up her arm and toward her heart.

She was slightly less certain about the symptoms of tetanus. She knew there were shots for that one and she'd probably had one in the recent past; but sometimes people called tetanus "lockjaw," and that sounded much more disturbing. She opened and closed her mouth as wide as she could, over and over again — testing to see if anything was seizing up, or getting stiff.

She really didn't want to show it to anybody, despite Terry's insistence that she get some proper medical attention. And of course, he had a suggestion. Terry *always* had a suggestion.

According to him, the high school's nurse moonlighted at a CVS clinic during the summer. Her name was Ms. Radlein, and when she wasn't patching up kids at Rudy Lombard High, she was doling out vaccinations and advice in the pharmaceutical section of the nearest drugstore.

By all reports, she was a popular and reasonable woman, and she had been known to be discreet. "Anyway, she's a friend of my dad's," he'd finished. He'd given her directions to the bus that would take her there, and then he finally gave up trying to make her go — telling her to do whatever she wanted, but not to come crawling to him when she dropped dead.

Denise wasn't too keen on the idea of dropping dead.

She also wasn't keen on the idea of her mom and Mike finding out about this, so she sucked it up, and first thing in the morning she took the bus to the drugstore. It was less than two miles away, but she was glad for the sticky cool air of the bus, because outside it was far, far worse. She'd had to wait until Sally was across town, arguing with the bank about when the next disbursement of the loan would be coming down the pike — and Mike was sleeping in, doped a little on painkillers and worn out from his traumatic experience.

Denise left a note, just in case. It was a vague note. It promised little, except that she was alive and she intended to return. If she was lucky, she'd be back in time to wad it up and throw it into the trash — and no one would ever read it.

The drugstore was on a block with a strip mall that was brand-new, but half-empty. In addition to the CVS it held a cash-for-gold place, a cell phone shop, and a laundromat. The other three slots were vacant, but a sign promised a chain pizza joint: COMING SOON!

Denise got off the bus and stood in a freshly paved parking lot with jet-black asphalt that felt like the surface of the sun, even through her flip-flops. She checked her hand for fresh swelling or streaks, took a deep breath, and pushed the glass door to let herself inside.

The AC was as new as everything else; it hit her in the face so hard and so fast that it dried out her eyes. She blinked until they worked right again, checked the signs above the aisles, and headed to the back right corner of the store — where the drugs were doled out and the nurse allegedly lurked, ready to stab people with needles. Or whatever.

She arrived at the small lobby area in front of the pharmacists' window, where everything smelled sterile and new. It was quiet back there too. No one was waiting for a prescription, and the people in the white lab coats were all busy in the shelves, setting up medicine for absent customers.

Around the fake wall that didn't even reach to the ceiling, she could hear a woman's voice explaining something calmly. A moment later, out stepped the girl whose name Denise was pretty sure was Dominique. She was stuffing something into her backpack, and when she realized that she'd been spotted, her eyes flashed. She zipped up her bag.

She wouldn't even look up as she fled.

The nurse followed behind her. She was tall, thin, and white — with short silver hair and a gray pantsuit under an unbuttoned lab coat. She checked around, and saw that Denise was standing there, alone and shifty-looking. "Do you need tampons too?" she asked. "I know it gets tricky when school's not in session, so I keep a stash. Are you new here? Did Dom or one of the other girls send you?"

"No ma'am. That's not . . . what I need." She suddenly felt very self-conscious. "And yes ma'am, I'm new. I didn't mean to . . . I wasn't trying to . . . I can get my own tampons, thanks. We're not rich, but we're not that bad off. Yet," she added.

"All right then, what can I do for you?"

She had a funny accent, one Denise couldn't quite place. It almost sounded like a northern city accent, but she suspected that it wasn't. She shifted her weight from foot to foot, feeling more awkward than if she really *had* come to collect some tampons.

Denise pulled her hand out from under her backpack, where she'd gotten used to hiding it. "I . . . I hurt myself, at home. I can't tell if it's getting infected . . . ? I don't know." She peeled off the bandage and waved her hand a little, shaking off the sting.

The woman, whose name tag confirmed that she was "Nurse Radlein," assumed an expression of cautious concern. She took Denise's hand and turned it over, checking the entry and exit punctures. "How did this happen?"

"Rusty nail. My mom and stepdad are fixing up an old house. It's a craphole," Denise said, preemptively. It was becoming a defensive habit. "I wasn't paying attention. Nobody's fault but my own," she added. That part was defensive too.

"The nail went right through, didn't it?"

"Yeah. I've been trying to keep it clean, but . . . I don't know. Am I going to get blood poisoning, or something?"

"When was your last tetanus shot?"

"I'm not sure."

Nurse Radlein released her hand, and withdrew toward the nook around the wall — motioning for Denise to follow her. "It can't have been *too* long ago. You have to provide vaccination records before enrolling in school. You're not homeschooled, are you?"

"No ma'am. Public school, but I've been in Texas." She stood there uncertainly, squeezing her hurt hand with her unhurt hand and wondering if this was really such a good idea.

Nurse Radlein glanced up, and then waved her closer. "All right, well. Go ahead and sit down."

The nurse sat on the edge of her desk, motioning for Denise's hand again. When she had it in her grasp once more for an up close and personal inspection, she said, "This isn't bad at all, and I don't see any signs of infection. You've done a good job taking care of it. When did it happen?"

"Yesterday."

"Then I wouldn't worry too much, because it's looking good. But in case it's been a few years since your tetanus booster, you might want to get another one, just in case. It can't hurt, and might help."

Denise shook her head. "Naw, I can't do that."

"Why not?"

"Because my parents . . . um . . . they don't know about this. I didn't want to worry them. We don't have much money, and my stepdad already had to go to the urgent care place."

"You've got money enough to fix a house. Money enough for tampons over the summer, apparently."

"I didn't . . . I wasn't being all *judgy* about that." Denise's eyes narrowed. "Look, we barely had money enough to buy that house, even though it's practically condemned. I know there's kids who are broker than us, but we aren't flush."

"I didn't say you were. All I meant was —"

"We've got every last dime tied up in this awful old place, and it'll probably fall down anyway, before we can prop it up good. Don't act like tampons and tetanus shots are the same thing. Just 'cause I can swing one doesn't mean I can have both."

"I *understand* that," the nurse insisted. "But I can help you with free tampons, and not a free tetanus shot. That's what I'm trying to tell you: Your resources may be limited, but you've got more to work with than some people — and I can help you juggle them more wisely."

Denise gave the nurse a long, hard look. She wasn't sure if she believed her or not. Finally, she sighed. "Forget it. I appreciate the offer, but I can't take you up on it. I *can't* tell my parents. It's not just the money . . . it's the house. And whoever's still in it." She slung her bag around, and turned to leave. "I'm sorry. I shouldn't have come here. I need help, but you're right. I don't need it that bad."

"That's not the message I was trying to convey. Here, at least let me bandage you back up . . ."

"I've got my own Band-Aids." She wrapped her hand back up again as best as she could while on the run, and fled the makeshift office just like Dominique had, embarrassed for different reasons — reasons she couldn't quite put into words. She squeezed out around the fake wall, into the soft mumbling echoes of the drugstore with its rows of greeting cards, housewares, vitamins, and shampoo.

She hustled away from the pharmacy toward the front door. Around the first corner she went, her flip-flops squeaking on the floor, one after the other, going so fast that by the time she rounded the last aisle past the makeup counter, she was almost running.

That's why it hurt, when she plowed into Dominique.

The other girl wasn't coming from the other direction; she wasn't moving at all. She stopped Denise cold, with the force of just standing there.

Denise bounced back — partly by reflex, partly by physics. "Sorry," she said fast, and she meant it. "I didn't mean to. I'm sorry about that — I didn't see you."

"I know."

"Were you . . . were you waiting for me? You're . . . you're Dominique, right? From Crispy's?"

"Yeah, that's me. What were you doing in there? Were you asking for stuff? Stuff you could buy your own damn self?"

"No," she told her. "I swear, I wasn't. I wouldn't take advantage."

"You know Miss Ginny buys it for us. Out of her own pocket, sometimes — especially over the summer when we can't just go to her office in the school."

"Nurse Radlein . . . is Miss Ginny?"

"To *us*, not you."

Dominique took a step forward, and Denise took a step back — stopping against a L'Oreal display that she couldn't afford to mess up. She held up both of her hands, showing the bandage. "I went to the nurse for help, all right?"

Dominique looked at the half-bandaged covering there, and saw a spreading red dot. "Oh, crap. What happened?" she asked, like she honestly wanted to know.

Denise closed her hand and felt it growing damp. The puncture wound was bleeding again, a sharp little stigmata that just wouldn't close all the way. "I got hurt, all right? I can't tell my parents. I thought I needed a tetanus shot."

"Why won't you tell your parents? Go to your doctor, or something."

"We don't *have* a doctor! We don't have money, either. *God*," she said, using the hem of her tee to apply pressure. The shirt was black, and it wouldn't show. "All we have is a craphole of a house and a ghost that's trying to kill us."

The door's greeting bell rang louder than a gunshot, and a cop strolled inside, taking off his sunglasses and tucking them into his pocket. He was white, with hair that was almost white too, in a crew cut that said he meant business — probably all the time, whether he was in uniform or not. He gave the girls a side-glance.

They straightened up and fake-smiled for all they were worth. Dominique batted her eyelashes and said brightly to Denise, "Look, they have that new mascara. Is this the kind you wanted?"

Denise had been watched by enough security guards in enough makeup aisles to know how this worked. "Oh yeah, that's it. Do they have anything except that blue-black? That stuff looks like crap on me; my hair's too light for it. The dark brown looks better."

Dom flipped through the offerings, pretending to look. "I see brownish black. Is that close enough?"

"Might be. Let me see . . ."

After a few seconds of suspicious observation, the cop gave them a nod of his head, the kind that said he was going to walk away, but he was still watching them. Then he lost interest and headed somewhere else in the store.

Dominique was rattled.

Denise was rattled too, but not quite the same way. "I hope he didn't think we were stealing."

Dom leaned in and whispered: "Don't even say that, not so loud. You don't want him coming back, do you? *Jeez.*"

"No, I really don't," she mumbled back.

Dominique had already turned away. She pushed her way past the glass door, and was gone.

Denise thought about going after her, but she saw the bus pulling around the corner, so she went to the stop instead, feeling a little lost. She looked for Dominique but didn't see her, and she gave up when the bus drew up to a halt and the doors split open.

Inside, she gave the driver her transfer and took a seat right behind him — where she fiddled with the dirty little bandage and used her next to last fresh Band-Aid. It didn't want to stick. Her skin was too messy from dried blood, or too damp with the blood that hadn't dried yet.

She tucked her hand into her shirt and tried not to look as gross as she felt.

Back home, she tossed the note she'd left behind, because Mike was still snoring in the bedroom and her mom's car was nowhere to be seen.

Then she washed her hands and very, very carefully applied her final sticky bandage.

When she was as first-aided up as she was going to get, she sat down at the dining room table with a Coke and poked idly at her phone.

As it turned out, her old school friends in Texas were mostly talking about some kid from her class who'd died in a car wreck. It was no one she'd known very well. He'd been a face in the hall, and she might've recognized him on sight, or then again, she might not. It was a surprise, but not a catastrophe. It happened a million miles away, to someone she barely recognized.

But jeez, everybody back at her old school was in crazy mourning, at least online. She shot Trish a text asking about it, hoping for details.

What kind of car wreck? She asked. *Was it his fault, or somebody else?*

Trish responded immediately, and briefly. Nobody knows yet. Rumor has it he ran a stop sign or something. Will let you know if I hear anything for sure.

Didn't know him very well but it's sad, Denise added.

He was a friend of Kierons. You should reach out, say something nice to your dear old ex.

No. She shook her head as she texted. It'd be more trouble than it was worth.

Then Trish said something about getting ready to catch a matinee, and turning off her phone, so Denise started to close hers too, but then her email pinged to say she had something new. She tapped the icon with her thumb, and frowned with confusion, then smiled.

Hello Miss Farber, my name is Eugenie Robbins. My father was Marty Robbins, and yes, a long time ago he was Joe Vaughn's literary agent. As you may have learned by now, Joe disappeared decades ago. (And I regret to say that my father is now deceased.)

I was very excited to see the images you sent! I'm not familiar with that particular Lucida Might story, but Joe wrote so many of them. It doesn't mean that *Lucida Might and the House of Horrors* was never published.

Your message mentioned that you live in New Orleans, and you're afraid that you live in the house where Joe died. I suppose you might? I don't know exactly where he was found, but I will try to look up an address for you. All I remember, off the top of my head, is that the house belonged to an older woman, and no one really knew why Joe was in her house.

I'd love to see the whole manuscript—if you have the time or interest in scanning it for me. Joe's comics are all out of print, and no one remembers the TV show anymore, but a lost manuscript might revive interest in his backlist. As far as I know, Joe had no heirs or near relatives; at least, no one ever came forward to claim his estate.

I'm not saying that you're sitting on a gold mine by any

means, but there might be some money to be made—you never know. I'd be happy to talk about representing the project for you or your parents, if you're interested in shopping it around. My agency manages my father's surviving clients (or their estates), and in all honesty, the thought of handling one of Dad's authors (even indirectly, after all this time) makes me very, very happy.

It's funny, my dad used to say that Joe sometimes hid "Easter eggs" in his stories, little pieces of autobiography, here and there. Does the house in the comic look anything like yours? That would be fascinating, wouldn't it? Maybe that's why he was there. Maybe he used it as an art reference. He must've known the lady who owned it.

Think about it. Let me know. Feel free to be in touch, and by all means, enjoy the reading!

At the bottom of the email, she'd included her office address and phone number.

"Huh," Denise said out loud.

A grumble of gravel suggested that her mother's car was pulling up beside the house.

She closed her phone and tucked it into her back pocket.

Around noon, Norman showed up for his new side gig with a large pizza. "Unclaimed at work," he explained, deploying the box to the middle of the dining room table with a casual flip of his wrist.

"I love this guy!" a freshly awakened Mike declared with honest enthusiasm. "What are the toppings?"

"They're *free* toppings," Denise guessed. "The best toppings of all."

Sally came down the stairs, shaking her head all the way. "No, no, no. Don't be silly. Thank you, Norman — that was very thoughtful, but of course I want to pay you for it. You didn't have to bring lunch."

"No way, Mrs. Cooper. I got it for free, so you get it for free. My only condition is that I get a piece. I'd ask for two, but I had one at work already."

They gathered around, pulled up chairs, and split up the free pizza.

When it was successfully reduced to crumbs, Mike slowly helped clean up, moving stiffly. He'd come home with stitches and an order to stay off his feet, but he wasn't paying much attention to that order. He was still doing all the same stuff as before — just slower, and more carefully.

Norman leaned over and asked Denise quietly, "His foot's still not any better?"

"It's not his foot anymore," she whispered back. "He fell through the porch and got hurt."

"Holy crap. This place ought to come with hazard pay . . ."

On her way to the kitchen, Sally said, "Norman, today we're going to pull down the rotted trim in the extra bedrooms upstairs, and prep for painting. There's still some wallpaper that needs to come down, and probably some plaster in need of patching."

"You name it — just point me at the supplies!"

She disappeared into the kitchen to grab some paper towels, and Denise's phone buzzed on the table.

"Anything interesting?" Norman asked.

"Maybe?" She wasn't sure if she should tell him about Lucida Might, but then again, she couldn't see why not. "See, the other day I found this manuscript, up in the attic. It's a comic book," she explained. And then she told the rest as fast as possible, concluding, "Supposedly this guy's papers are archived out at Tulane. Didn't you say you work there, sometimes, during the week? At the cafeteria? Maybe you could show me where the library is. I've never been there before."

"Yeah, sure. I can do that. It's only a couple of buses and a little walking. Can I see the comic book, if I take you out there?"

"Sure."

"Cool. Then what are you doing this weekend?"

"Not a thing."

He bobbed his head from left to right. "We can do it on Saturday. Meet you at the bus stop outside the school?"

"Sounds awesome. What time?"

"How about eleven? We can change buses down by the market—and pick up some lunch or something, if you want."

Oh, yes. She definitely wanted.

CHAPTER TWELVE

How are ur ghosts? Still ghosty?

Denise grinned down at the text. She'd only told Trish the bare basics of the spook situation. *Still ghosty, but quiet ATM. Mike is doing better, I think. Not quite so grunty and stiff.*

That's good. I hope nobody else gets hurt. By ghosts or whatever.

She could only agree. *Me too.*

So what about school next year? UR still coming back, rite?

Planning on it. Got a good roommate waiting back in Texas.

Trish replied, **Awwww. You mean me? You had BETTER mean me.**

Always you, yes — you big dork :)

Eventually, after a slow-growing headache from staring at her ancient phone, Denise gave up and decided to hoof it down to Crispy's. She badgered Sally to pick her up when summoned via text, and her mom agreed — just to get rid of her, Denise was pretty sure.

She brought two bucks because that's all she could scare up. It was only enough to get a drink and a small order of fries, but that was okay. She wasn't really hungry for anything except Internet.

She generally avoided the smattering of other kids who were hanging out in the dining area — all of whom were doing pretty much the same thing she was. One or two had phones, a couple had laptops open. One guy kept jiggling his power cord's connection, and Denise knew that feeling. If she didn't have hers positioned at just the perfect angle, it'd pop out easy as pie.

When she'd collected her food on a tray and picked a seat against the wall, she turned on her phone — but the only new message was a late closing volley from Trish, who declared herself QUEEN OF THE DORKS and don't u forget it

The door chimed, and someone came in. Someone hung out in Denise's peripheral vision, hovering. It was Dominique, acting like she wanted to say something.

"Hey," Denise said. "What's up?"

"Nothing," the other girl said back, but she worked her way a little closer. "Except, I was gonna say sorry about the CVS thing. I didn't know you were hurt, and then you played along later, and I appreciated it. So . . . are we cool?"

"Sure. We're cool." She wasn't sure how to ask what prompted the apology, but she wanted to know so she stumbled around the subject. "You um . . . you mean about the cop?"

"Oh, that guy's a jerk. He harasses us all summer — but I was standing next to you, in the white privilege zone," she said with a grin. "Anyway, my grandma will kill me if I get banned from the drugstore, for stealing or mouthing off, or anything else. She sends me down there all the time, running her errands and buying her smokes."

"But you weren't stealing."

"No, but that might not've stopped him, if he'd been in the wrong mood. Or if I'd been by myself. Or . . . I don't know." Dominique looked relieved and kind of embarrassed. "Anyway, that's all. I just wanted to say that."

"I'm just glad you're not mad."

"No, I'm not mad. See you around." Dominique melted back into the lobby to join somebody else she knew, and then Denise was on her own again.

Until Terry arrived.

He strolled into the joint and made a beeline for her. He didn't go to the counter to buy anything, but parked himself into the swivel chair across the table from where Denise had — once upon a time — had every intention of getting some sweet, sweet Internet-and-AC time.

He asked, "How's your hand?"

She held it up and waved it around. "It bleeds a little, sometimes, but the nurse said it looked fine. Hey, I was gonna ask you: Do you have any extra Band-Aids lying around at your house? I'm running out, and I still haven't told Mom or Mike what happened."

"All we have is one first aid kit. My dad stocks it from work, when he can. We don't have any extras, not Band-Aids or anything else. Sorry."

"No, I understand. I um . . . I shouldn't have asked."

"The nurse didn't give you any?"

"The nurse and I disagreed over whether or not I should tell my parents about the whole thing. She says they should take me to get a tetanus shot, just to be on the safe side. I said we couldn't do it, not after Mike's accident."

Terry nodded knowingly. He politely refrained from saying, 'I told you so.' "How'd your stepdad turn out, anyway?"

"They gave him a bunch of stitches, and he has some pretty bad bruises. He's taking it easy for a few days so he doesn't bust any of the sutures. Mom's waiting on him hand and foot, and telling him not to get used to it. If I'm lucky, she'll come and give me a ride home when I text her."

"If she doesn't, I'll walk back with you."

"Thanks, man. If she does, I'll get her to give you a lift home too. If you want."

He smiled, and his cheeks were as round as apples. "You're awesome. So . . . have you read any more of the comic?" he asked, his voice dripping with the hint.

"Nope. I stuffed it under my bed."

"You have a bed now? Not just the mattress on the floor?"

"I quit waiting for Mike to assemble it, and put it together myself."
A smidge of pride seeped into the declaration. "It took me half the
afternoon, but I did it."

He stopped hinting. "Go you. So . . . if you want, I could come over
and we could read it together. If you want."

She relented. It was easier than fighting him. "I'm sure it's fine."
Her phone buzzed. It was Sally, saying she'd have to walk home on her
own after all. "Great. Mom says she's not going to pick me up. So it's
foot-power for both of us. What the hell. Let's go."

Terry predicted that the trip wouldn't take them ten minutes, and he
was right. They arrived at the Agony House before anybody'd sweated
through their clothes too badly, and they found the place empty.

Sally had left a note on the dining room table.

*The power's on, so you can run your AC. Electricians are
done for now. Plumbers are barely started, but they should be
gone by the time you read this. They'll be back tomorrow.
Sorry I'm not home, and sorry you had to walk. I trust you survived the journey. I'll be back soon. Mike blew out a couple of
stitches, so I'm running him back to the doctor for a patch-up.*

"Great," Denise declared, with great sarcasm. "Now I *definitely* can't
tell them I need a tetanus shot."

"Maybe they won't charge him, if it's only a couple of stitches. Since
they already got paid to do it once."

She ignored his optimism, knowing it was useless. "I don't think it
works that way. I swear . . . by the time we're done with this house,
that doctor will be able to buy himself a yacht. Maybe I should change
my major and go to med school. I could use a yacht."

"You don't have a major yet. You're still in high school." Then he
paused and frowned. "Right?"

"I'll be a senior this year: Rudy Lombard, or bust. And I *will* have a major, pretty soon."

He dropped his bag on the table, beside hers. "What will it be?"

"Law," she said. "I'm going to be a lawyer."

"Everybody hates lawyers."

"I know. That's why I'm going to be one." She explained, "Me and Mom, when it was just the two of us . . . we got screwed over a bunch. Our landlords were always cheap bastards, or crooked bastards. They'd take our money and let the place go to hell, or refuse to give us our deposits back, so we couldn't move to a better place. First and last month's rent is hard to pull together when you can't get your deposit back."

"Tell me about it."

"They always had some BS reason for it, and they always would send us letters from their attorneys, kicking us out or saying we owed more money than we ever agreed to. It was a racket," she declared, echoing something her mom had said years before. "There was one lawyer who tried to bleed us dry, when my mom got served for driving without insurance — and another lawyer who charged us a bunch of money when Mom got hit at a stoplight. Some dumb girl was texting, and plowed right into her. It tore up Mom's shoulder and neck real bad, but all the money we got from the girl's insurance went to the lawyer's fees. Mom needed physical therapy for months. We could only afford it for a couple of weeks."

Terry scrunched up his face, like he wasn't entirely sure where she was going with this. "So . . . if you can't beat 'em, join 'em?"

"Exactly! If we'd had a lawyer . . . if we could've afforded a *real* one . . . things would've been different for us. Once I'm a lawyer, I'll make sure that kind of BS doesn't happen again. Not to my mom, or me, or anybody else who needs help but can't pay through the nose to get it."

"You'll be a lawyer for free?"

"Not for everybody—only for the broke folks. Or that's the plan. Now come on, I'll drag out the comic since it's just you and me."

"You promise you won't get creeped out again, and slam it shut?"

"Yeah, I promise. Let's see what this ghost has in store for us next. Forewarned is forearmed, right?"

"I have no idea. I don't even know what that *means*."

WHERE AM I?

HANG IN THERE, DOUG. I'M COMING TO SAVE YOU!

Terry leaned back against Denise's bed, and let out a little laugh.

"What's so funny?" she asked him.

He pointed at the open manuscript. "See? The comic isn't predicting what's going to happen. Unless you seriously think you've got goblins, in addition to rats and spiders. And ghosts."

"So far, we have absolutely zero goblins. No rats, either. I think? I haven't seen any. Plenty of spiders, though."

He nodded gravely. "Oh, you definitely have rats. *Everybody* has rats, around here. But it'd be worse if we were any closer to the river."

"Please do not tell me these things."

"I'm only trying to help."

"Stop. Stop trying to help," she urged. "Forget what I said about being forewarned. What I don't know won't hurt me."

"Oh my God, you are *so* wrong."

THEY CAUGHT ME BY SURPRISE THIS TIME, BUT IT WON'T HAPPEN AGAIN!

I'VE PROBABLY LOST MY ELEMENT OF SURPRISE. I'D BETTER STAY ON GUARD, AND BE PREPARED FOR ANYTHING.

HEAVEN KNOWS, DOUG WON'T SAVE HIMSELF!

WHAT AN ODD KITCHEN. OH, NO, I HOPE THAT'S NOT DOUG!

SURELY IT *CAN'T* BE . . . ?

NO. THERE *MUST* BE TIME TO SAVE HIM!

Denise smacked her hands triumphantly on her knees. "That is *totally* our kitchen, in that scene right there. Look, it's the same layout, with the sink under the window, and the door's in the same place, and the walls look similar."

Terry's eyes went wide. "You have a fireplace in your kitchen? Holy crap. I've got to see this . . ."

She stopped him before he could leap up from the floor and dart down the stairs. "No, dummy. We don't have a fireplace, or a cauldron full of boiling bones, either. But the window is in the same place, and I bet there used to be a fireplace where the cauldron is. For cooking or whatever."

"I only barely saw your kitchen for a minute the other day. I'll take your word for it."

She touched the panel with the table and chairs. "The dining room is pretty much the same too, though it's tough to tell."

As if on cue, tires ground into the grass and gravel beside the house.

"It sounds like they're home." She went to her bedroom window. She stood in the full blast of the AC, enjoying the chill for another few seconds before turning the dial down to "low." If Sally thought she'd been blasting it ever since she got home from Crispy's, Denise would never hear the end of it. She watched her mom get out of the driver's side quickly, then run around to the passenger's side and open the door for Mike. He climbed out carefully, one arm clutching his chest, and let Sally lead him up to the house.

"I'd better go see how he's doing." She turned to find Terry on his feet, the comic in his hand.

He set it on her bed. "I'm sure he's good."

"Me too, but I want to hear it from him."

Together they headed downstairs, greeting Mike and Sally at the door.

"Hey there, Terry," Mike said with a lopsided grin. "Nice to see you again."

"Thank you, sir. Nice to be back."

Denise looked him up and down. "You blew out some stitches, huh?"

Sally rolled her eyes. "I told him to lay off the handyman stuff, but he didn't listen. My beautiful dumbass thought he'd take a crowbar to the wainscoting in the dining room, and it was more than the sutures could take."

"I just wanted to pull it off before the electricians reach it tomorrow. It's in good shape," he insisted. "We can put it back up later. They'll just tear it loose or cut right through it. We should try to save it."

"*I* should try to save it," his wife corrected him. "Or we can ask Norman to take care of it tomorrow. *You* should go lie down."

"I can't. I'm too hungry."

Sally shook her head. "Aw, dammit. We were going to run past Wendy's, and I forgot."

"We could order pizza . . ." Denise suggested. The mention of Norman had made her think of it.

"Pizza," her mom agreed wearily. "I don't have the energy for anything else. Terry, are you sticking around?"

Politely, he demurred. "I don't have to, ma'am. Y'all already fed me once. I should probably go home and make something for myself."

"And your dad?" Denise asked.

"He's doing a double shift. He won't be home until after I'm in bed."

Mike waved away the boy's protests. "Then that settles it. You're not eating home alone, not while we've got pizza on the way. Sally, hand me your phone." He shot Denise a wink. "Maybe Norman is working the delivery routes again, eh?"

She rolled her eyes and said, "Come on, Terry. Let's go upstairs."

Once in Denise's room, they settled in with Lucida Might again — but as they opened the manuscript, Denise changed her mind and picked up her phone to check her messages.

"Do you have to do that right *now*?" Terry complained.

"Settle down, you addict. I was just going to show you this email I got, from an agent. Her dad used to represent Joe Vaughn. She wrote me back."

"Who wrote you back?" Denise and Terry jumped. They looked up and saw Sally standing in the doorway. "Sorry, I didn't mean to startle you. I just came up to say the pizzas will be here in another twenty minutes."

Denise's stomach growled in response. "Good," she said, and opened the email before her screen went dark.

"Is it something important?" Sally asked. "Is it about a scholarship?"

"*Mom* . . . no, stop it. It's something else." To Terry, she said, "She wants me to get in touch with her."

"*Who* wants you to get in touch?" Her mom came inside, and tried to get a look at the phone.

Denise held it out of her reach. "This lady, okay?"

"Some stranger on the Internet?"

"Yes. No, I mean. It's not like that."

"And since when are you into comic books?" she asked, suddenly noticing the open manuscript lying on the floor between Denise's and Terry's folded knees.

"Since I found this one in the attic. It's not a real comic book, exactly. It's a manuscript for one, but I don't know if anybody ever published it." She looked back down at the email. "Don't make fun of it. It might be valuable."

Sally was unconvinced. "Yeah, I bet."

"This lady in New York wants to look at it. Her dad was the writer's agent, a long time ago. She thinks this might be a lost manuscript. Someone might buy it, or pay us money to publish it."

"That's fine, but I don't want you making phone calls to any internet randos. And if the comic book is valuable, don't let that lady see it without paying you first."

"I don't think that's how it works, Mom . . ."

"What's this?" Mike appeared in the doorway. "We have something valuable in this house? You can't be serious."

"It's just some old comic book." Sally gently smacked him on the arm. "Don't get too excited about it. Dee says she found it in the attic, so it's probably just a waterlogged mess, anyway."

"No, it's not," she insisted. "It was wrapped up real good, in plastic."

"If you say so, dear." Sally squeezed out the door past Mike. "I'll be downstairs, scaring up enough dollar bills to tip the pizza guy."

"Check my wallet. I think I have a couple of ones." Mike told her. Then he asked Denise, "Can I see it? I like comic books."

She shrugged, and pushed it forward. "It's called *Lucida Might and the House of Horrors.*"

"Lucida Might . . . that rings a bell." Gingerly, he sat down cross-legged across from Denise and Terry, and turned the manuscript around so he could look at it upright. He flipped back to the beginning, leaving one set of fingers sandwiched in the pages where they'd left off reading. "Joe Vaughn," he read from the cover page. "Yeah, I've heard of him."

"You have?" Denise asked.

"He had a TV show, years and years ago. If this is one of his manuscripts . . . I wonder when he wrote it? Hell, I wonder what it was doing in our attic . . ." he added, shuffling quickly through the early pages, taking in the artwork.

She cleared her throat. "Um . . . I don't want to freak you out or anything, but I think he died here. In this house." She told him all about her Internet research, and her suspicions. "And on top of that, I think he's still haunting the place."

"Really? You think we have a ghost?"

"I think we have *two* ghosts," she confessed. She looked at Terry, who gave her an encouraging nod. "I think they're probably Joe, and the old woman who used to own the house. She disappeared before he died, and nobody knows what he was doing here. But this agent I talked to online—she said that maybe Joe was using the house for an art reference. I mean, the house in this comic sure *looks* like our house."

Terry had her back. "No way it's a coincidence!"

Mike made some more murmurs that said he was thinking, as he checked the thing page by page. "Ghosts, eh? I didn't know you believed in ghosts."

"I didn't, either. Wait, do *you*?"

He shrugged, still gazing down at the pages. "I've never seen much evidence for them, or against them."

"Terry has," she said, before he could volunteer the information. "He takes recordings. It's crazy, but he's picked up some really strange voices."

Mike looked up and eyed Terry. "Is that so?"

"I'd be happy to play them for you, sir! I didn't bring my recorder today, but next time . . ."

"Next time, then. And stop calling me 'sir,' would you? It's just Mike," he smiled. "If I've got two ghosts on the premises, I'd like to know more about them."

Denise watched her stepfather warily. "You're being awfully cool about this whole 'haunted house' thing, Mike."

The look he gave her in return was guarded. "Let's just say I've seen and heard some weird things myself, since we got here. And leave it at that."

"What about Mom?" she asked. "Has *she* seen or heard anything unusual?"

He shook his head. "If so, she hasn't mentioned it. If this house *is* infested with ghosts, I say we keep it to ourselves for now. Your mom has enough on her plate. Don't give her one more thing to worry about, please? I can worry for the both of us."

Denise wanted to tell him not to worry, that it wasn't a big deal — the ghosts were friendly! Probably! But she didn't think it was strictly true anymore. If he could worry for Sally, then Denise could worry for Mike. They could share the worry load, and maybe everybody wouldn't be scared to death all the time.

Was that how it worked?

Denise said, "Ghosts aside, I want to let this agent see the manuscript. I don't expect free money or anything, not that it wouldn't be awesome to have some. Do you think . . ." she began, almost shyly. "Mike, do you think it would be okay, if I talked to her?"

Downstairs, there was a knock on the front door.

Mike gave her a grin. "If it were me, I'd call her in a heartbeat. But this is your book. You found it, so you decide what to do with it. If you want to, go ahead and call the lady up. See what she has to say." They all heard Sally greeting the pizza guy, who turned out to be a pizza girl. No surprise visit from Norman, oh well. "But do it tomorrow. For now, let's eat."

After pizza, Denise went back upstairs to the meat locker (as she'd begun to almost lovingly think of her nice, cool bedroom) and she banged out a quick response to Eugenie Robbins's email. She didn't want to call because she hated talking on the phone, but she wanted to reach out — and an email was a good compromise.

Thanks so much for getting back to me. I really appreciate your time, and your interest in representing the comic book for publication. If you're sure that no one else owns the rights, I guess there's no good reason not to try and sell it. I am off to college next year, and then to law school. I could definitely use the money — any money at all. I hear the textbooks are expensive.

I can take more pictures and show you the pages, or maybe if you're in New Orleans anytime soon, you can come see the book for yourself.

She almost included her address, but restrained herself. One thing at a time, just in case this lady wasn't who she said she was. She closed out the email and hit SEND, and then sat back, wondering if anything would come of it.

She knew the hard way that maybe-money was no better than no-money-at-all.

It was even worse, if you got your hopes up.

OUR VILLAIN HAD A FAMILY, ONCE. I WONDER WHAT BECAME OF THESE PEOPLE.

GOOD HEAVENS . . .

. . . THE CHILD LOOKS JUST LIKE MY DOUG! THIS COULD BE A PORTRAIT OF HIM AS A LITTLE BOY. HOW STRANGE . . .

DOUG, ARE YOU IN THERE?

HELP...ME...

MY DARLING!

I KNEW YOU'D COME FOR ME...

STAND
BACK!

CHAPTER THIRTEEN

Mike paused, and poked his finger at the image of Doug. "Wait, who's this guy?"

Denise said, "He's Lucida's useless boyfriend. You should just read this from the beginning."

"I will, one of these days. This is crazy, how you just found it . . . I've never seen anything like it."

They were sitting together on the floor, their backs braced against the foot of her bed. Terry had gone home after pizza, and Sally was entirely disinterested in anything comic book related, so it was just Denise and Mike. The book was open with one flap on her leg, and the other on his.

"I've never seen anything like it, either. Nobody has, apparently."

"Hey, I've been meaning to ask you," he said, nodding his head at her hand. "What happened? What's with the Band-Aids?"

Denise tried to play it off. "I got into a knife fight with a pirate."

"And that's all the damage you took? Well played. But come on, kiddo. What gives?"

"It's no big deal." She tried to say it cool, like this was obviously nothing to get excited about. "I poked myself with a screw, while I was putting my bed frame together."

"Will you let me take a look?"

"These are my last Band-Aids. I'll show you after I take a shower, but for what it's worth, I showed a nurse, and she said it was fine."

He gave her a long, hard look. "Okay," he said. And he let it go.

Mike lifted his head and looked around. "Wait . . . do you hear that?"

Beneath their feet, they could feel a rumble. They could *hear* a rumble. Denise smelled grave dirt and sulfur with a dash of mold. "Where's Mom?" she asked frantically. Before he could answer, she yelled out, "Mom?" and scrambled out of the bedroom ahead of Mike, who was still moving a little slowly.

She was halfway down the stairs when she heard two things at the same time: her mother shouting, "Jesus!" and what remained of the ceiling collapsing into the parlor.

"Mom?"

"Sally?" Mike cried from the top of the stairs.

Denise was already at the bottom. Dust filled the room and dirtied up her eyes — some of it was powder like drywall, and some of it was brown and fluffy. She could hardly see. Everything smelled awful, and she wasn't sure where her mother was. "Mom?"

"Over here." Sally coughed and waved, like she could banish the filthy air with the back of her hand. "I'm fine. It missed me. Mostly. I think." She sounded creaky and uncertain, but she was definitely alive. The ceiling was on the floor, and a big jagged beam leaned down from above, its bottom end jammed through a rug at Sally's feet.

Sally made for one of the windows, wading through several inches of poop-colored fluff, and forced open the only two windows that worked. The air cleared a little. The stuff on the floor waved and swirled, like the grossest, driest snow anybody ever saw.

"What *is* this stuff?" Denise asked, wanting to run to her mom, and not wanting to step in any of that garbage.

Mike came down the steps behind her, covering his mouth and nose with the bottom of his shirt. "Insulation. Maybe . . . vermiculite? Or rock wool? Whatever it is, don't touch it. Don't breathe it, if you can possibly help it. We should get out of here."

Denise followed Mike's lead, pulling up her collar so she wasn't flashing her bra at anybody. "Oh my God, yes. As fast as possible."

"Why?" Sally demanded, even though she was wiping at her eyes and coughing.

"Best case scenario, there's mold and bug crap in this stuff. Worst case scenario, it's asbestos," Mike said unhappily. "In a house this old, the odds are too good to risk it. Everybody, to the bathrooms and wash up — then go pack an overnight bag. We're getting a hotel."

"With *what* money?" Sally asked, loudly, and with a shrill undertone of despair. "We can barely pay the electricians and the plumbers and I just bought pizza for the neighbor kid . . . and now this?" She stood in the wreckage of the parlor, where all the holes in the floor were covered by drifts of brown muck. More quietly, and with more exhaustion than sorrow she added, "I'm all tapped out, and we can't get the next portion of the loan disbursed until the pipes and the wires pass code."

"I've got some space on a credit card," Mike told her softly. "I'll find us a Motel 6 or something. Let's not panic just yet. The electricians already told me that there wasn't any asbestos in the walls, so there might not be any in . . . in whatever this brown stuff from the ceiling turns out to be, either. I'll go to Pete's hardware and get a test kit tomorrow, and then we'll know for sure."

"They make kits to test for asbestos?" Denise asked.

"Yes, they do," he confirmed. "And we'll spend one night in a hotel, as a precaution. Tomorrow, we'll know if we need to borrow more money, or if we just need to use the Shop-Vac. We'll figure it out. Now go on, get out of here. Both of you," he extended the gentle command to his wife, as well. "Nobody needs to be breathing this junk. Let me get my phone, and I'll find us a place to crash."

Denise didn't like how tired he sounded, and how hard he was trying to sound strong and positive; but somebody needed to keep cool, and her mom was wound up so tight you could bounce a quarter off her. "Mom?" she said. "Be careful, don't forget there's a hole in the —"

"I know there are holes in the floor," she snapped. "I'll find my way to the bedroom without breaking an ankle, don't worry." With that, she waded through the dry, dirty debris and off to her bedroom.

Denise looked up at Mike, who was still standing on the stairs a little bit above her. She wasn't sure what she wanted him to say, or do. He was already saying and doing everything he could. She really, *really* appreciated it, and she hoped that the look in her eyes got that message across, because she was too close to tears to say anything out loud.

"Go on," he said. "I'll take care of your mom."

She whispered, "Okay. Thanks." He stood aside to let her pass.

Up in her room, she was all alone but she felt like she was being watched and it drove her crazy. She wanted to check under the bed, and in the closet that still didn't have a door.

She didn't check. She grabbed her messenger bag, and picked up the old duffel she'd thrown on the floor in a corner. She selected a black tee from the shirt box, a pair of long shorts from the bottoms box, and to hell with it — a pair of flip-flops from that pile of shoes by the door. She had enough makeup in her purse to fake it for tomorrow. A fresh pair of underwear and her toothbrush topped off her whirlwind of packing, and that was it. Even a Motel 6 would have some soap, right?

She was ready to go. Her duffel was slung over one shoulder, and the messenger bag weighed down her other one. *Lucida Might and the House of Horrors* was lying facedown on the floor at the foot of her bed, right where she'd tossed it when the ceiling caved in downstairs.

Just like the ceiling in the story.

She didn't want to touch that book. But. She couldn't leave it lying there, not like that — all rumpled and upside down. Not if someone was going to pay money for it, and that lady in New York wanted to read it, so . . . she couldn't just walk away from it.

She picked it up off the floor, and smoothed the pages back down.

She closed it, and before she could change her mind, she stuffed it into her bag and zipped the whole thing shut.

The voice on Terry's recorder had said, "I keep what's mine." Was the ghost talking about the book? What would happen if she took it out of the house? Would the terrible coincidences follow her, even to a hotel?

Out in the hall, the dust from downstairs had wafted and settled on the floor, the doorknobs, and the handrail leading to the stairs. It wasn't the grime that made her throat go dry, and it wasn't the musty smell. It was the footprints leading to her room: broad, flat, square-toed imprints, made by a large man's dress shoe.

The footprints went in. They didn't come out.

Denise fled to the top of the staircase and took the steps down to the living room as fast as she could.

But she stopped near the bottom, because she heard her mother talking softly. She didn't mean to overhear her, but when someone talks softly, you have to listen hard to hear them. So you *do* listen hard, even when you're not supposed to.

"I don't know *what* I heard. All I know is what I *think* I heard, and I don't know what to make of it."

"Well then, what do you *think* you heard?" Mike asked, using his best sympathetic ear voice.

"I thought I heard a woman, and I know I *smelled* a woman."

"I'm sorry, say that again? One more time?"

Sally took a deep breath. "I heard a woman say, 'Get out of the way!' and I felt something shove me. Something . . . somebody . . . I got *pushed*, Mike. Right out of the way, like some kind of dang guardian angel was watching out for me, or something."

"And you smelled this guardian angel?"

"Yeah, she smelled like . . . like perfume. Roses and lilies. Old lady perfume."

"Your guardian angel is a pushy old lady. Got it."

"Sweetheart . . ." Sally was tired and exasperated. "I don't know. All I'm saying is, something moved me, and if it hadn't? That big support beam would've cracked me right in the head."

"You swear you aren't hurt?"

She cleared her throat. "No, I'm fine. It just scared the bejeezus out of me, is all. You know, if there's asbestos up there —"

"No, don't go down that road. Not yet. Don't borrow trouble. We'll find out tomorrow, for sure."

Denise didn't like to eavesdrop . . . or at least, she didn't like to *look* like she'd been eavesdropping, so she slowly descended the last handful of stairs. She cleared her throat to get their attention, and cautiously poked her head around the wall at the bottom.

"Mom? I don't think you have a guardian angel. I think we have a ghost."

"A ghost?" Sally narrowed her eyes. "Is that what we've come to, making up ghosts?"

Denise hopped off the bottom stair and into the living room, where she sheepishly stood in the wreckage of the ceiling. "Are ghosts any crazier than angels? Look, there are two dead people still hanging around this house," she explained. "I'm basically sure of it."

Sally looked at Mike, who hemmed, hawed, and said, "Sweetheart, hear her out. I've heard some weird things too."

"Both of you? You both think we've got ghosts? Were either of you planning to tell me about them?"

"I'm telling you now, okay?" Denise said, trying to head Mike off at the pass. She could take the damage on this one. She didn't mind. "Don't be mad at him; it's not his fault. I told him not to say anything," she fibbed.

"She's been doing research," Mike said, trying to lend a hand. "Tell her what you learned, kiddo."

Quickly, before Sally could spend any time getting mad about feeling left out, Denise said, "One of our ghosts was a guy named Joe

Vaughn, who died here back in the 1950s. He's a jerk, but there's another ghost — a lady. I don't know her name, but she's nice. I bet she's the one who pushed you. And I bet Joe's the one who brought down the ceiling."

Sally held very still and did not argue, but her eyes flickered between her daughter and her husband and the gaping chasm above their heads. "I *knew* something funny was going on," she finally said. "I keep smelling perfume, and finding stray nails lying around the house — in places they shouldn't be, places where they could hurt somebody."

Denise was both delighted and appalled to hear that her mother had discovered more nails. "Joe was a carpenter, supposedly," she said. Now that she thought about it, Desmond Rutledge was a developer. That was kind of the same thing, wasn't it?

"And a jerk," her mother confirmed.

Denise bobbed her head. "A total jerk. So you believe me?" She didn't mention her own encounter with the nails. Give her mom one new thing to worry about at a time, that was her thinking.

"More or less," Sally said, not quite ready to commit to having confidence in the afterlife.

But it was good enough for her daughter, who smiled feebly. She said, "Well you two, I'm all packed up. It's getting late. Mike, did you find us a hotel?"

Mike reached around the corner and collected a duffel bag. "Yeah, but it's a couple miles away. You're right, we'd better get going."

The hotel was more like ten miles away, and it wasn't a Motel 6 — but a mom-and-pop place with a neon sign that was half burned out, advertising GLF SD OTL rather than GULF SIDE HOTEL. They parked between a Dumpster and an old ice machine that looked like a great place to hide a dead body.

The room itself was clean enough, but nothing matched — not even the soap and shampoo samples. Still, when Denise checked all the sheets for bedbugs, she didn't find anything. She took one of the beds, and

Mike and Sally took the other. By the time everyone was settled in, it was after eleven o'clock.

The lights went out, but Denise couldn't sleep.

Over the roar of the old AC unit, she heard the honks of boat horns and the rumble of car engines on the busy street nearby. Flashes of head-lights peeked around the curtains, and the hissing hum of the neon sign buzzed, fizzled, and turned the room orange when it flickered.

She reached over the side of the bed for her bag, and pulled out *Lucida Might and the House of Horrors.* She also retrieved her phone. As quietly as possible, she pulled everything under the covers, and drew the blanket over her head. One thing she'd give the GLF SD OTL — the AC was powerful enough to keep her chilly, even with the blankets all tented up.

She called up the flashlight app, and turned it on.

THERE'S SOMETHING FUNNY ABOUT ALL THIS . . .

WHAT DO YOU WANT WITH DOUG? WHAT DO YOU WANT WITH *ME*?

DOUG BELONGS TO ME,

AND I KEEP WHAT'S MINE.

Denise's reading was interrupted by a text message from Trish, saying good night and that she hoped that the ghosts didn't bite — a message accompanied by the traditional ghost emoji with its tongue hanging out.

Denise didn't reply to that one. Not even with a lazy thumbs-up.

Her phone battery was running low, so she closed out the flashlight app — then found the outlet beside her bed and plugged it in. She pushed Lucida Might onto the nightstand, and fluffed her pillow, trying to make it feel less like a flat feather rock. When it was as comfy as it was going to get, she dropped her head down, and closed her eyes.

On the next bed over, Mike was snoring softly and Sally wasn't making any noise at all, so she was probably awake. She probably knew that Denise had been up too late, reading under the covers. She must not have cared. For all the trouble her family was taking to keep worries off her plate, she still had too many other things to worry about.

Denise's brain itched. It was hard to sleep when the AC unit rattled and howled a few feet away, and the neon light fizzled through the curtains. It was difficult to nod off when the bed was lumpy and the sheets smelled not so faintly of bleach.

She thought about Lucida Might. It was better than thinking about this miserable hotel room, or the Agony House, or tetanus shots that should've happened — but didn't. And as she finally drifted off to sleep, she considered how weird it was, how the villain talked about Doug like he was an object, and not a person.

But that was silly, wasn't it?

Unless Joe Vaughn wasn't really talking about a character named Doug. Maybe he was talking about something else. As Denise finally, restlessly drifted off to sleep, she couldn't help but wonder *what*.

CHAPTER FOURTEEN

The hotel alarm clock went off at oh-God-thirty and Denise shot awake in a panic, wondering where she was. She sat up in a tumble of sleep-pressed hair and dried drool, flailed around for her phone, found her phone, realized her phone wasn't making the alarm noise, and then slammed her hands up and down along the nightstand, trying to find the source of the buzzing horror.

Mike found it first. He rolled over and slapped it silent.

Only then could Denise stop freaking out, and take a moment to remember what was going on, and why she was in a hotel, and how come the alarm had gone off and it was still so early.

Was it early? It felt early.

"Oh yeah," she mumbled. Her brain gradually came back online.

Groggily, Denise groaned and stumbled into the bathroom, where she skipped a shower because to hell with it, that's why. She was only going to the po'boy place to kill time with the Internet over breakfast; she wasn't glamming up for a beauty pageant.

That's what they agreed to, over arguments on who was brushing whose teeth first.

"I don't know how long the test takes, and you seem to like it there," Mike said. "I'll give you five bucks and you can get some breakfast. Let's get this cleared up as soon as possible, so we can go back to work on the house, cleaning up that mess."

Crispy's did breakfast, mostly biscuit-related or beignet-related, often with eggs thrown into the mix. Mike's five bucks felt like all the money in the world at that hour—Denise could even get one of the small combo meals with that much. Did she want coffee? She needed coffee. But she'd rather have Coke, so that's what she ordered.

She took her tray to the table which was becoming "hers," if possession was, indeed, nine-tenths of the law. A couple of kids who recognized her as a regular tossed her a head-nod when she sat down. She gave them a bob back, and pulled out her laptop. She plugged in her phone to let it charge, and felt very sorry for herself — and for everyone else who was up this early in the middle of summer.

Norman was up early.

He appeared with a loaded-down tray, boasting two big bacon-egg-and-cheese biscuits and hash browns too. Smoothly he slid into the bench beside her, dropping a messenger bag on the floor. He pushed it under the table with his foot. "Hey there. Fancy meeting you here."

"Hey there, yourself. What are you doing here at this hour?"

"At this hour? It's not that early," he argued. "Sun's up and everything. I've already been down at the river, taking pictures. You ever see the sun rise over the delta?"

"I have not. And I have no desire to, either."

"Your loss."

"Sunset, maybe," she said. "You ever take pictures of sunsets?"

He nodded. "Used to. But I think the sunrises are prettier, and I'm usually not working a pizza shift through those."

"Fair enough," she told him.

They settled in to eat, fussing about old houses and joking about crappy working conditions. Norman asked about her hand, and Denise was evasive. He asked what she was doing there so early, and she told him about the mess with the ceiling and the maybe-asbestos. "And that's not the worst of it. On top of everything, we have ghosts."

"Ghosts?"

"One bad, one good. If we're um . . ." She was pretty tired. "If me and Terry are reading the situation correctly. Terry, he's this kid . . ." she began to explain.

"I know Terry. *Everybody* knows Terry," he said with a grin.

"Why am I not surprised. But what I'm saying is, if you're gonna keep working in the house with us, you should *definitely* ask my stepdad for that hazard pay you were joking about."

"I ain't afraid of no ghost."

She chucked a packet of salt at his head. "You should be afraid of ours. One of them is a real jerk, and I think he's been setting up all these crazy little accidents. I think it's Joe Vaughn, the guy who wrote that comic book we found in the attic."

He plucked the packet out of his lap, where it'd fallen, and tossed it onto the table. "Dang, it sounds like you've had a crazy couple of days."

"And gross. You should see the floor of our living room and parlor."

"I've got some free time today, if they want to spring for the help. I can use the money, and I'm not afraid of gross stuff from the ceiling. Especially if there's hazard pay involved." He waggled an eyebrow.

"I'll mention it. But if it's asbestos, there's no way they'll ask you to help shovel it out. Hazard pay or not."

When they were mostly finished eating, Norman asked if she'd brought the comic book.

Denise nodded as she chewed her final bite, wiped her hands down like she needed them for surgery, then topped off with a smidge of hand sanitizer. She handed him her extra napkins and the tiny travel bottle of sanitizer. "I've got it right here, but your buttery hands can't touch it. Clean up, man."

"Do I need a fancy pair of white cotton gloves?"

"No, but I don't want butter on it. Or cheese," she added, pointing out an orange spot on the side of his hand. "Just ask Terry: I like to keep it clean."

He accommodated her with exaggerated caution. Clean hands achieved, he wadded up the napkin and tossed it on his tray—then pushed the whole thing out of the way. "Now can I see this majestic manuscript?"

Denise reached down and brought her bag up onto the bench. She dug down deep into the satchel and pulled out the book, then set it down on the table — edging her butt over so he could see it better.

"Dang . . ." he said with a touch of awe. "How did it survive up there?"

"It was wrapped up in a bunch of plastic. It's got some mildew on the corners, but mostly it's okay."

"That's a miracle."

"A *cool* miracle." She opened the cover and showed him the first few pages. "There's an agent in New York who's asked to see it. Her dad used to represent Joe, a long time ago."

They flipped through the pages together for a few minutes, when Denise's phone buzzed on the table beside her. "It's . . . look, it's my mom. Apparently I have to go back to the house. Or . . . I *get* to go back to the house? Sounds like there's no asbestos. Just filthy garbage . . . hooray."

"Are you sure you don't want me to come with you?"

"If you're not afraid of no ghosts, or no probably-not-asbestos . . . you're welcome to join me. All they did was run a test they bought at Pete's. Who knows how reliable it is. It's not like they hired a professional or anything."

Norman wasn't too worried about it. "Everybody has asbestos, around here. If it's not in the ceiling, it's in the walls, and if it's not in the walls, it's under the floor. You're lucky if it's under the floor. Usually those are just tiles. You can break those up, and pull them out yourself."

She didn't ask him why people didn't get the rest of it removed. She already knew why.

Asbestos, old wiring, rusty lead plumbing . . . if it wasn't going to kill you right that second, you went ahead and lived with it — just like she and Sally had quietly lived with it, in one of their crappier apartments back in the day. Asbestos and mold had lurked all over the place, but the mom-and-daughter duo knew they wouldn't be there long. They could ignore it for six months at a time.

You add up enough six-month stretches, and eventually you've got years and years of pretending it isn't there, and figuring that if it was gonna hurt you, it would've done it by now. After a while, you forget it was ever there. You forget you were ever worried about it.

But Denise and Sally and Mike couldn't forget about this one, this time. This time, everything had to be up to code.

Denise and Norman tossed their garbage and started walking, but they didn't get very far before Dominique joined them. There wasn't much room on the sidewalk, so Denise and Norman stopped.

Terry came running up behind them. "Hey Denise, Norman. Hi Dominique," he said, covering all his bases.

Dominique smiled at him. "Hey there, Tee. You doing good?"

"Yeah, just walking home. Or to the nail house, to see if Denise was there." He flipped a thumb at her. "But I saw y'all walking, so . . ."

"So come on, and walk with us." To Denise she said, "Terry told me all about your ghost."

"I gave her the rundown," he said modestly. "Hope you don't mind."

"Nah. It's no secret, I guess. Everybody knows that somebody famous died there."

The rest of the way to Argonne Street, Denise gave Dom a few more details on Joe and his afterlife — with Terry chiming in when he felt the need to elaborate. Dominique didn't look like she understood the need for laser thermometers, voice recorders, or EMF readers any better than Denise did . . . but she was game to listen, and she made appropriately impressed noises at all the right times to keep him happy.

Norman, on the other hand, got nerdy about it. "You got a recorder? With real EVPs? I love that stuff on TV."

"I'll play them for you, later! Oh wait, Denise!" he interrupted himself. "You were having electrical work done on the house, right?"

"I'm not sure if they're finished yet or not. Every time I think somebody's done with something, it turns out I'm wrong."

"If you ever get a chance, ask an electrician for an EMF reader. Maybe they'll let you keep one overnight."

"I wouldn't know what to do with one."

"*I* would!"

"Got it: You want me to borrow an expensive piece of equipment so that you can come to my house and play with it."

He beamed at Dominique. "See? I told you she was kind of smart. She's going to be a lawyer."

Norman said, "Sweet! You and me will have to stay in touch. You never know when you'll need a good lawyer."

"Why? You planning to go committing any crimes?"

"Like you've got to break any laws, in order to need a lawyer."

Denise nodded approvingly. "I knew I liked you. You *get* it."

Dominique laughed a little. "Yeah, my cousin here — he's all right."

"Yeah, he is." Then she said, "You um . . . you want to come see the house? It's kind of gross and full of grumpy spirits, but if you wanted to see inside . . . ?"

"You had me at gross, and lost me at spirits. I don't do ghosts, man. I leave that stuff to Terry. It freaks me out. But thanks for the invitation, and I'll take you up on it one of these days . . . in broad daylight, with all the lights on. Hey, this is where I turn to my street, so I'll catch you later."

"Your cousin?" she asked Norman.

"Second or third, if you want to get technical," he said. "I was going to head over to your place after breakfast, Dom, but do me a favor, would you? Tell Grandma I went to work in the nail house early. Tell her about the ceiling, and that they're cleaning up. Tell her they need a hand."

"You real sure? She was hoping you'd swap out her old AC unit today."

"Oh yeah, I forgot about that." He gave Denise a pained look.

"Don't worry about it," Denise told him. "My parents would probably die of embarrassment, if you saw the place right now. It's pretty bad."

"I've seen worse, but whatever makes you happy." He gave her a smile followed by a little salute, and walked off with Dom.

Terry waved good-bye, and Denise threw them a head-nod that was supposed to look cool, but probably looked like a spasm.

Terry left her at the next block, because ghosts or none . . . he had no great desire to wade through the ceiling garbage. Not even for Lucida Might. Denise didn't blame him.

It was only one more block to the house, so she walked it in summer heat that was absolutely choking. "Sunscreen. I need sunscreen," she muttered to herself, feeling the back of her neck turning pink. "Better yet, a parasol."

Her sunglasses had a crack on the right lens, but they were cheap and she hadn't expected much from them in the first place. She rubbed them on her shirt to clean them off, and mostly got them even sweatier. She gave up and stuffed them into her bag, just in time to step into the shade of the rickety porch with its weird baby blue underside that her mom called "haint blue," though Denise didn't know what that meant. Something about good luck, or keeping bad spirits out.

It obviously didn't work.

She glared at the house and said, "All right, Joe. Just so you know . . . if it comes down to you or us . . . *you're* the one who's outta here."

Nothing in the house responded, so she stomped up the first two stairs . . . and tiptoed up the next two, remembering what had happened to Mike. In the porch floor the hole was still there, wide and ragged, but covered with plywood and a handwritten warning sign that said HOLE IN FLOOR. In case anybody came to the house and didn't know already.

The door was only sort of locked, with a dead bolt that was set — but a broken sidelight through which any idiot could just stick her hand and unlock it. The sidelight was supposed to be fixed by now, but so were a lot of other things.

Denise used her key, anyway.

This time, the note on the dining room table said that Sally and Mike were at the bank, signing off on some paperwork that would release more of the mortgage money. Apparently the plumbing was officially good to go.

One of the electricians was still present, packing up his bag. He was a short white guy, round faced and blond. He had a crack at the back of his shorts that Denise tried not to stare at. "Oh, hi there," he said when he realized she was present. "Don't mind me, I'm just wrapping up."

"How's it going?" she asked.

"Got a late start, after your parents cleaned up most of the ceiling insulation, but we're getting there. These old houses, man. They'll eat you alive, won't they?"

She wasn't sure if that was a joke or if she was supposed to laugh, so she just gave him a weird look until he cleared his throat and continued.

"I've got the new circuit boxes coming tomorrow, and then I'll be ready to finish the rest — probably within a couple of days. I know it seems like it's taking forever, but we'll be done soon. Listen, I'm gonna leave this stuff here, rather than haul it all to the truck, okay? I'll be back first thing in the morning."

Denise silently thanked God that Terry wasn't there to explode like a fistful of nerdy confetti. "Go for it. No one will bother them." She had gotten an idea. She stood still and listened as he drove away.

Denise didn't want to steal any of his tools, but maybe she'd borrow one. She realized she didn't have the faintest idea what an EMF reader looked like, so she pulled out her phone to google them.

"Okay," Denise said to herself. "I can find that."

It was red, with a little window on top and a needle that moved back and forth. Now she just needed to know how to use it. For a second she thought about calling Terry. Then she thought no, this was *her* house. She could do a little ghost-hunting on her own.

How hard could it be?

She ran a quick search on how to use the EMF reader, but that got real complicated, real fast. So she narrowed the search to "using an EMF reader to look for ghosts" and turned up some helpful sites with terrible graphics. One had a cackling skeleton GIF that rocked back and forth. One had some bats that flew out of a window. It was all tacky Halloween stuff, circa 2003.

But the information looked legit.

She flipped a switch on the side, and the little yellow light behind the needle lit up. The needle bobbed back and forth along a scale of "mG," with a range from zero to fifty. It settled around the left-hand side, barely registering 1 mG, whatever an *mG* was supposed to stand for.

According to the most promising website she found on the fly, anything between 2 and 7 (without an obvious electrical source) might indicate a paranormal presence. Appliances ought to read much higher, from maybe 10 to 30 mG. You were supposed to take test readings around your TV, microwave, and maybe your electrical outlets.

She turned in a circle, and the thin blue needle bobbed across the red scale, lifting off the "1" position and wobbling. There was no TV to check, and Denise didn't know how long it would be before her parents got home, so she didn't bother testing for a baseline.

She just dove in.

"All right, spirits." She cleared her throat. The meter's needle didn't move, so she moved instead, slowly circling the dining room. "I know there are two of you. Joe Vaughn, I think you died here. Are you the one who's been trying to hurt us?"

She didn't know why she was talking out loud. It wasn't like she was holding a voice recorder, but what else was she going to do?

"Come *on*, Joe," she added under her breath. "Talk to me. Why do you want to chase us out of the house? Or if *you* don't want to talk . . . um . . . lady ghost? Are you there? I think you helped my mom yesterday. I think you're trying to protect us. Was this your house?"

The needle twitched.

She thought maybe it twitched when she was facing the parlor, but she wasn't sure — so she went that direction and got another twitch in the hallway. A big spike, up to about 8, then it settled down around 7. She turned to the living room, and the needle dropped again. Another turn, and there was another bump — one that stabilized around 11 — when she stood in the parlor doorway.

"Got it. It's like . . . playing hot and cold."

It had to be. There weren't any electronic devices anywhere in the parlor — not even power tools, switched off. All of those were stashed around the living room and the back of the kitchen.

"Seven is supposed to be high . . ." she said to herself. "Eleven has to be even better, right? Even more . . . electromagneticky?"

One careful foot at a time, she crept into the parlor and swung the EMF reader slowly one way, then slowly the next. A couple of lights blipped, and the needle jerked — all the way up to 16.

"Is that . . . good? Is there someone here with me?" She wasn't shaking, not exactly, but it was hard to hold the meter steady when her hands were so sweaty and she was looking up and down, back and forth between the room at large and the device she was holding. "If there's anybody here, please be a nice old lady. The kind who wears flowery perfume, and doesn't try to scare anybody. Please don't be a mean man. Joe . . . you weren't mean, were you? You wrote a cool comic, about a cool girl detective. Maybe I'm talking to somebody else."

Her voice wasn't exactly shaking, but it didn't sound steady, either. Not even to her.

"Hello?"

She thought she smelled flowers. Expensive soap, or a funeral bouquet.

"Hello, is someone there?"

She followed the scent, and she followed the bouncing EMF needle. It shook and leaned, farther and farther to the right, as Denise grew closer and closer to the fireplace. An alert buzzer went off, and Denise leaped like she'd been snakebit. She dropped the reader and let it lie where it fell, its needle straining to burst through the little window.

It wanted her to look in the fireplace.

The fireplace was not quite a ruin. Its mantel was intact, if dusty, and the tiles that surrounded it were a pretty shade of turquoise blue, mottled with gold. Across the opening where a fire ought to go, a cast-iron cap was fixed. Mike had told her it was called a "summer cap," and they used to put them over the fireplace when it wasn't being used — to keep birds and mice from coming down the chimney. It was decorated with a fleur-de-lis and some scrollwork, and it looked a little bit thin and rusty.

If she touched it, it might crumble to dust.

She touched it anyway. It didn't crumble, but it creaked a little. There was a knob in the center, and one on the bottom. They were handles, or so she figured out real quick when she gripped them. She crouched, lifted with her legs, and wiggled the cap loose, then pulled it away. It smacked down hard on the floor — it was a lot heavier than it looked.

She let it lie down flat. It rocked back and forth, and stopped with a groan.

Inside the fireplace there was darkness and soot, swirling in soft, black poofs — disturbed by the cap's removal. When the soot settled, she saw naked bricks with crumbling mortar. She smelled flowers. She heard a whisper, coming from somewhere up inside.

Denise fumbled for her phone. She pulled it out and found the flashlight app, then turned the phone upside down. She slipped it inside the recess, and shined it around. More brick. A large chunk of fallen stone or something, up above. It dangled down into view, almost.

Keep looking.

Her head shot up so fast, she clocked it on the underside of the mantel. Not hard enough to see stars, but hard enough to make her eyes water. She rubbed at the back of her head with her free hand. She asked aloud, "Is somebody here . . . ?"

Then she saw it: around the fallen chunk of brick, or stone, or whatever it was. Something hung there, just on the other side of it. There was a little hole, big enough for a hand. A lady's hand. Denise's hand. She held her breath and reached inside, trying not to touch anything. Still touching everything. It all felt like gravel and dead bugs and sand and dust. It felt like paper.

Paper? Kind of.

She wrapped her fingers around something brittle and pulled it out. It was waxed paper, and it was wrapped around something, secured with an old rubber band. She tried to unstretch the rubber band but it snapped off and fell to pieces.

She tucked her phone under her armpit, unfolded the waxed paper, and found a small cache of folded, yellowed letters.

The first one had brown stains all along the seams, where mildew had worked its way past the butcher paper that'd been used to protect it. She straightened it out between her palms.

I really wish you would reconsider. The CCA won't last forever (I don't believe it CAN), and you told me you weren't finished yet—you said you had a dozen more LM stories, bubbling on your back burner. You're just going to drop it like this? Let it all go up in smoke, because some pencil-pusher made some rules you don't like? You're bigger than that. LM is bigger than that! People still love her, and want to read more. You're cutting off your nose, to spite your face. You can fight the power from the inside.

Maybe we should talk about licensing. LM can live on, maybe in film—maybe a cartoon, wouldn't that be something? So the TV show didn't pan out, big deal! TV shows fail all the time, and that doesn't mean they weren't great, or that nobody loved them. It just means Hollywood is a crapshoot, even worse than comics.

You could try something different. You could take LM a new direction, maybe get her and DF married off at long last, and that would take the edge off the CCA complaints. You could even make the little putz the hero once in a while. It wouldn't be the end of the world, and it wouldn't be the end of Lucida Might.

Please, talk to me. Call me, for God's sake. Stop avoiding me. Stop avoiding this.

It was signed "Marty."

"Marty." Marty Robbins, the agent. There was a second letter, hidden behind the pages of the first. It was falling apart, but Denise put the pieces back into place and smoothed them out flat on the floor, so she could read it. It looked like Joe's reply.

I wish I could say I believed you. about the CCA — but we both know how the world works. and we know they're here to stay. at least for the foreseeable future. By the time that foul organization follows the dodo into the great beyond. it'll be too late for me. It's already too late for Lucida Might.

I appreciate that you're trying to save my bacon, and save your own while you're at it. but I wish I could make you understand: To change the dynamic between Doug and Lucida is to change the heart of the story. I never wanted to tell the story of a weak boy becoming strong. There are plenty of those stories already. I wanted to tell the tale of a woman, strong already — but accepting of (and even loving toward) a partner who can't keep up. Apparently that's as baffling and obscene as the gory undead.

You're not wrong, and there's a story to be wrung from a partnership's shift in power dynamic, but that's never been the intent of Lucida Might. Lucida Might must be a challenge to the usual, not a capitulation toward some loathsome standard. But the loathsome standard is law of the land, and I'm already so beaten down by the nasty business between you-know-who and I (which I fear has not yet found its end. God help us). and I simply lack the stamina to struggle onward and fight both him and the CCA on top of everything else.

I'm getting old. and life is short. Marty. It's just too damn short.

Denise sat on the floor and put the pages in order, one letter and then the other, side by side. She read them over and over again, while the faint whiff of flowers faded from her nose. The soft whispers of soot and ghosts from the fireplace retreated, and there was only a residue of black grime that coated the mantel, the tiles, and the old pages themselves.

Word by word. Line by line.

If this wasn't Joe's house . . . then why were these letters stashed in the fireplace? Was the mystery lady keeping them to blackmail Joe? Denise considered the possibility. Maybe she'd stolen the manuscript too; maybe there was something incriminating written inside. If so, Denise hadn't found it yet. She didn't see anything incriminating in these letters, either — nothing she couldn't have gathered from her limited Internet research.

Joe was unhappy, so Joe was quitting. Marty didn't want him to quit. Joe was quitting anyway.

Then what about the lady? Who was she? What was her role in this weird vintage drama?

Denise didn't know, and she had no idea how to find out.

CHAPTER FIFTEEN

Come Saturday, Denise told Sally and Mike that she was going to visit Tulane, and they didn't quite believe her. "I thought you were hell-bent for Houston," Mike said.

Sally hushed him. "Stop it. If she wants to go visit Tulane, then by all means let her go forth and research. How are you getting there? Are you going by yourself?"

"What prompted this?" her stepdad added, more suspicious of her motivations than eager to see her off.

She answered her mother first. "I'm taking the bus, so can I have a few bucks for fare and lunch? And no, I'm not going by myself. I'm going with Norman. His mom works there, and he said he could show me around."

"But *why* are you going there?" Mike pressed.

"Because I want to look at their library," she said truthfully. "I read something that said they have some archives of Joe Vaughn's stuff."

"The comic book guy?" Sally asked. "Our resident dirtbag ghost?"

"Yeah. If he died outside my bedroom door . . . then I want to know more about him. Maybe I'll find out why he's such a jerk."

Sally was looking at Denise through narrowed eyes. "All right," she relented. "Fine. You can go, as long as you promise to answer your phone if I call — and you swear you'll be home by dark."

"We could always drive you two," Mike suggested.

"Oh, for crying out loud," said Denise. "I ought to learn the bus system anyway, right? I'll just . . . I'm meeting him at the stop near the school. If we get stuck or lost somewhere, I'll call one of y'all to pick us up."

Mike relented, and Sally told her to take a few bucks out of her purse and to have a good time. Denise went straight for Sally's purse before she could change her mind, and pulled out an overstuffed wallet that was mostly full of baby pictures, shopping lists, receipts, discount cards from assorted stores, a pen that didn't work very well, half-sucked cough drops wrapped back up and saved, reminder cards for various appointments that were at least a year old, and Band-Aids.

So that's where all the extras went. She pocketed a couple of those too. On principle.

Inside this wallet that was roughly as fat as a sandwich, she also found about three dollars in change and eleven one-dollar bills.

She pulled out all the quarters, and took six of the ones. She hoped it wasn't too much, and Sally wouldn't regret giving her permission to raid her bag, but she didn't want to look too broke if they got lunch at the market. After bus fare, five bucks ought to be enough to get at least a pastry and a soda. She could always say she was on a diet.

"Thanks, Mom!" she shouted on her way out the door.

Her messenger bag was slung across her chest, and her flip-flops slapped up and down as she ran down the front steps.

It was hot as hell outside. Maybe as hot as literal hell, for all Denise knew. She wasn't halfway to the bus stop in front of the school before she started wilting and wishing she'd remembered the sunscreen — but it was too late for that, and she wasn't sure that they even had any. Six ones and some change wouldn't buy any. Not even a sample size from a drugstore, if she planned to buy lunch too.

She wiped her forehead, and swabbed at the back of her neck with the rolled-up sleeve of her button-up. It was mostly white with a hint of black plaid, and very soft, and although the extra layer trapped a little heat, the cotton kept the worst of the sun off her shoulders. Her hair was tied up and back in a ponytail because there wasn't anything else you could do with it, in that humidity.

The bus stop near the school had a rickety-looking shelter over it, covered with graffiti both scrawled onto and scratched into every inch. It also had Norman, who grinned when he saw her. "Hey!" he called out, and he stood up. "You made it!"

She smiled back, and wiped a line of sweat off one cheek. "When does the bus come?"

"Another five minutes, if it's running on time. On the weekends they're pretty reliable, but during the week, they're crowded and kind of iffy. Did you ride the bus much in Houston?"

"All the time." She took a seat on the bench beside him. "For about a year, we were in this place where the school bus ran really late in the afternoon — like, if I took the school bus home, I wouldn't get back until after dark, so I took the city bus instead. It usually got me home before the sun went down."

He nodded. "Right on."

"I had to change buses downtown, at the main depot. Sometimes, I'd skip the last bus and walk down to the library instead. I'd call my mom and tell her I'd missed it. Then she'd have to drive out and pick me up."

"I bet she loved that."

"Totally. But there was this creeper who took that second bus, and sometimes I just didn't feel like dealing with it, you know? The driver never did anything to stop him." She wasn't sure why she was telling him that part, but it was true.

"Did your mom believe you?"

"Yeah, but she was working ten-hour days at this hotel restaurant, and when she was done, she wanted to go home — not drive all the way downtown to collect my sorry butt. I tried not to do it too often."

He nodded again, and stared straight ahead. He had a pair of sunglasses perched on top of his hair. He pulled them down onto the bridge of his nose. "Creepers gonna creep. Dom got a guy kicked out of school for like, a week, for being a creeper on the school bus last year."

"Oh, that's right, she's your cousin."

"We have a grandma and a great-grandpa in common. Or we did, but grandpa died in the Storm."

Denise nodded, and shifted her legs so that her shorts covered most of the bench underneath her. It was as hot as everything else, and she didn't need the chicken-fried thighs. "My grandma did too. And my dad. We didn't lose anybody else, though."

"I'm sorry about your dad and grandma."

"I'm sorry about your great-grandpa."

The bus picked that moment to come around the corner, so they both stood up. The big, rumbling vehicle stopped, the doors opened, and a thin drool of cool, damp air rolled down the steps. "After you," Norman generously offered.

"Thanks." She asked for a transfer, and went back to the first seat that was empty enough for two.

Norman joined her, settling down beside her.

The bus pulled forward. They both lurched, then settled back.

He asked, "So what did you mean? When you said you didn't lose anybody else?"

"Oh, you know how it goes." She shrugged. "When the water hit, everybody went in a million different directions. My aunt and uncle ended up in Atlanta, and my mom's cousins went to Minnesota. Mom's half sister went to Chattanooga. We don't see very much of any of them, not anymore. We're Facebook friends with everybody, but . . . nobody's home for the holidays, if you know what I mean."

"I know how it goes. I've got two uncles who are still in Fort Worth. They just . . . never made it back."

"We've got a couple of cousins who came back, but I don't know them real well. And one of my aunties got us the real estate agent, and helped find the house."

"How's it working out? Living in that big old house?"

"You say that like it's fancy or something." She smiled without showing her teeth, and without meaning it. "You know good and well it's just a big craphole."

"But y'all own it. It's *your* craphole."

"Sort of. My mom got some kind of historic business mortgage for it, because of the bed-and-breakfast. But if people keep getting hurt, I don't know." She waved her still-bandaged hand. "Everything feels so dirty, all the time."

"Sounds typical to me," he said with a knowing bob of his head. "Mom and me live in a duplex that used to be a single house. She goes crazy trying to keep it clean, but there's mold in the walls, so it always feels kind of dirty and wet."

It was Denise's turn to nod. The mold remediation in the Agony House was technically finished, but she was still pretty sure there was more mold lurking around somewhere. She could always smell it in the bathroom, no matter how much bleach she used.

Before long, Norman pulled the string to signal he wanted the next stop. "The market's right up here. Have you been to it yet?"

"No. I haven't really been anyplace."

"You're gonna love it."

When she stepped off the bus, back into the heat, she was prepared to believe him. The sidewalks around the market were bustling with shoppers, and the outdoor seating was all occupied, despite the late morning warmth. A few trees and a handful of umbrellas offered shade around the tall, long building that looked freshly restored from top to bottom.

It made Denise think of an old train depot, with all its windows and two stories' worth of height. The front entrance on St. Claude Avenue added to that feeling when she followed Norman through big double doors, into the market proper.

Inside, the lovely high ceiling was supported by a row of painted white columns, with vendors on either side of a central dining hub. All around, Denise heard tourists chattering about the seafood, and locals asking what was new, and sellers announcing the daily specials. Coffee grinders and juice machines hummed and ground and blended in the background. Kids ran back and forth between the front and rear, trailing balloons, or beads, or paper streamers and laughing their heads off, begging for a visit to the booth with all the sweets. She swiveled her head around, taking it all in. She almost lost Norman, but his back was moving ahead of her, ducking and weaving around the kids, the tables, the shoppers, the tourists with their too-big bags and goofy sunglasses. She followed him farther into the center.

The air was still too warm, but it was too warm everywhere and all the terrific collection of smells stirred and stewed. She got a whiff of coffee from over here, and a sharp note of the salty catch of the day from over there. Chocolate too — and the fluffy light sweetness of meringue. A quick gust of spiced rum, not that she was supposed to know what that smelled like, but it was one of Mike's favorites.

Norman stopped in the middle, between two white tables with black metal chairs. "Well, what do you think?"

"It's pretty great," she said. What she didn't say, was that she hoped she could find something she could afford to eat.

Almost as if he'd heard her thoughts, he said, "There's some pricey stuff here, but there's also a lot of stuff you can get on the cheap. What do you like?" he asked, gesturing around at the vendors of po'boys, and seafood, and candies, and booze.

"What do um . . . what do you like? I've never been here before. What's good?"

"Everything. I usually go to the Haitian guys, down over there," he pointed. "Good island food, if you're into that kind of thing. They've got . . ." He squinted around. "Tex-Mex too. Over there. You came from Houston, right?"

"I moved *back* here from Houston."

"That's what I meant."

He pointed out a counter that offered all kinds of promising and familiar food. "You can get street tacos pretty cheap. And chips and salsa, that kind of stuff. The guac is good too. Then you've got, juice and salads, crepes, and have you ever had Vietnamese food?"

"Nah, never. Maybe the Tex-Mex?"

"Okay, sounds good. I'll meet you back here . . ." he waved his arms around to indicate the general vicinity of these particular tables, ". . . in a few minutes."

She ended up getting two street tacos, a side of guacamole, and a glass of water. It didn't look like a lot of food, but by the time she'd finished it, and Norman had killed off some crawfish étouffée that probably didn't come from the Haitian vendors, she actually felt pretty full and pretty awesome.

"Thanks for this," she said to him as they bused the contents of their table into the nearest trash can. "I'm really glad I got to see this place."

"Me too. You ought to get out more. Get to know the neighborhood beyond the golden fried food of Crispy's. Which is great, don't get me wrong. But you should see the rest of it sometime too. Don't hole up in the nail house, just because it's weird."

"What's weird?"

"Oh, come on," he said, ushering her back out the door and toward the bus stop.

She had a feeling she knew what he meant, but she didn't want to say it herself, so she let him do it. "What do you mean?"

"White girl, coming from Texas, moving to a black neighborhood. A mostly black neighborhood," he adjusted, probably thinking of Terry. "Then your parents go off and buy a big house — even if it's not the world's greatest house, it still looks like money coming in from outside. Nobody around here could afford to buy it at all, much less get the money to fix it up. Nobody but the gentrifiers."

"Please don't call me that."

"I didn't." He took a deep slurp through his straw, finishing up all his water and maybe sucking up a little bit of melted ice. Then he chucked the cup into a trash can beside the bus stop. "But that's what happens around here. People come in from someplace else, they buy up crapholes and turn them into mansions. Everybody used to think it was funny. We used to joke about them."

"How come?"

"Oh, they'd take one house on a block and fix it up real nice, and then it was the *only* nice house on the block. They'd try to sell it for ten times what any other house would go for . . . and it'd sit for a while, nobody living in it. Finally, maybe they'd get a renter. Usually some white family, on a mission to save the city from itself, coming in after the Storm like they're gonna make a difference. Then maybe those renters buy a place, and maybe they bring some friends. Pretty soon, you've got a little block like an island, like a fortress. Bunch of people who see a couple of black guys waiting at a bus stop and call the police, like we're casing their houses or something."

Denise blushed. "But it's good if they're fixing the old houses, making the neighborhood nice again, right?"

"Good for somebody," he said, and stood up to announce that the bus was pulling up. "Not for everybody. I mean, look at this market, right? It was just about demolished, and now they've fixed it back up again. Now it's fancier than it ever was before the storm, and that's pretty cool—but now a lot of the locals can't afford the food."

Denise handed the driver her transfer and went to go sit down. Norman joined her.

"You know we're not like that. You know I'm not."

"I know you don't mean to be, but you might turn out to be. Your momma turns that place into a bed-and-breakfast, who's gonna come pay to stay there? More tourists who want to gawk at what the Storm left behind, and more white knights."

"I hope not." But the more she thought about it, the more worried she was that he could be right. And she didn't have any idea what to do about it, so she asked. "What should we do, then? How should we make the nail house part of the neighborhood?"

He thought about it a minute, and said, "Hire people *from* the neighborhood to work on it, and work *in* it when it's finished — and pay them what they're worth. That'd be a start."

"Well, they hired *you*." She didn't know if they were hiring neighborhood professionals for the pricey stuff, but she resolved to bring it up to her mom and Mike later on.

"That's true! And I'm worth every penny."

The number 90 bus headed uptown, to a stop in "Carrolton," or that's what she thought she heard over the intercom. The next one was for the university, and that's where she and Norman got off.

They climbed down off the steps at the bus's back exit and stepped into a sidewalk beside a bright, clean campus. Rows of bicycles were locked up on long metal racks outside each building, and everything looked very new.

Denise said, "Wow, this place is nice!"

"It doesn't all look like this. Don't get me wrong, the rest of it ain't bad," he added, "but some parts are nicer than others. Come on, I'll take you to the library."

"Do you want to stop by and see your mom, first?"

"She's off today."

Denise felt stupid. "I forgot it was Saturday."

"Sometimes she works on Saturdays. A lot of students live in the dorms and stuff, and school runs year-round. They've gotta eat every day, right?"

Okay, well. She didn't feel quite so stupid. "I guess that's true. Where does she work again?"

"Bruff Commons, at the dining area there. That's where I work too, when I'm off from the pizza place. I clear tables and empty trash, and sweep up. Here, we're going around this way." He pointed at a sidewalk, and led the way. "To the Howard-Tilton Memorial Library."

He said that last bit with a fancy flair that it seemed to require. "I've only been inside it a handful of times. I don't have a library card or anything, because I'm not a student. My mom gets some perks for working here, though. She wants me to enroll when I graduate. If I can get in, and if I can get enough student loans, but I don't know, man. It's a lot of money, and my grades are good, but . . . it's just, it's like. It's *so* much money. I keep my eyes open for art and photography scholarships and stuff, on the off chance anybody wants to help foot the bill—but so far, I haven't had any luck."

"My mom wants me to come here too," she confessed.

"It's a real good school."

She said, "I know, but like you said . . . it's a lot of money. I was thinking I'd go back to Houston when I graduate. I got friends there. I know my way around. School's cheaper too. I can probably still get in-state tuition."

"Sure, but you're making friends here too, and I'm showing you around. Maybe this place will grow on you."

"You saying we're friends?"

"Yup. Me and Terry, we're your friends. Dominique too. If you give her a minute. It's not the whole city, but it's a start."

She wasn't so sure about Dom. "I don't think your cousin actually likes me very much."

"She doesn't like anyone much, but she thinks you're okay. You should take it. It's worth something, when she decides she's on your team."

Around another corner, and the library came into view. It was three stories tall and made of concrete. It looked like it came right out of the 1980s. Inside, it smelled like every other library Denise had ever seen: like old books, strong air-conditioning, carpet cleaner, and a dash of mildew.

"What are we looking for exactly?" Norman asked.

"The special collections librarian."

He frowned. "Do they have one of those?"

"Wikipedia says they do."

They asked at the big central desk and got sent to a different desk, on the third floor.

The plaque on the special collections librarian's desk said he was Casey Pines. His name may have sounded like a nursing home, but he was a slender, handsome black man who was probably in his thirties. He had cute little glasses and a shiny shaved head.

"Excuse me, Mr. Pines?" Denise began.

"Yes, can I help you?"

She introduced herself and Norman, who waved awkwardly, and told Mr. Pines about Joe Vaughn and the comic manuscript in the attic. "I saw online that you have an archive of his papers."

Mr. Pines snapped to his feet with a broad smile of enthusiasm. "First, I must tell you not to take everything the Internet says at face value, because it's my job to warn you — but on this occasion, it's at least part right! Yes, yes, yes. Let me take you to the stacks, and I'll show you what we've got."

They followed him into a very quiet section of the library with half a dozen shelves that went all the way to the ceiling, and a wall that was stocked with boxes that looked like they belonged in a law office. Each one had a faux wood grain printed on it, and a white label with catalog numbers and letters scrawled in black Sharpie.

"This is the special collections?" she asked.

Mr. Pines said, "Some of it. We have more important things on lockdown — this is mostly local history of a more recent, less valuable variety. Come in to this room here, if you would please, and I'll bring you the box of Joe's archives."

She peeked through the door. It looked like a perfectly normal conference room. "Are his papers valuable?"

"All of our archives are valuable in some respect or another. Are Joe's papers worth money? I'm not sure. But he's dead, isn't he?" He didn't wait for a response. "Signatures of dead people can be worth money, and so can old comics."

"We don't need to see the comics. We're mostly interested in any articles about him, or letters, or that kind of thing," Denise said.

The librarian nodded. "I'll see what I can do."

Denise and Norman took chairs at the table, side by side, and fidgeted while Mr. Pines disappeared and rummaged someplace in the special collections stacks. Or boxes, or file cabinets, or wherever they kept that kind of thing.

She was a little disappointed when the librarian didn't return with a box at all, but a manila folder.

He placed it on the table in front of her. "Except for the comics . . . this is all we've got, I'm afraid. It's not much to go on, but if I recall correctly, Joe Vaughn was a rather private man — and not much is known about him. I think he used to be a woodworker, or something?"

"A carpenter, that's what I read," she told him.

"It may or may not be true." He shrugged. "Frankly, I'd be surprised if that was even his real name."

Norman cocked his head, looking more closely at an old copy of a Lucida Might comic that had tagged along with the material in the folder. "This is definitely the same artwork as the one you've got," he said to Denise.

Mr. Pines took a seat at the end of the table, and collected the pieces that Denise and Norman put aside. "I would leave you to this," he explained, "but without a student ID . . . I'm not really supposed to bring you back here at all, you understand. Please forgive me if I hover."

"Sure, sure," Norman replied without looking at him. He was engrossed in the folder's contents. "What are we looking for, exactly?" he asked Denise.

She sighed down at the folder. "I'm hoping I'll know it when I see it. Wait, what's this?" She pulled out a thin, brittle piece of paper the color of sand.

You've been a hell of an agent. Marty. and you've always done right by me. I owe you. and I owe you big. We've had a great run. and yes—I have more lucida Might in me...but not as much as I'd thought. It deserves a wrap-up. a send-off. a final chapter. doesn't it? Well. I've written one. and I've drawn it up.

I don't think I can ever publish it. It's a shame it'll never see the light of day. but I feel better for having done it. You might call it a confession. of sorts. Everyone feels better after confessing. right?

At any rate. I've written my manifesto. Maybe I'll box it up. and stuff it in a safe deposit somewhere. Maybe I'll burn it. (I probably won't. but with my mental state these days. I can make no promises.) Maybe I'll just hide it so no one can take it away from me. You know who would take it away. if I gave him half a chance. He enjoys playing the part. and the money that's come with it all this time. but all good things must come to an end.

Thank you. Marty. Forgive me. Marty. But my life has become a house of horrors. and my time in the business is over.

Mr. Pines cocked his head. "I don't get it."

"Check out that last line." Denise flipped the page over. There was nothing on the back. "He says his life has become a house of horrors. That's what my comic is called."

"Really? That's amazing!" Mr. Pines looked genuinely tickled. "Well, if you ever think of donating it someplace, I do hope you'll think of us!"

"Absolutely!" she fibbed.

Norman took the letter gently from her hands, and scanned it for himself. "He talks like he's having trouble with somebody."

"Yeah, that's the second time I've seen him make a reference to somebody he just calls 'you-know-who.' I wonder who it is? Wait, here's another letter. Or part of the same one . . . ? No, I don't think so." She pulled out another page. The paper was a different color, and it began mid-sentence.

what will happen. Things are coming to a head here. and Marty. I don't know what to do. I'm afraid. I don't know what he'll do. He's taken the news so badly.

"This doesn't feel right," Denise protested. "None of it feels right."

"Where's the rest of it?" asked Mr. Pines.

But there wasn't any rest of it. Just the single fragment. Apart from a few more comics, there wasn't much else: an envelope addressed to Marty Robbins in New York City, an award notice from some comic industry group, and a royalty statement that made it sound like Joe Vaughn didn't really earn much money at all.

"Those are 1950s dollars," the librarian noted. "It's more money than it sounds like, and this is only for the newspaper syndication, if I understand the statement correctly. It doesn't include the comic sales, or the cash from the TV show."

"Oh. Well, I guess that's everything in here. It's not a lot to go on, but thank you, Mr. Pines. I've learned a lot."

"I'm always happy to help young researchers find their way around the shelves," he said modestly. "Perhaps you two will come back as students, and I can give you the official tour!"

Denise and Norman walked back to the bus stop and discussed their theories all the way home, but neither one of them knew what to make of any of it. By the time they were back at the stop in front of the school, they were both stumped and silent.

They stepped out of the bus and the doors closed behind them.

"Thanks for everything, Norman. I really appreciated it."

"It was fun. Right?"

"It *was* fun." She smiled tiredly. "Seriously, thanks for getting me out of the house. I'll see you soon."

Later that night after supper, she sat on her bed, in her room with the water stains on the ceiling. The air-conditioning ran loud and cold, and she knew she ought to get up and turn it down, but she didn't. Instead, she texted Trish the latest on the ghost situation, and Trish sounded one-hundred-percent down to hear about it. And have opinions about it.

POLTERGEISTS did I spell that right

Denise grinned. *I think so? I don't think Joe's a poltergeist. Just a jerk.*

what's the line between a pissed off ghost and a poltergeist tho

Throwing things? Hurting people? Well, if that was the case, maybe she was wrong. Maybe Joe was a poltergeist after all.

why is this guy such a jerk

I do not know. But I'm trying to find out.

Let me at im. I'll defend you. Send him packing.

She laughed. *Don't say that. What if you chase him off, and he follows me back to Texas next year? You want a poltergeist in the dorm room?*

Yes. WE can sell tickets. Write our memoirs and people willmake movies about us. We will be zillionaires with the help of your jerk ghost.

She laughed again, and said, *You've got a point.*

Ive still got a roommate too. Right?

Denise stared down at her phone. *Um, YEAH. What have I told you that would make you think different? I want out of here. Someplace where nobody died on the floor.*

Terry picked that moment to crash the party. His text alert popped up over Trish's message: **Any new ghost sightings to report? Or ghost smellings? Hearings?**

She switched over to his message real quick. *My dude, I would tell you if there was anything spooky going on. You're probably the FIRST person I would tell.*

Then Trish asked: **Is there a gross stain?**

Back to Trish. *No.* She said it without even glancing out the door. If there'd ever been a stain, it was gone now. She'd checked a hundred times already. *And no, I don't want to stay in NOLA. I want to go home, and room with you and your rich-ass self. We will have a swank dorm room, right?*

Trish didn't really need to live in the dorm, but her parents had some money and she had some demands. She had been promised a dorm room, so long as she had a parentally approved roommate. Denise — with her test scores and willingness to tutor — was parentally approved.

Terry was back. **First person? Rlly?**

Yes, she told him. *First person, I swear. Feel all special and stuff.*

Trish returned to the conversation, fantasizing about their future dorm room. **Itll be the swankest of all time, you no it. I still want to see this haunted house of yours. And this comic book. You won't keep itall to urself would you?**

Terry was ecstatic. Denise could practically hear it through his next text. **I do! Feel special! You shuld sleep with a recorder, or camera. Do you have a camera? How about your phone?**

She replied, *Phone would probably go into standby if I just left the camera or recorder running.* Wouldn't it? She thought so. *Evenif I left it plugged in.*

Then quickly, back to Trish: *You are welcome here, of cours — but wait until we don't have holes in all the floors. I have an AC unit in my bedroom, so you know it is POSH up in here.*

Trish liked this idea. **Count me in!**

Terry had thoughts about batteries. **Maybe we could find a motion-detecting camera on ebay. Wouldn't use that much power.**

Yeah, she said. *I'll keep my eyes open when I'm finished rolling them. That stuff's expensive.*

I dare to dream! she concluded.

By then, it was getting late, and everyone was ready to call it a night. But not Denise. She was awake, and she had some battery life left, so she pulled up the Internet on her phone.

She went back to Wikipedia and started clicking around through the sources cited at the bottom of Joe Vaughn's entry. That's when she learned that the *Times-Picayune* had an archive, and although it wasn't online, someone had been kind enough to post a JPEG of the story about Vaughn's death. This someone was an earnest nerd, somebody with a Tumblr that was dedicated to the real-life people behind pre-CCA comic books.

"Truly, all information is contained within the Internet," she murmured to herself. That's what one of her old history teachers used to say. He said that the *real* trick was knowing how to find it.

She scanned the photo, struggling a little because it wasn't very big and the text was kind of fuzzy. But she got the gist easily enough. Joe Vaughn, local artist and author, had fallen down a flight of stairs and broken his neck. He was found in a house belonging to a lady named Vera Westbrook. Miss Westbrook had been missing for several days.

"Vera Westbrook! Nice to finally have a name to go with the perfume and the footprints." And nice to have a new lead. How had she not stumbled on this before? "Whatever happened to you, Vera?"

As far as the Internet could tell, nobody knew.

Vera Westbrook had disappeared off the face of the earth. The article with Vaughn's death by misadventure was the next to last mention of her that ever appeared in print. Her final appearance came in a city auction a few months later, when her house and everything inside it was put up for sale.

Vera Westbrook. It *sounded* like an old lady name. An old lady who wore roses and lilies to church every Sunday. An old lady with tiny pointed shoes, and a lilting voice that hummed a strange tune, just barely audible.

"Did Joe know what happened to you, Vera?" she asked aloud. Vera didn't answer, and neither did anyone else. "Did *anybody*?"

The Internet couldn't help her with that one, but Denise had an idea.

She was developing a theory.

CHAPTER SIXTEEN

Denise spent Sunday morning trying to text Terry, but he never did respond, and when she texted Norman, he replied that he was stuck at his grandmother's for church and potluck, then vespers that evening — so he was no good to her, either. If she'd had her number, Dominique might have been game to chat. She knew about the ghosts now too.

But she didn't have her number, so it was just Denise and her parents. They braced themselves for a day of vacuuming out the last of the fluffy gray goo, and probably water damage, and maybe bugs, by donning the longest gloves and the tallest boots they had — plus some paper face masks that Mike had picked up at Pete's. Denise felt ridiculous, her hands and feet were sweating buckets, and she sounded like Darth Vader when she breathed, but she *did* feel sufficiently protected.

"From everything but the ghosts," she added, when Sally asked her opinion on the safety gear.

"Screw the ghosts," Sally replied. "This is our house now, and they can lump it."

Mike chuckled awkwardly. "Let's not say such things quite so loud, eh? They might be listening."

"Good," his wife declared.

"Yeah. Like Mom said, this is *our* house now. Besides, I don't care if Vera stays — she's all right. It's Joe we've got to worry about. He's the jerk."

"Who's Vera?" Sally asked. "Or is that what we're calling the old lady ghost, for no particular reason?"

"Vera Westbrook, that's her name. Or that's the name of the lady who owned this house, back when Joe died like a chump. I did a little more digging, and turned up her identity."

"Was she his girlfriend or something?" Mike wanted to know.

"I haven't a clue." Denise picked up a trash bag and shook it open. "And nobody knows what happened to her, either. She vanished before Joe died."

Sally shook her head. "This whole thing gets weirder by the day."

Mike plugged in the Shop-Vac and made sure it was set to "suck" instead of "blow." "As long as *one* of the ghosts isn't trying to kill us, I'll call it a win."

"But you're fine if the other one is a homicidal maniac," Denise said wryly.

"I'm not fine with it, but I'm saying it could be worse. They could both be out to get us."

They spent the rest of the morning vacuuming and bagging trash, picking up the last of the ratty brown insulation that had come from the ceiling, and wiping the residue off every available surface. They'd gotten the worst of it earlier, but today was the fine detail work, and it was going to be never-ending as far as Denise could tell.

The fluffy stuff in question was indeed vermiculite, according to some guy at Pete's who Mike had chatted up on the subject. Nothing to get excited about, but wear gloves when you pick it up. Wear masks when you mess with it. It'll get into your chest and make your lungs all itchy.

When all that was done, they moved on to the wainscoting and wallpaper, those two miserable projects.

Mike and Sally were happy and a little day-drunk, playing dorky 1990s songs from Mike's playlist again while they scraped wallpaper in the dining room by electric lantern light, since the fixture still wasn't working.

Denise needed a break. She declared this loudly and scraped

together enough change for a soda and a beignet, and promised to be back in an hour or two.

Then she hiked down to Crispy's with her laptop, planning to wait around until someone she knew showed up.

Surely someone she knew would show up. Eventually.

Yep. Church had let out, and everybody'd finished up lunch at home. Now the little restaurant was collecting the usual suspects, wanting Internet and some freedom. She recognized most of the kids her age, but didn't know them well enough to chat them up. She thought about asking to sit with them, but chickened out at the last minute and took her usual table against the wall.

Finally, Terry arrived. She grabbed him before he could even order any food, and dragged him over to her table. She leaned forward and said, "Guess what: I think I know the name of the old lady ghost."

"Really?"

"It's *Vera Westbrook*. The house belonged to her, and get this: She vanished, not long before Joe died. Nobody knows what happened to her, but I'm pretty sure she's dead, and she's the second ghost—the one without a hit list."

"Hey y'all two." Dominique brought a tray from the front counter and slipped it into the slot next to Terry like she was sliding into home plate. It held a clear cup for holding water, not soda, and a ninety-nine-cent order of beignets. "Any more news about the ghosts?"

They caught her up on the Vera Westbrook development, and Denise concluded, "I think Joe was having some kind of fight with Vera Westbrook too. He might've even killed her. It sounds like she doesn't like him much. Maybe when Terry comes back over with his recorder—"

"Not if, but when!" he declared happily.

". . . then maybe we can get Vera to tell us what happened to her. She's been helpful before; she might be helpful again."

"You let me know how that goes. I want to know," Dom told her firmly. "But I don't want to be there, when you find out. I just want the download when you're done, got it?"

Denise liked how Dom didn't argue with her, or tell her there was no such thing as ghosts, or act like this was stupid. "I will. I'll tell everybody. Maybe I'll write a big Tumblr post about it, and tell the whole world." Then she told her about the agent, Eugenie Robbins. "You never know. This lady might get me enough money for a decent laptop."

Norman joined them then, adding his tray to the assortment that now covered the entire table. He'd paid extra for a second corn dog, and brought a plastic Aquafina bottle from home, so she guessed the potluck hadn't filled him up. "Been refilling it here for a couple of weeks," he explained. "Hello, ladies and Terry."

Together, they discussed theories of ghosts, probabilities, and how to find further evidence until the restaurant manager started to give them the side-eye about hanging around for so long without buying anything else. Denise had already texted her mom and told her she'd walk back soon, and after she promised Norman that she'd update him tomorrow, he'd headed back in the direction of his own home. Dominique and Terry kept pace with her as she walked back to the Agony House.

"Hey, Denise, listen," Dominique began. "If you've got a minute today . . ." She trailed off.

"If I've got a minute, what?"

She cleared her throat, and hemmed, and hawed, and generally acted like she was very uncomfortable about what she needed to say. "See, my grandma wants to know if you'll come talk to her."

"What?"

Terry perked up. "Mrs. James? How's she doing?"

"She's good, Tee. Same as always. So . . . what do you say? I just live a couple of blocks away from you. Grandma wants to ask you about your place, that's all. She wants to talk about the nail house."

Denise shrugged. "Sure, I guess. Let me text my mom that I'm running late, so she doesn't worry." She pulled out her phone and fired off a text begging an extra twenty minutes to find her way home. She hit SEND and pocketed the phone again. "Let's do this."

Dominique's house was long and narrow, with a single story and tall front shutters on either side of the front door. The porch was close to the ground, just two short steps that sagged like the ones at Denise's place. There was even a haint-blue ceiling, like it was just something everybody around there had. The porch was clean, and so was the living room, where a couple of antique chairs flanked a couch that once had been a very fancy velvet, and now looked a little too lived-in to call fancy anymore.

Before they went inside, Dominique turned to Denise. "She's going to ask you about ghosts, I just know it. She loves all that spooky business. I don't know what's wrong with her."

"Spooky business is fun business!" Terry declared.

"Yeah, says you. Fun to hear about, that's all. I like for my dead people to stay good and dead."

"What's the fun in that?" he asked.

"The fun of not getting your butt scared off." Then she cleared her throat, and said loud enough to project all the way to the back door: "Grandma, I'm home — and I brought that girl from the nail house!"

A voice came from the kitchen. "Good, I'm glad to hear it." Mrs. James poked her head around the corner and said, "Give me just a second, if you would. Take a seat, and make yourself comfortable. Terry? You came along too? Nice to see you, son. Can I get either one of you a Coke?"

"No thank you, ma'am," said Terry.

"No thank you, ma'am," Denise echoed.

Everybody sat down, and a moment later their hostess joined them, wiping her hands on a dish towel. "I'm glad you were willing to come around, dear. Remind me your name?"

"Denise, ma'am. Denise Farber. Dominique said you wanted to talk about the house."

"That's right." She took the chair that faced them all the best, and folded her hands across her belly. She was a thickset woman with sharp eyes and a kind expression. She could've been forty or seventy. She just had one of those faces, where it was hard to tell. "Your folks picked up the old nail house, over there on Argonne."

"Yes ma'am."

"Well, I asked Dom to bring you here because I know your parents are doing all that work on the place, and I wondered if you'd . . . *found* anything."

The very picture of innocence—or possibly confusion—Denise asked, "Like . . . what?"

Mrs. James's eyes just about twinkled. "Like anything . . . or any*one* . . . hidden inside that place. My momma always said the house was abandoned because someone disappeared, and was never found. When I was a kid, we used to dare each other to go inside, looking for a body."

"I think my stepdad found a dead possum in the bathroom wall, but that's been the worst of it."

The older woman laughed gently, then looked a tad embarrassed about it. "I can't decide if that's good to know, or a little disappointing. There were so many stories, and we all wanted to get inside so *bad*—but we were all so scared. Just looking inside the windows was enough to make us squeal. You'd see lights in there, sometimes. People walking past the windows."

"Yikes . . ." Denise whispered.

"Just squatters or trespassers, I figure. It'd been boarded up for so long, before that last fellow bought it—the one just before y'all picked it up. He said he ran out of money, but I heard through the grapevine that the place spooked him too bad to keep working on it. Like something inside that house don't want anyone looking around too much. Like it doesn't want anyone to stay."

Terry opened his mouth, but Denise gave him a kick on the leg that wasn't particularly discreet—but effective. He closed his mouth again.

Denise cleared her throat. "I don't know why the last guy left the house like he did. It sure *looked* like somebody got started and ran out of money, so that's probably all it was. As for us, like I said — we found that dead possum."

Mrs. James nodded. "But your parents, they're remodeling, aren't they? Gonna open it up, like a little hotel? Haunted hotels in New Orleans are a dime a dozen, but people love 'em. You should play that up, if you ever get it off the ground."

Denise sighed hard. "God knows we're trying to get the place in order, but it's falling apart at the seams."

"It's not much to look at anymore, if you don't mind me saying — but it can't be that bad on the inside."

"Ma'am, the inside's no picnic. The other day, we had to spend a night in a hotel because the living room ceiling caved in. But there weren't any corpses up in there, either. Nothing that used to be alive except for a snakeskin or two."

"Well, you keep your eyes open. For years and years everybody talked like there was a body inside, someplace."

"Probably just because Joe died there," Terry said helpfully.

"Joe?" she asked with a very keen look on her face. "Joe who?"

"Joe Vaughn," Denise answered. She sure did wish that Terry could keep his mouth shut. "He was a comic book writer, back in the 1950s. He fell down the attic stairs and broke his neck, but I'm pretty sure they took his body away and buried it. It's definitely not at the foot of the stairs anymore, so . . ." Her voice faded out.

"Maybe that's it," Mrs. James agreed. "Neighborhood lore can get tangled up something awful, with little bits of truth and little bits of lies all mixed in together. You never know for sure what's real, and what somebody made up to scare a bunch of kids away from a dangerous old house. Have you opened all the walls yet?"

"The plumbers and electricians did. It took a few days."

"*All* of the walls?" she pressed.

"All of 'em with wires or pipes inside, so that's . . . just about everything, right?"

"I suppose." She leaned back and looked at Denise hard, like she was trying to decide if she was telling the truth. "But you're saying there's nothing in that place? Not a single haunt or haint? Not even . . . a whiff of perfume? The fellow before you said he kept smelling roses and lilies," she said, and the twinkle in her eyes was now a gleam.

Denise held her breath. When the phone in her pocket buzzed and pinged, she let it out in an unladylike gasp. "I'm sorry," she sputtered. "It's my mom, I'm sorry. I really have to go. Thank you," she said as she stood. "Mrs. James, thank you for the hospitality, but I have to run. Terry, Dominique . . . I'll catch y'all two later."

When she got home to Argonne Street, she stood out front, like she did the very first time she saw the house. Mouth half-open, feeling glum, wondering if it could be saved. Or if it was even *worth* saving. But before she could drag herself up the porch, Sally opened the front door. "There you are. I was starting to wonder."

"I took a detour. I sent a text, didn't you get it?"

"It was a vague text." She stood aside to let Denise up the steps and around the hole on the porch, which still hadn't been fixed. "Come on inside, if you want something to eat."

Dinner was seafood, something that wasn't quite the fast-food junk they'd mostly eaten for days. Sally had picked it up from a po'boy place somewhere that wasn't Crispy's, but Denise didn't care. She'd never had a proper po'boy from Crispy's, anyway.

"Not that I'm complaining," Denise said as she pulled out a foil-wrapped sandwich the size of a baby's head. "But when are we going to have a working kitchen?"

"Soon," Sally said. "The electricians are almost done."

"I keep hearing that."

"So do we." Mike pulled off his face mask and drew up a chair.

Sally passed out napkins. "We're getting there. Gradually. We've got that next chunk of money approved, and it should hit our bank account this week . . . but it's supposed to go to the next round of work. Maybe we'll take a couple hundred bucks and scare up a stove with more than one burner mostly working, and an oven that doesn't spit fire. Maybe we'll even spring for one that was made in this century."

"I'd settle for last century, so long as it worked." Mike bit down on a full, golden bun and chomped through the fried shrimp stuffing.

Everyone ate in silence after that, because everyone knew they were eating all the money they'd set aside that wasn't for the house. Nobody needed to say it out loud.

After food, Denise excused herself and went upstairs, where she turned the AC unit up half a notch past the agreed-upon setting, and pulled out her phone.

Trish had sent her a row of ghost and skeleton emojis, so apparently she'd found a Halloween stash someplace.

Denise grinned and typed back. *Did I tell you I saw Tulane the other day? It's a pretty campus. Library is great.*

After a pause, a typing bubble appeared, and then her friend replied: **ur not chickening out on me, are you? still coming home to be my roommate?**

Obvs. Just saying, is all.

She put the phone away, not entirely sure of what, exactly, she was just saying. Even if she could, she didn't really want to stay in Louisiana, did she?

Forget it. She didn't want to think about it.

She was almost finished reading *Lucida Might and the House of Horrors*, so maybe that would distract her. Only a handful of pages remained. She might feel a little bad about finishing up without Terry, but she'd already read pretty far ahead of him, and she could always invite him over to let him finish on one of these afternoons when the house and its ghosts weren't actively trying to kill anyone.

She fished the manuscript out of her bag and settled into bed — sitting on top of the covers, propped up by all her pillows.

CHAPTER SEVENTEEN

Denise looked up from the book. She smelled something.

Flowers. Roses and lilies.

She sniffed until she was sure; it was very faint, but it was definitely perfume. Soon, it would be dark outside, so she flipped on the bedside lamp that sat atop a box beside her. It wasn't dark yet, but the room was gold and dim, and she wanted every bit of light she could get.

The air didn't just smell funny, it *felt* funny. It felt like it was buzzing. Like music with nothing but the bass turned up, somewhere far away. Like the damp, brittle humming of the sky when there isn't any rain, but any minute, there will be lightning.

Denise closed *Lucida Might* and set it aside. She only had another couple of pages to read, and then she'd be done with it — but then again, that's what she'd thought when she'd picked it up half an hour ago.

She thought of the previous night, when she'd been reading about a ceiling collapse, and downstairs, that's just what had happened. She thought of Mike falling through the porch. Windows that fell shut and almost crushed hands. Nails that appeared in stair rails. Bricks that crashed onto feet.

Slowly, she reached for her phone. She pulled up Terry and composed a text. She wasn't sure who else to ping.

Something weird is going on. I mean, EXTRA weird. Are you there?

She wasn't sure what she expected him to say or do, but she needed to say something, to someone. Trish was too far away to do anything but worry; Norman might think she was crazy, and she didn't think she knew him well enough to pass off crazy as charming. Dom might be intrigued, but Denise had brain-farted and forgotten to ask for Dom's number, and anyway—Dom didn't want to get in the middle of any ghost drama, she'd made that clear. On the one hand, she wanted to respect her wishes, on the other, she would've just about killed to have her there . . . oh well. It was nobody's fault but her own.

She'd have to settle for Terry. He was most likely to understand, and he was adventurous enough to respond to her summons. She hit SEND.

Unhooking the phone from its cable, she slid out of bed and poked her toes through the slots of her flip-flops. She dragged her feet and the foam-bottomed shoes scraped across the rough boards.

The roses and lily scent faded, and something else took its place. The new smell was sour and dark.

"Mom?" Denise called out. She reached her bedroom door and hung on to it, looking down at the hall's carpet runner and checking for footprints. There weren't any. "Mike?"

Nobody answered.

The smell grew stronger. The air grew thicker, and Denise felt light-headed. She let go of the doorframe and stepped into the hall, then took the rail and stood near the top of the stairs.

"Mom? Mike?"

Nothing was going on. Nothing was weird. If there was a terrible smell, it was in her imagination — or else it was in the attic, where there were plenty of terrible smells to go around. Just a draft, that's all. Just a rush of air pushing down under the door, into the rest of the house. Just some ghost with a grudge, or a different ghost with a pleasant odor and gentle warnings.

She kind of wished she had Terry's recorder handy. She wondered if anything was trying to talk, and she just couldn't hear it. Surely *something* was trying to communicate.

Her phone was a solid lump in her shorts pocket. She pulled it out. Terry hadn't texted back, but the phone had a voice recorder feature buried in it somewhere.

Still standing on the stairs, she poked at the screen until she found what she was looking for. She pressed the icon to turn on the mic. She held it out like she'd seen Terry do, away from her body, away from the static noise of her clothes, her breathing, her heartbeat.

"Is there anybody here with me?" she whispered. "What do you want?"

The buzzing got louder, or it felt louder. She couldn't really hear it, so much as she could feel it moving on her skin. Under it.

A voice answered, "Denise?" but it was just her mom, calling from downstairs. "What are you doing up there?"

Denise came down the steps, half-dead from relief. "Nothing, why?"

Sally wasn't in the living room or dining room. Denise didn't know where she was, because she couldn't see her. "Then what's that strange noise? Are you playing music?"

Denise followed her mom's voice down to the parlor, and found Mike there too. They were both looking up at the light fixture, one of the last old pieces that remained. It was probably just glass and not crystal, but it would be real pretty when they got it cleaned up.

The light was probably not rocking back and forth, swaying like a pendulum. It was probably not keeping time to some odd humming that sounded more like a grumble than a song.

"You hear it too," Sally said with a gulp. "Don't you?"

"What the hell is going on?" Mike asked without taking his eyes off the fixture. Then he looked over at Denise, who hadn't answered her mom yet. "What are you doing with your phone?"

She quit holding it out like a torch, and dropped her arms to her sides. "I was looking for a good signal," she explained, in case they would think her EVP recording efforts were weird. They probably weren't working anyway, so she tucked the phone into her pocket and wandered back into the living room.

Sally wrinkled her nose. "What's that smell? *Please* tell me nothing is on fire. The electricians supposedly took care of the knob-and-tube a couple of days ago . . ."

"Mom, I don't think it's fire."

The light fixture rattled, its glass bits clinking together. The windows rattled too.

Denise backed out of the room, in case another section of the ceiling was going to drop. She left it just in time to see a dark, nebulous shape spill slowly toward them, slipping down the stairs. It took her breath away. She literally couldn't answer Mike, when he asked if New Orleans ever got earthquakes. Even if she knew, she couldn't have told him. She couldn't say a word. She opened her mouth, and nothing came out.

The dark shape didn't have much shape to it at first — it was a blob about the size of a person, and then it sprawled and spread. It poured along the floor in every direction, pooling around Denise's ankles and leaving them cold. She shivered, even though it must've been eighty-five degrees down there.

It could've been hotter than that, and it wouldn't have mattered. She froze anyway.

She watched the tall, ragged shape take form — assuming the shape of a tall, heavyset man with hunched shoulders, and long arms, and big hands. He didn't have much of a face, just a pair of eyes that were holes in the smoke, white and bright. He stayed put on the stairs, but the dark fog around his feet sprawled toward the parlor. What if it got Mike, or her mom? What would it do to them?

She unfroze herself. Scared beyond words, she tore her eyes away from the figment on the stairs and darted back to the parlor. "Mom, we have to get out of here!"

"You're right . . . that smell. It might be a gas leak, or poisonous fumes, or . . ." Sally stopped at the "or" because she'd just noticed the putrid swirl of darkness moving across the floor.

"Out," said Mike. "Everybody. Now. We can come back later, when we figure out what's going on."

Joe had other ideas.

The windows rattled harder, and the doors all shook, thundering in their frames. Outside, something huge clapped against the house. A second something followed it. Then a whole volley of bangs, one after the next.

It was the window shutters. Every last one of them slammed shut.

Glass broke, and sprayed inside. Sally shrieked, and when the power went out in a loud, grand poof of sparks, Denise screamed too.

She felt around in the dark—it was so *very* dark, with the windows all covered up, and the lights all turned off—but she found the parlor entrance and knew that the front door was just a few steps to the left. All she had to do was reach it, throw it open, and get the hell out.

Mike and Sally had the same idea. They were right behind her, pushing her even as they felt along the wall.

Denise found the doorknob. She grabbed it, twisted, and yanked. The door swung inward about a foot. "Everybody, come on!" she said, but it wasn't that easy. Hard and fast, the knob yanked itself out of her hand and the door shut itself again.

Mike pushed her aside. "Here, I've got it."

He didn't have it. He pulled until the knob popped off in his hands and a smattering of nails fell across the floor. He kicked them away and announced, "I'm going to break a window! Those shutters are rotted out—they're practically cardboard. We can kick right through them."

She sensed her stepfather moving past her. He was in a rush, looking for something big enough and solid enough to chuck right onto the front lawn. "Bash them in! Use the dining room chairs!" she suggested.

To her right, there was a clatter.

To her left, there was a knock on the door. Denise nearly jumped out of her skin.

Everything went quiet. Her mother breathed hard and fast, and her stepdad stood with the skeletal shadow of a chair in his hands.

"Hello? Is anybody home? It's me, Terry . . ."

Of *course* it was Terry. All it took was a text saying something weird was afoot, and it was like Denise had raised the Bat-Signal. She flung herself at the door, knocking back with both hands. "Terry, can you hear me?"

"Yeah, open the door."

"I can't! We're trapped in here!"

Sally joined her at the door. "And the power's gone out!" she added.

Denise almost told him to call the cops, and then she remembered her own phone. She whipped it out of her pocket. The microphone was still running, but she minimized the app and pulled up the call function. She entered 9-1-1, and hit SEND.

Nothing happened.

She tried it again.

"Denise?" Terry called.

She tried to sound calm when she told him through the door: "Terry, my phone isn't working. You have to go get help."

"You want me to call the police? What do I tell them?"

Sally answered, "Tell them we're stuck in our house!"

"Trapped," Denise corrected her. "Tell them we're trapped, and there's an intruder."

"There's an intruder?" Terry sounded suitably appalled.

"There's a *something*. Just make the call!" she yelled, trying not to think about the looming, lanky figure of Joe — who was surely stalking around them, even as she spoke. Just because she couldn't see him, that didn't mean he wasn't there.

"I'm calling, I'm calling . . ."

Then he was crashing. She heard the boards break and she knew, suddenly and with great horror, that he'd fallen down in the same hole that almost ate Mike. How could he have seen it? The porch light was out, just like everything else. "Terry!" she screamed, and she pounded on the door with her fist, and with the useless cell phone. It didn't matter if she broke it. "Terry, are you okay?!"

Mike swung the chair again and again, but could only break more glass. The shutters were holding. "I swear and be damned!"

Okay, so Denise couldn't make any calls. Could she turn on the flashlight app? Her screen had a big, fresh crack in it, but she found the light and called it up.

It was blinding for a few seconds. Her eyes adjusted, and she saw her mother squinting, holding her face away from the light. "Jesus, girl. That's bright, but good thinking. Mike, we're coming with a light."

"Light won't make a difference," he said. He huffed, puffed, hoisted the chair, and took another swing. This time Denise could watch him. This time, she saw the chair break against the rotted wood shutters that should've splintered into dust if you sneezed on them. His face was tight with fear and maybe pain. He was bleeding through his shirt.

"Honey, I think you've popped your stitches again . . ."

"I don't care!" He threw what was left of the broken chair at the wholly intact shutter, and leaned over, putting his hands on top of his legs and breathing too hard. "What is going on?" he asked the universe at large. "What do we do?"

Denise swung the light around the room, and could not tell which shadows were only shadows, and which ones were moving with slithering, nasty grace along the floors. Or the walls. The pattern on the paper seemed to move. She blinked, and wasn't sure that was it at all. "I think we're asking the wrong questions."

"What do the right questions sound like?" Sally's eyes tracked the mobile darkness. She watched it climb, crawl, and creep around the corners until it took the wobbly, loose shape of a tall man once again. Mike put his arm around her, in turn, and guided her toward the foyer. It was the middle of the first floor, and farthest from any corners.

"What would Terry do?" Denise said for starters. "God, I hope he's okay." She thought of Lucida Might, and how that fictional heroine had found a tunnel under Desmond Rutledge's porch. Terry knew about that scene. She crept back to the front door and peered around — it looked like Joe had faded back into the swirling black. Thank god. Maybe he couldn't take the shape for that long? She pressed her ear against the door. "Terry?" she called again, as loud as she could. She dropped to her knees, and called down to the floor, and to anything underneath it. "Terry, can you hear me?"

No response.

Mike was shaky all over when he asked, "Well? What *would* Terry do?"

"And why does it matter?" asked Sally.

Denise said, "Terry's got some funny ideas, but he gets results." She pulled out her phone, and tried to dial 9-1-1 again. It didn't work. She returned to the microphone and, yes, it was still recording. She held it up again, and asked in a slow, clear voice — like she was trying to explain math to a Saint Bernard: "What . . . do . . . you . . . want?"

She counted to ten, listening to the persistent rushing buzz that filled the house, and filled her ears, and made her forget that she'd ever been able to hear anything else. Then she replayed what she'd recorded. Her own words were too loud, because she kicked the volume all the way up.

"What do you want?" she heard herself ask.

Fizz, static, hum.

I keep what's mine.

Sally and Mike jumped, but Denise yelled at the darkness. "That's all you ever say! You have to be more specific! Tell me *what* you want!"

She heard something else, something below. Some rustling noise, and it might've been Terry, rallying from his fall. She prayed that it was Terry, and she didn't pray very often, so she wasn't sure she was doing it right. But she did it with all her heart, as she held up the phone and counted to ten. She held her breath, and played back the last few seconds.

Fizz, static, hum.

A different voice, this time — a woman, her words as soft as petals: Let me out so I can help.

"Who is that talking?" Sally demanded with a shrill note of hysteria. "Who's saying that? Is it Vera?"

Denise didn't answer. She tried again, counted to ten, and played back the clip.

Fizz, static, hum.

The man spoke this time: . . . bring this house down. Destroy everything . . .

"I heard that. I heard that loud and clear!" Mike's words quivered around the edges.

Denise rewound and pressed the button. She wanted to hear the woman again.

. . . Let me out, so I can help . . .

"This is the craziest damn thing I ever heard. Where's my phone?" asked Sally. "Yours don't work to call the cops, but mine might."

"Where'd you put it?" her husband wanted to know.

"In my purse. It's in our bedroom. Where's yours?"

Mike was so shaken, he wasn't sure. "I can't remember."

. . . let me out . . .

Something moved in the walls, or under the floor. Denise shined the phone-light all around, but she couldn't see anything except the swirling murk. "Please be Terry. Please don't be a rat, or something worse," she whispered to the scrambling noise. Then she called out, "Vera Westbrook!"

. . . so I can help . . .

Mike and Sally were retreating, clutching each other, fumbling toward the bedroom in search of Sally's purse.

"Vera, don't let him do this!" A whiff of perfume tickled her nose — a tiny tendril of sweetness that cut through the god-awful gloom and the stink of death that otherwise filled the house. Something about the soft smell of roses and lilies chased out some of the terror. Something about the thought of it, the hint of it, the clue of it . . . jogged something loose in Denise's head. Something about Eugenie Robbins, and Lucida Might.

Two snippets of text tumbled around in her skull, knocking against each other, making sparks.

My dad used to say that Joe sometimes hid "Easter eggs" in his stories, little pieces of autobiography, here and there.

"You're the biggest liar of all! You hide behind a man's job, with a man's title and a man's gun.

"All you need is a man's name."

Denise gasped.

Everything clicked together.

CHAPTER EIGHTEEN

Something banged underneath the floor. Denise jumped, spun around, and almost dropped the phone—but held it fast and firm. Carefully, she kicked a response, like she was knocking "shave and a haircut."

"Terry? Is that you?"

A muffled, "It's me," made it up through the floorboards. "I'm okay. My phone's busted, but the screen still has a little light."

"Terry, oh my God—hang in there." She turned to look for Mike and Sally, but they must've made it to the bedroom to hunt for their phones. She could hear them rustling around, looking for Sally's purse in the dark. "Mike! Mom! Terry's under the floor! Get a saw—we can cut him out, and leave through the hole in the porch!"

The whole house shuddered at this announcement. Joe Vaughn was angry, but Vera was in there too; the roses and lilies stayed and rallied, faint but pure. Reassuring, but hardly strong enough to mount a challenge from wherever she was.

. . . find me . . .

. . . said the voice on the recorder.

. . . let me out, and I *will* help . . .

Mike came charging back in, Sally's phone aloft. "The phone's not working, but the light is fine." He demonstrated this by shining it right in Denise's face. "There's no Internet, either. No signal of any kind."

"We're in one heck of a dead zone." Denise let out a short, maniacal laugh. The house groaned, and something large, somewhere unseen, cracked with a noise as loud as a gunshot.

Sally was right behind Mike. "Terry's okay? Where is he?"

She tapped the floor with her foot. Terry said something loud, but unintelligible, confirming his continued survival and strange location. "He went under the house, just like Lucida Might did, in the comic."

"What's a Lucida Might?" Sally asked.

Mike said, "She's the girl detective from that comic Denise found in the attic."

"Me and Terry have been reading it together. Mike, come on — get him out of there. This house can't hold up much longer."

"There's no power. The Sawzall won't do us any good."

"Where's the pry bar?" Sally asked.

"Over there. Give it to me," he gestured with his free hand.

"No, I'll keep this. You take the sledge."

Denise got down on her hands and knees, and spoke into the floor. "We're coming for you, Terry. Get away from this spot — we're coming through the floor."

It was easier said than done. Mike and Sally reasserted Denise's warning to move away from the chosen demolition spot, then set to work prying, pulling, and slamming the sledge into the old wood floors that they'd thought about trying to save and refinish, just a week before.

Denise held back and aimed Sally's phone-light while they swung and pulled and swore. She tried not to shake, but it was hard. It was cold in there — as cold as she'd ever wanted the AC to make it — and the house wouldn't stop moving, moaning, and vibrating.

One-handed, she pulled out her own phone and loaded up the microphone again.

"Denise, *don't.*" Her mother said, then jammed the pry bar between two boards and leaned her whole weight on it.

"But I can't hear them without it," she protested, and before Sally could say anything else, she called out to the house, and anything in it: "Vera, I don't know where you went!" Ten seconds passed. Fizz, static, hum.

And the woman came through, her soft voice answered with a southern white lady accent: I never left . . .

Everyone stopped. Even the house stopped. Mike and Sally stared at Denise's phone.

"Vera again," she explained weakly.

From under the floor they heard Terry ask, "What did she say?"

Denise flashed Mike and Sally a worried look. Her phone pinged. She looked down and saw that the microphone had been recording. She pressed the playback button and heard Vera again.

. . . house of horrors.

She couldn't tell if Mike or Sally had heard the message or not; it was faint, and hard to hear over the loud, angry sorrow of the house as it strained to hold itself together. She handed her mom's phone back to her, turned on her heel, and ran for the stairs with her own phone's light bobbing madly, showing the way. "Sometimes there are Easter eggs!"

She heard Mike ask, "What?" but didn't catch her mother's response. The sound of her footsteps stomping up the steps drowned it all out. The vivid white light rocked back and forth as she climbed, clinging to the rail with one hand, and trying to steady the phone with her other.

Her foot caught something small and rolling, and she almost lost her footing—but they were only nails, lying loose across the stairs. Then there were more, pounded into the step, ready to trip anybody coming or going.

"Dang it, Joe! You're such a jerk!" she said as she dodged them. "You and all these stupid nails . . ." *Nails are supposed to hold things together,* she thought. They weren't supposed to drive people away. Joe sure did have a lot of things backwards.

The hall at the top of the stairs was blacker than black, even when she thrust her phone forward. It was a knot of the shadows that wiggled and writhed. She put out her hand and could feel them, cold and clammy, like the air that spills out of a freezer unit. The shadows pushed back. She pushed forward. She pushed harder. She took a deep breath and closed her eyes. Her room was a straight shot to the right, and that's where *Lucida Might* was waiting—on her bed, where she'd been reading it, certain she was almost finished with it.

She held her breath. She closed her eyes.

She pushed through the sticky, slimy shadows and ran—both hands outstretched to catch herself, in case she fell.

Her legs collided with something soft. She stopped, knees knocking against the side of her mattress, and she almost sobbed because she'd made it. Her bedroom was dark, but only dark in the ordinary way. It smelled like roses and lilies, and her phone-light showed no twitching shadows. Only fresh cobwebs, and boxes of clothes, and an unmade bed with an old comic manuscript lying open across it.

"I think I've got it, Vera," she breathed.

She climbed onto the bed and flipped the book open. She couldn't be sure but the last few pages looked more quickly drawn. They'd been done in a hurry.

I TOLD HIM THAT OUR LITTLE RUSE WAS UP, AND HE COULDN'T PRETEND ANYMORE.

HE DID NOT TAKE IT WELL.

I DON'T KNOW WHAT WILL HAPPEN NEXT.

BUT IT WON'T BE PRETTY.

Denise slapped the book shut and the house shuddered, like she'd slapped it too. She tucked *Lucida Might* under her arm, and ran. The hallway felt like a fun house, dark and wobbly, rocking back and forth. She fell and caught herself on one hand. She didn't drop the book. By the time she was back on her feet and headed down the stairs, she could hear Terry loud and clear. He was saying, "Ow," a lot, and thanking Mike and Sally for getting him out of there.

"One more board ought to do it," Mike said. He swung the sledge down, got the end under the next plank, and pulled back, straining against the stubborn wood. It split and popped free of the nails, making a hole big enough for Terry to climb through.

With a little help from Sally, he hauled himself up over the edge and lay on the floor, panting. He was even whiter than usual — ghostly and blanched, from fright or blood loss. No, not blood loss. Denise ran her phone-light over him from top to bottom. She saw a lot of dirt, some bruises, and a couple of scrapes on the palms of his hands. "Dude." She leaned over him, and put her hands on his shoulders. "Get up. You're fine. I need your help."

"Give me a minute . . ."

"We may not have a minute!"

Mike nodded, and leaned on the sledge. "Pull yourself together, Terry. We're getting out of here. Sally, help me grab another couple of boards. I'm not a kid, and I won't fit through that hole."

"You want me to go back down there?" he squeaked.

Sally whacked at the hole with the pry bar. "Yes!"

"No!" Denise argued. "Terry, get up. I finished the book. I know what Vera's trying to tell us."

"What's going on in here?" he finally asked, like he'd only just noticed that the house was shaking itself apart, and there was no electricity, and the living room buzzed with that otherworldly hum. He sat up and looked around. "Is this the ghosts? Denise, are the ghosts doing this?"

"One of them is, and I think I know how to shut him up."

He asked, "How are you going to do that?"

"I'm gonna let him pick on somebody his own size. I mean . . . his own . . . level of deadness. Um. Just follow my lead." She shoved the book into his hands, so she could grab him by the wrist and hold her light at the same time. "Vera wants us to find her, and let her out. She wants to help."

With this, the swirling blackness that had filled the floor grew even colder; it felt like hands scrambling around her ankles. She squealed and turned around, looking for the shape of Joe and finding it in the doorway, twisting and forming, and reforming around those dead, empty eyes.

She smacked Terry on the shoulder and started running. "Come on!"

Over her parents' protests she fled back up the stairs, Terry hustling in her wake. He stumbled, but she helped him up and they both kept going. At the top of the steps, she turned a hard left and stopped at the attic door. "She's up there."

"You think Mrs. James is right? You think there's a body up there after all?"

"I'd bet money on it. I'd bet my whole *life* on it." She grabbed the knob and pulled. It stuck. She pulled harder, and she said out loud, "Or I'd bet somebody's life, anyway. Vera! If you can hear me up there, let us in!"

A small gust of air puffed out from under the door.

"Do you smell that?" Terry asked, wrinkling his nose, trying to figure out what he was sniffing.

"Yup. That's Vera. She's stuck up here." Denise took another crack at the knob and this time, it opened as smoothly as if that's what it always did, every time anybody tried it. Then she thundered up the narrow, dark steps, her phone's light waggling wildly. She caught herself on the wall, bouncing back and forth; she tried not to break the phone in her hand as she stayed upright by luck and force of will and some lingering memory of gymnastics tumbling, back in middle school.

She reached the top, just as the first curls of black mist tickled the bottom step behind her.

Terry reached it half a dozen seconds later, wheezing all the way. "We already . . . looked around . . . up here . . ." he said between deep, ragged breaths. "All we found . . . was the book."

"Give it here," she commanded. He forked it over. She flipped to the next to last page, with the drawing of the attic interior. "See?" She tapped it. "In *real* life, Vera Westbrook is the one who wrote the Lucida Might stories!"

"Then who was Joe Vaughn?"

"Some dude," she said. "I guess she didn't want to go to the conventions, or public appearances, or whatever. Maybe she had another job, and she didn't want people to know she was writing forbidden comics on the side. Who knows? The point is, Joe Vaughn didn't create any of this stuff. Vera did, and when she told him she was pulling the plug, I think he killed her. He wanted to keep the comic going, and take all the credit for it. Take all the money for it too."

"How do you know he hid her body up here?"

"Because they found *his* body at the bottom of the stairs. *Those* stairs." She pointed back at the stairwell. "He hid her in the attic, then he tripped and fell on the way back down."

"Evil *and* clumsy. Wow."

"Yeah, he was a real winner."

Frantically she looked from the page to the stuffy attic interior; she shined the light back and forth between them, and the vast, mostly empty room where four columns of brick rose up from the floor below, and went up past the roof overhead. Downstairs, these columns led to fireplaces. Above the roofline, they became chimneys.

Denise squinted down at the attic scene. "I think he stuffed her inside one of the chimneys."

"What!?"

She held the manuscript up, and shined her light on it. "It's obvious that she based the house of horrors on *this* house, right? Well, there are *four* chimneys here in real life, and only *three* in the comic book."

"So?"

"So, at the bottom of each chimney is a fireplace, right? We have one fireplace in the parlor, one in the living room, and there used to be one in the kitchen."

"Okay, then where's the fourth fireplace? I don't think I've ever seen it."

She held the light under her chin, and smiled like a maniac. "Terry . . . we don't *have* one."

He was swift on the uptake, she had to give him credit. He lit up like the Fourth of July, and immediately ran back to the narrow stairwell. He stumbled and tumbled down — yelling all the way, "Mr. Cooper, Mrs. Cooper — we need the sledgehammer!"

Then he said, "Oh God . . . oh wow . . ."

"Oh God what?" she hollered.

"This black stuff . . . it's everywhere . . ."

"Just get the sledgehammer!"

While he ran that quick errand, Denise pondered which tower of bricks wasn't original, and didn't match up to things downstairs. The house wailed and sighed on its foundation; the frame itself squeaked as the old timbers twisted and stretched. "I'm coming for you, Vera. I'll get you out of there, so you can save your house. So you can save *us* . . ."

She closed her eyes and pictured the house's layout.

The brick tower to the right, and a bit behind her . . . it would go straight down to the parlor. The extra wide one looked like it'd bottom out in the kitchen. The other two . . . it was harder to say. They were rather close together.

Either one might go down to the living room.

But when she ran her light over the bricks, they weren't the same at all. One column was made with red bricks, and one was built with brown bricks. The mortar was different too. Was one newer than the other? How was she supposed to tell?

Around her shoes, she felt a cold gust that coiled tight, and there were footsteps on the stairs. Big, heavy ones. Slow ones. Not Terry, and not Mike, and not her mom — she would've known their feet. This was somebody else. Something else.

"Joe," she whispered, and she kicked her feet like she could shake off the frigid squeeze. It didn't work. "Joe, knock it off." She shivered and shuddered. Her eyes darted from chimney to chimney. "Where are you, Vera? Help me. Help me, Vera . . ."

She didn't need the microphone, this time. The voice came soft as a sigh, in her left ear: This one, dear.

Terry came storming up the stairs, and from the sound of it, Mike and Sally were coming up behind him — but her friend was the one precariously waving a heavy sledgehammer like a victory flag. He traded Denise the hammer for the book.

She took her first swing at the indicated column as Mike and Sally arrived.

"What the hell are you doing?" her mother demanded.

It was too late to answer. Chunks of brick broke and flew, and when Denise swung again — then again — she opened a hole the size of her hand. A low, horrible gasp poured out of that hole, followed by a soft whistle and a tune that had become almost familiar.

Denise jumped back, and dropped the hammer to the floor.

The gasp kept coming, and it smelled like something worse than death. It smelled like hidden rot and funeral arrangements. It was sorrow and outrage, and loss and missed opportunities.

It was not only flowers, but *fire*.

It flowed like Denise had punctured a balloon, and not a chimney tower. It whistled as it came — soft at first, and then stronger, and stronger. It swept through the attic and around it, in some terrible small hurricane of fury, of burning lilies and scorched roses. It whispered fiercely, and something answered it. Terry held up his recorder and braced himself, planting his feet and narrowing his eyes against the weird maelstrom.

"What is this?" Mike hollered his question into the wind.

But Denise was too triumphant to answer. She pumped her fist and shouted, "Go get 'im, Vera!"

A thin, sour smell of rot and mildew threaded through the perfumed air — it writhed, and fought, and argued, and it was crushed. It was smothered. It was snuffed out with a pop of everybody's ears, and a groan from the floor and ceiling, and a creak and crack from the nearest small window that looked out over what was left of the Argonne block in St. Roch.

The house stopped shaking.

The dull hum faded, until it was so dull that no one could hear it anymore. The rush of air slowed, until it was only a whisper — and then it was only a secret. Only silence.

The house settled. It sighed. Then it was silent too.

Everyone stared at the hole in the chimney that wasn't a chimney at all — but a tomb. It was dark in there. Too dark to see anything at all, until Denise held up her hand all shaky, and shined the phone-light into the hole. She saw dust, and a deserted wasp nest. She saw the other side of dirty brown bricks.

She saw a faded pattern of crochet and buttons.

Like the kind you'd see on an old lady's sweater.

CHAPTER NINETEEN

A small white car pulled up to the house. It hung out by the curb, engine idling, until the driver finally backed up and pulled around to park behind the first of two police cars. A woman got out, and shut the door behind herself. She stared at the key fob until she found the right button to lock the doors with an electronic beep.

"Who's that?" Terry asked. He took a bite of breakfast burrito and chewed. Sally had run to McDonald's, and once again, Terry was present for the fast-food feast. It was early. He was opportunistic. Nobody minded.

Norman had brought his own breakfast — a little baggie of beignets from Crispy's. He sat between Terry and Denise and got all powdery while the three of them watched the woman walk away from the car, looking back and forth between a piece of paper and the house. He said, "She doesn't look like a cop."

Denise swallowed a bit of biscuit and took a swig of orange juice from a paper cup. "She looks like she's lost."

It was a white woman in her forties, probably. She had short red hair and black-framed glasses. She was dressed for daytime in a laid-back office. Jeans and sandals, but nice jeans. Heeled sandals. She stepped sideways to go around the freshly reopened hole in the porch.

The kids couldn't see her through the dining room window anymore, but the woman didn't knock right away. Denise figured she was likely trying the doorbell, but it didn't work, so that wouldn't get her anywhere. It would be a few seconds before she realized her mistake.

Then the woman knocked, hesitantly at first. She knocked again, louder, more firmly. Like she had business there.

Mike called, "Denise, could you get that?" He and Sally were still talking to the one police officer in the living room, while the other one was upstairs taking pictures and looking for extra evidence in the attic.

"Yeah, I've got it."

Denise got up and opened the door. "Hello?"

"Hello," said the woman. She appeared almost surprised, but Denise didn't know why. "Um . . . is this 312 Argonne Street? I didn't see any numbers on the house, but . . ."

"This house is missing a lot of things. You've found the right place."

"Great! Okay. Great. So . . . is there any chance you're Denise?"

"There is a very, very good chance I'm Denise." She frowned, and cocked her head. "Do I know you?"

"Yes! Oh God, I hope this isn't weird. My husband said it was weird." She laughed nervously. "I'm Eugenie Robbins — we've been emailing a little bit? Back and forth? It looks like I've come at a bad time, though. I'm sorry. Is there any . . . um . . . are your parents home?"

"Yes, they're here. But they're talking to the cops. Did you *seriously* fly all the way from New York? Like . . . today?"

"I took a red-eye. There's a big independent booksellers' conference starting tomorrow, and I thought I'd see if I could squeak in early, and catch a word with you."

Denise stood aside, opening the door wider. "How did you find the house?"

"I went rummaging through Dad's old paperwork and found some correspondence between him and a police officer here in New Orleans. It all had to do with Joe's death — the cop included the address of the house where he was found, and asked if Dad knew who lived there. I don't know what my father told him, but I thought I might as well drop by, in case this was it."

Denise laughed. "Well, this is it. These are my friends, Terry and Norman," she added. "Terry was here for the whole show last night, just about. Norman just got wind of the excitement, and came over to see what was up."

"And to make sure everyone was okay!" he protested. "We all heard the ambulance and the cop cars . . ."

"Hi Norman, and hi Terry. It's nice to meet all of you. Wow . . . I can't believe I found this place. I can't believe it's still *standing*." Eugenie Robbins talked fast, like her words were all in a race to get out of her mouth.

Denise led her inside. "You and me both, lady. Especially after last night."

"Yes, I mean . . . good heavens. Ambulances? Police? What happened here?"

Mike, Sally, and some cop whose name Denise hadn't caught all looked up when they came past the living room. Sally rose, in case this was a proper guest who needed proper hosting. Denise headed that off at the pass. "Mom, this is Eugenie Robbins. I told you about her. Her dad was Joe Vaughn's agent."

The cop looked from person to person, trying to decide what was going on, and if it was important. Finally, he asked, "Who's Joe Vaughn?"

Offhandedly, Denise replied, "She's the lady wrapped in the rug upstairs." To Eugenie, she added, "We found Vera Westbrook's body in the attic last night. This was her house, and she was the *real* Joe Vaughn. I mean, kind of."

"Maybe I need a word with *you*," the cop said, a pen held aloft and a notepad in his hand.

"Sure thing. But first, I'm going to take her up to my room." She jerked her thumb toward Eugenie. "And show her my comic book."

Upstairs and down the hall to the right, Eugenie followed them. The whole way, her eyes scanned every inch of the place, taking in all the wonder and glory of the decrepit scenery — which now had a bonus layer of plaster dust and splinters on every surface . . . and a webbing of police tape across the attic door. "Good god . . ." she gasped, her mouth hanging open.

"Vera didn't do this," Denise clarified. "It was the other guy—the one who took credit for all her work. Vera wrote about him, in a round-about way, in this book." It was lying on Denise's bed.

Eugenie sat down on the mattress beside it. "May I?"

"Go for it."

She flipped through the pages with great care, reading quickly and absorbing the art. She skimmed at a crazy speed, admiring everything as she went. Finally, she reached the last page, and scanned all the way down to the signature at the bottom.

"Oh, wow. *Wow.*"

"Vera drew the comic herself, and wrote it too. But for some reason, she didn't want the whole world to know about it. She let Joe Vaughn pretend he was her—I think she even paid him. He's the one who showed up for all her conferences and public appearances," Denise told her. "But Lucida Might *belonged* to Vera, and Joe got mad when she ended it. Your dad did his best to help. I found one of his letters hidden here, in the house. Let me get it."

She offered the old pages to Eugenie, who took them with reverence. "Dad always wanted to help," she whispered. "He must have known all along . . ."

"There's another letter or two at Tulane, in the library archives. I should've taken a picture to show you, but you get the idea from this, right?"

She nodded in response, her eyes never leaving the old letter.

Terry could hardly contain himself. He stood up and half paced, half bounced around the room. He said to Denise, "We'll have to go back to Mrs. James's place. She'll want to hear about the body in the attic because you *know* Dominique will tell her about it. It's going to be all over the neighborhood tomorrow."

"It'll be all over the neighborhood in another hour," Norman corrected him. "The neighborhood grapevine is faster than Wi-Fi."

Denise considered this. "I can't decide if that's awesome or terrible."

"A little of both?" Terry was still tickled pink. Literally. His round, freckled cheeks were flush with glee. "It's totally stranger than fiction. Stranger even than *Lucida Might*. But everyone will have to believe you! I was there — and my dad was there too."

His dad had been half of the responding EMT team, when they'd finally gotten the cell phones working again. Terry wasn't really hurt, but he was the one who'd called it in. His dad had freaked out and come right over, ambulance wailing and lights flashing.

Eugenie Robbins pulled out her phone and started taking photos of the last few pages. "My father would have loved this." She sighed, and held the book across her lap. "I'm positive that he never saw this manuscript. It definitely wasn't published; I learned that much from the material sent over."

"How?" Denise asked.

"Oh, there's an archivist in Texas — a guy named Jess Nevins — who's basically the king of the pop librarians. In his downtime, he compiles bibliographies of comics, pulps, and genre media. He had a complete listing of all the Lucida Might stuff that was ever published or otherwise produced, and he was very, very helpful." She paused and lifted her face. "Wait. What's that? Does anyone else smell it?"

Denise could smell it. One glance at Terry and Norman told her that they could too.

"Flowers . . ." Eugenie breathed.

"Roses and lilies," Denise agreed.

"Where's it coming from?"

Along with the flowers, came music — soft and vague, and then a little louder. Somehow it still sounded very far away, but very clear. Denise wondered about this odd little song . . . the one that Vera liked to sing when she wandered through the house leaving tiny, neat footprints in the dust. It was a cheerful, simple string of notes. They lifted and fell at the farthest edge of her hearing.

Eugenie looked around the room, trying to pinpoint the source. "Do you hear that? It sounds like . . . like someone singing."

Terry slowly reached for his bag, on the floor by the bed. He pulled out his battered recorder, pressed a button, and held it up.

"I know that song," Eugenie whispered.

Denise asked, "You do?"

She nodded, vigorously and with wonder. "Did you ever see the *Lucida Might* TV show? Anywhere online? It must be on YouTube somewhere." She hummed the notes herself, louder and for anyone to hear as clear as a bell. "You don't know that tune?"

Denise and Terry both shook their heads.

Eugenie's eyes were a little damp, but she was smiling anyway and squeezing the brittle paper between her fingers. "Oh, guys. The TV show. This was its theme song!"

Norman grinned from ear to ear. "I like this Vera lady. She's cool."

"She really saved our butts last night," Denise agreed.

Terry added, "I'm still not sure how, but she chased the other guy away and now . . ." He toyed with the recorder. "Now I think she's free and clear to hang around if she wants, or follow the light, or whatever."

"I hope she stays," Denise declared. "If we're going to have a bed-and-breakfast, it might as well be haunted by somebody famous. Maybe they'll put us on one of those ghost tour thingys."

Downstairs, there was another knock on the door.

It was Dominique, wild-eyed and fresh out of bed. She was still wearing a pajama top that said GIVE ME ALL THE ZZZZZZS with a pair of shorts and flip-flops when she came running up the stairs. At the top landing she paused, not knowing where to go, until Norman hollered, "In here, Dom. Everybody's in here."

She slid into the room and froze, looking back and forth between her cousin, Denise, Terry, and Eugenie. Rather than ask about the new lady, she said breathlessly, "The whole neighborhood wants to know what happened last night, and dammit . . ." she grin-scowled at Terry and Norman. "I thought I was going to find out first."

"My dad was the EMT who came to the scene!" Terry chirped.

"My mom was headed into work early, and saw the cop lights," Norman explained.

And Denise said, "We really did have poltergeists. Or . . . one poltergeist, and one badass old lady ghost who saved the day. We found her body upstairs, bricked up in a fake chimney."

"Oh my God!" Dominique looked back out into the hall and noticed the tape over the attic door. "Oh my God!" she said again and pointed. "Is that the attic, over there?"

Terry said, "Yep!", Norman nodded, and Denise said, "Yeah, but I wouldn't climb those stairs if I were you. They're a hazard. That's how the poltergeist died — he fell down them and broke his neck. His body was lying right . . . about . . . where you stepped when you got off the stairs," she teased.

The thought of it didn't bother her so much anymore, now that he was really gone. Gone-gone. All of him, even the nasty leftover parts that wanted to bring down the house and everyone in it.

It bothered Dom, though. "Well that is just plain gross." She clutched her own arms, then suddenly noticed the AC. She said with a smile that teased in return, "Hey, you've got your own unit! I thought you said this place was a craphole."

"I've got the only one in the house!" Denise said proudly. "Come on in, and have a seat on the bed if you want. The comic is a little scary, but not, like, corpses-in-the-attic scary. I'll turn up the air, if you won't tell my mom, and we'll get you all caught up."

Dominique agreed to this, and Eugenie Robbins made room on the mattress. Norman and Terry held back on the floor, and everyone enjoyed the dramatic reading and interpretive gestures that ensued.

By lunchtime, the agent had excused herself in favor of lunch and a nap before her convention began, and Terry's dad had picked him up and taken him home. Norman and Dom were getting ready to leave too, but Mrs. James showed up before they got the chance. She introduced herself to Sally and Mike, who invited her inside to sit in the living room while they rounded up the kids.

"We don't need rounding up," Dom announced as she descended the stairs. "We're all just hanging out in Denise's room. She's the one with the good AC. If y'all had any sense, you'd come up here, instead of asking us to come down there."

Norman and Denise followed behind her.

"Hi Mrs. James," Denise greeted her. "Nice to see you again."

"Nice to see you too, and to know that you were bluffing me about not having any bodies in the attic!" she said with something perilously close to glee.

"In my defense, I had no idea she was up there — not when I talked to you the other day."

"You knew there were ghosts, though. I know you did. It was all over your face, but you didn't want to say so." She accepted a soda that Sally brought around from the kitchen, and gave Denise a wink. "But that's all right. I'll forgive you."

Everybody piled inside and pulled up seats, even if those seats were just crates or wooden pallets. The living room seemed smaller that way. It also seemed warmer and safer. The fresh drywall looked like a promising start, rather than a work in progress. The newly plastered ceiling looked clean instead of plain. The capped-off wires that hung from the ceiling felt like a logical progression, not an unfinished chore.

The hole in the floor . . . well, it was still a hole in the floor, but somehow it looked less permanent.

"Mrs. James, you didn't have to come all this way to pick up Norman and Dominique," Mike said, once he understood the general relations. "I would've been happy to drive them home."

"That's sweet of you to offer, but I don't have a car and that's not what I'm here for. I just wanted to get the scoop!" She told them what she'd told Denise, about being a kid and daring her friends to sneak inside, years before. "And I wanted to see how the place was coming together," she admitted frankly. "Everyone is curious, you know. The house has been standing for so long, looking so sad. It's nice that a family has bought it, and good that you're working to bring it back."

Denise prepared herself for another conversation about gentrifiers — right here in her own house, in front of God and everybody. But Mrs. James stopped there and looked at Sally and Mike.

Sally mustered some excitement, even as they all knew they were sitting in a half-finished, half-rotten space that still had a long way to go. "Yes! That's the plan, eventually. My mother-in-law — she died in the Storm, but she was a wonderful cook and hostess, and she always wanted for us to buy one of these old places and fix it up. Well," she blushed a little. "She wanted that for me and my first husband, but he died in the Storm too."

"Sally, I am so sorry to hear that. You're in good company, though. I suppose this means you're coming *back* to town, not just coming in."

"That's right." She rehashed the old story about leaving, meeting Mike, and returning. "So here we are . . . just barely. This is all we could afford, but we're doing our best to bring it back to glory."

Mrs. James made some encouraging oohs and ahs, admiring the things that were original and the things that were halfway to being fixed. Then she said, "You know, there are plenty of professionals right here in the neighborhood. You can always talk to Pete and the boys down at the shop; they'll tell you who's good, and who's shady. It would be a nice thing, if you could keep the work and keep the money close to home."

"That's our goal," Mike told her, "And we're happy to pay fair, but we can't pay much. The bank is mighty stingy with the payouts, and we're stretched to the limit as it is."

"Oh, everyone here understands how tough it is. If you're willing to work with people, more often than not, they'll be willing to work with you. Oh!" She remembered something, and snapped her fingers. "Once you get things up and running, you should talk to Norman's mother. She's been in charge of the kitchen at Tulane for years, and they don't treat her with half the respect she deserves. Or half the money, either."

"That would be wonderful!" Sally exclaimed. "If she's interested, when we finally find our footing. We'll have to have her over for pizza or something," she said to him. "Or I'll just cook, if we ever get the kitchen in shape."

"You ought to throw a shrimp boil or something like that, it's a good way to meet the neighbors . . ." Dom hinted.

"So's church," her grandmother said back, but she didn't ask any questions, or make any assumptions. "Honestly, if you need resources, if you need recommendations, or extra hands . . . you send one of these two"—she waved at Dom and Norman,—"and I'll come around. I know everybody, and I enjoy putting people in touch with one another."

Norman agreed to be a messenger, and added, "When it comes to this neighborhood, if you want to do right—if you want to be part of the solution, not part of the problem—all you have to do is ask. Then, I mean, you have to listen."

Dominique agreed. "What happens after that is up to you, but the neighborhood is watching. And the neighborhood doesn't forget."

Sally looked a little embarrassed when she said, "We really do appreciate how kind everyone has been—and how helpful you've been, Norman. I know it seems like we've been keeping to ourselves, but the house has eaten up so much of our time and energy . . . we've had so many appointments, so many workers coming and going . . ."

Mike nodded along to what she was saying. "It must look like we're hanging out on our own private block, but I promise, that's not how we want it. Shoot," he said with a little half laugh. "After last night, we've got one hell of a conversation starter!"

Mrs. James laughed too. "That you do! So why don't you start with me? Tell me everything. I'm dying to hear all about it!"

When the last of the police had gone, and all the neighbors had returned to their corners of St. Roch, and the AC was buzzing a little too loud in Denise's room, she climbed into bed.

She didn't smell old lady perfume, but she didn't smell the primordial funk from the attic, either, and when she listened for ghosts, she didn't hear anything that worried her. Maybe there was a faint hum, an old TV theme song trailing through the halls. Maybe small, ladylike feet tripped up and down the stairs, bothering nobody — happy to roam the whole house once again.

Denise had a pretty strong feeling that Vera approved of their work. She also had a feeling that Joe Vaughn had left for good. Now that his secret was out and Vera's body had been found, he had nothing left to hide or protect.

"Vera," Denise said quietly as she snuggled under the covers and picked up her phone. "I hope you stay. I hope you haunt this place like crazy, and we get write-ups on ghost-hunting sites, and people pay us all kinds of money to spend the night in the attic. I hope you give everybody the scare of a lifetime, and I hope it makes you laugh."

She called up Trish's last text message.

"I hope you like us, and you won't try to chase us away. I hope you loved this house and this neighborhood . . ." She turned the phone sideways, for easier typing. "As much as my mom and Mike do."

Then she took a deep breath, and let it out slow. She stared at the glowing screen until it dimmed a little, in an effort to save battery life. She tapped it, and brought it back to full brightness.

Today has been really nuts, and if you're up, I could tell you about it.

No response, and no typing bubble to suggest that one was immediately forthcoming. Well, you couldn't catch Trish at the phone all the time, Denise supposed. She was thinking about calling it a night, when someone else pinged her phone.

It was Norman. **How you doing? You okay tonight?**

Aw, how sweet. She answered him: *Everybody's good. It's been quiet. Maybe it'll stay quiet.*

Then she realized someone else was looped in on the message. A bubble with Terry's name on it replied, **Maybe it won't!**

Such an optimist. A third bubble appeared, but it just had a number — and Denise didn't recognize it. She was about to ask who it was, when the bubble expanded to say, **This is Dom. Norman gave me ur number.**

Cool, Denise replied. Then she sent a little hand-waving emoji.

Dom sent a hand wave back.

Denise was about to continue their chat, when Trish finally replied. **TELL ME ALL ABOUT UR NIGHT. Especially if there were ghostsin it.**

She switched back to Trish. *DUH of course there were ghosts. Maybe when you hear how crazy haunted this house is you'll REALLY want to come see it. What I'm thinking is*

She accidentally sent the text mid-composition, and started again.

Is I could show you around. I def want you for a roommate next year, don't worry, but maybe you could humor my parents. Sometime before school gets too crazy

She couldn't believe she was saying this, but.

You could come visit, and check out Tulane.

Trish asked, **How far is your house fromTULane?**

Dom was back. **Terry played me some of the ghost voices. That's messed up!**

Denise smiled, and responded: *Extremely messed up! You want to come over and try next time? See if we can get Vera to say hello?*

I'll come too, Norman promised. Me and Terry. WE'll get the whole scooby gang together.

She liked the idea, and she told them so. *It's on!* Then she switched back to answer Trish's question, *Tulane's just a bus ride away. No big deal. You could be my roommate in my house, easy as a dorm. Room would be bigger. Got my own AC unit too. Or you could have your own room.*

Not the one with the wasps tho, rite

She forgot she'd mentioned it, during one of their midday chats. *Not unless you want them. I would save them for you, if you do.*

Terry again. There are other haunted houses in the neighborhood.

Denise asked, *Do people live in them?*

Some of them. We could start a ghost hunting club. We could ask for permission.

Dom wasn't so sure. Let me start slow. I like this old lady ghost, let me just talk to her first. She seems nice.

No one will give us permission to hunt ghosts in their house, Denise protested.

Norman disagreed. Terry's good at asking for stuff. You let him hunt ghosts in YOUR house.

Well he was very persistent.

Terry added, I don't take no for an answer!

"Truer words were never spoken," Denise muttered. "Or texted. Whatever."

Trish said, I've never been to NOLA.

No time like the present. Or like, kind of soon, Denise said. *U might like it. If you don't, oh well. But I want you to see it.*

The wheels in Trish's head were turning. Denise could practically hear them rolling around, all the way over in Texas. Parents would be pissed if I left the state, but NOLA isn't that far.

Right, Denise agreed.

I could come look. No promises.

Denise wasn't asking for promises. **No promises.** Just options. Just possibilities. Just a chance to come home, and be home — if that's what this was — and bring somebody she loved along for the ride.

Trish signed off: **Ok then. Good night. Sleep tight. Don't let the ghost-bugs bite.**

Denise told her good night, and then told the other kids the same. It'd been a long day. But tomorrow, she promised everyone, *We'll pick up where we left off.*

She plugged her phone in and flopped back down on her bed. From there, she stared around and realized she needed some wall art. Posters, or pictures, or blown-up pages of comic books that no one ever published. That and a few throw pillows, maybe a couple of cute rugs, and a lamp, and it wouldn't be the world's most embarrassing place to have a guest.

It wouldn't take much. Just a little time, and a little money. Or a lot.

"Good night, Vera," she mumbled sleepily to the room at large. "Thanks for everything."

Then she turned off the lamp and fluffed her pillow, punching it into a shape that worked, and she did not notice the shadow that perched on the window seat. She did not smell any perfume, and she did not hear any music. She didn't even hear a woman's voice, not then. But later, when she checked her messages in the morning, she'd see that someone had turned on the microphone again — and then she would know that she wasn't alone, and this time, that was all right.

Good night, dear girl. Thanks for everything, yourself.

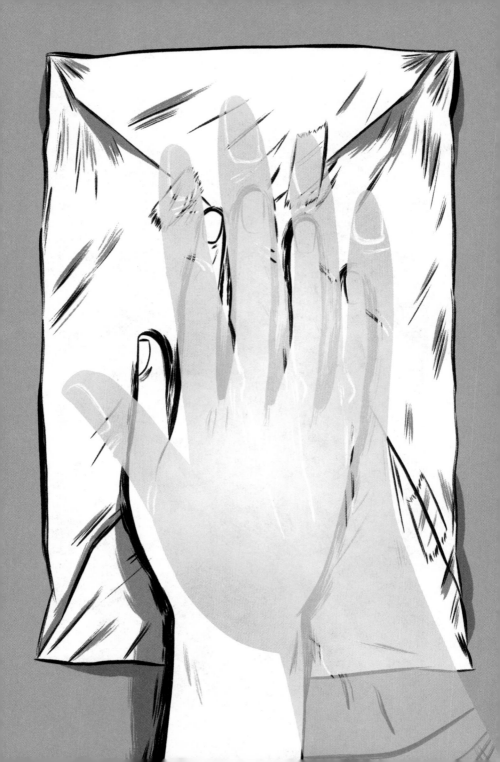

ACKNOWLEDGMENTS

This book has been a group effort from day one—and it never could've come together without a veritable host of folks including (but by no means limited to) the following great people: Cheryl Klein, the editor who helped me develop *The Agony House* in the first place; editor Nick Thomas, who dove right in to help me pull it together and push it over the finish line; talented and speedy artist Tara O'Connor, who did such a killer job of the comics; art director Phil Falco, who shepherded all the visuals with aplomb; and my outstanding agent Jennifer Jackson. Many thanks to them, and to everyone else who's helped me along this spooky little road.

CHERIE PRIEST

is the author of *I Am Princess X,* her debut young adult novel, which earned three starred reviews and was a YALSA Quick Pick for Reluctant Young Adult Readers. She is also the author of more than a dozen adult science fiction, fantasy, and horror novels, including *Boneshaker,* which won the Locus Award for Best Science Fiction Novel. She lives in Seattle, WA, and can be found online at cheriepriest.com and @cmpriest.

TARA O'CONNOR

is a comic maker and illustrator currently residing in the New Jersey wilderness. When she's not drawing or teaching comics, she's probably working on an illustration of some sort. She is the author of *Roots* and *The Altered History of Willow Sparks.* You can find more of Tara's art online at taraocomics.com

This book was edited by Cheryl Klein and Nick Thomas and designed by Phil Falco. The production was supervised by Rachel Gluckstern. The text was set in Alisal, with display type set in Bureau Agency. The book was printed and bound at LSC Communications in Crawfordsville, Indiana. The manufacturing was supervised by Angelique Browne.

Introduction

Heart Full of Love by Colleen Coble
Eden Walters is a nurturer. When she was eight, her brother and two sisters were ripped away after their mother died. Since she can't care for her own family, she takes in foster children to give them the love she never had. One in particular has her heart. She's adopted Katie, but if Katie's uncle Josh has his way, Katie will be ripped away from her as well.

Ride the Clouds by Carol Cox
Crista Richmond was only three when she started being shuffled from one temporary home to another. The foster family who left her feeling abandoned also gave her the message that Christianity was a farce. Can Brad Morgan help Crista find a sense of belonging in God's family?

Don't Look Back by Terry Fowler
With so much loss in her life, Angelina Collier's motto has become "don't look back." She is determined to do whatever it takes to keep her family together, never totally placing her faith in Jesus Christ. Wes Robbins has learned to give his worries to the Lord and is dedicated to enjoying life. He's determined to help Angelina do the same.

To Keep Me Warm by Gail Gaymer Martin
Tim Richmond, a widower, is left ⋯⋯⋯⋯ oung disabled son. Separated from ⋯⋯⋯⋯⋯⋯ ed by an aunt, Tim longs to ⋯⋯⋯⋯⋯⋯⋯⋯⋯ determined to give his s⋯⋯⋯⋯⋯⋯⋯⋯ nditional love. His purpose an⋯⋯⋯⋯⋯⋯⋯⋯ s to be needed. Though he is drawn t⋯⋯⋯⋯⋯⋯ independent Julie, he knows there is no hope ⋯⋯ relationship. She doesn't need him. Or does she?

Home for

CHRISTMAS

*Love Reunites Four Orphaned Siblings
in Interwoven Novellas*

Colleen Coble
Carol Cox
Terry Fowler
Gail Gaymer Martin

BARBOUR
PUBLISHING, INC.
Uhrichsville, Ohio

Heart Full of Love ©2001 by Colleen Coble.
Ride the Clouds ©2001 by Carol Cox.
Don't Look Back ©2001 by Terry Fowler.
To Keep Me Warm ©2001 by Gail Gaymer Martin.

Illustrations by Mari Goering.

ISBN 1-58660-242-X

Published by Barbour Publishing, Inc., P.O. Box 719, Uhrichsville, Ohio 44683 http://www.barbourbooks.com

 Member of the
Evangelical Christian
Publishers Association

Printed in the United States of America.

Home for
CHRISTMAS

Heart Full of Love

by Colleen Coble

Dedication

For all the young adults in our
Lifebuilders Sunday School Class.
You've brightened our lives and given us purpose.

Chapter 1

I've come for my niece."

Eden Walters' smile faded, and she took a step back from the man's overwhelming presence in her doorway. Though she barely came to his broad shoulder, he would soon find he couldn't push her around.

"You—your niece?" Her thoughts ran through the children squealing in laughter behind her. The older children were playing Candyland while two-year-old Katie and infant Braden slept upstairs. Five children, three of them girls, but she had no idea which one this man wanted. She tilted her chin in the air, leery of handing any of her children over to this bulk of a man who oozed self-confidence that would put an emperor to shame. He was probably used to getting what he wanted with his size and dark good looks.

"Katie Leland. I'm Josh Leland." He thrust his hands in his pockets and stepped inside, shutting the door behind him.

"Now see here, Mr. Leland," Eden began.

"Isn't there somewhere quieter we can discuss this?" Eden compressed her lips and reminded herself she was a professional. "Very well, follow me." She led him to the library across the hall from the front parlor where the children played. Tugging on the pocket doors, she was panting by the time she managed to close them and turned to face Josh Leland.

His warm brown eyes took in the gap where they didn't quite close, then traveled around the room. Eden saw it afresh from his eyes. Stained and torn wallpaper that she wished she could afford to replace, old furniture she'd bought at Goodwill, and a threadbare carpet on the floor. She felt a bit like Jo in *Little Women* and suppressed a smile at the errant thought.

Those brown eyes were regarding her now, and she knew what he must think. A short young woman with flyaway blond hair, curves that were too generous, and clothes as shabby as her house. A warm flush started up her neck, and she forced her eyes up to meet his.

"I'm quite busy this morning, Mr. Leland. If you check in with Child Welfare Services, you will find you have no legal right to see Katie. Even if you really *are* her uncle."

He ran a broad hand through his thick brown hair. Eden always noticed hands. His were muscular with long fingers and neatly clipped nails. She pushed away the stir of attraction. His expression told all too clearly what he thought of her. Disapproval radiated from every pore of his immaculately clothed being.

"I don't want a visit, I mean to take her permanently. I've been to Child Welfare, and they tell me you have already filed adoption papers. Surely you can see it would be better for her to be raised by her uncle than by a stranger."

"I'm no stranger to Katie! I've cared for her—and loved her—since she was three months old. You, Mr. Leland, are the stranger. She is two years old. Where were you when her mother brought her to the welfare office and dumped her like an unwanted suitcase?" Eden clenched her hands to keep from slugging him. "You're the stranger, Mr. Leland."

Her barb struck home for he colored and lost a bit of his superiority. "I didn't know about Katie," he mumbled. "Last I heard, Mandy was in college and nearly finished with her degree in accounting. Then I was called and told she'd died." His face paled. "Drugs, they said. The college sent her stuff to me. That's when I discovered I had a niece. I chucked my job with Sutter Petroleum in Saudi Arabia and came straight here."

That explained the tan. Eden pushed a strand of hair out of her eyes and bit her lip. His bald recitation of the facts touched her more than she wanted to admit, but facts were facts.

"That's all very interesting, Mr. Leland, and I'm sorry for your loss, but I'm afraid you're too late. The adoption papers were signed yesterday."

"Yesterday?" He paled beneath his tan and sank onto the sofa. He breathed deeply, then raised his gaze to hers. "May I see her?"

Eden flinched at the thought of allowing this man to see her daughter. A surge of fear rushed up her spine. Katie was *hers*, in heart and legally. But would the welfare officials see it that way if he challenged the adoption?

"She's sleeping right now."

"I won't wake her. Please."

11

"I fail to see what good it would do."

"She *is* my niece, Miss Walters. Our parents are dead as well. Surely you can see I'd have some feelings for the child."

"And she's *my* daughter."

"I'm not leaving until I see that she's well cared for." He waved a hand around him. "You hardly seem old enough to be caring for a house full of children. And look at this place. It's practically falling down around your ears. I know foster care is hardly a decent living for you, let alone all the things a little girl needs. I could at least offer some financial assistance."

The fury Eden had been holding in check spilled over. "I don't need your money, Mr. Leland! This may be an old house and not up to Leland standards, but it's a house full of love and laughter. We have God to watch over us, and that's worth more than all the money you've made in the oil fields!"

A small hand rapped at the door. "Eden? Katie was crying so I brung her to you."

Eden nearly groaned but had no choice except to go to the door and shove it open. Ten-year-old Samantha, rail-thin with haunted gray eyes, held chubby Katie. Eden took the toddler and touched Samantha on the cheek. "Thanks, Sweetie, you're a good helper."

Samantha colored with pleasure, then cast a frightened glance toward Josh and scurried away. Eden turned slowly with Katie in her arms. The little one's chubby arms were around her neck, and Eden breathed in the sweet scent of her.

Josh stared at Katie with hungry eyes. "She looks a lot

like Mandy," he said. The muscles in his throat moved as he swallowed.

Was that a film of tears in the big man's eyes? Eden's tender heart smote her. She'd given no thought to how he must feel with his sister dead and his niece ripped from him before he even knew he had a niece. She could afford to be generous. God had given her Katie as a daughter.

Eden stepped closer to him. "Would you like to hold her?"

His eyes widened, and he nodded. He slipped his big hands around Katie and drew her to his chest the way he might hold a basket of eggs.

"She won't break."

"She's so little," he said. Katie regarded him solemnly, then reached up a chubby hand and pulled on his nose, released it, and peered inside one nostril.

Eden chuckled at the panicked expression on Josh's face. "She's fascinated with noses right now."

"I haven't been around many children," he said. "But she doesn't seem to be afraid of me. Is this normal?"

"It is for Katie. She's very secure and outgoing. She loves people."

He shuddered. "Makes me frightened for her in this world."

"Wabash is a nice town to raise a family in," Eden said. "I'll take very good care of her." She fought the words struggling against her lips, but they came out anyway. "You're welcome to stop in and visit her sometime. Just call first. Katie has plenty of love to share." She held out her hands for her daughter.

A muscle twitched in Josh's jaw, and his fingers

tightened around Katie. He took a step back. "I mean to raise her myself, Miss Walters. I give you fair warning."

Eden's olive branch was sliced in two, and the hair on her neck stood. If it was a fight he wanted, he'd get one. There was nothing he could do. The adoption papers were signed. "Give me my daughter," she said evenly.

With obvious reluctance, Josh handed Katie back to her. "I'll be back, Miss Walters."

"Look, Mr. Leland, I'm willing to let you see Katie. I think it's important for an adopted child to have as many roots of her heritage as possible. But Katie is happy here. Surely, you can see that. What's to be gained by disrupting her life now?"

Josh hesitated, then shook his head. "That's not enough, Miss Walters. She's all I have left of Mandy, and I mean to have her."

"You're not thinking of her, only of yourself."

He clenched his jaw. "I can give her much more than you can."

"Money isn't everything, Mr. Leland. You admitted yourself you were unused to children. What about caring for her when she's sick or fixing her hair and teaching her to bake cookies? I don't see a wedding ring, so I assume she won't have a mother. A girl needs a mother."

"And a father. I see no ring on your hand either. What do you propose to do about that?"

Eden felt the hot blush on her cheeks. "Neither situation is perfect," she admitted. "But you need to face the facts, Mr. Leland. Katie is my daughter now, and there's nothing you can do about it."

"We'll see." With that last parting shot, he brushed by

her and stalked to the front door. His brown eyes were haunted when he looked back. "I lost my sister, Miss Walters, I'm not going to lose my niece, too." He slammed the door behind him.

Her throat tight, Eden ran to the door and locked it. As if that could shut away the danger. "Don't worry, little one," she whispered. "I won't let him take you."

She still remembered the horror of being ripped from her brother and sisters. Eden was still tormented with nightmares about that time. She couldn't let that happen to her Katie.

Chapter 2

His eyes burning, Josh strode along the sidewalk on Canal Street toward the law office. His jaw hurt from clenching it. Eden Walters was an infuriating woman. Why couldn't she see the advantages he could offer Katie? She had obviously buried herself in those foster children. It was too bad, though. She could be attractive if she ditched the sloppy clothes and did something with her hair. Maybe then she would find a husband and have her own children instead of stealing Katie away from him.

His jaw softened at the thought of Katie. She was the most beautiful child he'd ever seen. Soft blond curls ringing cherubic cheeks he wanted to pinch. Looking into her blue eyes had been like seeing Mandy again. He couldn't lose her.

The bell on the door tinkled as he pushed into the waiting room of Grover Law Offices. The sound brought back memories of the old corner grocery with the jars of licorice and the old freezer full of Popsicles and fudge bars. And the Victorian storefronts along the street had set the mood well. Most hometowns didn't retain the flavor of

Wabash, Indiana. Too bad he wouldn't be staying long. It would have been a nice place for Katie to grow up.

An hour later he stalked those same streets back to his car. The attorney had not held out much hope that he could overturn the adoption. Preference was given to foster parents! After only six months? And Katie had been with Eden Walters almost two years now, since she was three months old.

His only hope was to get the woman to agree to give her up. He had to convince her it was best for Katie. After all, he could provide the best education and a stable home life where she was the adored only child—unlike growing up in a run-down foster home. He appreciated what Eden was trying to do, but let her take in some abandoned urchin without an uncle who wanted her.

He drove to his room at the Wabash Inn and planned his strategy. The first thing would be to run some paperwork to show her his assets. Maybe if she knew Katie would be his sole heir, she would relent. She didn't seem an unreasonable young woman.

He spent the evening jotting down reasons Katie would be better off with him and printing out financial information to show Eden. Eden. What kind of a name was that for a woman, anyway? But she looked the type to have an old-fashioned name. Maybe that was what drove her to take in all those kids.

The next morning he dressed in khaki chinos and a carefully pressed navy shirt. His shoes were buffed to a high shine and matched his belt. He wanted to make sure he looked the part of a conscientious father.

As he walked up the path to the front porch, he took

note of the house this time. An old Victorian Queen Anne, it was large enough to house an army, but sorely in need of a man's hand. The paint was peeling, and the porch railing had some missing spindles. He would point that out to Eden—in a reasonable way, of course.

He rapped on the door. Inside the house, he could hear screams and the clatter of something falling to the floor. When no one came right away, he debated about letting himself in and seeing if there was a problem. But before he could overcome his reluctance to barge in, the door opened, and a little boy of about five regarded him with sad green eyes.

"Hello," he said. "I'm Katie's 'Uncle Josh.' "

The little boy's eyes widened in alarm, and he started to shut the door.

Josh put a foot in it. "Is Miss Walters around?"

The little boy nodded. "She's in the kitchen." With an obvious show of reluctance, he opened the door wider and stepped aside. "You'd better come in. She can't come out here right now. Katie choked on a spider."

Choked? Alarm raced up Josh's spine, and he followed the little boy through the labyrinth of rooms to the kitchen. Eden crouched over his niece with her finger down Katie's throat. She paid no attention to him but probed and peered inside Katie's mouth. Katie wailed and thrashed, trying to escape the unwanted attention. Beside her were the soggy remains of a very large spider.

Josh shuddered. He hated spiders. His respect for Eden went up a notch that she could handle such an event with that competent air.

Katie saw him, and her wails increased in volume. She held out her arms to him, and he felt a stab of delight.

"What's going on here?" Josh scooped his niece away from Eden's attentions.

Dressed in a denim skirt and pink cotton sweater that had seen better days, Eden's fine blond hair was wadded on top of her head in a haphazard way that was very becoming. Wisps of hair trailed against her flushed cheeks, and she compressed her lips when she saw him.

"Mr. Leland, I expressly asked you to call before you came by. Right now is not a convenient time for callers."

His good intentions for peace blew away like a stray feather. "I can see that. My niece is being raised in a house overrun with giant spiders. If I hadn't stopped by unexpectedly, I never would have known how dangerous this place is." His arms tightened around Katie. "And there are spindles missing on the front porch where she could easily fall through. I don't think this is a safe house for children, Miss Walters."

Eden's green eyes flashed, and the color rose in her cheeks. "It was just a spider, Mr. Leland, not a monster. Katie is never on the front porch without me. I have the spindles, but I haven't had time to install them yet."

"You mean to install them yourself?"

"I am a woman, but I'm quite competent, I assure you."

He regretted his hasty criticisms. All he'd succeeded in doing was getting her back up. He wasn't going to get anywhere by taking this tone with her. He suspected the welfare authorities would fail to find a dead spider a reason to remove Katie from Eden's care.

He cleared his throat and softened his voice. "I'm sorry, Miss Walters. Please, can we start over? And call me Josh."

The angry sparkle in her eyes didn't dim. She looked

all too delectable to Josh, soft and round like a woman should be. Pressing his lips together at his flight of fancy, he shifted Katie to one arm and held out his other hand. "Truce?"

Eden hesitated, then nodded. Her handshake was firm, and her small hand had calluses on it. She was an enigma to Josh—so feminine, yet not afraid of hard work, and not easily cowed by a challenge. He didn't want to admire her. She was all that stood between him and Katie.

"Would you like a soda or a cup of tea, Mr. Leland?"

"Josh."

"Josh," she amended. "I have cola and iced tea as well as hot tea."

"Cola would be fine."

She poured the soda into a Mickey Mouse glass, then poured a glass of iced tea into a Cinderella glass. It didn't look to Josh like any of the glasses in the cupboard matched. She handed the soda to him and led the way to the parlor.

This room was in a little better shape than the library. The wallpaper was still intact, and a newer rug covered the oak floor. A Candyland game was on a table near the fireplace, and he nearly tripped over a small fire truck.

Eden had just sat down when a wail from upstairs echoed down the hall. She stared at Josh with appraising eyes. "May I have Katie, please? I need to see to the other baby."

Josh felt a stab of irritation. "I'm no baby thief, Eden. I want only what's best for Katie. Go see to the other baby. Katie and I will be right here when you get back."

She stared a moment longer. "Are you a Christian, Josh?"

At least she cared about such things. "Since I was ten." He held up his hand. "And an Eagle Scout. I promise you can trust me."

She nodded. "Excuse me a moment." She hurried from the room, and he heard her tennis shoes tread lightly on the stairs.

Josh stared at his niece. This place was like Grand Central Station. There was not a moment's peace. The sooner he got Katie to some quiet place, the better. Katie gave his nose one last pull, then slipped from his arms and went to play with the fire truck.

Josh watched her play until Eden came back down the stairs with an infant in her arms. The baby's tuft of hair stood straight up on end, and it was sucking its thumb.

"This is Braden," Eden said. "Could you hold him a minute while I fix lunch?" Without waiting for a reply, she plopped the baby in his arms and hurried from the room.

Josh stared into the baby's blue eyes. He started to pucker, and Josh hurriedly stood. "There now, don't cry. Er—your mama will be back in a minute." He jiggled him, and Braden gave him a shy smile. The triumph Josh felt was all out of proportion to the smile, and he shook his head at his own reaction.

Slipping a hand under the baby to adjust how he carried him, he felt a suspicious wetness. "Uh, oh," he said. He held him away from him. Dismay swept over him at the wet stain on his shirt. Now what was he supposed to do? Holding the baby away from him like a naughty puppy, he carried him to the kitchen.

"I think he needs changed," he told Eden.

"The diapers are in the changing table in the bathroom across the hall," she said.

"You expect *me* to change him?"

Eden stopped stirring the bowl of some kind of gluey-looking stuff, and he colored at the amusement in her green eyes. "Katie isn't potty trained yet. If you expect to spend any time with her, you'd better learn to change diapers."

"I've changed diapers before," he said stiffly. She didn't need to know it had been thirty years ago when Mandy was a baby and he was five.

"Good. There are wipes on the changing table as well." She went back to stirring that tasteless-looking concoction.

Josh stared at her, then shrugged and found his way to the bathroom. He laid the baby on the changing table and rolled up his sleeves. Surely it must be like riding a bike. He could do this. Gingerly, he unsnapped Braden's sleeper. Disposable diapers. That should be easy, at least he wouldn't have to worry about sticking the little guy with a pin.

He loosened the tabs and pulled the diaper down. The odor that met his nose made him cringe. Great. It was a dirty one. With one hand on the baby, he flipped open the box of wipes and pulled one out. Braden cooed as Josh swiped his bottom. Still keeping one hand on Braden, Josh bent to grab a clean diaper when it happened. A pale yellow arc of urine hit him squarely in the face.

Eden stood in the doorway with Katie in her arms. Her green eyes sparkled with amusement. "I can see you've done this often," she said.

Chapter 3

Braden sucked contentedly on his bottle while Josh played on the floor with Katie. She had her dollies displayed for his admiration, and he had Katie's favorite, Bubbles, on his lap with a plastic bottle stuck in its mouth. Eden sneaked a peek and tried to hide her mirth.

Eden didn't know what to think about Josh. There was a gentleness about him in spite of his size. He seemed lonely to Eden, as though he searched for a place to call home. Of course, he'd been drifting all over the world for the past few years, so it was no wonder he seemed a bit lost.

Eden ventured another look. Katie looked a bit like him. It was in the shape of her mouth, that firm determination in her upper lip. Her eyes were shaped like his, though hers were blue. And Katie's hands had his long fingers and well-shaped nails. She didn't know what to do about him. He couldn't take Katie, but he was not the kind of man to give up easily.

The bottle plopped out of Braden's slack mouth, and Eden stood. "I'll just pop this little fellow into his bed and be right back down."

"I'd need to sleep too if you'd forced that concoction down my throat."

Eden chuckled, then glanced at Katie. "You want a nap, Katie?"

Katie's droopy eyes flew open. "No!" It was still her favorite word.

"Uncle Josh will read you a story." Josh stood and held out his arms for Katie.

Uncle Josh. Eden frowned. He had not even asked if he might identify himself to Katie as her uncle. She would have to talk with him about what role he would be allowed to play in her young life. Suppressing a sigh, she led the way up the wide staircase. She pointed out Katie's room to Josh then went farther down the hall and slipped Braden into his crib. He didn't stir, so she backed out of the room and pulled the door partway shut behind her.

When she entered Katie's room, she found Katie tucked into her bed with Josh sitting beside her. He was reading *Green Eggs and Ham*. Katie's thumb was corked in her mouth, and she had one arm around her Pooh bear. Her eyes closed and didn't open again.

" 'I do not like green eggs and ham. I do not like them, Sam I Am.' "

Eden chuckled, and Josh looked up. His eyes, as dark as a buck's, narrowed at her smile, but an answering one tugged at his own lips.

"She's asleep," Eden said.

He glanced down at his niece and nodded. Rising from the bed, he put the book on the bedside table, and they both tiptoed out of the room.

"Can we talk?" Josh asked when they reached the bottom of the stairs.

A prickle of unease ran up Eden's spine at the somber tone. She nodded. "You want something else to drink?"

"No, I'm fine."

His pacing made Eden's pulse race. He was a formidable opponent, but he would soon see he couldn't push her around. She crossed her arms over her chest and stared at him. "Sit down, you're giving me a headache."

He shot her a curious look, then dropped into the worn leather armchair by the fireplace. "How are we going to work this out?"

"There's nothing to work out. Katie is my daughter, legally and of the heart. I know this has been a shock to you. You thought you could waltz in here and take her with you, but that's never going to happen. I'm willing to allow you to see her, though. I think it's important for an adopted child to have access to her—her heritage." Her voice broke, and she looked away.

He cocked his head and stared at her curiously. "Why did you say it like that?"

Eden bit her lip. "I was a foster kid myself, Josh. Somewhere out there, I have two sisters and a brother that I'll probably never see again. I don't want Katie to have the pain of knowing she has blood relatives she's been ripped away from."

"Then surely you can see she would be better off with me," he began. He began to rummage in his briefcase. "Here, look at these financial figures."

She held up her hand. "I'm not interested, Josh. Katie is my daughter. I'm the one who nursed her through chicken pox and pneumonia. I'm the one she calls for in the night. She's just a link to your sister for you. I'm not saying that's bad—those links are important. But raising a little girl is not about remembering who her mother was; it's more about finding out who she is and helping her to realize she's special because God made her that way. It's about listening to her dreams, teaching her she's special in God's eyes. It's about seeing her go to school on that first day, then crying with her when her heart is broken by her first boyfriend."

His face grew more sober as she spoke. "Was your foster mother like that?"

Eden clenched her fists as the traitorous tears flooded her eyes. "I had a succession of foster parents. None of them replaced my mother. She taught me all I needed to know about mothering in the eight years before she died. The last foster parents adopted me, but they never took the place of my own parents. I know what it's like to be ripped away from the only life you've ever known, and I'll not subject Katie to that."

He stood to his feet. "Then I suppose there is no more to say. But I'm not giving up, Eden. Katie belongs with me. My sister and my parents would expect her to be with me. I'll be in touch."

Disappointment sharpened her tone. "Make sure you call first. I can't have you dropping by whenever you feel like it. Katie might begin to depend on you, and then you'll go flitting off to the Middle East or somewhere else. I don't want her hurt."

His jaw tightened, and he nodded curtly. "I'll call." He slammed the door behind him.

Eden sighed. That had not gone well. But everything she said was true. She knew what it was like to cry at night from missing her family. Katie couldn't be allowed to experience that heartache. Not while there was something Eden could do about it.

The next few days seemed particularly lonely to Eden for some reason. Twenty-four years since she'd seen her sisters and her brother. Where were they? The question never left her mind for long. With Mama sick so much, the children's care had fallen to Eden as the oldest.

Her arms still ached to hold Crista, the baby of the family. She yearned to braid Angelina's thick hair again, to see Timmy's face when he smelled the chocolate chip cookies she and Mama used to bake. Did they remember her at all? They were so young. Little Crista had been only three when they were separated.

How could anyone do that to children? To rip them apart from one another and send them to different homes, to change their names so they couldn't find each other. Not that she had tried very hard lately. The roadblocks bureaucracy had thrown in her way had left her feeling hopeless and alone. It wasn't fair. But God had never promised life would be fair. She had to remind herself of that all the time. He had gone with her through every trial, every heartache.

But what if I never find them? The question rang in her head, and she hunched her shoulders and reached for her Bible. She couldn't think thoughts like that. Someday she would find them. She knew this in her soul—if not here on this earth, in heaven. Their mother had prayed for them, and she had to believe her prayers had taken root. Those prayers had led her to Jesus, and she had to believe that Angelina, Timmy, and Crista had come to know Him as well. Without that hope, she couldn't go on.

The front door slammed, and the older children rushed in from school. Samantha had her book bag slung over her shoulder, her ribbon missing and her braid half undone. Cory immediately sat at Eden's feet. Amelia's shoelaces were untied, and her new blouse was stained with ink. Eden sighed.

"Eden, we seen Mr. Leland outside. I invited him for supper, is that okay?" Samantha dropped her book bag and stared at her with hopeful eyes.

Great. Just what she didn't want to have to deal with. And he hadn't called first, in spite of her admonition. Before she could answer Samantha, the doorbell rang. Eden's heart gave a funny hitch, and she frowned. She couldn't be attracted to the man, could she? He was the enemy. She would do well to keep that in mind.

She would act as though their harsh words had never happened, she decided. It was best for Katie if they could get along. Josh would eventually come to realize this was for the best. She pinned her smile in place and went to the door and opened it.

Josh looked good this evening. Too good. He was impeccably dressed, as usual, and she caught the faint whiff of his cologne, a spicy, masculine scent that reminded her of the woods. He carried a laptop computer and a briefcase, and she felt a stab of alarm. Was he serving her with papers or something? But that was silly, the sheriff would be the one to serve papers.

He smiled faintly when she raised an eyebrow and glanced to the briefcase. "I won't put you on the spot and demand supper. But I *was* invited."

Eden chuckled and stepped out of the way. "Come in.

If you like vegetable soup, there's plenty to share."

"With cabbage in it?"

"Lots of cabbage. It's cheap," she said, shutting the door behind him.

"I'll stay." He followed her to the parlor where Samantha sidled up to him and took his hand.

The little girl was quite smitten with him. Eden decided she might have to watch that. Samantha's feelings were easily bruised, and she'd been through a lot in the past six months.

Josh sniffed. "Smells good."

"Thanks." Eden didn't know what to say to him. Why had he come back, again without calling? And how long did he intend to hang around Wabash?

She went to the fireplace and lit her Yankee candle. She never had the money for such frivolous things, but her secret sister at church had bought it for her. The spicy aroma would soothe her frazzled nerves.

"Want me to make a fire?" he asked.

"You know how?" He didn't strike her as the outdoorsy type. Too urbane and sophisticated.

"You forget I'm an Eagle Scout. I live for my times in the woods."

He kept surprising her. "Be my guest."

He went to the fireplace and found the kindling. Within moments he had coaxed a flame and then piled three logs on the grate. He put the screen in front of the grate and went to the sofa. "I have some things to show you," he said.

Eden swallowed hard. She was afraid to see what he had in his briefcase. She had a feeling it might change her life.

Chapter 4

Josh found it hard to think with Eden's green eyes on him. They were darkened with trepidation as though she didn't quite know how to take him. And how did he know if his suggestion would be welcome or not? Maybe she didn't want to know. Some people didn't. Possible rejection was hard to handle.

He cleared his throat and opened his computer. "Where's a jack I can plug into?"

"Right beside you. The phone has a place in the back of it."

He snapped the connector into place while the computer booted up, then clicked on the Internet icon. The computer dialed up and took him to the site he'd looked at earlier in the day. He thought Eden would be impressed.

He patted the space beside him on the sofa. "Sit here so you can see."

Her eyes widened but she didn't object, just moved from the rocker and sat beside him. She smelled sweet, like vanilla maybe. Her gaze focused on the screen. He heard her slight intake of breath but was almost afraid to look at her. The last thing he wanted to do was offend her. But his uncertainty vanished at the sight of her eyes widened in delight.

"I've heard of these adoption bulletin boards, but I've never been able to afford a computer to check them out. And with two babies, the library was out of the question." She moved closer and peered at the screen.

It was all Josh could do to drag his gaze from her animated face with that delightful dimple flashing in her cheek. "I would need to know all the information you have about your family. Do you know your family name?"

"Richmond. I was eight when Daddy left me at the preacher's so I remember quite a lot. My parents were John and Anna Richmond, and we lived in Covington, Kentucky."

"Kentucky, huh? You're not so far from your roots. Have you ever gone back there?" He tapped at the keys.

She shook her head. "There's never been the money for it. I called and talked to a woman at the state office, but she said my sisters and brother were sent out of state and wouldn't tell me more than that."

"Let's go to the Kentucky site first and see what their laws say." He selected the state and peered at the screen as the information scrolled up.

"This says siblings can petition the court to search for each other!" Eden grasped his arm in her excitement.

Josh glanced at her small hand on his arm and was shocked at his own desire to take it and hold it in his own. These inappropriate feelings toward his niece's care-taker had to stop. He cleared his throat. "As long as you're all over eighteen," he pointed out.

"We are. I'm the oldest, and Crista is the baby. She's five years younger than me, so that would make her about twenty-nine." Her voice grew dreamy. "Wouldn't it be wonderful if they were looking for me, too?"

Eden was thirty-four then. She had a freshness to her skin and eyes that had made him guess her to be still in her twenties. He dragged his gaze from the petal-softness of her cheeks and began to read the screen again.

He could sense Eden's excitement, and he felt a bit uneasy. What if he'd raised her hopes for nothing? His plan could backfire on him. If she failed to find her siblings, she might cling even tighter to Katie. He couldn't allow that; he had to find them.

"I'll call and request a form to begin the search," he said. "Now let's go to the bulletin board and post the information. Tell me everything you know."

"John and Anna Richmond. Four of us kids. Mama died of cancer." Eden's voice trembled, and she bit her lip. Tears shimmered in her eyes, but she blinked several times. "I loved my daddy, but he changed when Mama died. Then he lost his job and left us with Mama's preacher."

"How long were you with him?"

"A few months. Word came back that Daddy had died. I'm not sure what happened, I suppose I was too young to hear the full story. Anyway, his sister, our aunt Selma, came to see us. But she was a widow with no inclination to try to handle four kids who were still grieving for their parents. She kept Timmy and sent the rest of us to foster care."

Eden bit her lip and shivered. Josh had to fight to keep himself from putting his arm around her. She'd gone through so much, he could understand why family was so important to her.

"Crista was the first to go. When I heard that the state was allowing her to be adopted, I threw up, then cried for three days. Angelina was next. By then, I was numb. Too old to be appealing to childless couples, I was shunted from one foster home to another. But I never forgot my brother and sisters. And I never will. They're out there somewhere—I know it."

A lump formed in Josh's throat. There was a steadfast integrity about Eden that drew him. He cleared his throat and looked back to his computer screen. "Let's get this posted. Read this and see what you think."

Seeking Richmond siblings.
Parents, John and Anna Richmond, died in 1975.
Eden, the eldest, seeks three younger siblings,
born in Covington, Kentucky.
Last known names: Timothy Richmond,
Angelina Richmond, and Crista Richmond.

Eden touched the screen with a trembling hand. "Do you really think this might work, Josh? And why do you care? Why are you doing this?"

Josh tried to ignore the questions. "What's your address and phone number?" He typed in the information she gave him. When he looked up from the screen, Eden's green eyes were focused on him.

"Why are you doing this, Josh?"

How could he tell her his motives were so selfish when she gazed at him with such trust in her eyes? He felt dirty and longed to escape from the piercing light of goodness in Eden's face. Looking away, he shrugged. "At least they're still alive," he said.

Eden's face softened even more. "I understand," she said softly.

What a jerk he was! Leading her to believe he was doing this for altruistic motives. Josh had never felt so low. He would find her siblings and tell her the truth as soon as possible. He didn't feel good about misleading Eden; she was so innocent and had been hurt by so many. He cringed inside at how she would feel if she knew his true motives.

He clicked the Send button, then shut his computer down. "It will probably be a few days before we get any response."

Eden's eager smile faded. "If we get a response. They may not even remember or care."

"They would care about finding a sister like you." His gaze locked with Eden's. He almost felt as though their souls touched in that moment. Hastily dropping his gaze, he got to his feet. "Where's that vegetable soup with cabbage I was promised?"

Was that disappointment in Eden's eyes? Had she felt a special something that had stretched between them like a physical touch?

She stood and went toward the kitchen. "I'll put it on the table. Would you get Katie up from her nap?"

"You sure she won't be frightened?"

Eden put her hands on her hips and laughed. "Josh Leland, you can't tell me you haven't noticed how you've stolen the hearts of my children!" She shook her head. "She won't be frightened of her uncle Josh."

Uncle Josh. The sound gave him a warm fuzzy feeling. He grinned. "I'll get her."

"And change her diaper before you bring her down," Eden called.

Uh-oh, another diaper. But this was on a girl, and it was less dangerous. Josh took the steps two at a time and strode down the hall to Katie's room.

Lying on her back with her bare feet kicking the foot of her crib, she smiled when she saw him. She quickly scrambled to her feet and held up her arms for him to take her.

"Well, you are rather angelic, just as your mama said," he told her.

She corked her thumb in her mouth and regarded him soberly.

He felt her diaper. Rats! It was wet. But at least it was only wet. He laid her on the changing table and managed to change her without a hitch. Her diaper drooped slightly, but not so badly as Braden's had yesterday. He must be getting a handle on this diaper business.

He started down the hall, then heard noises from Braden's room. Josh peeked inside, and the baby began to bounce excitedly at the sight of Josh and Katie.

"I guess you're awake." How did he handle two of them at once? How did Eden do it? He put Katie on one hip, then scooped Braden up in the other arm and balanced him on the other hip. It seemed much more awkward than the way he'd seen Eden do it. And there was no way he was going to attempt to change Braden, too.

Biting his lip in concentration, he managed to get down the steps without a mishap. Katie gripped his ear with one chubby hand while Braden inspected Josh's teeth. There was more to this parenting business than he'd thought. But he would learn. He was not giving up Katie to anyone. Not even Eden.

Chapter 5

Eden tried to tamp the rising excitement as she ladled the vegetable soup into bowls. There was no guarantee they would really find her brother and sisters. But this was the first time she'd really had hope in all these years. And she owed that hope to Josh. Her heart thawed toward him like the first glimpse of spring. Katie had a good uncle.

Josh came in carrying the two babies. Samantha's face brightened when she saw him, and she sidled up to him and gazed at him with adoring eyes. Cory backed away and hid behind Eden.

She touched Cory's head with a reassuring pat. He was still frightened of men, and no wonder. The bruises from his stepfather's blows still darkened his legs and buttocks. "It's okay, Cory," she said softly.

Josh raised one eyebrow and softened his voice. "You want to help me with these babies, big guy? They're a little more than I can handle by myself."

Cory regarded him with sober dark eyes, then hid his face against Eden's leg.

"He's had a rough time," Eden mouthed.

Josh nodded. "You want to take Braden for me, Sam?"

"She doesn't like to be called Sam," Eden said hastily. The last time someone had called the little girl "Sam" she'd thrown a vase and sulked in her room for two hours.

"He can call me Sam," Samantha said. She smiled hesitantly at Josh and took Braden from his arm. "I like it now."

Eden managed to hide her astonishment. Josh had quite a way with her kids, and she suspected it was innate. Kids just gravitated to him naturally. He'd make a wonderful father and a caring husband. Her face burned with mortification, and she turned away to finish supper. Where had that thought come from? She wasn't looking for a husband. Change was the last thing her children needed. Familiarity was key, and she'd see they got it. Any thought of romance was ridiculous.

Josh put Katie in her high chair. "Should I put this thing on her?" He held up Katie's Pooh bib.

"Please. She's a messy eater."

Eden managed not to laugh as he coaxed Katie to put her arms through the bib armholes. She hated her bib. He finally succeeded, then tied it in the back and sat in the chair next to Katie.

"I warned you, she's messy. If you sit beside her, you'll probably have to wash up afterward."

Josh's grin of nonchalance changed as Katie banged her spoon into the bowl of soup, and it splashed everywhere. He sprang to his feet and wiped a streak of soup from his cheek. Then to Eden's surprise, he sat back in the same chair.

"I've already been baptized. I might as well guard you

from the onslaught," he said with a grin. He made a credible job of containing Katie's mess through supper and kept the other children entertained as well.

"You should have a houseful of kids yourself," Eden said. As soon as she spoke, she wanted to retrieve the words.

Josh shrugged, and his gaze wandered to Katie's face splotched with vegetable soup. "I've never been in one place long enough to meet the right kind of woman. For the last five years I've been in Saudi Arabia, traveling from one city to the next. But I'm almost thirty-five; it's time I thought of a permanent home."

Eden's breath caught in her throat. For just an instant, she imagined what it would be like to have him come home from a hard day's work to her and Katie, to have Katie running to greet him and calling him "Daddy." Her face burned with humiliation. If he could read her thoughts, he would be out the door so fast an Olympic runner couldn't catch him.

She glanced up to find his dark gaze on her. Was that longing on his face? She was likely reading her own silly dreams in his expression. Glancing away, she rose. "I'll do the dishes. You want Mr. Leland to help with your homework, kids?"

"Yes!" Samantha and Amelia shouted. Cory's face whitened, and he shook his head without looking up.

Eden sighed. She didn't know what to do with poor Cory. He couldn't seem to get over his terror of men. Maybe having Josh around would be good. Cory would learn that all men weren't like his mother's new husband.

Before she could reassure Cory, Josh knelt beside the

little boy. "I'm not very good at spelling, Cory. Do you suppose you could help me?"

Cory bit his lip and shook his head. Huge tears hung on his lashes, and he cast a desperate glance toward Eden. "I'll dry the dishes."

Josh touched Cory's head, and the little boy flinched back. "I won't hurt you, Cory." Josh's voice was low and soothing. "I'd like us to be friends."

Cory slid out of his chair and ran to Eden. He buried his face in her lap. "Make him go away, Eden. Make him go away."

Eden ran her fingers through the little boy's rough curls. "Mr. Leland is Katie's uncle, Cory. He likes little boys, too."

"That's what Tom said." Cory's words were muffled in her lap. "But he didn't. He didn't."

The last words were a wail of despair, and Eden gathered Cory up into her arms. She looked to Josh and bit her lip. "Why don't you take the rest of the children in by the fire. Cory and I will do the dishes and join you later."

A muscle twitched in Josh's jaw. "Some man hurt him, right? What kind of person could hurt a little boy like that?" He stood and thrust his fists in his pocket.

"You'd be surprised what horrors adults inflict on children," Eden whispered. Cory was literally shaking with terror, and she hugged him closer.

"I'd better never meet the man who hurt Cory," Josh said. He took the washcloth and wiped Katie's hands and face, then lifted her out of the high chair. He set her on the floor, then cleaned Braden's face and picked him out of his chair and carried him toward the door to the living room. Samantha took Katie's hand, and they all paraded after Josh.

Eden sank onto her chair and rocked Cory for a few moments. This was not a new occurrence. Sometimes she despaired of repairing the damage Cory's stepfather had done. But with God's help and her love, she thought the tide might be turning. A few weeks ago, he wouldn't have even managed to stay in the same room with a man.

Josh was unusual, though; she had to give him that. She'd never met a man as good with children as he was. There was a loneliness in him that answered the yearning in her own heart. She was afraid to hope he found her as fascinating as she found him. Katie was the real draw. In her heart, Eden knew this. But it didn't stop her from being drawn to the man whose heart seemed to be as big as his physique.

By the time she and Cory finished the dishes, the girls were done with their homework and had coaxed Josh into a game of Fish. They all lay spread out on the rug in front of the fireplace, the lamps casting a glow over the picture that made Eden think of Norman Rockwell prints. She swallowed the lump in her throat and sank into the rocker by the fire.

"Go fish," Josh said with a cheeky grin to Samantha. She groaned and snatched a card from the pile. "These girls are smoking me," he told Eden. "They should be sent to bed right now so I can claim victory. It's the only way I can win."

Samantha's face clouded, and with the next hand she played recklessly. Josh gained some of the ground he had lost, and he cast an amused glance to Eden. It was obvious

Samantha was throwing the game to him.

By the time the game was over and the kids had been bathed, prayers heard, stories read, and tucked in bed, it was eight-thirty. Josh's hair stood on end where he had swiped a wet hand through it after bathing Braden. A warm glow enveloped Eden as she and Josh went back to the parlor. She could get used to evenings like this.

Josh sat on the sofa and patted the place beside him. "Let's fire up the computer and see if there happens to be an answer."

"So quickly?" She sank beside him and watched as he went to his E-mail.

"Probably not, but it couldn't hurt to check," he said.

A box appeared that said it was downloading five messages. Eden caught her breath. Maybe there was a response already.

Josh frowned as he scanned the list of downloaded messages. "Most of it is junk mail," he said. "But this looks promising." He clicked on the message with the subject RICHMOND FAMILY.

Eden's heart sped up, and she clenched her fists in her lap. Maybe this was the news she'd waited twenty-five years to hear.

Chapter 6

Josh heard Eden catch her breath. Should he even have started her down this path? What if the search became fruitless? He would hate to be the cause of more pain in her life. She'd already had a lifetime's worth. But it was too late to turn back now. He'd opened this particular Pandora's box, and they would both have to live with the consequences.

He moved the cursor so they could read the message on the computer screen.

> *Pastor Markus Brittan once cared for a Richmond family after the mother died and the father disappeared. Could this be the family you mention? If so, I can give you Pastor Brittan's address and phone number.*

Eden's hand clamped on Josh's arm, and he nearly winced at the fierce grip. "I remember a preacher," she whispered. "I couldn't remember his name, but we went to church all the time. He had a cat named Spooky. It was all black with a white spot at its throat and used to leap on my legs when I went down the stairs."

Josh clicked Reply To Message and typed in a request for more information. "Let's see what the man has to say."

Eden groaned softly.

"What's wrong, Eden?"

He and Eden turned at Samantha's frightened voice.

Eden squeezed the little girl's hand and gave her a reassuring smile. "What are you doing up, Sweetie? Mr. Leland and I are just trying to find out some information about my family."

"Were you—adopted?" Samantha's face grew whiter at the dreaded word.

"Yes, Sweetie, but don't be frightened. Your daddy is working hard to get you back. You just saw him last week, remember?"

The terrified expression in Samantha's eyes faded, and she nodded. "He got a new job."

"That's right. You'll be with your daddy again soon. Now scoot back to bed."

What was the full story behind Samantha's removal from her home? He would have to ask Eden when the little girl wasn't around. Had her mother abandoned her or had she died? He glanced at Eden. There was one mother who would never leave her family. He'd never met anyone with a more nurturing soul. Her heart was so full of love for the children, he felt a little jealous. He watched her escort Samantha to the staircase.

Josh pulled his straying thoughts up short. Where had that come from? He'd best keep his mind on business. Eden had her life, and he had his. But she was so very appealing with her baby-fine blond hair curling around her face and those remarkable green eyes. If he were to hold her, that soft hair would barely reach his shoulder.

He dragged his gaze from her and turned back to the computer. The sooner he found her family and succeeded in retrieving Katie, the better. A new daughter would be enough of a change to his life; he wasn't ready for more than that.

Clicking the Send And Receive button, he leaned forward. "I'm bushed. I think I'll shove off."

"But what about the answer to the message you just sent? That lady might reply right away. It's only nine."

"And what is there to do tonight if she does? You can't go to Kentucky tonight."

"No, but you could call."

He caught the fact that she'd said *he* could call. She must be terrified. "I can stay awhile, I guess. But only if you fix some popcorn."

Relief lightened her face. "You've got a deal."

She hurried from the room, and Josh leaned back against the sofa. He was getting more and more entangled in the lives of this turbulent family on Hill Street. But he didn't remember any time he'd had more fun than he had tonight. Sitting around a family table with spills mixed with laughter, romping on the floor with a passel of children, watching the firelight spill red-gold over Eden's face had awakened a strange hunger in his heart. The feeling wasn't entirely pleasant, it was too new and filled with the trepidation of the unknown.

The aroma of popped corn wafted from the open kitchen door. The tinkle of ice in glasses followed, then

Eden walked back to the living room. She clutched a bowl of popcorn to her chest as she balanced two glasses of soda.

He leapt to his feet. "Let me help you."

"I've got it." She handed him the 101 Dalmatians glass and set her own Cinderella glass on the coffee table. She sat down, put the bowl of popcorn between them, and dug out a handful.

Josh scooped a handful of popcorn. For some reason, the fact that they ate from the same bowl touched him. He hadn't done that since he was a kid, and he and his sister shared popcorn with their parents.

Eden must have caught the nostalgia in his expression for she smiled. "We've talked about my past, but what about yours? What kind of upbringing did you and Mandy have?"

The pain that had subsided to a dull ache flared again at the mention of Mandy. *His fault.* "I don't want to talk about Mandy," he said.

"I think you need to. Katie is not your sister, you know. She may look like her, but she's her own little person. If you hope to find your sister again through her, you're making a big mistake. One that could hurt you and her terribly."

"I thought you were just a poorly paid foster mother. Since when did you get a psychology degree?"

Eden's face clouded, and he felt a shaft of shame. "I'm sorry, I had no right to say that," he said. He took a deep breath. "I suppose you're right. I should talk about it, but it just hurts."

Eden's green eyes softened. "You need a friend. I'm a pretty good listener."

She'd certainly been a good friend to his niece, a friend and a mother. Maybe he needed to talk about it. It couldn't be any worse than turning it over and over in his mind.

"I couldn't protect her," he said. "I tried when we were kids, but I was too little to stop him."

The color faded from Eden's cheeks. She looked older, filled with care and weariness. Josh knew she'd heard this same story many times in her profession. Shame tied his tongue, but he pressed on. "To the outside world, we looked the perfect family. Mom, Dad, nice house in the suburbs. Then *he* came to live with us."

Eden's eyes widened, and he knew she'd thought it was one of his parents who'd hurt Mandy. He rushed on, incapable of stopping now.

"Our uncle. He came back from Vietnam with bitterness that crouched on his shoulders like some vulture. He was always after Mandy to go places with him. At first she was happy to do it. She remembered the uncle John who'd gone away to war, the lighthearted, laughing uncle who brought us candy and presents."

He drew a breath and wished he could stop, wished he could erase the shameful knowledge of his own failure. Though Eden was silent, he could sense the waves of compassion flowing from her. He wanted to take her hand but was afraid he'd crush it as he told the rest of the story.

"I came home from school one day. The house was quiet. Mother and Dad were both at work. I called out, but no one answered. I poured a glass of milk and grabbed a handful of cookies, then went upstairs. I heard a noise, a cry maybe. I pushed open Mandy's door. Uncle John was there with Mandy. He had her by the arm. She was crying.

I shouted at him to leave her alone. He dragged her out the door past me. The whole time she was begging me to help her, to save her. I ran after them and tried to pull Mandy from his grasp, but I was only twelve, she was ten. Two little kids fighting some kind of demon that never let loose. He shoved her in the car and took off with the tires squealing. I ran back inside and called my mom. She came right home, but it was three days before we found Mandy. She called us after Uncle John took a bottle of pills and was dead. We drove to Missouri to get her, and she wasn't the same little girl who'd left. She was never the same again. And it was my fault."

A crushing weariness weighed him down. "And now she's dead. All I have left of her is Katie. Only Katie."

He started at the light touch of Eden's fingers on his. She took his hand and pressed it. He raised his eyes, and his gaze locked with hers.

"It's not your fault, Josh. You were a child, there's nothing you could have done."

"I should have saved her. Dad had a gun in his room. I could have gotten it or hit him with something." He raked a hand through his hair.

"Samantha's mom shoved her out of the bathroom, then slit her wrists and climbed in a tub of hot water and bled to death. Could she have stopped her?" She sighed, and the sound was filled with tender compassion. "Adults do terrible things sometimes, Josh. We don't know why God allows children to be hurt by their actions. It's one of the things I struggle with most. But I know this one thing. Though we suffer sometimes, God can use it to make us stronger."

"It didn't make Mandy stronger. She destroyed herself trying to erase the memories."

"But we have to let God make the difference. I could have wallowed in what happened to my family, but instead I chose to try to make some small difference in the lives of other children who suffer as I did. God made that difference. He could have made that difference in Mandy's life if she would have let Him."

"I wrote her once about trying to let go of the past, and she never answered."

"It's never easy. I went through a period of blaming God for my misfortune, too. But Mandy would have gotten back on her feet and forged through this. You have to believe that, Josh."

Exhaustion slowed his muscles, and he nodded. "In my heart, I do believe that." If only she'd lived. But all the regrets in the world wouldn't change what was finished.

"But God left Katie motherless."

"She's not motherless. She has me," Eden said. "And she always will."

Maybe he should tell her now he still intended to take Katie. He regretted the pain it would cause her, but he needed Katie. She would have to see that sooner or later. She was his lifeline.

Chapter 7

Eden glanced at Josh, and the veiled look of pain in his eyes made her want to take him in her arms and kiss away his hurts the way she might with Cory. The thought surprised her. He was an adult, but he still carried the scars of his childhood. The same way she carried them. No wonder he had wanted Katie so badly.

She could tell by the stiffness in his shoulders that he had erected his wall of defenses again, and she felt inadequate to scale it. She glanced at her watch. Nine-thirty. Such momentous revelations in only half an hour.

"Let's check the E-mail again, then I'll head back to my hotel." He took his laptop from the coffee table and clicked the Send And Receive button. Nothing.

Eden's keen sense of disappointment surprised her. This wouldn't happen overnight. And she'd waited this long to find them, what was a few more weeks or months? At least she was doing something about it now. Thanks to Josh.

He switched off the computer and stood. "Thanks for the great evening. Could I take you and the kids to dinner tomorrow? Just so you don't have to cook for me again?"

His teasing grin did funny things to her breathing. "Would you like to come to church with us in the morning?"

He grinned. "I was hoping you would invite me and I wouldn't have to invite myself."

Eden laughed. "You want to follow us or ride in the kid-mobile?"

He hesitated, and she laughed again. "Such a decision. Peace and solitude or sticky fingers and chattering voices."

He chuckled. "I'll take the sticky fingers and chattering voices. Peace and solitude sound boring. What time do we leave?"

"Nine-ten. Sunday school starts at nine-thirty, and our church is in the country about ten minutes away. It takes me a few minutes to get them all to their classes and Katie to the nursery."

"I'll bring donuts at eight and help you get them ready."

The shock of pleasure that went through her at his words brought her up short. Did he have any idea what a treat that would be for the children? There was rarely enough money for such an extravagance.

And she was enjoying his presence way too much. She needed to keep in mind that he would be leaving soon. He would soon tire of commotion and the small, daily trials of children. One day soon he would go back to his real life. She didn't want to be nursing a broken heart when he did. But, oh, how good it felt to have someone to share all this with, someone who thought of what the children needed besides her. She allowed herself to bask in the pleasure of it for a moment.

She shut the door behind him, took the remains of the popcorn and empty glasses to the kitchen, then turned off the lights and went to bed. Tomorrow she would try to remember this sharing of their lives was temporary, a chasing after the wind. Her life was here with these children who needed her so badly. His life was oil fields and the hectic world of business. Too different to ever meld.

In spite of her resolve, Eden saw her own flushed cheeks in the mirror the next morning and shook her head. The thought of spending the day with Josh had given her a glow anyone but an idiot would recognize. She took extra care with her makeup, then dressed in a grass green suit that slimmed her hips. Not that mere clothing would hide those extra pounds she couldn't seem to lose. She swept her hair on top of her head and let the curls fall in disarray.

Standing in front of the full-length mirror, she nearly groaned. She looked like a green sausage with a blond topknot. Josh could have his pick of glamorous women— real beauties who knew how to flirt and hold a man's interest. He would never be interested in a homebody like Eden who looked like she'd made too many cookies. But making them wasn't the problem, it was eating them.

The children were stirring. She turned from the mirror. Her appearance would just have to do. Josh wasn't interested in her anyway, so she could just quit obsessing. Eden changed Katie's and Braden's diapers, then got the older children dressed for church. Samantha brightened when she heard Josh was going with them, but Cody cowered. She wished she knew how to break through his fear of men.

The doorbell rang, and her heart jumped. She hustled down the stairs with Katie under one arm and Braden under the other and opened the door.

"We got another message!" Josh stepped inside with a white box of donuts in one hand and his computer in the other. He strode past her into the living room. Setting the box of donuts on the coffee table, he turned and enveloped her in a hug.

All thought left Eden's head at the feel of his strong arms around her. For the first time since she was a child, she felt safe and protected. She wanted to burrow against his chest and savor the sensation. But she felt him stiffen and realized what he would think. She pulled away hastily.

He dug in his pocket and pulled out a scrap of paper. "Here's the phone number and address. But rather than call, why don't we just go there?"

"To Kentucky? What if it's the wrong people?"

"They're the right ones, don't you feel it, Eden? When he sees you, he might recognize you. I have a feeling you haven't changed much since you were eight. You're not hardly bigger than a minute now."

Eden nearly choked, but she wasn't about to argue with him. Maybe he hadn't noticed her generous proportions, and she wasn't about to point them out. But Kentucky!

"I looked on the map; Covington is on the east side of Cincinnati. That's only three hours from here. We could leave after church, stop for lunch, then head to Covington. We could be there by four at the latest. I'll buy the gas."

"We may get back late. And I can't take my foster children out of state without permission."

"Can you get someone to watch them?"

She bit her lip and gazed into Josh's intent eyes. "Are you sure you want to go to the bother? What if he's not there?"

"He's a preacher. He'll be around on Sunday."

"All right, then, if you're sure. I'll see if Rick and Belinda can come. They've done it for me before."

"We can take Katie, right?"

She nodded. "Why are you doing this?" Eden asked Josh. "I really appreciate it, but it really isn't your concern."

He averted his eyes, and a flush stained his cheeks. Could he possibly be coming to care for her? She couldn't imagine any other reason for his reaction. She warned herself not to jump to conclusions, but it was hard to squelch the thrill of hope that lightened her heart.

"Take some clothes to change into for you and Katie. You pack, and I'll feed the kids their breakfast. It'll be a fun day." He took Katie and Braden from her arms and strode toward the kitchen.

Eden blew her bangs out of her eyes, then went to pack a change of clothes. Josh was a take-charge kind of guy. She supposed it was from being in command of others in his job. It was a nice change to let someone else have that role.

By the time she got downstairs with a satchel of clothing, Josh was washing faces and clearing away the breakfast things. Even Cory had eaten, though he watched Josh with a wary gaze as the man moved around the kitchen. Still, Eden thought he might be beginning to thaw.

"If you dress Braden, I'll dress Katie." Josh didn't wait for an answer but handed Braden to her and headed toward the stairs.

Eden followed with Braden in her arms and a frown

on her face. She was beginning to dislike the way he took control of Katie. The adoption was final, but maybe Josh was still unwilling to accept that. She shook her head. She was overreacting. He would naturally want to spend time with Katie; after all, she was his niece. And there was nothing he could do to change the situation.

She dressed Braden in a navy-and-red sailor suit and combed his hair. He kept snatching at strands of her hair that fell forward, and she knew she looked a mess by the time he was ready. She checked on the other children, but they were all ready.

Pushing open the door to Katie's room, she found Josh struggling to comb Katie's hair. She hated to have her hair combed and was trying to escape. The bow he'd managed to get in her blond curls was lopsided and barely hanging on.

Eden chuckled and handed Braden to him. Josh watched while she gave Katie a toy, then took out the bow and repositioned it.

"I'm new at this girl stuff," he said.

Though he laughed, Eden thought she detected a note of chagrin in his voice. "We'd better go," she told him.

He nodded, then scooped up Katie and carried both children to the entry. She and Josh popped the children into their jackets and went to the minivan. A twelve-year-old model, it was the best Eden could afford. Though the paint was faded and rust showed through in spots, the engine was sound, and it got her and the children safely where they needed to go. And the stains from their sticky fingers didn't matter so much on the worn upholstery.

At New Life Church she waved to her friend Tatiana,

then got the kids to class. Tatiana's husband, Gabe, took charge of Josh for her and led him off to the Life-builders class. She knew the class would make him welcome. Though Gabe and Tatiana Salinger were newlyweds, they were the ambassadors of the group. Tatiana had come from Russia to marry Gabe, and she was always conscious of making newcomers feel welcome.

Eden found Belinda in the nursery, and she readily agreed to come to the house to watch the foster children. Her daughter Andi was Amelia's age, and the girls were best friends. Eden was in such a flurry of excitement, she found it hard to concentrate on the lesson. Today she might find her brother and sisters. The thought made her giddy. She wanted to hug the knowledge close. She prayed all through church for God to give her the strength to face what she might find in Kentucky. Good or bad.

Chapter 8

You want to drive?" Eden asked Josh. She'd changed into jeans and a sweatshirt, then changed Katie's diaper and dressed her in pants as well. Josh had also changed into jeans. His hair was a bit rumpled, and his eyes sparkled with excitement and adventure.

"Sure." He took the keys from her outstretched hand. "Actually, I wondered if we ought to stop by and get my SUV. You think this old rattletrap will make the trip?"

"It hasn't failed me yet. What's the matter? You too good to be seen in this old tank?" She grinned to show she was joking, but his answer mattered more than she was willing to admit to herself.

"If you'd seen what I drove for five years, you wouldn't ask that. This is a rental. I drove a twenty-year-old Range Rover in Saudi Arabia with no bumpers and practically no paint. This is a luxury vehicle compared to it." He took Katie from her and buckled her into the seat belt.

Eden felt a rising sense of excitement. For too long she had followed the same schedule day after day, month after month, year after year. She was in a rut, and it felt good to break out, to smell the fresh air, to see something beyond the city limits of Wabash, Indiana. She clambered into the front passenger seat and fastened her seat belt.

Josh pulled into a fast-food drive-up lane and got them all a sandwich and fries. He glanced at Eden's face and grinned. "I'm too excited to eat here. I don't normally eat while I'm driving, but today I'll make an exception. It looks like you'd strangle me if I suggested a delay."

Eden's cheeks burned. "Does it show that much?"

"You just look like a kid on her birthday. And I have to admit I kind of feel like that myself. When is your birthday, anyway?"

"December fourth."

"Dare I ask how old you'll be?"

"A gentleman never asks a lady her age," she said primly.

"You look like you're about twelve with the way your eyes are shining." He pulled onto the highway and took a bite of his hamburger.

"My foster parents always forgot my birthday," she said. "I try to make birthdays special for my foster kids because of it. It's sad to think no one cares if you are alive or not. At least that's the way it always seemed to me." She looked down at her hands. "I want my foster kids to always know I consider them a special gift from God."

"You said you were eight when your mother died. Surely your parents celebrated your birthday. Do you remember much about them?"

"Oh, yes. Some things are fuzzy, but I remember one birthday I got a red wagon. I think Daddy might have found it in the junkyard, but he'd painted it and tightened all the wheels. I thought it was wonderful. A brand-new wagon wouldn't have meant as much as knowing the love that went into all his work. When he pulled me down the sidewalk in it, I felt like a princess. My daddy's princess." The remembered pain of her loss tightened her throat, and she struggled not to cry. "We didn't have much money, but we were happy. Mama was always smiling and cheerful, no matter what. We played games in the evenings, and she always read us a story before bed. I remember baking cookies and her teaching me how to crochet. Lots of memories." The sting of tears in the back of her throat stopped further speech.

Josh reached across the seat and squeezed her hand. "We'll find them again, Eden."

"I'm afraid to hope," she admitted. "After all these years, it seems almost impossible to track them down."

"I have a good feeling about today."

"I hope you're right." Eden leaned back against the seat and sighed. Josh's optimism was rubbing off on her. She needed to guard her heart in case of disappointment, but she was tired of doing that. She'd done that for years. It was time she let go and risked her heart. She'd never felt so reckless, so ready for adventure. She slanted a glance at Josh, and gratitude swelled in her heart. It was so kind of him to pursue this for her.

Before she knew it, they were merging into traffic around Cincinnati. She directed Josh where to turn, and they soon found the street. The houses were all small ranch homes from the forties with no garages or porches, just cracker-box houses that were all alike save for the occasional splash of color from an enterprising homeowner.

"There it is!" Eden's heart began a taut staccato beat

against her chest. She bit her lip and tried to slow her breathing. "What if it's the wrong pastor?"

"It isn't."

Josh's calm voice quieted her fears. She nodded. "This looks vaguely familiar. I can't put my finger on just why."

Josh put the car in park and turned it off. He glanced into the backseat. "Katie is asleep. Want me to stay in the car with her?"

At the thought of going to the door by herself, her throat grew tight. Josh must have seen the panic in her face, for he patted her shoulder. "Never mind. I'll carry Katie." He opened his door and got out. Slipping Katie from her seat, he cradled her against his chest where she hung in a dead weight like a rag doll.

Eden took a deep breath and opened her door. Her heart hammered against her ribs, and her blood pounded in her ears. Licking her lips, she shut her door and started up the walk behind Josh. He strode purposefully to the door and turned to make sure she was with him. The doorbell pealed inside.

Eden ceased to breathe. She swallowed hard and clenched her hands together. What if he didn't remember anymore?

Josh turned and gazed at her. "I just realized—there's no car in the drive or at the street."

A woman walking a small poodle with a pink bow on its head stopped in front of the house. "Are you looking for the Brittans?" the woman asked.

Eden turned to stare at her. The woman was about her age with bright red hair and a dusting of freckles across her friendly face. Eden felt a sense of recognition; a memory, faded but still full of warm feelings, came over her. A little girl with red hair and a smile that never dimmed. She couldn't tear her eyes from the woman's face.

"I'm Molly Larson. I live across the street. The Brittans are on vacation in Florida. They won't be home for a couple of weeks."

Eden barely heard the woman's words. The sense of familiarity grew. Molly. The name heightened the feeling that she should know this woman. A little girl's features began to overshadow the woman's. "Molly? Um, have you lived here long?"

Molly tilted her head and stared at Eden. "You look familiar to me."

"I'm Eden Walters. I lived with the Brittans for a few months. I used to be a Richmond."

Molly gasped. "Eden! I remember!" She rushed across the grass with her hands outstretched. "I thought of you just the other day. Let me look at you! Where did you go? You never answered any of my letters." She rushed on without waiting for an answer. "Remember the tree house we built in my backyard? It's still there, and my kids play on it."

Eden took her hand and squeezed it. The years fell away as if they had never passed, and she was eight years old again. "You were the best friend I ever had, Molly. I still have the diary you gave me when I went away."

Molly's smile was bright. "The Brittans aren't home, but I am. Let me get you a soda, and we can sit and get caught up on news."

Eden followed her across the street, barely conscious of Josh trailing behind with Katie. She should have introduced them, but she was just so shocked, she couldn't think.

The house was the same one Molly had lived in as a child. The carpet and kitchen had been updated, but when Eden asked to use the rest room, she found the same pink tile on the floor and walls. The sight brought the past back so vividly, Eden felt almost physical pain.

Katie was still sleeping in Josh's arms when she made her way to the kitchen. Molly was chattering to him as she dropped ice into glasses and poured soda out of a two-liter bottle. Eden sank into a chair and watched her old friend. She felt as though Molly might disappear and leave her bereft again.

Molly handed them each a glass and sat in the chair beside Eden. "Now tell me what you're doing here," she demanded. "And why didn't you answer any of my letters?"

"Letters? I never got any letters. I lost your address, and my foster mother said it was just as well, that it was best to break with the past."

"I sent you a letter every week for months." Molly frowned. "Do you suppose she kept them from you?"

"It's possible," Eden said slowly. "She was afraid to let me get close to anyone from school. I think she knew I wouldn't be there long. She taught me to iron and clean, and I was so busy I didn't have time to miss not having any friends. But I never forgot you, Molly."

"I even wrote your aunt once to see if she'd heard from you. She sent me back a very nice letter but said she hadn't heard a word and didn't expect to."

Excitement threatened to choke Eden. She gripped Molly's hand. "You have my aunt's address? I can't even remember her name. I only met her the one time."

"Oh, Eden, I don't remember either now!" Molly

slapped her forehead with the heel of her hand.

Eden's burgeoning hope faded, and she felt near tears.

Molly bit her lip. "Wait! I might still have the letter. My husband says I'm a hopeless pack rat, and I have a whole box of childhood mementos and letters. Let me look." She jumped to her feet and dashed down the hall.

Eden looked at Josh. "Hang in there," he whispered. "Don't give up hope yet."

She nodded, but her throat was too tight with unshed tears to speak. All this way for nothing. But no, not nothing. She'd found Molly. That was something.

A shriek echoed down the hall. "I found it!" Moments later, Molly came running down the hall. "Here it is, Eden! Her name is Selma Johnson, and she lives in Michigan." She held out a tattered envelope.

Eden reached out a trembling hand and closed her fingers on it. It was a link to her family. Her only link.

Chapter 9

Josh watched the play of emotions across Eden's expressive face from the corner of his eye. The van hummed smoothly across the highway, trundling toward Wabash. Eden smoothed the letter from her aunt across her lap as though caressing a treasure. And he supposed to her it was. His own emotions were running high, so he could only imagine how Eden felt. They would be home soon, and then they could decide what their next step was.

Home. Already he was beginning to think of that dilapidated Victorian as home. Though shabby, its fading grandeur was enhanced by the warm presence of this woman beside him. Eden could make any house a home. She had a presence about her, a calming competence that set people at ease. He'd just seen her do it with Molly. People took to her right off, children and adults alike. Josh had never met anyone like her.

No wonder Katie adored her. He felt a stab of guilt at the thought of his plans to gain custody of his niece. Where was his trust, his faith in God? He'd been scheming and laying his own plans without even consulting God.

The problem was, he had a feeling God wouldn't slap a rubber stamp labeled APPROVED on his plan to take Katie. He knew Katie needed to be with family, but in his heart he admitted Eden was a better mother than Mandy would have been. It ached to admit it to himself, but it was true, nonetheless.

Eden's soft voice broke into his tortured thoughts. "You don't think we'll find them, do you? I thought you'd be glad we've gotten this much information."

"I am." He forced a note of cheerfulness into his voice. "I was just thinking about my future. Of course we'll find them. This is a great start. When we get home, I'll hop on the Internet and see what I can find out about your aunt."

"Your future?"

Was that alarm in her voice? He nodded. "I can't be unemployed forever. I have enough money to last a few months, but I need to be looking for a job."

"Where will you look?" She bit her lip and turned to look at the passing landscape. "I'd hoped you'd join us for Thanksgiving."

"I'm not talking about leaving this week. But once the holiday is over, I really should start sending out some résumés. I doubt there are any jobs around here for someone with my background. I'll probably have to go to Texas."

She barely nodded, and Josh's fingers tightened on the steering wheel. For a crazy moment he wanted to put his arms around her and tell her he'd never leave her and the children. What had gotten into him? His aching heart seemed to find solace and comfort in Eden's presence, and it had to stop. He answered to no one, and he liked it that way. This woman would tie him in one place, and he'd never see the world again.

I've seen all the world I need to see. He shrugged the thought away and concentrated on the road. He liked his life just fine the way it was. There was no reason to let a woman's green eyes tempt him from the life he'd chosen years ago. With just Katie, he could still pack up and move whenever he pleased. Eden would just complicate matters.

They stopped for supper at a truck stop near Indianapolis. The parking lot was full, so Josh knew the food must be good, though the place looked like it would have been right at home along Route 66 forty years ago.

Their table and every other one in the place had a small jukebox on it, back against the wall. The waitress, her jaw working as she popped her gum, took their order, then brought a high chair for Katie.

When their food was brought, Katie threw her green beans on the tile floor and refused to eat more than a few bites. Eden cleaned her up and shrugged. "She's not a good traveler. She likes her own bed and the other children."

"She'll learn to travel better," Josh said. He nearly winced when he realized what he'd said.

Eden looked at him strangely, a question in her eyes. "I don't travel much," she said. "She has no reason to get used to it."

"Do you want her to just see the four corners of Wabash? Don't you want her to experience the world and not spend her whole life in a little backwater town?"

"You're still planning to take her, aren't you?"

Eden's voice was soft, and Josh dared a glance at her. The steely glint in her eye was at odds with her gentle voice, and he knew she would never let Katie go without a fight. He didn't want to fight with her.

Josh's shoulders tightened. "Yes," he admitted. "I love her. She's all I have left of Mandy; she's the only family I have."

"I'm sorry, Josh." Eden laid a hand on his arm. "I'm sorry you lost your sister. But Katie belongs with me. I'll never give her up. Never."

The finality in her words struck Josh like a blow. He'd only been deceiving himself. There was no way to convince her to give Katie up without a fight. And he didn't want to fight with Eden. He was beginning to care way too much about her. His thoughts shied away from that direction again.

He forced a smile. "You've said your piece. Are you ready to head for home?"

Eden plucked Katie from the high chair. "Let me take her to the rest room and change her diaper first."

They were silent on the trip home. Josh mulled over his options. He could find a lawyer and take it to court. He thought he might have a good chance if the jury realized he had no family left except for Katie. But the thought of doing that to Eden hurt. No, his best bet was still to find her family. If she had her own kin, maybe she would realize just how important it was for Katie to be with him.

Light spilled from the windows of the house, and Josh felt a warm glow of homecoming. He stopped the van in the driveway and got out to lift Katie from her seat. Eden held the front door open for him, then shut it behind them.

Belinda was curled up on the sofa. The fire flickered in the fireplace, and the scent of the apple candle burning on the mantle added to the homey glow of the room.

Belinda put her book down and smiled at them. "There you are. Rick came and took Andi home with him, and the children are all asleep."

"I found my aunt's address!" Eden burst out. "She lives in Michigan. That's where Timmy is."

"What about your sisters?" Belinda stood and stretched.

"Molly heard Crista went to Arizona, but she has no idea where or who took her. She hadn't heard anything about Angelina."

"Well, at least it's a start." Belinda hugged Eden, then picked up her coat. "Maybe you'll find some of your family by Christmas. What a holiday that would be!"

Eden nodded. "I'm almost afraid to hope for that." She walked Belinda to the hall.

While Eden saw her friend out, Josh carried Katie to bed. She slept heavily, her thumb in her mouth. He pulled her shoes off and slipped her out of her coat. Trying to decide if he should put her in her pajamas and risk wakening her, he didn't hear Eden come up behind him.

She went to the bureau and pulled out a pink fleece sleeper. Josh lowered the side of the crib and laid Katie down. He watched while Eden deftly changed her without waking the sleeping toddler.

"You're good at that," he said. Again, doubts assailed him. Eden knew so much more than he did about raising a child. He'd had no experience. But he had a lot of love. He could learn.

She smiled. "Katie is a sound sleeper. You go on down and see what you can find on the Net. I'll be down as soon as I check on the other children."

Josh nodded and went down the hall to the stairs. He almost tripped over a fire truck on the stairs but caught the railing just in time. He picked up the toy to make sure Eden didn't stumble and carried it with him to the living room. Within minutes he was looking for Eden's aunt on the Internet.

Eden came in the room, yawning and stretching her back. "Any luck?"

He shook his head. "No trace of her."

"Could we go to Michigan and talk to some neighbors?"

Her eyes sparkled with determination, and he hoped he wasn't setting her up for a major disappointment. "I'm game if you are." Anything to keep that sparkle in her eyes. And as long as he felt needed, he wouldn't leave. The time of his departure could be pushed back once again. He wasn't ready to walk away from Eden. Josh shied away from examining just why that was true.

Chapter 10

The aroma of roasting turkey filled the kitchen. The tart scent of cranberries mingled with that of pumpkin and cinnamon. Eden had tied balloons everywhere to add a festive touch. She loved Thanksgiving. This year she had something to be even more thankful for. Her heart filled with thankfulness to God for the gift of Katie. Her daughter. The thought sent chills of joy up her spine. This would be their first holiday as a real family.

And Josh would be here as well. Eden knew the camaraderie would soon be gone. One day he would decide it was time to move on, find a job, and settle down somewhere. The thought deflated the bubble of joy she'd been enveloped in, and she sighed. Picking up the wooden spoon, she began to beat the pumpkin mixture for pies.

The doorbell rang. "Samantha, would you get the door?" she called.

She heard Samantha's footsteps echo along the oak floors. A couple of minutes later Josh's broad shoulders filled the doorway. He wore black jeans with a garnet sweater. His hair was still a bit damp from his morning shower, and the spicy scent of his cologne added to his masculine presence. Eden forced her attention back to her pies.

He sniffed. "Smells great. I really appreciate your taking pity on me today. This will be the first real Thanksgiving dinner I've had in over ten years. Can I set the table or something?"

"Sure. But just set it for four."

He raised an eyebrow. "I thought the house seemed quiet. Where are the rest of the kids?"

"With their families for the day."

"Even Cory?"

She'd been trying not to think of that. "I tried to talk social services out of it. Cory's advocate said his mother had assured her the stepfather wouldn't be there today."

"And they believed her?" Josh's voice raised.

"They want to give her a chance. The goal is always to get the family back together."

"It shouldn't always be. When they hurt the child like that man hurt Cory, they lose the right." Josh scowled. "I'd like to get my hands on him."

So would Eden. She forced a smile. "They've been warned they'll go to jail if any harm comes to him. And that would be the least of their worries once you and I found out."

Josh's worried frown didn't dissipate. "We'd better pray for him today, the other kids too."

Eden had already done just that, but the fact that Josh felt comfortable enough with her to suggest they pray together touched her. She wiped her hands on her apron, then took both Josh's hands in hers and bowed her head.

The strength of his fingers calmed her heart. Josh cleared his throat. "Lord, we know You love these little ones even more than we do. We ask that You protect them today, give them a good day with their parents, and work in the lives of those families to help them come together again. In Jesus' name. Amen."

"Amen," Eden echoed. Josh didn't release her fingers, and she raised her head, catching his gaze with her own. His dark eyes seemed filled with an emotion Eden was afraid to name, even to herself.

"You have flour on your cheek," he said in a gentle voice. He let go of her left hand but kept a tight grip on her right. His fingers brushed her cheek, and he rubbed the smudge away with his thumb.

The moment drew out between them, and Eden was almost afraid to breathe. He pulled her into his arms and rested his chin on the top of her head. It felt right, as though she fit there, as though his arms were made for her. She breathed in the scent of his cologne and wrapped her arms around his waist without thinking. His heart thumped beneath her ear, a slow, steady beat that filled her with confidence. This was a man who wasn't afraid to be tender, who could laugh at himself yet knew when to be serious. A man who loved children and wasn't afraid to show it. Her man.

The thought shocked her, and she dropped her arms and would have stepped away, but Josh tipped her chin up, and his lips claimed hers. Eden closed her eyes again and tasted the sweetness of his kiss. Tentative but tender, his lips were firm yet soft. She cautioned herself not to read too much into it. Men kissed women all the time without promising anything. She had to guard her heart.

His gaze flickered over the strands of hair trailing around her face. "Eden, I—"

"I'm hungry!" Samantha stood in the middle of the kitchen, her hands on her hips in a belligerent pose.

She was jealous. Eden could see it in her resentful glance. She smiled at her foster child, but Samantha's stern gaze didn't falter. Her defiant gaze flickered from Eden to Josh, then she bit her lip and looked at the floor.

"It's almost ready." Eden stepped away from Josh. Trying not to wonder what he had been about to say, she turned and slid the pies in the oven, then set the timer.

"I'll get Katie," Josh said. "Want to come with me, Sam?"

The little girl's face brightened, and she shot Eden a triumphant glance before practically skipping out of the kitchen with Josh. Eden managed not to smile. Bless Josh for knowing just how to soothe the little girl. He had a knack with children that was unusual in a man. Maybe Katie *did* belong with him.

The thought was a stab of agony to her heart. She'd just told him it was important for families to be together if possible. That was the goal she worked for, the aim she always kept in mind for her foster children. Just because she wanted Katie didn't make it right. She pushed the knowledge away. Katie was hers, she couldn't give her up. But guilt gnawed at her. God couldn't want that of her, could He? She wouldn't believe it.

Her hands trembled as she carried the food to the table. Tears blurred her vision, and she took a deep, calming breath. She was just being emotional because of the holiday. They would enjoy the meal, play some games afterward, and she would forget all about this prick of guilt. It was nothing.

By the time Josh brought Katie down from upstairs, Eden had recovered her composure. She mustn't let him know she'd even thought about giving up Katie. He would be all over that idea like a duck on a June bug.

Katie snuggled against Josh's chest like it was made for her. Eden knew the feeling, and a smile curved her lips. She turned away before Josh could see it and ask why she was smiling. Heat bloomed in her cheeks at the thought of explaining herself.

The meal passed slowly and amicably. Katie even managed to keep most of her food on the tray of her high chair. Samantha chattered to Josh and seemed to have forgotten her earlier pique. When the buzzer on the oven went off, Eden took the pies out to cool. They would have dessert a little later in the afternoon.

Josh and Samantha pitched in to help wash dishes, and Eden couldn't help imagining what it would be like for them all to be a family. She had to stop that kind of thinking. Josh would be appalled if he knew where her imagination had taken her.

When the kitchen was clean, they all went to the living room. Eden flopped onto the sofa. "I'm pooped," she said.

"Oh, no, you don't," Josh said. "You know what was always traditional at our house on Thanksgiving afternoon?"

"Resting and playing games?" she asked hopefully.

He grabbed her hand and pulled her to her feet. "Nope. Putting up the Christmas tree."

She started shaking her head. "I always buy a live tree. There's nothing open today."

"Wrong again." He pulled her to the front door and opened it. A magnificent Christmas tree leaned beside the door. It was at least nine feet tall with full branches and no holes.

"Where did you get that?" Eden held her breath in awe.

"I bought it yesterday and brought it over when I came. You get the decorations out, and I'll bring it in." He lifted the tree and carried it through the door Samantha held open for him.

"He told me about it," Samantha said smugly.

"You kept the secret well." Eden squeezed her shoulder as she passed, and Samantha smiled, all traces of her earlier fit of temper gone.

Samantha kept an eye on Katie while Eden hurried up the stairs to the attic. The attic steps were steep, and she paid attention to her feet as she climbed them. She'd stumbled many times on them. Josh came up behind her.

He looked around. "I love these old attics. They don't build houses like this anymore."

"Sometimes I come up here and imagine these boxes are filled with things from my grandparents. Silly, isn't it?"

"No, it's not." He draped an arm around her. "Family is important. And you've made a family here, Eden. This is a great thing you're doing, something to be proud of."

Heat touched her cheeks, and a matching glow filled her. Sometimes she wondered if she should give up the fight, get a real job instead of working for the state with these children. She'd seen the way people looked at her when she said she was a foster parent. The abuses in the system were legion. But she cared too much about the children to abandon them.

She turned away and began loading his arms with boxes. "I have so many ornaments the children made. Samantha will be glad to see the one she made for me last year."

Josh carried a load downstairs, and Eden followed with her arms full of boxes too. Samantha was nearly bouncing in her excitement. Eden put her load down and held out her arms for Katie.

"You'll want to help Josh decorate," she said. "This little munchkin needs to be up and out of the way."

Katie came to her willingly. As she watched Josh and Samantha decorate the tree, she wished this could be the first of a lifetime of Christmases spent together. She nearly gasped at the realization. She loved him! When had that happened? She couldn't love him. He would leave her just like everyone else in her family had done. It wasn't safe to love him. But how did she kill love once it began? He had the ability to rip her heart out and take her daughter as well. But what would he say if she asked him to stay, to find a job here, and help her raise Katie?

Chapter 11

J osh couldn't figure Eden out. Thanksgiving she had been so warm and sweet. Since then she'd kept him at arm's length. She avoided being alone with him, and her green eyes warned him to keep his distance.

He didn't want to keep his distance. Those minutes in the kitchen on Thanksgiving had awakened him to the fact that this emotion he felt when he looked at her was love. He was in love for the first time in his life. With a woman who smelled of baby powder and formula instead of expensive perfume and hair spray. A woman who thought watching a video with a roomful of kids more fun than going out to dinner. The realization astonished and delighted him. Eden was what he'd been looking for all his life. But how did he break through that wall she had around her?

Today might be a start. He glanced at Eden sitting beside him in the SUV. They had the whole day to themselves in their search for Selma Johnson. Belinda was holding down the fort, and it would be just he and Eden together today. They were nearly there, and Eden hadn't said two words to him.

She didn't look happy. Staring through the window, her profile was somber with no evidence of her dimples. Josh hadn't seen them since Thanksgiving. Had he gone too far with that kiss? Maybe she wasn't interested in him that way. His spirits sank at the thought.

"Penny for your thoughts," he said.

She turned and gave a halfhearted smile. "They're not worth that much. I wasn't really thinking, just staring out the window."

"Scared about your aunt?"

She shook her head. "I think I'll find my family eventually. I'm content with that."

"What's wrong between us, Eden? You've been acting strange since last week on Thanksgiving. I thought we had a nice time."

"I did, too," she said. She turned her head again. "Nothing's wrong. I've just been busy with making gifts for the children for Christmas. I'm sorry if I seem a little distant." She swiveled around to look at him. "Tell me, where are you planning to find a job?"

"Where did that come from?" No telling what thoughts were running through that pretty head.

"Do you plan to buy a house so you can have Katie stay occasionally?"

"I would like to find a large house like yours, one where she could feel at home. You might want some help with her once you find your siblings. You'll be busy catching up on old times."

She jerked her head up and stared at him through narrowed eyes. "Is that why you're helping me look for my brother and sisters?"

He felt his face burn, and he turned his attention back to the road. Guilt had to be written all over his face, for he heard her catch her breath.

"That's it, isn't it? That's why you've been spending so much time with us, why you're so determined to find my siblings. You think once I find them, I'll let you have Katie!"

"Look, Eden, maybe that was the reason at the beginning, but I soon learned to care about you and the kids. I really want to help you find your family." He needed to find a place to pull over. Driving down the road was no place to declare his love to a woman. It would have to wait.

"And I was feeling guilty for keeping Katie from you. I had even begun to think she belonged with you!" Eden's voice was choked with tears, and she bit her lip, then turned to stare stonily out the window.

How did he answer that? He swallowed and tried to think how to say he loved her. Did he just spit it out? Good grief, they were driving down the freeway! He wasn't going to propose in this kind of situation. He had it all planned, and this wasn't in the plan. He wanted them all to be together; he didn't want to take Katie from her.

"She's all I have left of my family," he said lamely. That would have to do until the right time.

She didn't answer him as he turned onto her aunt's street. It was lined with old oak and maple trees that hid modest, two-story homes. He gritted his teeth and pulled the SUV to the curb. Jumping out, he started to come around to open her door, but she hopped out before he could get there. He put his hand on her arm, but she jerked away.

"Don't touch me," she said. "You used me, Josh. You

used my need to find my family for your own purposes. I thought you cared about me." Her voice choked off, and she marched ahead of him to the house where her aunt used to live.

"Eden, please—"

"I don't want to talk to you right now, Josh. Let's stop while we're still civil." She rapped on the door, painted red with off-white trim.

Josh fell silent, and his own temper rose. Women! They wouldn't listen to reason.

❄

Eden masked her pain with anger. Josh's betrayal hurt more than she'd imagined. By the time she'd tried to protect her heart, it was already too late. He didn't deserve Katie. The sooner he was gone, the better. She could nurse her hurt and figure out a way to get over him. When they got back, she would tell him it was best if he left.

She felt him glowering at her back as she waited on the front stoop of the house. Straightening her shoulders, she rapped at the door again.

"I'm coming, hold your horses." Her gray hair scraped back in a bun, a short woman nearly as wide as she was tall opened the door and peered at them through thick glasses.

"Are you. . .Selma Johnson?" Eden heard her own voice quiver and bit her lip.

"Selma Johnson. Now there's a name I haven't heard in years." The woman took off her glasses and polished them on her stained apron. She perched the glasses back on her nose and opened the door wider. "Don't stand there looking like two possums in the porch light. Come in, and we'll jaw awhile."

Eden stared back uncertainly at Josh. Who was this woman? Obviously not her aunt. Josh gave Eden a slight nod, and she stepped through the door. The odor of sautéing onions hung in the air.

"Cooking liver and onions. I got plenty if you folks would care to join me for lunch."

"No, thanks," Josh said. "We won't be able to stay that long."

"You young folks, always rushing hither and yon," the woman grumbled. She pointed toward a chintz sofa, its once vivid reds and greens faded to a soft mixture of pastels.

Eden slipped off her coat and sank onto the sofa. "I'm Eden Walters, and this is Josh Leland. Selma Johnson is my aunt."

"Selma and I were neighbors for over fifty years. Maybe you heard her mention me. Gabby Summers."

Eden shook her head. "I'm sorry; I never knew my aunt. I only met her one time."

"Say, you must be one of them Richmond kids!"

Eden's heart sped up. "Yes, yes, that's right. I'm the oldest."

"It were a shame, splitting you young 'uns up like that. I told Selma it weren't right, but your aunt had a head as hard as a new walnut. It was hard enough for her to raise young Timmy, she said."

"Do you know where they are? Timmy and my aunt?" Eden put in eagerly. "I'm trying to find him and my sisters."

Gabby shook her head. "Selma's been gone near ten years," she said. "Timmy went off somewhere last I heard. I don't recall just where that was." Her voice trailed off in a mumble, and she stared vacantly toward the floor.

Eden shot a glance at Josh. He leaned forward and touched Gabby's arm. "Mrs. Summers?"

Her eyes focused again, and she shook her head. "It's gone, young Eden. Give me your number, though. If I happen to hear from Timmy or remember where he went, I'll call you."

Eden nearly gasped from the pain of disappointment. So close, and to come up empty-handed. It was almost more than she could bear.

Josh rose. "Thanks for your help, Mrs. Summers." He pulled a business card from his wallet. "I'm putting Eden's phone number here," he said, scribbling the number on the back.

"Sometimes things come to me in the night." Mrs. Summers took it, then turned away and tucked it into her purse.

Josh picked up Eden's coat, and she slipped her arms into it. All her bright hopes for the day lay in ashes. He squeezed her hand, and she choked back a sob. What was wrong with her? This lady might remember something. At least it was something to hope for.

Mrs. Summers led the way to the door. Eden paused in the doorway. "Was Timmy happy?" she asked softly.

"Oh my, yes. Such a lovely child. So well-mannered, good in school, very helpful. He used to rake my leaves in the fall and wouldn't take a penny for it."

Eden's eyes flooded with tears. "I don't suppose you have a picture of him?"

Mrs. Summers shook her head. "I'm sorry, little lady, I don't. But you keep your chin up. If I could just remember where he went off to, you might track him down through that."

"Thanks for your help." Josh laid a hand on Mrs. Summers's shoulder, then followed Eden through the door and pulled it shut behind him.

Eden stumbled toward the SUV. Gulping back her tears, she threw open the door and practically fell into her seat. Josh slid into the driver's seat. She felt his eyes on her face, and her lips trembled.

"Aw, Sweetie, don't cry."

Eden fished in her purse for a tissue. "I'm not crying," she quavered. "I never cry."

Josh touched the back of her head, and a sob escaped Eden. "She's dead. My aunt is dead and with her all hope of finding Timmy and my sisters."

He pulled her into his arms. "It's only a delay. We'll find them."

"You have to leave." With his arms around her and her nose buried in his chest, the tension in her shoulders began to ease.

"Not before your birthday tomorrow."

She pulled away and scrubbed at her face with the tissue. "How did you know December fourth is my birthday?"

"You told me, remember?" Regret twisted his lips, and his reluctance to let her go warmed her.

Eden sniffed. "I'd hoped to find them for my birthday." She laughed shakily. "Silly, isn't it? For some reason I thought my birthday would be the start of a new life for me."

"It's not silly. And you never know what tomorrow might bring." Josh turned the key, and the SUV roared to life. "Let's go home to our girl."

Chapter 12

Eden heard the children giggling with Josh in the kitchen. They had banished her to the living room while they prepared her birthday dinner. Josh had been acting strangely all day. She caught him staring at her several times with a bemused smile on his face.

He'd arrived this morning with his arms full of helium balloons. Katie had squealed with delight, and Eden was touched he remembered how much she liked balloons. Samantha had motioned him into the kitchen, and they'd scurried back and forth with their decorations.

Eden tried to occupy herself with wrapping Christmas presents. She'd been torn over whether or not to give Josh a gift. Then she had hit on the idea of making him up a scrapbook of Katie's life so far. Filled with pictures and cute captions, the scrapbook was almost too precious to give away. Josh would love it, though.

Smoke billowed from the kitchen. She jumped to her feet and ran through the kitchen door. "Where's the fire?" She grabbed the fire extinguisher by the back door.

Josh grinned sheepishly. "False alarm. I spilled some cake batter in the oven." The kids, including Katie, were busy decorating her cake. Katie had icing in her hair.

Eden wrinkled her nose, and he leaned over and kissed it. A rush of pleasure soared through her. What was with him today? She couldn't figure him out. He seemed carefree somehow.

"We're almost ready," he told her. "You go in the living room, and we'll bring the cake in there."

Eden laughed and went back to the living room. She didn't know when a birthday of hers had elicited such excitement. Usually there was no celebration other than a cake she baked for herself and the balloons she bought the kids. Now all these balloons were for her. The living room was full of them, bobbing from the ceiling, clustering around the Christmas tree, their ribbons hanging down like confetti.

She didn't have long to wonder. Josh came through the kitchen door carrying the cake. It canted to the left and drooped with runny icing. The candles flickered and sputtered wax over the top and left drips like wax petals. Eden bit her lip to keep from laughing.

Samantha and Amelia carried packages wrapped with more tape than paper. Katie's gift was clutched in her chubby hands, and the bow was now in her hair. The children placed them on the coffee table with a flourish.

"Sit down, Eden." Amelia clapped her hands in excitement.

Eden obeyed and sank onto the sofa.

"Mama," Katie said. Her dimples flashing, she offered her tattered package.

Eden took it. "Thank you, baby girl." Katie tried to help her open it, and Eden let her rip the wrapping paper. Inside was a candle. Katie sniffed. "It smells good, doesn't it?"

Katie nodded, then Cory sidled up to Eden and held out his package. "Uncle Josh helped me find it," he said.

Uncle Josh? Eden glanced at Josh and saw a smile of pleasure curve his lips. He'd worked so hard to get close to Cory. That was one of the reasons she loved him; he cared so much for others. His big heart had taken in all the children.

One by one she opened the packages from the children. There were bath salts, stationery, a lace throw for the piano, and a box of chocolates. Josh had gone to a lot of work with the children.

She sat back against the sofa and sighed with pleasure. It was the nicest birthday she could remember. Josh smiled and pulled the ribbon on a balloon in the corner of the room. He came toward her with a grin, but fear seemed to lurk behind his eyes.

He held out the balloon ribbon. "You'll have to break the balloon to get your gift from me."

"You didn't need to get me anything. You've already spent way too much money. We all know where the money came from for the gifts from the children."

"This is something special." He handed her a pin. "Give it a stab."

She laughed and took the pin. Poised over the balloon, she could see a stuffed bear inside. She held her breath and pricked the balloon with the pin. There was a loud *pop* then the bear dropped into her lap. Eden picked it up and hugged it.

"Mine!" Katie said. She tried to grab it, but Eden

held it away from her.

"No, Sweetie, it's Mommy's."

Josh was looking more uncertain. "What's wrong?" she asked him.

"Um, nothing's wrong. Did you see what the bear was holding?"

Eden glanced down at the bear in her hands. A small, velvet jewelry box was in the bear's hands. Her heart began to pound against her ribs, and she couldn't think.

Josh slid to his knees and took the box from the bear. Opening it, he held up a lovely marquis diamond ring.

Eden gasped, and tears filled her eyes. Her gaze sought Josh's, and the love she saw reflected on his face made it hard to catch her breath.

"I love you, Eden Walters, and I want to spend the rest of my life with you. Will you marry me? Before you answer, I want you to know I got a job here in Wabash so we won't be leaving our kids. I'm going to be working at Ford Meter Box in their export department. And I'm handy with a hammer. I can fix this old house up and make it a traffic stopper." He paused to catch a breath, and Eden laughed.

"All those things don't matter," Eden said softly. She cupped Josh's face in her hands. "I love you, Josh. And Katie loves you. The thought of your leaving has kept me awake nights. Yes, I'll marry you."

"Yippee!" Cory began to dance around the middle of the room, and Samantha and Amelia joined him. Katie tried to dance, too, but was only able to run to keep up with the older kids.

Josh leaned forward and kissed her. The love in his

kiss brought tears flooding to her eyes.

Josh pulled away and dug in his pocket. "There's one more thing," he said, pulling out a piece of paper. "I've got a lead on Crista. It looks like she might be in Arizona. How does Phoenix sound for a honeymoon? Warm sunshine, blue skies."

"You make the sun shine for me," she said, leaning forward to kiss him again. As he took her in his arms, she knew her haven in his arms was the home she'd longed for all her life. Wherever Josh and Katie were would be home.

COLLEEN COBLE

Colleen and her husband, David, have been married thirty years this October. They have two great kids, David Jr. and Kara. Though Colleen is still waiting for grandchildren, she makes do with the nursery inhabitants at New Life Baptist Church. She is very active at her church where she sings and helps her husband with a young adult Sunday school class. She enjoys the various activities with the class, including horseback riding (she needs a stool to mount) and canoeing (she tips the canoe every time). A voracious reader herself, Colleen began pursuing her lifelong dream when a younger brother, Randy Rhoads, was killed by lightning when she was thirty-eight. *Heart Full of Love* is her fifth novella. Her seven novels may be ordered from Barbour Publishing.

Ride the Clouds

by Carol Cox

"Sing to God, sing praise to his name,
extol him who rides on the clouds—
his name is the LORD—and rejoice before him.
A father to the fatherless,
a defender of widows,
is God in his holy dwelling."
PSALM 68:4–5

Prologue

C rista McDaniel eased her foot off the accelerator and brought her car to a stop on the shoulder of Deer Valley Road. Ignoring the hum of traffic on the interstate behind her, she settled into a comfortable position and opened the lid of her mocha latte. Sipping the steaming drink, she turned her gaze toward the mountains to the east. Long shadows took form amidst the saguaros and sagebrush between her and the jagged peaks and gradually swelled into rounded outlines. Lights flared, and the shapes rose from the ground with stately majesty and hovered above the earth, glowing in the predawn dimness.

One by one, the hot air balloons lifted into the lightening sky, their brilliant hues in vivid contrast to the pink streaks of dawn. Crista stared, transfixed, her gaze never wavering from the floating giants until they all hung suspended above her. With a lingering glance, she turned the key in the ignition and swung her car around to the on-ramp, joining the early morning southbound traffic on I-17.

Chapter 1

Remember, the three biggest time thieves you'll deal with are disorganization, indecision, and procrastination. See how they creep into your lives this week. Next class period we'll talk about how you can deal with them."

Crista straightened her stack of class notes with an efficient tap and looked across the lectern at her new students. When North Phoenix Community College first approached her about teaching short-term evening classes on time management, she'd refused abruptly. Providing training in a corporate setting was a far cry from teaching everyone from college students to harried housewives to retirees. The college's persistence and her eventual capitulation a year ago surprised her almost as much as her enjoyment of the class.

At the close of the opening class this second summer session, Crista felt gratified by the enthusiasm her students showed. She had seen lots of eye contact and plenty of note-taking, but not one sign of boredom.

"Please pick up a class syllabus on your way out." She set the papers on a small table near the door. "You'll find an outline of points I plan to cover in each session. Look them over and let me know if there's something you're interested in that isn't listed, or if you see a topic you'd like to explore in greater depth. I'll expect your input next time we meet."

She scooped up her teaching notes and filed them in her briefcase, smiling at each departing student. Quite a varied lot, she noted. Out of twenty pupils, only about half fit the profile she'd originally expected. Tonight's group included several business majors, at least two grandmothers, and several women who simply wanted help scheduling all the activities their busy families were involved in.

Funny how things worked out. As little as she'd wanted to begin teaching in the first place, the widely varied backgrounds of her students were what convinced her that a market for her services existed far beyond the traditional corporate setting. Without that seemingly unimportant step, she might never have broken away from her job to become a freelance efficiency consultant.

Crista snapped the locks on her briefcase and waited for the remaining student to leave so she could switch off the classroom lights. Instead, he paused in front of her. "I enjoyed the class," he said in a warm voice. "I can tell I'm going to learn a lot."

"Thanks." Crista found herself responding to the friendly light in his sky blue eyes. She tried to remember his name from the introductions earlier. "Brad Morgan, right?"

His smile broadened, forming creases in his cheeks. "Do you include memory-improvement techniques in the course, too?"

Crista matched his smile with one of her own. "Put that on your list of things you want to study. As I recall, you're here to learn ways to improve your business operations."

"Right again, and very impressive." His tone became more serious. "Actually, I need to learn more than just how to streamline things; I need to get a handle on the whole concept of being in charge."

Crista raised a quizzical eyebrow and reached for the light switch.

"Let me carry that for you." Brad picked up her briefcase and waited in the hallway while she locked the classroom door. "Would you mind answering a couple of questions on the way to the parking lot?"

Crista hesitated, then nodded agreement. They walked toward the exit while she waited for Brad to continue.

"I never intended to be a business owner," he explained, pushing open the outside door. A warm blanket of air enveloped them. "My uncle owned J&R Machining. He didn't have any kids, so when he passed away six months ago, he left the place to me."

"Had you worked for him for long?"

Brad grimaced. "I never worked for him at all." He laughed at Crista's startled expression. "Believe me, I felt the same way. The business was important to my uncle. He built it up from scratch. In a way, I think he nurtured it like he would have a child. He took great pride in it, and it's done well. His plan was to build it up further, retire in a few years, and let the income take care of his and my aunt's financial needs for the rest of their lives. The idea seemed to be working fine; he just didn't live long enough to reap the benefits."

Brad shook his head slowly. "Being asked to take over came as a total surprise to me, but he and I were always close. He knew I'd do anything I could to help him. He counted on me to see this through, and Aunt Rachel's depending on me. I just hope I can live up to their expectations."

Crista stopped beside her car and leaned against the driver's door. "You have quite a challenge ahead of you." She tilted her head and studied his face. "But you already know that. Being willing to admit you have a lot to learn is a big step in the right direction."

Brad grinned. "It looks like I've come to the right place to get started. Any suggestions on what I'll need to know in addition to the work you'll be assigning?"

"Good question. We'll cover a lot in class, but you'll need to learn much more. What's your background? Do you have managerial experience, or are you starting from square one?"

Brad raked his fingers through his dark brown hair and gave her a rueful smile. "Somewhere below square one, if you want the truth. You're looking at a rank beginner."

Crista couldn't keep her lips from twitching. "So we're talking about more than a slight deficiency here?"

"More like utter desperation. Do you take on special projects?"

Crista considered the prospect, then nodded. "I can loan you some books that will give you a start. We'll see where you want to go from there."

"Is there any way I can get them from you before the

next class? I don't think I have a minute to lose."

"Well. . ." She made it a policy not to socialize with her students, but his predicament touched her. "Where's your business located?"

"Twenty-first Avenue, just south of McDowell." He handed her a business card.

"That'll work. How about if I drop them off on my way to the airport Thursday morning?"

"I've run you out of town already?"

Crista laughed and unlocked her car door. "I do a lot of traveling. I have a seminar in Ohio this weekend."

His smile broadened. "That'll be great. See you Thursday."

❄

Crista strolled into J&R Machining, her nose wrinkling at the acrid smell of machine oil. The harried receptionist took a moment between calls to point out Brad's door at the end of the corridor. Crista took her time, noting the flurry of activity with both approval and concern. The business obviously had potential, but it needed a firm grip on the reins to keep it headed in the right direction.

She paused before knocking on the open door and took in the scene before her. Brad, shirtsleeves rolled up over muscular forearms, cradled the phone between his chin and shoulder and scrabbled frantically through the mound of papers scattered across his desk.

"Uh-huh, uh-huh." He tugged a paper from the bottom of a stack, then tossed it aside and renewed his search. "I'm sure we can beat that price. Just let me pull our spec sheet and get the particulars for you." His confident tone belied the increasingly desperate way he rummaged through the disorganized heap.

Crista leaned against the doorjamb, fascinated.

Brad's elbow dislodged a jumbled pile of papers, which slid to the floor despite his frenzied attempt to catch them. He vanished behind the desk for a moment, then reappeared holding a stapled packet aloft with an expression of triumph. "I have it right here," he announced in a matter-of-fact tone that made Crista bite her lip to keep from laughing out loud. "I'll fax it to you within the next few minutes."

He ended the call and glanced up, his eyes widening when he saw Crista. "How long have you been here?"

"Long enough to know you didn't sign up for my class a moment too soon." Crista handed him the books she carried.

Brad reached for them at the moment the phone rang. A haunted look crossed his face, and he walked past Crista to lean out of the doorway. "Bea!" he called to the receptionist. "Would you hold my calls for the next few minutes, please?"

He turned back to Crista and nodded at the books in his hand. "Thanks for taking the time to drop these off. Sorry about the interruptions. So what do these cover?"

"Some time management basics—setting goals and priorities, delegation. . ." Her gaze shifted to his desk. "Handling paperwork."

Brad followed her glance and winced. "My uncle Jess could lay his hands on anything he needed at a moment's notice, and the desk didn't look any better when he was here." He caught Crista's amused look. "Okay, a little better. But not much. I really am trying, but I just don't seem to be able to get a handle on everything the way he did."

His bleak look caught at Crista's heart. "There's hope," she promised. "And those books can point you in the right direction. At least you'll be making a start. Once you can put these things into practice—"

"Got a second, Brad? Oh, sorry." The stocky man who entered the office looked more irritated than remorseful.

"If you could give me just a few minutes, Nick." Brad's fingers raked a path through his hair.

"That's all right," Crista put in. "I'm just on my way out." She smiled and lifted her hand in a quick good-bye gesture, then started toward the exit. She had passed the receptionist's desk when Brad's voice echoed down the hall.

"Where do I start with these books?" he called. "Which one do I need the most?"

Crista glanced around. Bea spoke into the phone while two incoming lines rang insistently. Behind Brad, Nick drummed his fingers on the doorjamb. She gave Brad a gentle smile. "All of them."

The airliner banked left over Lake Erie. The runways and terminal buildings of Cleveland Hopkins International Airport slid into the distance, and the city itself dwindled into a miniature landscape. Crista settled more comfortably into her seat with a satisfied sigh. The workshop had gone well, she thought, remembering the invitation she'd received to return for a more in-depth seminar in the spring.

Her gaze shifted out the window, and she leaned forward, watching the rolling farmland of Ohio pass by thousands of feet below. Ohio, the state of her birth. She stared intently, searching the depths of her being for some sense of connection or any spark of recognition. Nothing stirred within her.

She sighed, whether from regret or resignation, she wasn't sure. Somewhere down there lay Hillsboro, where she'd lived after becoming a part of the McDaniel family at age five, before their move to Arizona.

With practiced determination, Crista stifled the pang of longing that shot through her. No point in worrying about the dead past or birth parents who hadn't wanted her. The McDaniels had treated her arrival as their daughter as a highlight of their lives and had let her know every moment of the past twenty-four years how much they treasured her.

Fleeting questions danced through her mind, questions she thought she'd put to rest years before. What made her birth family give her up? Why hadn't she been good enough for them?

Pictures from her earliest days as Crista McDaniel showed a winsome child with long curls and huge hazel eyes. As often as she pored over the snapshots as a child, Crista couldn't see anything that would have made her parents not want her. The one remarkable thing about the photos had been the hint of sadness in those wide hazel eyes, and Crista was at a loss to pinpoint its source.

She turned away from the window, pulling a magazine from her briefcase. Better to leave such questions safely buried where they could cause her no heartache. She found immense satisfaction in her career and she loved her family with a fierce devotion. Life was good. Organized. Under control. No need to stir up doubts that would only lead to pain.

Thumbing through her magazine, she spotted an article titled "Twenty Ways to Streamline Your Work Space." Her thoughts flew to Brad Morgan, and she wondered how his weekend had gone. Crista leaned back against the headrest and closed her eyes, smiling at the memory of Brad's attempts to make light of the chaotic state of his office. She hoped he'd taken her seriously and had spent the past couple of days immersed in those books. If ever anyone needed to learn how to manage his time, Brad Morgan fit the bill.

Crista's smile broadened. What a challenge it would be to take him in hand and get him and his business organized! Her lips parted and her eyes flew open. Where had that thought come from? She had her seminars and her college class to keep her busy. Besides, she had a policy of keeping her relationship with her students confined to the classroom.

Then why had she broken that policy and gone out of her way to loan books to this particular student? The question accused her like a pointing finger. Because his was an extreme case, and his business was in danger of falling apart without immediate help, she told herself, bridling at the feeling that she had to be on the defensive. She had offered to drop off the books without a second thought, in the same way she would stop to render aid if she witnessed an accident.

Thus mollified, she reopened her magazine with a snap, determined to read every word between its covers on the way home.

Chapter 2

Once again Crista watched her students file out the door. They chattered excitedly about the time wasters they'd identified this week, a sign they were putting classroom concepts into practice. She'd been able to meet her goal of matching all the names and faces by the second class of the session and had a better sense of which students had signed up for the class just for something to do and which would seriously pursue the strategies she would present over the course of the next few weeks.

Brad took his time putting away his notes and sidled up to her desk as the last students straggled out. "I brought these back." He held out her books. Crista suppressed a giggle when she saw the apple sitting atop the stack.

"Trying to bribe the teacher?" She raised one eyebrow in mock severity. Brad responded with a slow grin that sent a tingle up her spine. She took a quick count of the books and looked at him in surprise. "You've read them all already?"

"That's all I did this weekend except for going to church," he told her. "The more I read, the more I realized

I need all the help I can get." He shuffled his feet and cleared his throat. "Would it be totally inappropriate if I asked you out for coffee? There are a lot of things I read that I'd like to discuss, and it wouldn't be fair to the rest of the students to spend class time on my problems."

Crista hesitated, wondering whether she could take on this challenge and still maintain a professional distance between teacher and student. But it wouldn't be anything like a date, only the opportunity to give someone the extra help that might make all the difference between his failure and success.

"I knew things weren't going as smoothly as they should," Brad confided, stirring cream into his coffee. "No surprises there. The books did help me get an idea of where I've been making some mistakes. I'm already spotting some of those time thieves you talked about, but I still don't know how to deal with them. Any suggestions?"

Crista sipped her latte and took a moment to think about her reply. "Let me give you a couple of examples based on what I saw last Thursday. No matter how hard you try, you're never going to accomplish anything if you don't make some significant changes, and soon. The telephone, for instance—does it ring incessantly?"

Brad propped his chin in his hand and nodded wearily. "Sometimes I think I spend more time answering that phone than doing anything else."

"You're probably right. But does anything productive come of it?"

"Not so you'd notice. Mostly it's clients wanting information on pricing, status of orders they've already placed, that kind of thing."

"So why are you answering those questions? Let your receptionist deal with that, or at least have her screen your calls and route things like that to someone else who can handle them. You're the boss, remember? You've got a company to run."

Brad flipped his notebook open and started scribbling.

"For the calls that do need to come to you, let your caller know right up front how much time you can give them. Don't let them ramble; get to the point, then get back to work. You can do that in a businesslike way and still be polite."

"Good," Brad muttered. "I don't want to run off customers."

"No, but you can't let them use you as a social outlet, either. And don't waste time looking for information while someone is holding on the phone." She grinned, remembering Brad's frantic search for the spec sheet. "If you can't lay your hands on whatever you're looking for instantly, let them know you'll get back with them later. Then follow through on that. You'll show them you value their time as well as your own, plus let them know you keep your word. Are you getting all this?"

"Just don't talk any faster." Brad shook his hand and flexed his fingers. "Sounds like I need to do some immediate restructuring."

"While you're at it," Crista continued, "do something about that desk. Set aside an evening or a day this weekend. I'll bet you could throw over half of those papers away. The rest need to be organized and filed by subject so you can find what you need when you need it. You'll be amazed at the difference it makes." Her mouth curved up in a playful grin. "And think what fun it'll be to find out what the surface of your desk looks like."

❄

Brad shot a quick glance at Crista then let his gaze linger on her face. Those enormous hazel eyes, usually so solemn, sparkled with mischief, and her impish smile revealed an unsuspected dimple at the corner of her mouth. His own lips curved upward in response.

"Thanks for the tips. I'll make some changes on handling the phone calls, and I promise I'll tackle that desk sometime this week."

❄

That fleeting glimpse of Crista's playful side stayed with Brad throughout the following week. When he cleared the last piece of paper from his desk after an all-day sorting marathon on Saturday, he could imagine her standing nearby, applauding his efforts.

He closed his eyes to picture her more clearly. With every approving nod, her shiny brown hair would sway across her shoulders in gentle rhythm, and the hint of a dimple would show at the corner of her mouth. Yes, he thought, shoving the last folder into its proper file, Crista would be proud of what he'd accomplished in only a few short days.

Why did that matter so much? The question stopped him cold. Brad hauled a trash bag full of papers to the Dumpster in the alley, deep in thought. Teacher or not, he realized he'd like to get to know Crista McDaniel on a more personal level.

He propped up the heavy Dumpster lid with one arm

and tipped in the bag with the other. "This is a real shock, Lord. Am I just being drawn to an attractive woman, or is this from You?"

He let the lid drop and trotted back to the building to lock up. Was Crista a believer? Their conversations so far had dealt with time management issues. Spiritual matters hadn't come up at all. He thought back to their last visit to the coffee shop. She hadn't let anything slip that would make him think she knew the Lord. But he hadn't said anything, either.

On the other hand, her actions spoke of kindness and concern for others. When they left their table to go to the register, a little girl had careened between the booths, barging right into Crista. Instead of snapping at her, Crista knelt beside the child to make sure she wasn't hurt. The little girl slipped plump arms around Crista's neck, and Crista gave her a quick squeeze in return. That seemed promising.

And when they paid their bills—separate checks at Crista's insistence—the cashier had given Crista an extra dollar in change. She hadn't noticed it until they were out in the parking lot and went straight back inside to square accounts. Would an unbeliever be that scrupulous?

He stretched his weary muscles and headed for his car. A hot shower and a session of prayer seemed in order.

❄

Droplets peppered the window, and Crista pulled back the curtains to enjoy the rain. With Phoenix getting only seven inches of rainfall a year, even a light sprinkle was an event she didn't want to miss. She settled back into her desk chair and slit open the next envelope in her stack of mail. Her face lit up with pleasure when she saw the confirmation for another seminar. The choice to set up her own Web page seemed to be paying off. This would be her tenth out-of-state seminar since last Christmas.

Double-checking the location and date, she jotted a brief note on her calendar and set up a file for the event, pleased that she'd be visiting North Carolina for the first time. When she stopped to think about it, she had as ideal a life as anyone could want—a loving family, an organized routine, and a job she loved. She'd worked hard to reach this point in her career and would have to work even harder to stay there, but the effort had been worth it.

She pulled her road atlas from her reference shelf and flipped it open to the page for North Carolina. Just exactly where was Wilmington? A quick search located its position not far from the coast on the Cape Fear River. A slow smile spread across her face. Maybe she'd schedule in an extra day for sightseeing and spend some time on the beach. Growing up in dry Arizona made the allure of so much water too tempting to pass up.

She chuckled at her mounting excitement. She ought to be able to find some wonderful gifts to bring back for the rest of her family, too. They teased her about her penchant for doing her Christmas shopping year-round, but they had to admit it paid off in the long run.

Speaking of family. . .Crista turned her attention to her planner. They'd be celebrating Lindsey's birthday on Sunday. A smug expression crossed her face. Her sister's present sat on the hall closet shelf, wrapped and ready. Her brother Rod probably wouldn't remember he needed to think about a present until Saturday evening.

Crista grinned, remembering Rod's panicked calls for last-minute advice in previous years. The family had been aware of her fondness for planning and efficiency long before she decided to make it her career. She knew it seemed strange to them when they first heard she planned to make a living out of being organized. It didn't fit the typical young-girl goals of being a teacher, nurse, or flight attendant, but it gave Crista a sense of fulfillment unlike any other she'd ever experienced.

Being organized meant being in charge of her life. It meant security and control. The McDaniel clan had eventually accepted her choice, although she suspected most of them shared her father's opinion when he pushed his glasses up on his balding forehead and told her, "I can't say I understand it, Honey, but if that's what you want, I'm behind you 100 percent." Only her mother seemed to understand her consuming need for structure, but the rest accepted her decision. Rather, they accepted her. That was enough.

Brad Morgan seemed to accept her, too. She closed her eyes, remembering his friendly smile and open manner. She found it easy to relax in his presence. It wouldn't be hard to get lost in those sky blue eyes.

Crista pulled her thoughts from Brad and checked her watch. Good, she could take a few more minutes before she had to get back to work. She leaned her elbows on her desk and propped her chin on her cupped hands, taking time to savor the sights and smells of a desert rain. Her sense of contentment grew.

"God sends rain on the just and the unjust," an elderly neighbor used to say. Crista didn't know that God spent much time considering how the weather He sent affected people, whether they were good or bad. But if He ever did spare a thought about Crista McDaniel, she'd suspect He'd worked overtime to give her a good life.

Chapter 3

Brad loitered outside the classroom door. The more he'd prayed over the past few weeks, the more he felt God's urging to develop a deeper relationship with Crista.

It hadn't taken much persuasion. Tonight had been their last class meeting. If he missed this opportunity to move their relationship beyond the classroom level, he might not get another chance.

Two older ladies exited the classroom, talking a mile a minute. The one with tinted blue hair slowed her step and gave him a roguish wink. "Cliff had some questions she's trying to answer, but I'm sure she'll be out in a minute or two." Motioning to her companion to wait, she poked her head back inside the room and called, "Crista, you'd better get rid of that old geezer. There's someone out here who's a whole lot better-looking." Cackling gleefully, the two made their way to the exit.

White-haired Cliff appeared in the doorway and peered at Brad from beneath beetling brows. "You'd better be worth it, young fellow," he growled. With a playful poke in the ribs, he left Brad standing in the hallway.

Slowly, he reentered the classroom. Crista stacked her papers and packed her briefcase as efficiently as ever, but the spots of color high on her cheeks told him she hadn't been immune to the trio's needling.

"Are you up for coffee again?" he ventured, hoping their teasing hadn't scared her off.

He held his breath when she hesitated, then let it out in a whoosh of relief when she nodded assent and accompanied him to his SUV.

"How was your weekend?" he asked when they'd placed their orders, hoping a neutral question would break the uneasy silence.

She brightened. "Good. We celebrated my sister's birthday."

Finally, a topic that seemed safe. "Do you come from a big family?"

A faint shadow flitted across her face before she responded. "There are five of us. Mom, Dad, one son, and two girls. I'm in the middle."

Brad grinned. "As focused as you seem to be, I would have sworn you were a firstborn. So much for birth order." He took a bite of raspberry cheesecake and caught Crista's quick grimace. What was going on here? She obviously enjoyed spending time with her family. Why did talking about them make her so uncomfortable?

He tried another tactic. "Have you always lived in Phoenix?"

Crista blinked rapidly, then composed her features. "We moved here just before I started first grade. Before that, we lived in Ohio." She sipped her cappuccino and leaned against the booth's padded back, seeming more at ease. "My mom had problems with her health. Her asthma got so bad the doctor told my dad he needed to get her to a drier climate. You can't get much drier than Phoenix," she added with a grin.

Brad chuckled, relieved. Whatever had been bothering her, she seemed to have gotten past it. "That's the truth. My folks came from Oklahoma, but they moved here before I was born. My mom's taken up genealogy the past couple of years, and we've learned more about our ancestors than we ever really wanted to know. We tease her about it a lot, but I have to admit it's kind of nice to know about your roots." His smile faded at the dismal expression on Crista's face.

"What is it?" he asked, reaching out to cover her hand with his. "I feel like I said something wrong, but I don't know what it is."

Crista shook her head in a jerky movement. "It isn't you; it's me." She pulled her hand away and picked up her napkin, tearing tiny pieces from its edge. Without stopping her assault on the paper square, she looked up to meet his gaze. "The fact is, I'm adopted. I have no idea about biological ancestors, or roots, or anything like that."

A tiny smile played across her face. "I have the best family in the world, though, and I came to terms with the whole adoption thing a long time ago. I don't know what got into me just now. I'm sorry."

"You don't have any reason to apologize. I didn't mean to bring up a tender subject. Are your brother and sister adopted, too?"

"No, just me. They were born McDaniels. When I was four, I was placed in their home as a foster child.

They adopted me when I was five. Rod is two years older and Lindsey's three years younger, so I fit right in the middle. I really don't think about it much anymore. We're a family; how we got that way doesn't matter."

Brad felt a warm glow, surprised and pleased at her openness. "Do you know much about your birth family?"

The shuttered look returned. "No. I'm really not interested." Her fingers shredded more of the napkin into confetti. "So how are things going at your business?"

"I've made progress," he said, yielding to her obvious desire to change the subject. "I'm amazed at how much difference it's made just to have the responsibility for all those phone calls off my shoulders."

"Told you so." She patted the torn bits of paper into a neat pile. "What about your desk?" She raised a skeptical eyebrow.

"It's walnut."

Crista gasped delightedly. "You really did clear it off?"

"Of course. Didn't you expect your star pupil to follow orders?"

"No comment." Crista laughed and rose to accompany Brad to the register.

He laid his hand over hers when she started to open her purse. "This is my treat," he told her. "Tonight wasn't about business."

In the parking lot, he leaned against his fender, enjoying the balmy evening air. Crista joined him, only inches away. Brad wished he dared put his arm around her shoulder and pull her closer but refrained.

"Thanks for the coffee and the talk," she said. "I enjoyed it."

"Even if you had to listen to Cliff's heckling first?" he teased.

Crista laughed, a sound Brad decided he wanted to hear more often. "I guess it wasn't so bad." She twisted her fingers together. "And I really am sorry about getting so on edge about all that talk about my biological parents."

Brad frowned. "I wouldn't have brought any of that up if I'd known it would be a problem. I guess we all have issues that are sore spots."

Crista turned to face him. "You, too?"

Brad nodded, crossing his arms. "My dad is an alcoholic. He's a recovered alcoholic now, and these days we get along fine, but there were some times when I was growing up I'd just as soon forget."

Crista rested her hand on his arm. "That's a tough one. So how did you learn to handle it?"

"It wasn't easy. Nothing really worked. . .until I learned to turn the whole situation over to God." He studied her face, waiting for her reaction. When she stiffened and pulled away, he felt like he'd received a sledge-hammer blow to the heart.

"I'm glad it helped you." Crista turned to open the passenger door.

Brad reached around to open it for her, trying to think of the right words to say. How could someone with such a sweet nature be so prickly about a mere mention of God?

Crista stared out the window on the drive back to the campus, wishing the knot in her stomach would disappear. She'd hoped to get to know Brad better, and tonight things seemed to be progressing nicely. . .up until the point when he brought God into the conversation. The leaden weight of disappointment that settled in her chest unnerved her. What did his beliefs matter?

"I guess I said the wrong thing again." Brad's low-voiced comment brought her back to the present.

Crista sighed. "I believe in God. You can't look around and really think everything just happened by accident." She wet her lips. "But that's where it ends, as far as I can see. He started everything and put it into motion, but that's it. I don't see where He cares about any of us as individuals."

Brad didn't answer right away. "What about the people whose lives have changed because of Him?"

Crista pressed her lips together. "It's nice if they can pump themselves up and use that idea to help them through life, but I have my family. I don't need anything more."

"I see. You and your family seem really close." He paused, then added, "Did you ever go to church together?"

Crista relaxed, and a smile spread across her face. "At Christmas," she said. "Christmas is absolutely the best time of the year. All the giving, the sharing, spending time together. The tree and the lights." She sighed, lost in happy memories. "We used to go to the Christmas Eve service every year to watch the kids' program and hear the Christmas story."

Brad turned into the college parking lot and pulled to a stop beside Crista's car. "I don't get it." He swiveled in his seat to face her. "How could you enjoy the story of Christmas so much and still miss the idea that God cares about each one of us?"

Crista shook her head wearily. "Look, you spend Sundays going to church, right?"

He nodded, looking puzzled.

"You enjoy spending time with the people there?"

"Sure. Fellowship is a special part of it."

Crista smiled in triumph. "Well, that's what I do with my Sundays, too. I have fellowship—with my family—but I don't have to go to a church to do it."

Brad rested his arm on the steering wheel and leaned toward her. "There's more to it than just fellowship. I'm talking about a relationship with God."

The knot in Crista's stomach tightened. "And the people who know God are the ones you find in church, right?"

Brad hesitated, looking like he'd walked into a minefield and didn't know where to step next. "Right," he said, drawing the word out slowly.

"Then I'm not interested." She opened the door and got into her car before Brad could get out to help her.

She turned the key in the ignition and drove away, giving Brad only a brief wave of her fingers. By the time she reached her driveway, she was already rebuking herself for her rudeness.

"What is wrong with you?" she scolded, crunching across the buff gravel of her yard to her front door. "You blew a chance to make a good impression on him."

She let herself in and sank onto the couch. Brad seemed like a wonderful person and she felt a definite chemistry between them. Or did until she threw her temper tantrum, she reminded herself. But was it all her fault? Why did he have to bring God into their budding relationship?

If she hadn't been edgy about the adoption discussion, she probably wouldn't have overreacted like that. She needed to apologize. If the subject came up again, she'd have to hold her tongue. But maybe it wouldn't. Surely something like that couldn't dominate Brad's life.

❄

Brad stared at the ceiling, the twisted sheets attesting to his inability to sleep. "I guess that answered my question, didn't it, Lord?"

He punched his pillow and tried to find a comfortable position. He'd been so sure Crista believed. Her gentle spirit, her willingness to help. . .everything pointed that way. But her reaction tonight had set him straight. Now what?

There went the dating relationship he'd halfway mapped out. He'd seen too many friends ignore the biblical injunction against being unequally yoked and fall into the trap of dating an unbeliever. They'd been hurt or, worse, compromised their faith in situations that should never have been allowed to start. He'd consciously avoided entanglements like that and had been relieved at the trouble it had saved him.

But now. . .the sharpness of his disappointment surprised him. He'd only known Crista a brief time; surely it shouldn't be hard to forget her and move on.

"Then why can't I sleep?" He sat up and leaned against the headboard, wrapping his arms around his knees. Try as he might, he couldn't shake the feeling that God had brought Crista into his life for a purpose. Could it be possible that God intended him to know her strictly as a friend, as someone placed in her life to help lead her to Christ?

Brad sighed and dropped his head onto his arms. "If that's what You want me to do, Lord, I'm willing. But You'll have to help me dial down my feelings and be ready to just be her friend."

Chapter 4

C rista pushed open the door to J&R Machining and strode down the hallway to Brad's office, hoping her cool professional demeanor would hide her nervousness. How would he react to an unannounced visit after her behavior the other night?

She paused beyond Brad's range of vision outside his open door and surveyed the office. He really had cleared his desk, she noted with delight. More than that, he'd managed to keep it clean, a positive sign.

She raised her hand to knock, then dropped it back to her side, overcome by unaccustomed shyness. Would he think her unbearably pushy to show up this way? She knew she hadn't acted well during their last visit, but she'd felt so defensive with all his talk about religion. Now that she knew he had strong feelings in that area, she could steer the conversation away from that dangerous ground.

Unless he was some kind of fanatic, he wouldn't bring God into every discussion. Her attraction to Brad was undeniable, and she wanted to pursue their relationship. She knew that looking for perfection in anyone was unrealistic.

Everyone had some irritating flaw. If Brad tended to be overly interested in religious things, it didn't need to color their whole friendship. She could overlook it.

Lifting her hand before she could change her mind, she rapped on the doorjamb. Brad looked up, his face creasing in a smile when he saw her. Crista's heart lightened, then fell when his expression changed to a more formal one.

"I just thought I'd stop by and see how things were going," she told him, keeping her voice neutral. She nodded at his desk. "Looks like you've really made progress here. How's the situation with the phone calls?"

The ring of the telephone interrupted Brad's answer. He gave Crista a sheepish glance and picked up the receiver. After a quick exchange of words, he transferred the call back to Bea. "Delegated without a twinge of guilt," he announced. "How was that?"

She couldn't help but mirror his triumphant grin. "Not bad. Now what about—"

"Brad, we need to—" The stocky man she had seen on her previous visit burst through the doorway, stopping just before he barreled into her. He looked at Crista, then at Brad, and sighed. "Will you be long?"

Crista bristled at his tone. She could be a new customer for all the man knew. Brad's business wouldn't be helped if every visitor to his office met the same surly attitude.

"I'll call you just as soon as I'm through here, Nick." Brad looked at Crista apologetically when they were alone again.

"Nick's been the mainstay here since I can remember.

He knows more about running this place than anyone except Uncle Jess. Every time I wonder what on earth I'm doing here, I know that Nick is wondering twice as much."

Crista bit her tongue to keep from reminding Brad who was in charge.

"I can't fire him." Brad's comment paralleled her thoughts so closely she jumped. "I'll admit his attitude is irritating, but his whole focus is on how to make the business better. He's the biggest asset Uncle Jess left me."

"Even so," Crista said, "you have to protect yourself from interruptions like that. If Nick has ideas on improving the business, fine. But you need to establish a set time for doing that. Maybe you could discuss his ideas just before closing time every afternoon. If he knows you'll be here and ready to listen, he can save up all his suggestions for then."

"Good idea." Brad glanced at his watch. "I'm running late for lunch today. Have you eaten?" When Crista shook her head, he motioned her toward the visitor's chair. "If you'll wait here while I let Nick know we can talk later this afternoon, I'd like to take you to lunch." He gave her a friendly grin. "Call it payback for all the free advice I've been getting."

Crista settled into the chair, her heart pounding in relief. Brad hadn't held a grudge. Maybe they could get things back on track.

Brad pulled into the parking lot at Garcia's. "I hope you like Mexican food," he said, escorting Crista inside. He hadn't believed it when he looked up and saw her standing in his doorway. He hoped he'd covered up his joy quickly enough that he hadn't looked like a lovesick schoolboy. His focus was on friendship now.

They followed the hostess to their table. Crista had a point. He was the boss. He didn't have to clock in and out of the office. Today he was going to take a long lunch and not worry about what Bea or Nick or anyone else thought about it.

He ate at Garcia's often enough to know he'd order one of their incredible chimichangas, so he contented himself with studying Crista's profile while she looked at the menu. A stray strand of hair wisped across her forehead, and he stopped himself from tucking it back into place.

Friends, he reminded himself. *Just friends.* Crista's spiritual status had to be the important thing here. Resolutely, he determined to squelch his feelings and keep things on a platonic level. Nothing had ever been said or done to imply otherwise. They could go on just as they had begun. Crista didn't ever have to know he once intended to pursue something deeper.

❄

Crista watched Brad bow his head briefly when the waitress brought their meals, and her brows tightened in a quick frown. He hadn't made a big production of it, though, hadn't prayed out loud, or asked her to join him. Her forehead smoothed again. If he didn't try to drag her into praying with him, she could ignore it.

His gaze locked with hers as soon as he raised his head. Crista lost herself in the depths of his eyes, marveling at how much he could stir her feelings after such a brief acquaintance.

Already a special connection seemed to exist between them. A connection Crista realized she'd be happy to see grow and flourish. She couldn't name one negative quality Brad had, unless she counted his preoccupation with God and church. But surely she could wean him away from that.

A thought struck her. He spent his Sundays at church because he enjoyed being around people he felt comfortable with. Why not get him involved with the most special group of people she knew? She realized Brad was talking and focused her attention on him.

"I'm curious," he said, eyes twinkling. "What's the schedule of an efficiency expert like? I know you have your evening classes and do some seminars out of state, but what do you do the rest of the time?"

Crista smiled, enjoying his interest in her. "I do a lot of workshops and corporate training sessions here in the valley. In fact," she added, trying not to sound boastful, "I'm pretty well booked for the next six months. That's really exciting to me because I've only been working freelance for the past year. When I started, I figured I could use my savings to help me get through the dry spells until I got established, but it hasn't been necessary."

Brad's eyebrows raised admiringly. "Pretty impressive. So how do you manage to fit it all in?"

"It isn't hard. Really," she insisted, laughing when Brad rolled his eyes. "Just a matter of organization. I schedule my local work during the first part of the week to leave weekends free for trips out of state. When I'm not traveling, I read trade journals, study, or plan upcoming seminars. It's simple."

Brad gave her a quizzical look. "What about evenings. . . on the nights you aren't teaching, that is?"

"That's when I take care of household details—paying bills, shopping, things like that."

"No time for yourself?"

She shrugged. "I love my work. I'm very happy doing things exactly this way."

"But what about fun? Don't you ever schedule in some time to relax?"

What an opening! Crista couldn't have set it up better if she'd tried. "As a matter of fact, I do. Want to see for yourself?"

Brad grinned. "A chance to watch scheduled relaxation? I wouldn't miss it."

"You're on. I'll be in Wisconsin this weekend, but how about dinner at my parents' the Sunday after that?"

Brad raised one eyebrow. "That's your big day out?"

"Trust me. You'll see how much fun it can be. Straight up noon, all right?"

Brad shifted uncomfortably. "Church doesn't let out until twelve or a little after."

Crista tensed. Couldn't he let go of church for one day? "I'll talk to Mom and see if we can put it back a little. Say between twelve-thirty and one?"

Brad smiled. "That'll be fine." He glanced down at his plate, then back at Crista. "Why don't you come to church with me? That way you can keep me organized and make sure I get to your parents' house on time."

Crista didn't miss the challenging glint in his eyes. She tensed, then relented. Fair was fair. If she showed a willingness to meet Brad halfway, maybe he'd be more inclined to see things from her point of view. What harm could one church service do? "Okay," she said, squaring her shoulders. *But don't get used to it,* she added to herself.

✻

Crista took her time dressing for church, trying on three different dresses before she settled on one she hoped would be suitable. She smoothed the flaring skirt over her slim hips and checked its lines in the full-length mirror. Why had she let herself in for this? "Because you're looking at the long-term goal instead of one day's discomfort," she told her reflection.

She placed clothes to wear after church—jeans, a polo shirt, and sneakers—in a canvas bag and waited for Brad to pick her up. Remembering the undeniable flicker of interest her parents had shown when she informed them she would be bringing a male guest along, she hoped she wasn't sending out the wrong signals to her family.

Surely not. Her family had always kept an open house to her acquaintances. She and Rod and Lindsey had invited plenty of friends over before. And Brad was quickly becoming a close friend.

Her thoughts turned back to their lunch together. After the way things had gone so well, she'd half expected him to kiss her good-bye when they returned to his office, but he'd only squeezed her hand and promised to pick her up for church today.

Crista had to admit their relationship confused her. She sensed Brad felt as attracted to her as she did to him. He lit up when they were together and seemed to enjoy her company. Why, then, did he pull away emotionally at times?

She picked up her brush and ran it through her shoulder-length hair for the fourth time, making sure the ends curved under in smooth lines. Her reflection showed an oval face framed by soft brown waves. A face with the regulation two eyes, one nose, one mouth, all in their proper places.

Maybe she wasn't anything exceptional, but she couldn't see anything drastically wrong. Yet her birth parents had found something so unacceptable they didn't want to keep her. The knowledge gnawed at her. Did Brad see the same thing? Did that explain his emotional distance?

She heard his SUV pull into the driveway and sighed. Time for church.

Chapter 5

Brad watched Crista fidget in the pew beside him. He knew she didn't have much church background, but he'd never expected her to be this edgy. She tried hard not to show her uneasiness, but the constant tiny motions she made with her feet and the whiteness of her tightly laced fingers gave her away. It couldn't be more evident that she wished she could be anywhere but here.

He frowned. What kind of unbelieving nonsense had her family instilled to make her so antagonistic toward the things of God? And what kind of afternoon did he have to look forward to with people like that?

Not for the first time, he wondered how wise he'd been to accept Crista's invitation. At first it seemed like a way to get to know Crista better and open further opportunities to share the gospel. But would it come across to her family as having more than a friendly interest in her?

They stood for the last hymn. Brad tried to forget his misgivings about their afternoon together and pour his heart into the song of praise. Beside him, Crista barely moved her lips. Her stoic expression tore at his heart. If she could only get past whatever hurdles her family had placed in her way to discover the freedom found in knowing Christ.

Brad had envisioned a lively discussion of the morning's sermon on the way to her parents' house, but they made the drive in near silence. Crista spoke only to direct him and to point out the house when they arrived. When he pulled to a stop in their driveway, she grabbed her bag and bolted from the vehicle.

Brad followed slowly, trying to prepare himself for whatever lay ahead. He surveyed the house and yard. In contrast to Crista's easy-care desert landscaping, this lawn flourished green in spite of the late summer heat and showed the results of meticulous grooming. The stucco house looked equally well kept.

"Hi, Hon. Come on in," called a voice in response to Crista's knock on the screen door. "We're back in the family room."

Crista led him through an airy living room done in earth tones and into a large informal area. Three people rose from the massive trestle table to greet them. "We missed you last week, Sweetie." The older woman enveloped Crista in a warm hug, then turned to smile at him. "You must be Brad," she said, squeezing his hands. "We're so glad you could come."

"Thanks." Brad had barely responded to her welcoming smile when a meaty hand enveloped his own.

"Good to have you here, Son." The stocky, balding man clapped him on the shoulder with a force that knocked his breath from him.

Crista chuckled. "We aren't much for formal introductions, Brad. You've just met my parents. And over here," she nodded at the athletic-looking brunette watching the scene with unconcealed interest, "is my sister, Lindsey."

"Nice to meet you." Lindsey stepped forward and shook Brad's hand, then pointed out the large windows overlooking the backyard. "That's our brother, Rod, out there, trying to keep up with his munchkins." She indicated a slender, dark-haired man chasing a Frisbee with three little girls. Lindsey turned to Crista. "Mary's out of town visiting her mom, so Rod gets to baby-sit today."

"It'll do him good." Crista laughed. "He doesn't look any too upset about it."

"Nope. Rod's a terrific dad. Just like Steve's going to be someday."

"Where is Steve, anyway?" Crista asked her sister.

Lindsey grimaced. "He had to work this weekend. Kind of like someone else I know," she said, slanting a playful look at Crista. "Steve's my fiancé," she informed Brad, "and Mary is Rod's wife. So today you're getting the full effect of the McDaniel clan without any of their softening influence." Her sparkling eyes made it clear that she didn't mean her words to be taken seriously.

Crista went off to change before lunch and came back looking much more relaxed in her casual clothes. Mrs. McDaniel seated Brad between herself and Crista and kept his plate filled with pork chops and mashed potatoes until he had to beg her to stop.

Rod's three daughters kept up a lively conversation all through the meal. Afterward, Mrs. McDaniel insisted on cleaning up while the rest went to the park across the street to "work some more of the steam out of those youngsters," as Mr. McDaniel good-naturedly put it. He settled himself in a leather recliner and disappeared behind the Sunday paper.

Crista and Rod tossed the Frisbee to the kids and each other, leaving Brad and Lindsey to seek out the only shade available under the spindly branches of a paloverde tree. They settled themselves on the sparse, sun-bleached grass. "So what do you think of our family?" Lindsey asked, leaning back against the paloverde's pale green trunk.

"I think you're all pretty wonderful." Brad's answer to her direct question came without conscious thought, surprising him with its truth. What happened to the dysfunctional clan of his imagination who had turned Crista against church and the things of God with their ungodly ways? He'd never felt so at home with a group of strangers in such a short time.

"Have you and Crista been seeing each other long?" Lindsey's casual tone didn't match the quick look she shot at him from beneath lowered lashes.

"We haven't. . .we aren't exactly 'seeing each other,' " Brad said. "Not in a dating sense, anyway. We met in one of the night classes she teaches, and we've become good friends." He wasn't prepared for the pang of disappointment this reminder brought.

"Oh." Lindsey sounded as deflated as he felt. "Crista said the same thing when she told us you'd be coming, but I'd kind of hoped. . .well, never mind." She grinned at him, sweeping her long dark hair back with both hands and twisting it into a knot. "I'm glad she has you as a friend. I just thought it would be nice if she'd finally let herself get interested in someone."

"What do you mean, 'let herself'?" Brad asked, ignoring the twinge his conscience gave him at his nosiness. Lindsey seemed to have no compunctions about discussing her reserved sister. If he wanted to understand Crista better, this might be a good way to get the information he needed.

Lindsey shrugged, seeming to search for the right words. "Don't get me wrong. Crista's a great sister and a wonderful person. It's just that she holds on so tight to her feelings. We've shared everything since we were kids, but even with me, there are areas of her life that she keeps to herself. I think maybe she's afraid of getting hurt." She turned a concerned gaze on her sister, romping with their nieces, then looked back at Brad with a rueful smile. "I guess making a good friend is a start."

Brad shifted, crossing his legs and leaning his elbows on his knees. He hated probing like this, but if Lindsey was in a sharing mood, maybe he'd find out as much as he could while he had the opportunity. "You said something about getting hurt. Did she have a bad experience with a boyfriend?"

"Nothing like that." Lindsey shook her head in a decisive gesture. "Crista's always kept a bit of a wall around her, but she's built up a higher wall over the years. She loves spending time with the family, but she doesn't have much of a personal life besides that, have you noticed?"

Brad murmured assent. Lindsey's revelation echoed his own observations. He drew a deep breath, wondering if he was venturing out on forbidden territory. "Do you think it has anything to do with her being adopted?"

"She told you about that? Good." Lindsey gave him a relieved smile. "I think that may have a lot to do with it," she said slowly. "But not in the sense you might think. She's a part of this family just as much as Rod and I are, and she knows that. But it bothers her that her birth family gave her away. I think it bothers her a lot. Sort of like she feels secure with us because we're the ones who love her, but if her original parents didn't want her, she's afraid to open herself up to that kind of rejection from anyone else. Does that make sense?"

Brad nodded, sorting this new information out in his mind. "I think it does. Does she know anything about her birth family? Anything that would let her know why she was placed for adoption?"

Lindsey paused before answering. "I think she knows some of the story, but not all of it. Maybe I'm wrong, but I have this feeling that if she could locate them and find out the truth, it might be the key to letting her relax and enjoy life." She plucked a blade of grass from the hard-packed ground. "I worry sometimes about the long-term effect this will have on her. She needs to deal with the past and forgive them and go on with her life, you know?"

The Frisbee clipped Brad on the shoulder and landed between them, followed by three squealing little girls. Brad filed Lindsey's comments in his memory, wishing their conversation hadn't been interrupted.

❄

"So what did you think about my family?" Crista leaned back in the seat, looking more relaxed than he'd ever seen her. She looked younger, he thought. More open, more vulnerable.

131

"They're great. I don't know when I've enjoyed an afternoon more." Brad stopped for a red light, then turned onto I-10.

"Even a Sunday afternoon?" She smirked and shot him a glance from the corner of her eye. "Okay, that wasn't fair. I admit it. But can you see now why I don't feel the need for church people to fill some so-called void in my life?"

Walk cautiously, Brad warned himself. "So Sunday's always been your family's day together?"

"Mm-hm. Ever since I can remember. When I was little, we'd go to the zoo, or spend the day at North Mountain Park, or pack a picnic lunch and eat it out by some petroglyphs Dad knew about. We always had something special going on." She sighed and leaned her head back against the seat. "You seemed to get along well with him."

Brad grinned. "Your dad? He's quite a guy. I really enjoyed talking to him. We seemed to be on the same wavelength about nearly everything."

"See?" Crista leveled her gaze at him. "People can be nice without being churchy."

Brad racked his brain and sent up a quick prayer for the right answer while he maneuvered his vehicle into Crista's driveway. "You're absolutely right. They can be nice. The trouble is. . . ," he paused, hunting for the words he wanted, "being nice just isn't enough when it comes to eternity."

Crista's brow wrinkled in consternation. "What do you mean?"

"You can be the nicest, most moral person on earth, but without Jesus as your Savior—"

Crista sat upright, her relaxed posture disappearing. "Come on, Brad. Are you trying to tell me just going to church makes it all okay? Be honest. Haven't you ever known one of those oh-so-pious churchgoers who was a real stinker at heart?"

Brad winced, able to think of several who would fit that description. "I won't argue that one," he conceded. "But you see, just going to church doesn't do it either."

"But you said—"

"I said that without Jesus in your heart, you're lost. . . for all eternity. Jesus—having a relationship with Him—is the key to the whole thing."

Crista pressed her lips together and seemed inclined to drop the subject. Brad decided to let it go for the time being. She'd probably had enough to think about for one day. He circled around to let her out, then walked her to her front door, searching for a neutral topic.

Her dangling earrings caught his attention. He reached out and tapped one with his finger, making the tiny bauble dance in the sunlight. "A hot air balloon? I don't think I've seen earrings like that before."

Crista touched her earlobe self-consciously. "I've always had a thing about them. Balloons, that is."

"Really?" Brad warmed to the topic. Here was something they could discuss safely. "I'm partial to them myself."

Crista studied his face. "Why don't you come in?" she invited, swinging the door wide open.

Brad stopped just inside the doorway, lips pursed in a silent whistle. "That's some collection." He eyed the room with interest. Dainty china balloons appeared ready to lift off from an oak coffee table. A three-dimensional needlepoint balloon complete with gondola and tiny passengers hung suspended from the center of the ceiling fan. Every available surface, from the lamp stand to the knickknack shelves held something relating to the hot air balloon theme.

Crista shoved her hands in her pockets. "People collect all kinds of things: owls, or horses, maybe even frogs. I collect hot air balloons." She shrugged and gave him a sheepish grin. "I don't show these to many people. Even my family thinks I'm a little crazy to love them like I do." She smiled and waved him to a seat on the couch. "Thanks for not laughing."

Brad returned her smile. "No way. I'm a little crazy about them myself. How many times have you been up?"

Crista blinked. "Excuse me?"

"How many times have you gone up in a balloon?"

"Gone up? Um. . .never."

Brad's eyebrows shot up toward his hairline. "Never?"

Crista folded her arms across her stomach and stared at the floor. "I. . .have a problem with heights."

Brad started to chuckle, then tried to cover it by clearing his throat when he realized she wasn't joking. "I don't get it. You fly all over the country. That isn't high?"

"It's a whole different thing. A plane is enclosed. It's almost like being in a building. I went to the top of the Sears Tower once, and it didn't bother me at all. But the idea of standing in a little basket hundreds of feet in the air with nothing between me and the ground. . .uh-uh. No way."

Brad held his hands palms up. "Then why the fascination with them?"

Crista raised one shoulder, a tiny smile tilting her lips.

"It's a puzzle to me, too, but I've loved them ever since I was a little girl. Something about them touches a place deep inside me. They make me feel peaceful and happy. Loved." Her cheeks grew pink. "Sounds pretty silly, doesn't it?"

"All that from a balloon?" Brad did chuckle this time, then touched her chin with his fingers, tipping her face upward. "No. It doesn't sound silly at all." The warmth of her skin sent an electric tingle through his fingers, warning him that he'd better get out of there if he intended to keep things on a friendship level.

"I had a good time," he told her, rising to leave. "Thanks for inviting me." He tapped his index finger on the tip of her nose. "Have a safe trip to North Carolina."

He drove home, mulling over the events of the day. Had he shared enough? Too much?

If she could find out the truth. Lindsey's words kept running through his mind. Why wouldn't Crista make the effort to find out more about her birth parents?

"The truth will set you free." The familiar verse took on a new slant. Could finding her parents set Crista free in more ways than one? The thought sent a surge of excitement through him as speculation became certainty. Learning the truth might be painful, but confronting it was the only way Crista could free herself from the past. If only he could convince her of that.

A new thought burst into his mind: Could he find Crista's parents for her?

Chapter 6

Wilmington was even lovelier than she'd expected. Glad she had given in to her urge to schedule an extra day for relaxation, Crista strolled along savoring the gentle breeze.

The cooler weather made a nice change, with Wilmington's 80 degrees in stark contrast to the searing Phoenix heat. At home, temperatures remained well above the century mark, despite the calendar's insistence that fall loomed just around the corner.

She slowed her steps, not certain what to do with her unaccustomed free time. She had wandered for several hours already. What else should she do with a day off? Maybe Brad had a point about her needing more time away from work.

Brad. Maybe she should spend some of her time trying to figure out where their relationship seemed to be heading.

Thoughts of him hadn't been far from her mind, even while presenting her seminar, and she couldn't decide whether that irritated or pleased her. He seemed interested only in being friends, and that was fine with her on one level. Another, deeper part of her longed for more. But she wasn't about to make the first move.

Crista stopped at the entrance of a red brick church. An unfamiliar urge to enter swept over her, and she pushed tentatively on one of the tall wooden doors. It swung wide at her touch, and she stepped into the tranquil interior. In that moment, a sense of peace washed over her. She spent a quarter of an hour examining the ornate pews and stained glass windows before she resumed her stroll. How sad, she thought, that she couldn't carry that peace along with her when she left.

A nearby strip mall caught her attention, and she strolled over to investigate. She hadn't yet purchased any gifts to take home, and this looked like a good place to remedy the oversight. In a shop that catered to the tourist trade, she found a book beautifully illustrated with photos of many of the city's historical buildings. Her mother would love it, she decided, carrying it to the register.

Several stores farther down, she spied a number of stained glass pieces. Intrigued, Crista went inside. The man behind the counter looked up. "Browse all you want," he called. "Let me know if you have any questions."

Crista smiled in reply and moved through strategically lit display units, resisting the urge to stroke the delicate pieces with her fingers. Their deep colors and unique designs took her breath away. She admired the variety of patterns, everything from bouquets of flowers to biblical scenes. Scanning the items arranged near the far wall, one captured her attention, and she caught her breath in a little gasp.

A hot air balloon in bright reds and yellows floated in a sapphire sky above rolling fields. Crista stepped closer, unable to tear her gaze away. Even inside the shop, the colors shimmered. With sunlight streaming through it, the effect would be gorgeous. She reached up to turn over the price tag and swallowed hard. The figure there wasn't as much as she'd feared, but more than she'd normally spend on an impulse purchase.

"You like balloons?" The voice came from so close behind her, she jumped.

"I do," she admitted, turning to face the beaming proprietor.

His smile widened a notch and he stared at Crista, then a tiny frown furrowed his forehead.

"Is everything all right?" she asked hesitantly.

He started, an embarrassed grin spreading across his face. "Sorry about that. You just made me think of someone I know." Crista smiled and the man's eyes widened. "You even have a dimple like hers. I can't believe how much you look alike! Do you mind if I call her? She works right next door."

Crista's smile froze in place, and she tried to keep from rolling her eyes. "Sure, I guess." She turned back to study the balloon piece while he went to the phone. Should she buy it? The more she tried to talk herself out of spending that much money, the more she wanted it.

She examined a collection of sun catchers hanging nearby. Several smaller hot air balloons dangled there, their vibrant colors sending prisms of light dancing across the walls. Maybe she should buy one of those instead. No, she decided, she would get one of the sun catchers for Brad. It would make a nice souvenir for him, symbolizing their common interest. And for herself. . .

Behind her, she heard the door open and the man speak excitedly. With a sigh of resignation, she turned to meet her "double." Her lips twitched when she saw the other woman, a petite, green-eyed blond wearing a white pharmacy smock. Just as she'd expected, the only resemblance was in the man's mind, despite his repeated protests. Her supposed twin evidently felt the same way, but graciously made an effort to gloss over the uncomfortable situation.

Crista mentioned the large balloon piece as a diversion, then realized that in her heart she'd already decided to take it home. She pulled out her credit card and made arrangements for shipping it after the other woman left.

She chatted with the salesman a few moments, then strolled out of the shop, Brad's tissue-wrapped sun catcher nestled safely in her shoulder bag. Funny, she mused, how many people looked alike in some way. As a young girl, she had looked for those similarities, fantasizing that someday she'd find someone related to her by blood. Even in her early teen years, spotting a person with similar features would cause her heart to race. Not long after that, though, she'd stopped looking. Similarities didn't make another person family. Love did, and the McDaniels had given her plenty of that.

She headed to her hotel to pack for the next day's flight back home.

Brad stared at his computer monitor through bleary eyes, wondering how many on-line hours he'd put in tonight. Typing in a request for Internet sites dealing with adoption searches yielded far more sources than he'd imagined. First he tried to peruse all the information on every site, but quickly realized he'd have to skim and hope he was reading the items that mattered.

Brad rubbed his weary eyelids and turned the computer off for the night. He wasn't quite ready to start his search for Crista's parents, but at least he knew what he needed to get started. That would be the tricky part. He couldn't very well come out and ask Crista for that information, but Lindsey might be willing to help. He'd call her in the morning.

✵

Crista put the finishing touches on her upcoming presentation and returned the folder to her file cabinet. Turning at the ring of the phone, she lifted the receiver and smiled when she recognized Brad's voice.

"Are you all rested up from your trip last week?"

"So much that I've actually gotten ahead of schedule." Crista basked in the feeling of accomplishment.

"Great. That means you can pencil me into that calendar of yours for Saturday. All day Saturday."

"All day? Doing what?"

"Something productive. Like finding out how to be unstructured for a change."

"And what's wrong with structure?" she demanded.

Brad laughed. "Not a thing, as long as you keep it in perspective. Learning those organizational skills from you has made my life easier in a lot of ways, and don't think for a moment I'm not grateful." He paused. "But you can't live your whole life by a planner."

Crista bristled. "I don't agree. I'm a lot more comfortable knowing what I'm doing ahead of time."

"Think how much you enjoyed taking that extra day in North Carolina just to look around."

"It's not the same at all. I knew I was going sightseeing. I didn't know exactly where I'd end up, but I had a basic plan."

Brad's voice softened. "Just give it a try, Crista. I think you'll be glad you did."

His pleading worked where persuasion had not. "You win. But you've got to give me some idea of what to expect."

She could tell Brad was smiling, even over the phone. "I'll tell you this much. Dress like you would for one of your family picnics and bring a jacket. I'll pick you up at seven."

Chapter 7

He appeared at Crista's door right on schedule and hustled her out to his SUV. "This should tide us over until breakfast," he told her, indicating the thermos and bakery sack between the seats. "I picked up coffee and croissants. I hope that's okay?"

Crista poured the steaming coffee into foam cups and handed Brad one of the flaky croissants. "Looks like you thought of everything. Now where are we going?"

He threw back his head and laughed. "Nope. I told you—this is the day you learn the joys of spontaneity. Just sit back, relax, and let the day happen."

He turned down Northern and took the northbound on-ramp for I-17. Crista munched her croissant. When they passed Deer Valley Road, she instinctively craned her neck to see if any balloons were being launched that morning. Not spotting any, she settled back into the seat and watched the scenery roll by.

She waited for Brad to take one of the exits at the north end of the city, but he didn't slacken his pace. Instead of city sprawl, they now drove through rolling hills thick with scrub brush and saguaros.

"It's easy to forget just how close we are to the wide-open spaces, isn't it?" she mused aloud.

Brad murmured agreement, then fell silent again.

Crista became so involved in watching the play of light on the stark mountains that nearly an hour passed before she remembered to ask where they were going. She had just opened her mouth to do so when Brad took the exit to Highway 69.

"Another thirty minutes and we'll be there." Brad glanced from the road ahead to Crista and gave her a warm smile. "With all the Sunday outings your family took, you must have come up this way before."

Crista shook her head. "We went south to Tucson a few times. Once we went to Tombstone and did the whole tourist bit at the OK Corral, but we seldom went north of Phoenix at all. I've only been to Flagstaff and the Grand Canyon once," she admitted.

Brad let out a slow whistle. "Then this should be even more fun for you than I thought."

He guided the four-wheel-drive vehicle around the sweeping curves. Crista noted the signs marking each community they passed through: Mayer, Dewey, Prescott Valley. She looked at Brad, puzzled. "We drove this far just to get breakfast?"

"Not just breakfast, a change of pace and some fresh air." Almost as soon as he spoke, the heavy fragrance of pines filled the vehicle.

Crista closed her eyes and inhaled the pungent scent. She opened them again to find turn-of-the century buildings rolling by, interspersed with more modern structures.

"Welcome to Prescott," Brad told her. He pulled into

a parking place in front of the Courthouse Plaza.

"It's beautiful," Crista said, eyeing the historic storefronts with delight.

"I'm glad you like it. It's one of my favorite places." Brad tucked her hand into the crook of his arm and led her across the street to the old hotel on the corner where they ordered a hearty breakfast.

Afterward, they wandered up one street and down another, with Brad sharing from his extensive fund of stories about the town. The small shops and gingerbread-laden Victorian homes charmed Crista, and she stopped to read every interpretive marker in front of the well-preserved buildings.

"I can see why you like it," she said, catching Brad's enthusiasm for the place. "It's really lovely."

He nodded contentedly. "I always thought I'd like to live here someday. Now that I'm running Uncle Jess's business, that isn't in the picture anymore, but at least I can come up on weekends."

He laced his fingers through hers in a companionable way on their walk back to the SUV. She paused in front of the Bashford Building, imprinting the tranquil scene on her mind. "Thank you for bringing me here," she said softly.

"Wait till you see what comes next," Brad said, helping her into her seat. "We haven't even gotten started yet."

Crista's stomach rumbled and she clasped her hands across it, embarrassed. "I hope there's some food in the offing. This mountain air is giving me an appetite."

He pointed the SUV north on the highway, turning at Ash Fork to head east on I-40 for a few miles, then taking off on a bumpy Forest Service road.

"Don't tell me there's a restaurant up here where we're stopping for lunch," Crista said between gritted teeth, bracing her feet to keep from being bounced against the door.

Brad smiled. "You don't expect me to tell you and ruin the surprise, do you? Just hold on and see what happens."

"I'm trying to hold on," she retorted, clutching the armrest.

They turned onto an even more primitive road before Brad stopped and turned off the ignition. "We're here," he announced.

Crista surveyed her surroundings, seeing only trees and grass. "Where's 'here'?"

Brad chuckled at her bewildered tone. "Fine dining in the outdoors." He opened the back hatch and pulled out an enormous picnic basket.

Crista closed her eyes and rubbed her temples. "Brad, what exactly are we supposed to *do* here?"

He spread an old quilt on the ground and opened the basket with a flourish. "Relax. It's time you learned how."

They took their time over their late lunch. Crista repacked the basket, assuming it was time to leave, but Brad went to the SUV and pulled out a canvas bag.

Crista lifted an eyebrow. "Another surprise?"

Without speaking, Brad took her arm and led her down the rutted road at an easy pace, pointing out the various types of trees and vegetation they passed. He stopped by what looked like a small pond.

"We're going fishing?" Crista eyed his bag skeptically. "Isn't that awfully small for a tackle box?"

Brad merely smiled. "Come on." He guided her to a large pine and scooped up needles to make a cushioned seat. He took two cameras from the bag and handed one to Crista. "You wanted something specific to do," he said in a low voice. "Okay, here it is. We're going to sit here and wait for wildlife to come in to this tank for water. You can just watch or take photos. Your choice."

Crista stared at him, dumbfounded. "We just sit? For how long?"

Brad glanced at his watch. "Shouldn't be more than an hour or two before we see something." She opened her mouth to voice a protest, but he placed his fingers gently over her lips. "Shh. You have to be quiet, or you'll scare them away." He settled against the tree trunk. "In the meantime, we get to practice one of my favorite Bible verses." He gave her a wink. " 'Be still, and know that I am God.' "

Crista sat rigid with disbelief. He wanted to sit and do nothing? For two hours? What a ridiculous waste of time! She started to speak, but Brad held up a cautioning hand and she subsided into a frustrated silence.

Made drowsy by the afternoon sun's warm rays, Crista's taut muscles relaxed in spite of herself. Little by little, the peace of the sylvan setting penetrated her soul. An hour passed. She saw Brad tense and followed the direction of his gaze. Two cow elk appeared from the island of trees across the meadow.

Crista watched, entranced by their calm grace. When they had crossed half the distance to the tank, Brad pressed his shoulder against hers and nodded toward the trees. A huge bull elk stepped forward and sniffed the air, his enormous antlers glinting in the late afternoon sun. Crista gasped and stared in wonder until the three stately animals had drunk their fill and left.

"That was amazing," she told Brad when they had loaded up and started for home. "I can't believe they came that close to us."

"Shows you the value of being still, doesn't it?" His teasing grin made her laugh.

"Except I was so fascinated by them I forgot to take any pictures."

"That's okay, I took plenty. I'll share." He reached over and gave her hand a gentle squeeze. "I'm glad you enjoyed it. At one time, I'd given serious thought to taking up wildlife photography professionally. There's nothing quite like experiencing them up close."

Crista's lips parted in surprise. "You're that good?"

"I've sold a number of photos to some of the better-paying magazines. But now I have a business to run." His voice trailed away.

Stars blossomed in the gathering darkness. Despite her best efforts to stay awake, Crista nodded, then dozed.

❄

Brad pulled into her driveway and turned off the ignition. He watched Crista for a moment, enjoying the sight of her delicate lashes fanning across her cheeks. He touched her shoulder and she blinked sleepily. She shook herself fully awake and stretched. "I can't believe how relaxed I feel. You may just have something there about taking a day off now and then."

Brad smiled in response, hoping her receptive mood would continue. He reached over the back of his seat and drew out a plastic bag, then opened it to reveal a gaily wrapped package. He placed it in Crista's lap.

"What's this?" She eyed the bright holiday wrapping uncertainly.

"Call it an early Christmas present." Brad chuckled at her suspicious expression. "You're not the only one who can shop ahead, okay?"

She pulled the paper loose, looking at Brad quizzically when she saw what lay within. "A Bible?"

"I can't think of a more appropriate gift for Christmas." He watched her trace the imprint of her name on the cover. "You said it was your favorite holiday. You need to get to know more about it than just the lights and tinsel."

Crista shot him a wary look but didn't hand the book back. Feeling encouraged, Brad went on. "I marked one of the verses." He flipped on the dome light and opened the Bible to a page marked by a navy ribbon. "Read it and see if that doesn't seem to be written just for you."

Crista scanned the words Brad had underlined. " 'Sing to God, sing praise to his name,' " she read in a whisper. " 'Extol him who rides on the clouds—his name is the LORD—and rejoice before him. A father to the fatherless, a defender of widows, is God in his holy dwelling.' " She turned to Brad, searching his face.

"That's what God wants to be for you," Brad said gently. "A Father. One who'll never leave you."

Chapter 8

Brad walked up to the stucco house, wondering if he was crazy for doing this. As far as the McDaniels were concerned, he barely knew their daughter. What gave him the right to pry into their family's affairs?

The door swung open before he reached the front step. "Come in, Brad. It's nice to see you." Mrs. McDaniel's warm greeting allayed some of his nervousness. She led him through the house to the patio, where a tray with frosty glasses of lemonade awaited them.

"Lindsey told me about your talk," she said, indicating a chair to Brad and settling in another. "If it will put your mind at ease, I want you to know that I think you're doing a wonderful thing."

Brad sipped his lemonade to give himself time to frame his reply. "Frankly, I wasn't sure how you'd take this. I know how close your family is, and I didn't want you to think I was intruding."

Crista's mother shook her head and smiled. "When you adopt a child, knowing they'll someday be curious about their birth family is something you have to accept as part of the package. I've tried to prepare myself for it from the moment she became ours."

She moved the bottom of her glass in circles on the table, studying the swirls the condensation left behind. A tiny crease appeared between her eyebrows. "This is something Crista should have dealt with long ago. She needs to resolve her bitterness toward her birth parents about being placed for adoption."

She looked up at Brad with an unflinching gaze. "It's something I can't help her with. That's why I'm glad you're willing to take on this project. I'm not completely happy about doing it behind Crista's back, but I doubt she'll give you any cooperation."

Brad straightened and leaned forward. Now that the door was open, he was eager to learn all he could. "Has she ever talked to you about her biological parents?"

"Once. A number of years ago." She stared at the trees beyond the back fence. "It was the year Rod graduated from high school, so that would have made Crista about fifteen. She sat down with me after supper one night and told me she wanted to know about them." A faint smile crossed her face. "She was so careful to try to phrase it so she wouldn't hurt my feelings and make me think she didn't love me and her dad."

"Did you have any information to give her?" Brad prompted.

Mrs. McDaniel's face darkened, and she caught her lower lip between her teeth. "I told her all I knew, but it wasn't what she wanted to hear. We had taken Crista in as a foster child when she was four, but it wasn't long before we knew we'd like to make her a permanent part of our family. She seemed like one of us right from the start." Her eyes grew misty with remembrance.

"In those days, very little information was given out to adoptive parents. All we knew was that she had been abandoned, and there were no problems getting her birth mother and father to relinquish their parental rights.

"I didn't tell Crista about that," she went on, "but she pieced it together from what came next. She asked me if I knew whether her parents were alive, and all I could tell her was what I'd seen on some notes in her file when we visited the agency in Cincinnati." She closed her eyes, as if to see the scene more clearly.

"The caseworker left the room for a few minutes. I didn't dare pull the folder over to me or get up and go around the desk, so I had to try to read upside down. In the brief time I had, I could see a last name: Williams. The first name looked like Melvin or maybe Martin. There were also several brothers and sisters listed, but I couldn't make out individual names.

"The only other thing I saw before the caseworker came back into the room," she said, looking at Brad again, "was a notation under the parents' names. Something about them being active in a local church. That's all I could tell her."

Brad suppressed a groan. No wonder Crista didn't hold churchgoers in high regard. "So her parents are still living?"

Mrs. McDaniel nodded slowly. "And they had other children. Children they apparently kept." She pressed her fingers to her lips and drew a shaky breath. "At that point, Crista told me she wasn't interested in finding them anymore, and that was the last she ever said to me on the subject.

"She's always been reserved, Brad, but after that she just seemed to put up a wall around herself with everyone but the family. Until you came along, anyway." She smiled and stood. "I wish you luck. I hope you can help her."

❄

The whine of the engines grew increasingly louder. Crista dutifully fastened her seat belt and waited for the 727 to take its place in line for takeoff, watching the runway lights glow against the growing dusk.

She relaxed against the seat back but shook herself awake before her eyes closed. The flight home from Dallas/Fort Worth International Airport only lasted a little over two hours. Tired as she felt after a grueling round of back-to-back seminars, napping now would mean she'd be too wide awake to get back to sleep at a decent hour. Instead, she opened her planner, pulled out a pen, and forced herself to focus on her schedule for the next month.

Halfway into the flight, her eyelids drooped despite her best efforts. Her fingers loosened their grip on the pen, and she drifted into a peaceful slumber.

Brad waited for her across a meadow, arms outstretched, the warm light in his eyes shining like a beacon guiding her home. Without hesitation, Crista flung herself toward him, wanting nothing more than to be wrapped in his embrace and know she belonged there. Twenty paces from him she stumbled, then stumbled again. What was getting in her way? No rocks marred the smoothness of the grassy expanse, but still she tripped. Brad seemed farther away than ever. Then the ground fell away under Crista's feet.

She sat bolt upright, straining against the taut seat belt.

Her momentary relief at knowing she'd been dreaming vanished with the realization that the ground was still falling away. Disoriented, she looked around wildly, but what she saw only frightened her further. Bodies sprawled across the seats and in the aisles. Panicked screams echoed her own sense of terror.

"We're going to die!" shrieked a woman across the aisle.

Crista believed her. She had no idea how long they had been falling or how fast, only that the plane was plummeting through the darkness and showed no signs of stopping. The time had come for her to face eternity. . .and she was unprepared.

"Dear God, please help us! I'm not ready to die!" Her involuntary cry mingled with the anguished wails of the other passengers.

With a lurch, the plane bounced, then settled. Crista wondered if they had hit the ground and rebounded, then realized they were still airborne. A moment later, she heard the pilot's voice over the intercom.

"That was quite a ride, wasn't it?" came the soothing Texas drawl. "You folks probably didn't expect a rodeo on this flight." His voice changed, becoming more clipped and professional. "Ladies and gentlemen, we've just experienced some unexpected turbulence. We seem to be past it now, but for your safety and comfort, I suggest you keep your seat belts fastened for the remainder of the flight."

A flight attendant pulled herself to her feet just behind Crista's row and attempted to reestablish her practiced smile. "Is everyone all right?" she inquired, giving each row a quick but thorough scrutiny.

Slowly the cabin resumed a semblance of normalcy.

Crista tuned out the nervous laughter and the solicitous tones of the flight attendants and stared out the window, reliving that moment she was sure would be her last.

Fear, pure and simple, had consumed her. She laced her fingers together, trying to keep her hands from trembling. Just how close had she come to facing eternity? And why had the plane's violent pitching stopped so suddenly? Could it be a result of her loud plea for divine intervention, or was there another explanation for their abrupt deliverance?

Crista couldn't even feel embarrassment about her uncharacteristic outburst. The cry had been torn from deep within her, responding to the deepest longing of her soul. All the things she had told herself about self-sufficiency and control vanished in that one moment of complete clarity. What did it matter if she had every moment of her life in perfect order if in the end she didn't have her accounts settled with God? She didn't see how she could dare go on another day of her life without Him. Or Brad.

That realization rocked her almost as much as the first. Had the near crash destroyed her reason? Brad wanted only to be friends; he'd telegraphed that message in a hundred different ways. The contentment she felt when they were together, that ache to hold him close and be held in his arms—Brad didn't share those feelings. If she wanted to maintain their friendship, she must put aside her yearning for something more and settle for what he did offer.

"Thanks. Sorry to have bothered you." Brad hung up the phone and penciled a line through the name on the notepad before him. Another dead end.

He pinched the bridge of his nose between his fingers. Some investigator he'd turned out to be. His Internet search had turned up a number of Melvin and Martin Williamses in Cincinnati, but none of them admitted to knowing Crista. Widening his search, he'd typed in the names of Cincinnati suburbs, this time including any first name beginning with *M*. He'd contacted them all, except for the last name on his list, Milton R. Williams.

Before making the call, he paused, assailed by Crista's own doubts. How could a family give away one of their children? Were these the kind of people he ought to bring back into Crista's life?

He punched in the numbers, conflicting thoughts flashing through his mind. Did he have the right to do this, not knowing what kind of Pandora's box he might be opening? *Lord, if I've misjudged Your direction in this, please don't let this call go through,* he prayed, counting the rings. One. . .two. . .

"Hello?"

Startled by the quick answer, Brad took a moment to respond to the soft voice on the other end of the line.

"Is this the Williams residence?"

"Yes." The voice took on a guarded tone, and Brad realized he'd better clarify his purpose for calling.

"Please don't hang up. I'm looking for the Williams family who lived near Cincinnati twenty-five years ago." He took a deep breath. "I'm calling about Crista." He waited, hardly daring to breathe.

The woman turned from the phone and called, "Honey, come quick! Somebody's calling about Crista!" She spoke to Brad again. "It's been so many years, I just can't believe this. Nothing's wrong, is it?" she asked, her excitement changing to concern.

"No, not at all." Brad's mind reeled. How could she sound so happy after two and a half decades with no efforts to contact her daughter? Of all the possible scenarios he had imagined, none of them had been close to this. "I'm looking for information about her adoption."

Mrs. Williams sighed. "It was the hardest thing we've ever done, letting that little mite go. She'd become like one of our own. We've never quit praying for her, even after all these years."

Brad blinked. "One of. . . Mrs. Williams, are you telling me Crista isn't your child?"

Her astonished silence confirmed his guess even before she spoke. "Well, of course not. What made you think she was?"

Brad scrubbed his forehead with the heel of one hand. "Something isn't adding up here. Let me start from square one. My name is Brad Morgan. I'm a friend of Crista's, and I'm trying to help locate her biological family. The only information her adoptive mother could give me was that they adopted Crista from an agency in Cincinnati and that her family's name was Williams."

Mrs. Williams clucked in dismay. "No, we only went to church with Crista's family. So sad when that poor woman died and left her husband with all those little ones. The pastor kept them all for awhile, but when their daddy didn't come back, he couldn't keep on doing it indefinitely.

"I taught Crista's class in Sunday school and knew what a sweet little thing she was. We wanted to help, so we took her. I'm afraid I don't know where the rest of them went," she added apologetically.

"How many children were in the family?" Brad asked, his excitement mounting.

"Three or four, near as I can remember."

"And none of the others went with you?"

"Goodness, no. We had four of our own. It was just that I knew Crista from my class, and the thought of that poor little thing being thrown in with strangers was more than I could stand. Although. . ." Her voice faltered. "I wonder now if they might all have been better off if they'd been kept together instead of being parceled out like that." She paused. "You say you're a friend of Crista's. How is she? What's become of her?"

"She's fine. She was adopted by a wonderful family, and she's done very well for herself. Has her own business, as a matter of fact."

"Well, if that don't beat all! Hard to believe she once lived with a family of factory workers, isn't it?" Her voice softened. "I feel better, hearing that. I'd always hoped we did the right thing in giving her up, but it was hard to know for sure. It looks like the Lord's hand was in it after all."

Brad spoke hesitantly. "You obviously cared for Crista a great deal. Do you mind me asking why she couldn't stay with you?"

A sigh echoed through the phone line. "Milt worked in the factory from the time he was fifteen, but loyalty didn't matter when they started laying people off. When he lost his job, we barely had a nickel to our name." She sighed again, then went on. "Having to watch those five little ones get by on one meal a day nearly tore our hearts out. We held on to Crista as long as we could, but as young as she was, we didn't think we had any right to take chances with her health that way."

Mrs. Williams paused. "I'm glad to hear she did all right. So very glad." Her voice grew brisk. "Now let's get back to the reason you called. You say Crista's trying to find her family?"

"Not exactly," Brad hedged. "Actually, I'm doing this on my own. She doesn't know a thing about it."

"Why are you doing it on your own?" Her voice held curiosity rather than censure.

Brad hesitated. Why indeed? "The only thing I can say is that I feel God wants me to."

Mrs. Williams gave a low chuckle. "Well, Honey, that's the very best reason there is. Is there anything I can do to help?"

"Yours was the only family name her adoptive mother saw. Do you know what Crista's last name was?"

"Well, of course. It was Richmond." She spelled it for him.

"Richmond." Brad jotted it on his notepad. "A Richmond family from Ohio. Thanks a lot; that will really help."

"Not Ohio, Hon, Kentucky."

"Kentucky?"

"Sure. That's where we all lived at the time. Just across the river in Covington. We didn't move to Ohio until Milt was laid off and we went looking for any work he could find."

"Kentucky," Brad repeated dully. "Thank you, Mrs. Williams. You've helped more than you know."

He hung up, then stared at his scribbled notes. Crista's mother was dead and her father had disappeared, but she had siblings. Siblings named Richmond.

Brad booted up his computer with renewed optimism and logged on to one of the adoption search message boards. He had a name and a state. The right ones, this time.

❋

Crista sat on the edge of her bed, staring at the open Bible in her lap. Her gift from Brad contained a wealth of study notes, and she had spent hours since her arrival home looking up passages pertaining to knowing God. She smiled in astonishment when she read that a person could be adopted into God's family. It all connected with her conviction that families were built on a foundation of love. The McDaniels had brought her into their family; God wanted to bring her into His. It was a concept so simple, yet so profound that she could barely take it in.

She returned to the notes in the back and reread the section on salvation. That was what she needed. Hadn't she cried out for that very thing when she thought the plane was going down? She slipped from the bed to her knees and lifted up a heartfelt prayer. "Oh, Lord, I want You to be my Father. . . ."

Chapter 9

B rad had gotten so used to scanning the entries without success that he almost skimmed past it. "Searching for siblings born Covington, Kentucky," it began. He read it again more slowly, then went over it a third time. "Parents John and Anna Richmond." The right name, the right area. His mouth went dry. Could it be?

This entry contained a link to a Web site. He clicked on the link and waited for the site to open. It told the story of Eden Richmond, her separation from her siblings and attempts to locate them, and her hope to reunite them all. Brad stared at the last paragraph. "One sister may have moved west, possibly to Arizona."

He noted the woman's E-mail address and began to compose a message:

> *My name is Brad Morgan. I'm helping a friend in Arizona look for her family. Her birth name was Crista Richmond, and she was born in Kentucky. If this sounds like anyone you're looking for, please give me a call.*

He added his phone number, then pressed the Send button.

✻

The minister moved into the final point of his sermon on deepening one's walk with Christ. Brad leaned back in the pew and glanced at Crista, seated beside him. He'd hardly believed it when she called and asked if she could accompany him to church this morning. As if he'd say no! Watching her, he marveled at the difference between her last visit and today. Gone was the fidgety behavior. She leaned forward slightly as though she didn't want to miss a single word.

Was God softening her heart and drawing her toward Himself? If only he could believe that.

When the last song had ended and the congregation began filing out, Brad remained seated and turned to Crista. The gladness shimmering in her eyes made him wonder if his prayers had already been answered. He hoped so, but he had to be sure.

"Something's happened, hasn't it?" he asked.

She nodded happily, tears glistening on her lashes. "I'm part of God's family now."

Her arms circled his shoulders in a joyful hug. Brad wrapped his arms around her for the first time, rejoicing with Crista and wondering if God was opening the door to answer yet another prayer.

"You were right," she whispered close to his ear. "I can feel the difference. This changes everything."

More than you know, Brad thought.

✻

Brad checked his hair in the mirror. It appeared as

well groomed as the last time he'd looked. And the time before that. He glanced at his watch. Crista should arrive any minute. Thank goodness she hadn't minded driving to his house. When negotiations over a major new contract ran later than he'd expected, he knew he'd never be able to get ready, pick up Crista, and still make it in time for their dinner reservations.

He patted his jacket pocket to reassure himself the tiny jeweler's box still nestled there. Crista's news had removed all but one obstacle to letting her know his feelings. He had to let her know about his search for her family, and he had to do it tonight, before he asked the question that could change their futures.

Tires crunched on the driveway. Brad hurried to the door and smiled at the sight of Crista in a teal silk dress. He could get used to seeing a sight like that every day of his life.

Crista looked around his living room, brightening when she spotted the sun catcher she'd given him. The smile faded and she turned to Brad, a solemn expression on her face. "Are we in a hurry? There's something I'd like to tell you."

Brad nodded and motioned to the couch. He sat beside her, close enough to take her in his arms. How he'd like to do that and have the waiting over with! He tried to pull his attention back to what she was saying.

"I've decided you were right," she stated. "If God has forgiven me, I have to forgive, too. I've decided it's time to start looking for my birth family."

Brad stared at her. He'd hoped for an opportunity but hadn't planned on leaping into it quite this quickly. "I have something to say to you, too." Taking her hands in his, he gazed into her eyes, steeling himself for her reaction. "The fact is, I've already started searching for them." He felt Crista stiffen and try to pull away, but he tightened his hold on her hands and went on. "I know it must seem like a terrible intrusion, but I felt like God was telling me to do this." Would she believe him?

Slowly she relaxed, although her expression remained troubled. She studied Brad's face. "So what have you found out about the former Crista Williams?" Her tone was light, but Brad could hear the pain beneath the surface and sense her fear of reopening the old wound.

He stroked the backs of her hands with his thumbs. *This isn't going to be easy, is it, Lord?* "Well, for starters, your name wasn't Williams." He watched her eyes dilate and waited a moment for the news to register. "You were born Crista Richmond, and your mother died when you were just a little girl. Your father left you in the care of his pastor, but I don't know what happened to him after that. I do know that a church family named Williams took you in later on. They loved you very much, but had some serious financial problems and weren't able to provide for you. Just after that, your mom and dad became your foster parents, and you know what happened from then on."

"You have been busy, haven't you?" Brad could feel her fingers tremble. He gave them a gentle squeeze. At least she was still talking to him. He might as well tell her the rest.

"There's more," he said, plunging ahead before he lost his nerve. "I may have found your sister."

The trembling spread through her whole body. "I

have a sister? Besides Lindsey, I mean?"

Brad smiled. "At least one, maybe more. There's no guarantee the woman I found is related to you, but I wanted you to know about the possibility."

Crista nodded, apparently at a loss for words. And who could blame her? Surely he could have dropped this on her more gently. He slid his arm around her and pulled her to him, cradling her head on his shoulder.

"Is there anything else?" she asked in a shaky voice.

Brad chuckled and stroked her hair. "That's it. Only one bombshell per day." *Unless you count a proposal.* Could he spring that on her now? Maybe he'd wait until after dinner and give her time to collect her thoughts.

"Do you still feel like going out to eat, or would you rather order in?"

Crista shook her head and pressed her hands to her cheeks. "Going out is fine. I just need a little time to assimilate all this."

"I don't blame you a bit. And you aren't angry with me?"

She shook her head again, a small smile lighting her lips. "Surprisingly, no." The smile widened into a grin.

Brad's shoulders slumped in relief. The evening hadn't been ruined. A sense of elation welled up inside him. There was still hope.

"In that case, what do you say we head for Mario's?"

Crista smiled assent and reached for her wrap. Brad held it for her and was just draping it over her shoulders when the phone rang. He looked at Crista apologetically. "Do you mind if I get it?" he asked. "It might be about that new contract."

"Go ahead." She smiled. "It'll give me a minute to catch my breath."

Brad hurried across the room and picked up the phone, expecting to hear Nick's voice. "Hello?"

"Mr. Morgan? This is Eden Richmond Leland."

Brad started. He shot a frantic glance at Crista, then turned his attention back to the phone. "Yes," he said cautiously. "This is Brad Morgan."

"I'm sorry I haven't called sooner, but I've been out of town and just got your message." She drew a deep breath, clearly audible over the wire. "I think your friend may be my sister. I'm the oldest, and Crista is the baby. She was born in Covington, Kentucky, and she'd be twenty-nine years old now. Does that sound like we're talking about the same person?"

Did her voice sound anything like Crista's? Brad couldn't tell. He risked another glance at Crista, hoping his expression wouldn't give him away. She was looking at the sun catcher, turning it to catch light from the lamp. Brad breathed again and turned his attention back to the phone.

"I think we might be," he ventured. "How can we find out for sure?"

Eden gave a nervous laugh. "I haven't the faintest idea. After getting this far, I have no idea what to do next. She was only three years old when our mother died. I don't know if she'd even remember me, so we can't go over shared memories."

Brad's fingers tightened on the phone. Everything checked out so far, but how could he be certain? He couldn't bear the thought of sending Crista's hopes soaring only to chance having them plummet again. "That does present a problem," he said. He shifted position so his back was toward Crista and lowered his voice. "Do you remember anything about what happened after your mother died?"

"It's all just bits and pieces, I'm afraid. Losing our parents and then being shuffled around like that was such an upheaval. I do remember that we stayed with our pastor for awhile, but then we all went with different families and our world fell apart all over again."

It had to be the right woman. There couldn't be more than one situation like that in the same place at the same time. "That checks out with what I've learned."

Eden yelped with joy. "I can hardly believe it! How can I get in touch with her? Do you think she's ready to talk to me?"

"Hold on a minute." Brad looked across the room at the woman he loved. The evening he'd planned so carefully had just crumbled into dust, but who was he to complain about God's timing?

"Crista," he called softly. "Your sister's on the phone. Her name is Eden. Would you like to talk with her?"

Eyes wide in disbelief, Crista moved across the room like a sleepwalker. Brad nodded with more confidence than he felt, then pressed the receiver into her hand. He stepped away, as much to get a grip on his own feelings as to give Crista privacy, and watched as she spoke to her sister for the first time in twenty-six years.

Thirty minutes later, Crista hung up and turned a radiant face to Brad. "God has been so good to me!" she exulted. She pulled another tissue from the box he'd handed her earlier and dabbed at her cheeks. "Can you believe it? Eden has been looking for me for ten months, and once I turned my life over to God, He worked it all out."

Brad crossed the room and wrapped her in a bear hug. She buried her face in his shirt and returned his embrace.

"I'm so happy," she said, looking up at him through a film of tears. "First I find God, then my birth sister. I feel whole for the first time, and it's all because of you. You're such a wonderful friend."

Brad's elation deflated like a leaky balloon. He'd been so sure Crista's feelings matched his own, but now he wondered. Had guiding her toward Christ and helping her locate her family been the only reason God placed him in her life? And if it was, could he accept that?

He'd struggle with that answer later. At this point, he only knew one thing: There would be no proposal this evening. He glanced at his watch. They'd missed their reservations at Mario's, but they still needed to eat.

He picked up her wrap from where she'd dropped it on the couch. "Let's go get dinner."

Chapter 10

How would you like to go cut your own Christmas tree this year?" Brad stretched one arm across the back of Crista's couch and cradled a mug of cocoa in the other hand.

Crista carried her own mug to the couch and settled next to him. "Could we? Where?" She'd heard stories of her parents cutting trees in snowy Ohio, but growing up in Phoenix didn't give one opportunities for treks in the woods.

"Up north, not far from where we saw the elk. I already have the permit," he told her with his slow grin.

"Not bad." She laughed. "You mean I finally have you planning ahead?" It felt good to hear that teasing note in his voice. In the three days since Eden's call, he'd seemed a bit subdued, although she'd been sure he shared her happiness.

"Yep. See what a good influence you are?" He wrapped his arm around her shoulders and hugged her close. "What are you doing the Saturday after Thanksgiving?"

Crista pulled away so she could stare into his face. "Thanksgiving? I always put my tree up a week before Christmas."

Brad's mouth dropped open. "You're kidding. You're missing out on an early start to the season."

"And having needles all over the carpet for weeks on end."

Brad pulled her back to his side and rubbed his chin against her hair. "Needles on the carpet are a traditional part of Christmas," he murmured, stroking her cheek with his thumb.

"A tradition you just created?" Crista snuggled closer, reveling in his nearness.

"Mm-hm," he admitted with a low chuckle.

Well, why not get an early start on her favorite holiday? This Christmas would be the best ever. She'd found her family, she had Brad in her life, and most importantly, she finally knew the Reason for the celebration. "Okay. The Saturday after Thanksgiving."

She sipped her cocoa, then rubbed her cheek against Brad's sweater. "Planned any resolutions for the new year yet, Mr. Organization?"

Brad straightened and placed his mug on the coffee table. "As a matter of fact, I have." He leaned back, lacing his fingers around one bent knee. "I've learned a lot about what makes a business work these past few months, not to mention a lot about myself. I've decided the best thing I can do for J&R Machining is to turn it over to Nick."

"What?" Crista couldn't hide her astonishment.

Brad nodded decisively. "He loves the company. He's been with it since the beginning, and he knows it better than anyone. Being able to have the final say in what happens without having to run everything past me will be the best thing that ever happened to him." He held her gaze with his own. "And getting out from under a job I was never suited for in the first place will give me the chance to see if I can make one of my dreams come true."

Crista cupped her hands around her mug and tried not to show how much his announcement had shaken her.

Brad's faced creased in a boyish grin. "Now that J&R is back on track, I'm going to use my new business skills to start a freelance photography venture. In Prescott."

"You're moving?" Crista's voice came out in a hoarse croak.

He nodded. "Right after Christmas. I want to enjoy life, not just get through it, and I need to slow down to do that. Not that I won't stay organized." He chuckled and gave her a hand a light squeeze. "I just want to go at an easier pace."

"I see." Crista drained her mug and stared into its depths.

Brad didn't allow his expression to change, but inside he felt like punching his fist in the air with a victory shout. More than her words, Crista's crestfallen reaction to his announcement told him what he needed to know.

Thanksgiving dinner with her family always brought more temptation than Crista could resist, but she'd out-done herself yesterday. She stepped out of her jeans and exchanged them for a pair of sweatpants with an elastic waist. Maybe having Brad there had boosted her appetite. She walked out to check her mailbox, smiling at the memory.

Bills, more bills, and some Christmas sale flyers. Crista

wrinkled her nose in annoyance. She always did her Christmas shopping way in advance, but here it was the day after Thanksgiving and she still needed gifts for everyone but her mother.

An envelope slipped from the stack, and she bent to retrieve it, frowning at the unfamiliar return address. Inside she found a Christmas card with a discount coupon from the stained glass shop in Wilmington. She tossed the rest of the mail on her counter and tapped the coupon thoughtfully, eyeing the shop's Web address at the bottom. She typed the string of characters into her computer and watched a dazzling array of photos appear on screen.

He'd added even more to his inventory. She made note of several items that would be perfect for her family and started to send an E-mail, then stopped. A phone call would be better this close to Christmas. If some of her choices were out of stock, she could ask him to recommend alternatives. The line was busy, so she propped the card next to her phone as a reminder. She had errands to run today, but she could call again tomorrow.

No, next week. Tomorrow would be spent with Brad, selecting the perfect Christmas tree. She wrapped her arms around herself, looking forward to another day with him, then sobered at the thought it might be one of the last times they had together.

She laid out clothes for the next morning. Brad planned to pick her up before sunup. When she protested the early hour, he'd alluded to some mysterious errand he had to take care of before they went in search of the tree. "It's just off the interstate, not out of our way at all," he assured her.

"This is your errand?" Crista stared doubtfully at the long shape on the ground as it swelled gradually in the predawn light, taking on a more rounded appearance. Flames shot from the propane burners, and the balloon slowly lifted off the ground.

She pulled her jacket more snugly around her and reached for Brad's hand. "I'm not so sure about this."

"You'll be fine." He smiled, giving her fingers a reassuring squeeze. "Trust me."

Crista looked into his eyes. She did trust him. That was one miracle. She glanced at the gaily colored balloon hovering overhead. If God would help her overcome her aversion to heights, that would make two.

The pilot jogged over to them. "Ready?"

Brad turned to Crista, one eyebrow raised questioningly. She drew a deep breath and nodded. "Ready."

Stepping into the wicker gondola wasn't so bad. She rested her arms on the leather-padded rim. As long as it sat on the ground, she could be quite comfortable. She could hear the whoosh of the burners behind her and swallowed, knowing that the increase in heat would produce the added lift needed for them to take off. She let her gaze travel up the steel cables to the load tapes, then on to the vivid hues of the balloon itself, hoping the ripstop nylon envelope was really as strong as Brad had told her it was.

Brad turned from conferring with the pilot and put his arm around her, pulling her close. "It's going to be okay," he promised. Crista closed her eyes and breathed a quick prayer. When she opened them again, she realized they were off the ground.

Brad laughed at her startled expression. "Not as bad as you expected?"

Crista shook her head in wonder. "I can't believe how smooth it is. I don't even feel the breeze."

"You won't," the pilot told her. "We're moving with the wind, so there's no sensation of it blowing. You won't even get any turbulence, the way you would in an airplane."

"Good," Crista said under her breath, the memory of her near disaster all too recent.

The gondola hung steady beneath the balloon. Crista leaned against Brad, finally prepared to relax and enjoy their flight.

"Beautiful, isn't it?" she murmured, watching the scene beneath them unroll in a living panorama.

"Absolutely breathtaking," Brad agreed.

She turned her head to find him watching her instead of the landscape. Their gazes locked. Brad cupped her face in one hand, stroking her cheek with his thumb. "I'm glad you came today," he said, his voice a husky whisper. "I'd like you to always soar above the challenges of life." He brushed his lips across her forehead, then tilted her chin up to receive his kiss.

"Crista," he said, clasping both of her hands in his, "I'd like to meet those challenges with you." Reaching into his pocket, he pulled out a small, square box and flipped open the lid to reveal a delicate ring set with a glittering diamond. "Will you marry me?"

Crista melted into his arms and sealed her acceptance with her kiss.

Behind them, the pilot cleared his throat. "Hard to

tell about people sometimes. They pay good money to ride in a balloon, then they don't even look at the scenery. Go figure."

Crista caught Brad's amused look, and they laughed together. Held in the warm circle of Brad's arms, she rested her head against his chest, feeling the steady beat of his heart keeping time with her own. They hung suspended between the heavens and the earth, the splendor of creation spread out before them.

" 'Sing to God,' " she said in a voice barely above a whisper. " 'Sing praise to his name.' "

Brad's voice joined hers. " 'Extol him who rides the clouds,' " they finished together. " 'His name is the Lord.' "

"Looks like we're starting our descent," Brad murmured in her ear.

Filled with unspeakable joy, Crista could only nod. Today she had ridden the clouds, both in the balloon and in her spirit. Even after they landed, she knew her heart would still soar.

CAROL COX

In addition to writing, Carol's time is devoted to being a pastor's wife, home-school mom to her teenage son and young daughter, church pianist, youth worker, and 4-H leader. The Arizona native loves any activity she can share with her family in addition to her own pursuits in gardening, crafts, and local history. She has had three historical novels published in the **Heartsong Presents** line as well as five other novellas from Barbour Publishing. Carol and her family make their home in northern Arizona.

Don't Look Back

by Terry Fowler

Dedication

To my brothers and sisters in Christ—
how glorious to be a member of the family of God.

Chapter 1

W e need to talk."

Rattled by the man's demanding tone, Angelina Collier lost count of the pills in the tray. "What can I do for you, Sir?" she asked, a hint of irritation in her tone.

"I want you to fire my daughter."

Fire his daughter? Angelina supposed that in the course of employing people to work in her store, his daughter might be in her employ. Still, she was curious why she should do as he requested. "Who's your daughter?"

"Melody Robbins."

Angelina gasped. Of all the possibilities, Melody was the one she most hated to think of losing. Back in mid-June, she'd taken the college student in, offering room and board and a small salary in exchange for a few hours of babysitting each week. The arrangement worked well for everyone.

In a short time, Angelina and her children had come to love Melody so much. She was more like the children's older sister than a stranger in their home. Angelina's parents had even adopted the young woman into their extended family.

Angelina took a moment to study Melody's dad. For the life of her she couldn't recall his first name. She'd been curious about him since seeing the photo of her parents on Melody's nightstand. Based solely on his daughter's age, she'd guess him to be in his early forties. Just under six feet, he appeared to be fairly health conscious, weighing in around 175 pounds. In keeping with the pleasant summer temperatures, he wore a golf shirt and shorts with worn sandals on his feet.

His thick, salt-and-pepper hair was combed straight back, neatly blow-dried and styled. The chiseled face contained strength to match penetrating brown eyes that had the luster of expensive mink fur.

"And exactly why should I fire her? She's the best employee I've ever had."

He beamed a bit at her words of praise, obviously proud of his daughter but intent on his purpose. "You're making her old before her time. She's too young for the responsibility you've placed on her shoulders."

"Responsibility?" Granted, Melody was spending longer days with the children over the summer, but they had already discussed the plans for when classes started. Based on her calculations, Melody would have the children on her own for around three or four hours a day in the afternoon.

"You always respond with a question?"

"Do you?"

"Look, Mrs. Collier, this is getting us nowhere fast."

"I agree, Mr. Robbins." From what Melody had told her, she knew her mother had died a couple of years before and her father lived in Atlanta. What was he doing here now? "Are you visiting Melody?"

"Call me Wes. Actually, I'm relocating to Wilmington. I don't like being so far away from my only child."

"Have you seen her yet?"

"I wanted to surprise her."

You'll do that, Angelina thought. She glanced at the two women approaching the pharmacy. "Excuse me. Your prescriptions are almost ready, ladies. Just one more minute."

❄

Wes stepped back from the counter and waited. He half listened as she directed the women on the use of the medication, thinking she had the perfect voice for her work. The soft tones would certainly soothe the sick.

Glancing around, Wes noted her stock included the standard drug store stuff. A display of summer items ran through the middle aisle—plastic rafts and beach toys inexpensive enough to be left behind after vacation and picnic supplies for those who cared to commune with nature. A couple of beige plastic bucket-shaped chairs sat nearby, momentary respite for those too sick to stand while they waited.

He took a moment to look over the display of suntan lotions, some with SPFs so high that even this woman's milky white complexion wouldn't burn. Wes considered making a purchase. He'd forgotten to pack his.

To say Angelina Collier was a bit of a surprise would truly be an understatement. Melody raved about the woman, her children, and even her parents. Studying her from the corner of his eye, Wes felt certain most men found her attractive. Far from the superwoman image his daughter had instilled in his head, he decided diminutive was the only word to describe the petite woman who probably weighed in at little more than one hundred pounds.

A true blond, she wore her shoulder-length hair pulled back in a clasp. Her facial features were perfect with the exception of a slightly tip-tilted nose that gave added cuteness and a dimple that winked when she smiled.

Maybe it was a bit of insecurity at seeing himself replaced as family that forced him to come here and confront the woman. Could it be that he was so afraid of losing his daughter's love that he wanted to break up the happy environment she'd created for herself the moment she moved out on her own?

No, that had nothing to do with the situation. He was definitely right about the level of responsibility Angelina Collier had put on his Melody's shoulders. She shouldn't be worrying about someone's children. She should be concentrating on earning her degree, enjoying her college years, and making friends.

"Mr. Robbins?"

He jerked out of his reverie at her calling his name. The line to the pharmacy had lengthened, and Wes realized he would have to talk with her after business hours.

"I'm going to be tied up here awhile. Perhaps we can continue this conversation later?"

"Tonight?"

"I have a church meeting. Tomorrow?"

"Fine. Here's the number at my hotel. I'm staying there until I finalize my moving plans."

"I'll be in touch."

A weary Angelina closed the etched glass front door and

locked it for the night. As if the marathon day at the store hadn't been enough, she'd spent the last two hours planning an upcoming church homecoming. Easing her aching feet from her shoes, she padded across the slate tile to the family room to find Melody on the sofa, the television playing low in the background.

Now that she'd met the father, Angelina could definitely see the resemblance between the two. The young woman wore her dark hair long, midway down her back. When standing, she towered over Angelina, at least as tall as her dad. The lines of her face were much softer, but her eyes were the same beautiful shade of brown.

"Everything go okay?" she asked, dropping into the green leather recliner that had once been her husband's. For the moment, the room was toy free, everything neat and clean. She knew Melody had enforced their nightly cleanup rule.

"They tried the usual delay attempts," Melody said, grinning broadly, "but I hung in there and only read them one story before lights-out."

"Good for you. They'd have you reading all night if they got their way."

"Your mom called. Said to tell you she can't go shopping with you tomorrow. The baby's sick."

Disappointed, Angelina asked, "Did she take him to the doctor?" She'd been looking forward to spending a few hours with her mother.

"She said he's cutting teeth and has been a real bear."

"Poor little guy."

"She claims there's no sense in taking him for the doctor to tell her what she already knows."

"It's not like she doesn't have a world of experience," Angelina agreed. Her mother had helped more than her share of infants through teething. "What did you do today?"

"We went to the beach. I slathered the kids with sunscreen, and Bee didn't burn this time."

Melody had learned about the fair-haired child's tendency to burn easily the hard way. She'd been right by Angelina's side, doing everything possible to comfort and cool Bee's heated skin, promising she'd never make that mistake again.

"What did you have for dinner?"

"We feasted on sloppy joes. There are leftovers in the fridge if you're hungry."

Angelina shook her head. She'd grabbed a grilled chicken sandwich on her way to church.

"Good movie?"

"I don't have a clue. After I read my E-mail, I turned the television on and fell asleep. The sun takes a lot out of you."

"Not to mention the kids. Do you ever feel it's too much?"

The young woman looked up, a curious expression touching her face. "What do you mean?"

"Everything. The kids. The chores. Do you ever feel I've placed too heavy a burden on you?"

Melody shook her head. "I love living here with you and the kids, Angelina. I knew immediately that I couldn't live with my friends, and truthfully, I don't much care for the idea of sharing a dorm room or an apartment with a stranger."

"But we were strangers," she pointed out.

"Not really. It's hard to explain, but from the minute we met, I felt like one of the family."

"You should be enjoying your summer. Hanging out with your friends."

Melody shrugged. "I do those things."

"And you play mom to two rowdy children."

"Is something wrong?"

Angelina sighed, worrying that she'd already said too much. "No, not at all. I suppose I should tell you that your dad came by the pharmacy today."

"He went to the store?"

"I take it you've heard from him already?"

"He called tonight. Wants to have breakfast to discuss his plans. What did he say to you?"

"He's concerned that I've placed too much responsibility on you for your age. I don't want to believe that's the case. You would tell me if it got to be too much, wouldn't you?"

Melody pushed her feet to the floor and sat up. "What is he trying to do? Dad knows how much I love my job here. Why would he make statements like that?"

Angelina reclined the chair, dropping her head against the cushioned back. "Probably because he's worried. He's entitled, you know. I suppose I'd feel the same way if someone told me my daughter had taken on two children in her spare time."

"Compared to the jobs some of my friends have, taking care of Rob and Bee is a walk in the park."

Angelina chuckled at the young woman's analogy. "Well, it is that, but it's also a constant battle of wills with a four and three year old."

"I'll talk to Dad. Make him understand how I feel about him interfering."

Fear welled up inside Angelina. She didn't want to be the cause of an argument between father and daughter. "Don't be too hard on him, Melody. He loves you and only has your best interests at heart."

"I'm a grown-up, Angelina. He needs to let me decide what's in my best interests. You don't know Dad like I do. When I was a child, he was never there. Now he wants to make up for lost time. But I'm not his baby anymore. He has to let me grow up."

Empathy for Wes Robbins's plight touched Angelina. "I suppose it's something you won't understand until you have children of your own, but parents can never totally relinquish their leadership role. He's doing what he thinks is in your best interests."

"How can he know what's in my best interests? He hasn't bothered to ask what I want."

She wanted to warn the young woman, tell her what was about to happen, but Angelina knew it wasn't her place. The two of them would have to deal with the situation, and she would have to do her best to remain an impartial bystander. *Yeah, like that would happen.* She loved Melody, and no matter what her father thought, she was fairly certain Melody loved them and her job.

"I'm sure you two will work it out. Just promise to let me know if things get to be too much."

"I love this job so much that if I didn't need the money, I'd do it for free."

Angelina knew the young woman was telling the truth. From the beginning, she'd been struck by Melody's generosity and honesty. Her parents had done a wonderful job with her. "You don't need to convince me. I know how good you are with the kids. I think you'll make a wonderful teacher."

The conversation drifted between them until she could hardly keep her eyes open. "I'm going to turn in. I still have to take the kids shopping tomorrow. Both of them are outgrowing their clothes faster than I can buy them."

"I heard there's a new gently used children's clothes store off College Road. Might be something you want to look into."

"Gently used?" Angelina repeated unbelievingly. "When have you ever seen Robbie and Bee being gentle with their clothes?"

"Well, their Sunday things are in pretty good shape."

"Robbie is growing like a weed. I can't believe he starts kindergarten next year. Where has the time gone?"

"Go to bed, Angelina, before you start fixating on your kids like my dad does."

Apprehension touched deep down inside. "Melody, I don't want to be the cause of trouble between you and your dad."

"You aren't. Dad's more than capable of stirring up things on his own."

Recalling his abrupt entry at the store, Angelina agreed Wes Robbins was that. "Enjoy your breakfast. If you want to spend more time with your dad, I'll be here with the kids."

"Kelly wants me to go with her to visit her grandmother, so I'll probably meet her after I see Dad."

"Have fun and be safe. Night."

Upstairs, Angelina checked on the children and then prepared for bed. Settling in the queen-sized bed, her thoughts drifted for a moment to Wes Robbins. Did the man really intend to attempt to force Melody to give up her job? The parent in her understood his concern, but she also felt Melody resented her dad's interference.

"Father, please help them," she whispered softly. "Guide Wes Robbins's actions so that he doesn't alienate his daughter, and guide Melody's so she doesn't hurt him. Help them to understand just how precious their relationship is—how lucky they are to have each other to love."

The prayer drifted into praise for all the blessings in her life, and soon Angelina's eyes closed in sleep.

Chapter 2

When the doorbell rang late the following morning, Angelina thought maybe her mother had changed her mind about the shopping trip. Instead, she was surprised to find Wes at the door.

"Hi. You've caught me at a bad time."

"When is a good time for you?"

She detected the note of sarcasm in his voice. "If you'd called, we could have set a time." Angelina knew he had the number. He'd called Melody on her direct line for weeks now.

"I won't take long. I just wanted to thank you for making my daughter angry with me."

"I didn't—"

"Save it," Wes interrupted. "Melody and I had breakfast. From the things she said to me, I'm fairly certain you shared our conversation with her."

"Not really. I did ask if she felt I'd placed too much responsibility on her."

"And now she's pretty upset with me."

"I'm sorry. I was addressing your concerns. I didn't see any other way to handle it than to ask outright."

"You think she's going to admit the job is too much for her?"

Perhaps Melody was right. Her father didn't seem to realize how capable she was. "I think Melody is a mature young woman with a good head on her shoulders. And yes, I do believe she was honest with me."

"I don't understand any of this," Wes declared, shoving his hair back with spread-eagled fingers. "All I heard for weeks were Melody's pleas to let her come to the beach and get an apartment with her friends over the summer. Next thing I know, she's moved into your house and taken a job as a part-time nanny. It doesn't make sense."

"Maybe she decided it was better to live free of charge and get paid, too."

Angelina didn't add her suspicions that Melody didn't care for the living arrangement with her friends. The young woman's comment about going a bit far in testing their wings led her to believe Melody's friends' lifestyle had been more than she expected.

"Perhaps," Wes agreed, shrugging his shoulders.

A loud crash came from the distant parts of the house. "Fereby?" Angelina yelled, racing in the direction of the sound.

Her daughter sat between an overturned coffee table and a jumble of sofa cushions.

"Mommy," the little girl called, holding out her arms. She touched one hand to her head. "Boo-boo."

"What have I told you, Bee? You're going to break your neck if you don't stop climbing on everything." She quickly checked her head, sighing relief when there were no cuts or abrasions.

"Who that?"

Angelina followed her daughter's finger to Wes. Swinging Fereby into her arms, she said, "It's not polite to point, Bee. This is Melody's father, Mr. Robbins."

"Mr. Wobbins?" the child repeated.

Wes walked across the room and touched the child's cheek. "Yes, Cutie. And who are you?"

"Fairbee," she announced.

"This is my daughter, Fereby."

"How old are you?"

Angelina smiled when the child worked her fingers until she held up three. She was just beginning to master the new age.

"I really do have to go. I have to pick up my son from day school and take them clothes shopping." She thought for a minute. "Tonight's pizza night. You're welcome to join us."

Wes's serious gaze rested on her face. "I think I will."

"See you around six o'clock then. We eat early because of the kids."

Wes watched the white SUV pull out of the driveway before starting his own car. Was there ever a time when Angelina Collier wasn't rushing around? He'd truly like to know.

The little girl was definitely a cutie complete with her mother's hair, eyes, and dimpled smile. No wonder Melody was so attracted to the child. It would be interesting to see how she interacted with this family. Perhaps being a member of a larger group was what appealed to his daughter.

Maybe by tonight, Angelina Collier would be able to

settle down long enough for them to complete a conversation. Meanwhile, he had lots of details to work out.

Wes honestly felt God had directed his path to this new city. He had prayed and asked how he could strengthen his relationship with Melody, and this had been God's answer. He would miss Atlanta, but in truth, he missed his child more and wanted to be where she was.

❄

"Daddy? What are you doing here?"

He kissed Melody's cheek. "Mrs. Collier invited me."

She looked puzzled. "Why would she do that?"

"I stopped by earlier today when she was rushing off, and she suggested I come back tonight."

Melody eyed him suspiciously. "You didn't say anything else?"

Wes thought maybe it was wiser that he keep his earlier accusations to himself. "I'm not happy about this, Melody."

The struggle between parent and adult child was evident in their stubborn expressions. "And I told you I want to keep this job."

"Melody? Is it the pizza delivery?"

Wes recognized Angelina's voice.

"It's my dad."

Angelina stepped into the foyer. "Wes. Come in. Can we get you something to drink?"

"Whatever everyone else is having will be fine."

"Iced tea it is. Unless you'd prefer milk?"

He grimaced at the suggestion. He hadn't drunk milk with his meals since he was a child. "Tea is fine."

After serving him, they all settled in the family room.

Melody sat in the corner of the sofa with the little boy curled up at her side while the girl chose her mother's lap.

"These your new sneaks?" Melody asked the sturdy little boy, rubbing her fingers over his freshly trimmed hair.

He must resemble his dad with that reddish blond hair and hazel eyes, Wes thought as the child launched into a description of how the new shoes lit up when he walked.

"Mel never had shoes like that," Wes said.

The child giggled and repeated the name.

"You didn't have to call me that."

"It's my pet name for you."

"I want a pet," Robbie announced.

"No, Robbie. A pet name is like when we call you Rob or Robbie. Dad, this is Robert Collier, Jr. Robbie, this is my dad, Wes Robbins. I think you've already met Bee."

"Nice to meet you, Robert."

"Robbie's my pet name," he said. "Robert's my daddy. He's in heaven."

"I'm sorry to hear that. I know you must miss him a great deal."

"Robert died last year following an extended bout with cancer," Angelina explained.

Wes knew all about the insidious disease that showed no respect for family as it ripped loved ones from their homes. "My wife died of cancer two years ago."

Angelina offered him a sympathetic smile. "Melody told me. It's a tragic loss."

Wes nodded, offering his daughter a small smile when she touched his hand.

The chiming of the doorbell alerted them to the arrival of dinner.

"First one to the door gets the cheese pizza," Melody called, jumping from the sofa. The two children raced after her.

"She always lets them win. I think she's on to something with her game. They eat better when they think they're winners."

"The things parents do to get food into their kids. Mel was quite a picky eater."

They returned to the room, Melody carrying the pizza boxes. "I don't think Angelina wants to hear about my pea-throwing skills."

Angelina laughed and moved to settle the two children at the coffee table. "Not in the presence of these two. Robbie, it's your night to say grace."

Wes was both surprised and entertained by the little boy's version of grace. Robbie didn't recite a standard prayer. Instead, he thanked the Lord for food and then shoes and a variety of things until his mother called his name softly. He hurriedly added his mother, sister, and Melody, and said amen.

Wes found himself enjoying being in the midst of a family again. The pizza was consumed amidst much laughter and talking. Melody was as quick as Angelina in meeting the needs of the kids, wiping hands and encouraging them to try one more bite, acting more like an older sister than a caregiver. Afterward, she set up the VCR for them and returned to the sofa.

"What did you do this afternoon?" Melody asked him.

"Looked at a house. One of those old places downtown. It has a private apartment if you're interested."

His daughter rolled her eyes. "You don't give up, do you?"

"Bee, Robbie, time for your baths," Angelina said, apparently attempting to give them privacy to discuss the matter.

He appreciated her sensitivity to the situation. Melody quickly foiled the plan.

"I'll take care of them, Angelina."

"Visit with your dad."

"We'll only argue. You should stick around and referee."

"Melody!" he blurted.

"Well, it's true. I like my life the way it is. What else did you do today? I bet you looked at stores, too."

He had rented the unit next door to the pharmacy. The shopping center seemed pretty active with a good mixture of businesses, and the unit was large enough for him to offer classes to small groups.

"I knew it. Don't you ever take time to reconsider an action?"

"Not after the Lord answers my prayers."

He noted the way Angelina's head popped up at that. "The unit next door to yours caught my eye when I was there the other day."

Melody flashed him an angry look. "Angelina was thinking of expanding into that unit."

"Sorry. I called, and it was a good deal so I snapped it up."

Angelina shrugged. "That's what being indecisive will do for you. What's your business?"

"Stained glass. I create and sell pieces and stock supplies. I plan to offer classes in small groups after I get open."

"I'll have to check out your work. I love stained glass."

"Maybe you should take a class and create some of your own."

"I work far too many hours to take on anything else."

"Daddy, about the house-hunting, a condo or town-house is all you need," Melody pointed out.

"I'm supposed to look at some places at the beach tomorrow."

"Now you're talking."

Wes grinned and directed his next words to Angelina, "Tell me I don't know my child. The beach is exactly why she chose to go to college here."

"Along with most of the other students," Angelina agreed. "UNC-W by the Sea is quite popular." The phone rang, and Angelina picked up the cordless from the end table.

"Hi, Mom. Sitting around talking. Melody's dad's here." From the way Angelina lowered her voice, Wes could tell the woman was asking questions. "Yes, he's right here. How's the baby?"

"Baby?" Wes repeated, thinking it strange that Angelina's mother would have a small child.

"The Atkinses have two foster children, Jeremy and Eddie," Melody explained. "The baby was running a temp last night. He's cutting a tooth."

"They live here in town?" Melody nodded. "Why don't the kids stay with their grandparents?"

"They do."

"No, I mean, why does she pay you to baby-sit when their grandparents are here?"

"Angelina doesn't feel right about asking them to take on her responsibility."

"But it's okay to ask you?" he inquired, lowering his voice.

"It's a job, Daddy. We've got the schedule worked out."

"And what about when classes start?"

"Robbie will be in half-day school, and his grandfather will pick him up afterward. Bee will stay with her grandmother. I pick them up when I get out of school and keep them until Angelina gets home around 6:30. Then we fix dinner and share the chores."

"Sounds pretty complicated."

"But it's not," she insisted stubbornly.

"You want to go house-hunting with me tomorrow?"

"Sorry, can't. I have the kids."

"When do you have another day off?"

"Sunday, but I usually go to church with Angelina and the kids."

"Mind if I tag along?"

"Not at all."

"Are you okay with my move?"

"Daddy, you know I love you. And I've missed you. I just want you to understand this is important to me."

Angelina replaced the receiver and moved to get the kids in motion for bedtime preparation.

Melody jumped to her feet and kissed her father's cheek. "Night, Daddy. I'll take care of their baths."

"I suppose I've been dismissed," Wes said when his daughter shepherded the kids from the room. "Thanks for your hospitality."

"You're welcome. I'm glad you could come."

"Melody seems to really love it here, but she's right about one thing. I don't give up. I'm going to encourage her to come live with me."

Angelina nodded. "If Melody tells me that's what she

wants, I won't stand in her way."

❄

After closing the door behind Wes Robbins, Angelina found herself thinking how nice it was to hear a man's voice in her home again. She missed Robert dreadfully. Even though they'd married in college, their time together had been much too short. Robert had been the type of husband women dreamed of having, always encouraging her to reach for her goals and never letting their family stand in the way of her accomplishments.

Not only had his loss left her lonely, it had left a hole in her security net. All her life Angelina had struggled with security, never able to fully trust anyone for fear she would be let down again. She had been a child the first time it happened, and the second time had been just as difficult. The feeling that she had to depend wholly on herself never left her.

She understood Wes's feelings about his child. Her struggle to combat the fear of providing for her children and herself made her accept that he would probably be victorious in his quest. But what Wes failed to see was that she loved Melody as well and only wanted the best for her.

Chapter 3

While working two weeks later, Angelina considered Wes Robbins's invasion of their lives. No matter where she went, he was there. He often popped into the pharmacy during the day after checking the renovation progress in his store and, under the guise of seeing his daughter, had slipped into the habit of spending time with the family.

That first Sunday Wes attended church with them, her mother invited him to dinner. He fit right in, cuddling the kids, teasing her mom, bonding with her dad, and turning them into his extended family.

Her plan to distance herself from the situation as much as possible was shot to pieces in the first few days after determining father and daughter required a mediator. In one sense, Angelina didn't feel it was her place, but then her mothering instincts kicked in, and she felt she had to be the voice of reason.

Though Melody didn't say so, Angelina knew he still encouraged her to give up the job and come live with him in the two-bedroom condo he'd found at the beach.

The phone rang and she answered, not the least

surprised to find Wes on the other end.

"Hi, Angelina. You busy?"

"Hello, Wes. What can I do for you?"

"Melody and the kids are helping unpack boxes."

She knew that. Melody had called to ask if it was okay to take the kids with her to her dad's.

He certainly didn't allow anything to slow him down. He'd flown to Georgia to pack up and put his house on the market and returned the night before driving a truck filled with his possessions.

"I'm not sure how much help Robbie and Bee are," she pointed out. Her two little ones were probably more of a hindrance than anything else. She should have suggested Melody check with her parents.

"We've got the kitchen and living room in passable condition and thought maybe you'd like to come over for dinner."

"You're too busy settling in," she argued. "I'll pick up the kids after work, and Melody can stay and help. You'll be finished in a fraction of the time."

"It's spaghetti. My mom's recipe. The sauce cooks for hours. You'll think you've gone to heaven," he promised. "Besides, you have to eat. I'm making garlic bread. Mel said the kids love spaghetti, and they sort of know what we're having for dinner."

Wes wasn't playing fair. Telling her children he was preparing their favorite food and making garlic bread, which was her weakness, seemed like calculated temptation to Angelina. Besides, after her long day, the idea of going down to the beach wasn't necessarily appealing, but then again, the thought of not having to cook more than made up for the drive. "Okay. How do I get there? And it'll probably be close to seven before I arrive."

"Perfect."

"How's the store coming along?" she asked, not sure why she felt the need to extend the conversation.

"Great. They promised to have the renovations completed by next week. I hope so. I've already got an order in for stock."

The old adage about time being money sprang to mind. When it came to business, every day the store was closed cost the owner. "I can probably loan you a corner if it arrives before they finish."

"I don't think that'll be necessary, but I appreciate the offer. Oops, better get back to my spaghetti. See you soon."

❄

"Why did you give me that second helping?" Angelina moaned as she laid her napkin on the table.

A knowing grin covered his face as Wes countered, "I don't recall forcing it on you."

She grimaced, resting one hand against her well-filled stomach. "I'm not sure I'm going to be able to move."

Melody picked up her plate and reached for Robbie's. "Sounds like you need a walk. Why don't you join Dad on his nightly constitutional? He has doctor's orders to walk every day."

"Doctor's orders?" Angelina repeated.

"I had a heart attack a few years back."

The news rocked Angelina to her core. He appeared to be in the best of health. There was no outward indication that he was less than robust. "That must have been frightening."

"I was lucky. It didn't do much damage. Of course, I had to change my lifestyle."

"Why don't we all go?" she suggested.

"No, you two go," Melody insisted. "I need to do the dishes, and the kids are tired. They've had an exciting afternoon."

"You're spoiling me, you know."

The two women shared a smile. "I know. I figure I'll hit you up for a favor soon."

"Hey, I cooked," Wes reminded. "Do I get a favor, too?"

"I'm walking with you, aren't I?" Angelina teased.

It was a beautiful evening. The warm night was only a hint of the hotter ones to come. Now and again the scent of Wes's aftershave tantalized her nostrils, and Angelina found she liked the manly scent.

They dodged an incoming wave. "I've been meaning to tell you how much I enjoy spending time with your family. I'm in awe of your parents. I can't imagine being a foster parent at their age. Then again, I can hardly recall what it's like to have small children."

"The grandchildren will come soon enough, and you'll get back into the swing of things."

"I'm hoping that's several years down the line for Mel. One of my biggest fears is that she'll decide to marry before she finishes college. I don't want her missing out on her education."

"Women can do both, you know," Angelina said, bending to pick up a tiny sand dollar. She brushed it off, pleased to find it wasn't broken. "Robert and I married in college. When he got his degree, he took a job at a pharmacy in Chapel Hill so I could finish my education. Robbie came along just as I was finishing up. Considering what happened to Robert, I'm glad we didn't wait."

"You've got a point."

"Don't worry, Wes. Melody dates, but she's never been serious enough to bring the guy to the house."

"That's good to know. I know she thinks of you and the Atkinses as her extended family."

"The Atkinses are good people."

"You say that like you're not one yourself."

"I'm an Atkins by the grace of God—the child of their hearts."

"You're adopted?"

"Yes. From what Mom told me, my real parents died when I was five or so."

"Did you have siblings?"

"Yes, but I don't know much about them."

"Do you ever think about finding them?"

"Sometimes, but then I've found it's not good to look back. The past holds a lot of sadness. For now, I've got to concentrate on making a good life for my kids."

"You only have to trust in God to provide. Psalm 118:8 reminds us it's better to trust in the Lord than to put confidence in man."

Trust in God. If only he knew how much she wanted to do that; but Angelina was afraid. If something happened to her, what would happen to her children? She didn't want them growing up in foster homes.

"We'd better head back," she said, ignoring his words. "It's late and I need to get the kids into bed."

❄

What was she thinking? Wes wondered as they backtracked

to the condo. He'd noticed the way she clammed up when he mentioned trusting in God. Wasn't Angelina a believer? She attended church regularly and unless she was putting on an incredible act, she obviously loved the Lord.

Maybe it was the past making her doubt. Whatever the case, Wes knew from experience that the only way he'd survived the rocky times was by remembering that the Lord loved him. The heart attack had been hard enough—knocking him to his knees—and then Laura's death had laid him flat. For weeks, he'd barely existed until Melody forced him to rejoin the land of the living.

Now he was thankful she had. She'd asked him if he thought this was what her mother expected of him. That had been more than sufficient to push him toward recovery. Throughout her illness, Laura had prayed for God's will to be done in her life. She was ready to go, but determined to fight the cancer to the very end. Tears wet his eyes at the thought of his courageous wife.

Wes pulled the door key from his pocket and unlocked the door, heeding Melody's shushing finger as they stepped inside. The two children were fast asleep on the sofa.

Angelina knelt by Robbie's side, tenderly smoothing back his hair before she shook him gently. "Time to go home, Sweetie." She didn't even try to wake Bee, just lifted the little girl into her arms. Bee sighed and adjusted her head more comfortably against her mother's shoulder. "Thanks for dinner, Wes. You were right about that spaghetti sauce."

"My pleasure. We'll have to do it again soon."

Melody picked up her purse and kissed his cheek.

"I'm going to follow Angelina home, Dad. Talk to you tomorrow."

Wes followed them to the cars, watching as they settled the children in Angelina's SUV. As he watched the taillights disappear around the corner, he admitted he already missed them all. Slowly but surely they had slipped into his heart and mind.

Chapter 4

A few days later, Wes stopped by Angelina's house to see if Melody wanted to have lunch with him. He was shocked to find four children instead of two.

"Why is he here?" Wes asked when she opened the door with the baby draped over her shoulder. Her hand never stopped its movement as she rubbed and patted. "Mrs. Ruth had a doctor's appointment, and Mr. Edwin wanted to go with her. I volunteered to baby-sit."

"Why do you always take on so much? You don't owe these people anything."

She smiled when the baby rewarded her with a loud burp. "They're my friends, Dad."

Why couldn't she see the truth? "I think they take advantage of you," he retorted somewhat angrily.

"Oh, please, you don't have a clue how cushy this job truly is."

"Cushy?" he repeated doubtfully. "I hardly think caring for two, sometimes four, active children is cushy."

"My friends are slinging burgers and waiting tables until the wee hours of the morning. Compared to that, this job is a breeze."

"So you keep telling me."

"I can see you're dying to talk to Angelina again. Just don't. Okay? Promise me, Dad," she insisted when stubbornness entered his expression.

"But, Melody, you shouldn't be tied down with all these kids."

"I'm exactly where I want to be. Why can't you understand?"

"Because I have no idea why a vibrant, beautiful young woman like yourself isn't out there making friends and enjoying what should be one of the best times of her life."

She turned around and walked into the family room, settling the baby in his car seat. "Maybe you've never understood me then, Dad. I never planned to turn my college years into a constant party. I have my friends from home and friends at church that I go out with occasionally, but I'm not interested in pledging sororities and stuff like that."

Wes had the suspicion he was fighting a lost cause. "I guess I'll head on to the store since you're busy. Can we get together for dinner or lunch soon?"

"Sure thing," she said, her attention diverted when the children ran screaming at the top of their lungs through the room.

❋

"Something wrong, Wes?" Angelina asked minutes later when she glanced up to find him strolling down the aisle toward the pharmacy counter.

"I don't understand my child."

She drew a deep breath. "What parent does?"

"I want to make her life easier."

"Let me guess. You've been arguing about her job again.

207

What happened this time?"

"She's baby-sitting the foster kids, too."

She chose her words carefully. "I see. I can assure you she's well-paid. Mom doesn't ask her to sit for free, though I will admit that if Melody had her way, she would. She loves babies."

Wes shook his head wearily. "I know. Do you have any idea why?"

Angelina lifted one shoulder and smiled. "No. Why does it bother you so much, Wes?"

"She's young. I'd like to see her out having fun."

"Maybe your idea of fun and hers don't match?"

"I have more fun than she does, and I'm an old man."

Angelina couldn't control her burst of laughter. "You're not old."

"Then why do I feel so old right now?" he challenged.

"Defeated, but you'll live to fight another day," she teased. A customer came to the counter, and Angelina broke away to talk to him. Wes lifted a hand in good-bye and headed out of the store.

As she worked, Angelina found herself thinking of him. Wes was a nice guy. She could appreciate that he didn't like his daughter's choices. Melody and her father were very alike, and she didn't hesitate to tell him to let her live her own life.

The phone rang and she answered, immediately recognizing his voice. "Wes?"

"If I asked you out to dinner, would you go?"

Stunned, she fumbled the pill bottle she held. Why had he gone back to his business and called? Why not ask her in person?

"I know I should have asked you while I was there, but I couldn't get up the nerve."

She caught the receiver against her chin. "To discuss Melody?"

"No," he said quickly.

"You want to consort with the enemy?" she asked, capping the bottle and checking the label one last time.

"I'm beginning to think I'm my own worst enemy."

"I don't understand."

"I'm so eager to have something I never bothered to work for when I should have."

"Huh?"

"Just past regrets. Are we on for tonight? Or do you need more time to make arrangements?"

"I probably should see if Melody is available to keep the kids."

"I'm sure she is," Wes responded matter-of-factly. "How about it?"

"Where did you plan to go?" She hadn't dated in a long time and wasn't certain she had anything in her closet that was date-worthy.

"How about the steak house over on South College? I've been there several times, and the food is great. I'll pick you up around seven."

"I'll check with Melody and let you know."

Angelina rang up the prescription and thanked the customer before reaching for the phone. Melody picked up on the second ring.

"Hear you've got a full house over there."

Melody sighed loudly. "What did he say? He promised."

"He didn't pick a fight," she reassured. "He's worried."

"Well, he can give himself a break. Your mom picked them up a few minutes ago. Said her appointment went fine."

"Thank God. Now, I've got a question for you, and I expect you to tell me nothing less than the truth."

"Is something wrong?"

"Your dad asked me out to dinner tonight. I said yes, but if you have a problem with it, I'll tell him I can't."

"Why would I have a problem? You two share something in common."

"What?"

"Me." Melody laughed at her pun. "Personally, I'd be thankful if you went. Maybe if Daddy got a life of his own, he'd leave mine alone."

"You're sure?"

"Positive. Where's he taking you?"

Angelina shared the restaurant name and time. "I'll run home and change. Are you sure you're not busy tonight?"

"No great plans. Kelly might come over for awhile. Robbie and Bee won't be any trouble."

"Would you like to order Chinese so you don't have to cook?"

"Sounds great."

The butterflies in her stomach must be some gigantic hybrid, Angelina thought as she waited for Wes's arrival. In the bedroom, she'd thought about what she was doing and wondered if it was the right thing. The doubts had been so overwhelming that she'd finally dropped onto the bed and prayed for God's guidance in the matter. She felt a bit more confident after finishing the prayer.

"Angelina, there's some old man here who claims he's your date," Melody called up the stairs.

"Why. . .I'll show you old, young lady." The sounds of muted laughter drifted up the stairs.

She stood and smoothed the lavender knit top. Did she look okay? One last glance in the mirror assured her she was fine. She joined the family in the living room to find Robbie and Bee being teased by Wes.

"Mommy," Bee cried out, running over to wrap her arms about her legs.

"Your mommy can't save you. I'm going to steal all her kisses." Wes laughed.

Her childish screams echoed throughout the room as she ran around behind her mother. Melody stretched out her arms. "Come on, Bee."

"No. Want Mommy."

"She's going out."

"Bee go."

Melody made a sad face. "You have to stay with us. We'll be lonely."

The child looked at her mother and said emphatically, "Wobbie and Meldee go too."

"No, Bee," Angelina said, lifting the child into her arms and delivering the next words with a hug. "Tonight's a grown-up night. Mr. Wes and I are going out, and you're staying home."

"I want to go," she insisted stubbornly.

"Not tonight."

She started to cry.

Angelina forced herself to discipline the child. "Fereby, what did Mommy say?"

"Bee not go."

"That's correct. I want you and Robbie to behave."

Melody took the child from her arms and said, "They're always good for me, aren't you?"

Bee nodded her head before tucking it into Melody's shoulder and sticking her thumb into her mouth. It was a habit the child reverted to now and again, when she felt insecure or didn't get her way. Angelina figured it was the latter tonight.

"We can stay here," Wes said when she glanced back as they started out the door.

"No. She needs to learn."

"Leaving them with others is hard. You're a stronger parent than me. That was the most pitiful expression on Bee's face. I would have given in."

Angelina settled in the car, taking advantage of the moment to study Wes. Was there some hidden meaning in his words? "We can go back."

"No way. You've already told her no," he said, quickly closing the door. He climbed into the driver's seat and asked, "You okay with the place I suggested?"

She nodded and soon they were seated in a booth, enjoying a blooming onion appetizer and iced tea.

"It's been a long time since I went on a date," Angelina said.

"Did you date a lot?"

"There were a couple of guys before Robert, but once we met, I decided he was the one. What about you?"

"Laura and I married right out of college. Then first

thing we knew Mel was on the way. Laura elected to become a stay-at-home mom, and I jumped on the fast track. I was even more driven to succeed after I had a wife and daughter to support. That was the biggest mistake I ever made."

Regret filled his eyes as he continued. "I can't begin to count the nights I came home long after Mel was in bed. I kept telling myself I'd do better, but something always interfered. All too soon she was nearly grown and didn't need to spend time with her daddy."

"That's why I feel guilty about leaving my two," she said. "I spend so much time at work and want to be with them as often as possible."

"You think they're willing to share you?"

She finished wiping her fingers and tucked the napkin in her lap. "Why Mr. Robbins, are you stating your intentions?" she inquired with in an affected drawl.

He chuckled at her playfulness. "And if I were?"

"I might ask what you intend."

"You're a beautiful woman, and I'd like to have you as my friend—and whatever else the Lord intends."

"Well, you leave no doubt."

"Don't you think a man should be straightforward?"

"Yes, I do. And, truthfully, despite our problems over me being Melody's employer, I do think of you as a very good friend."

He touched her hand. "Just a friend?"

"Well, that's important too," Angelina defended.

"Definitely. The best relationships start out that way."

"I find you to be a handsome, personable man with a delightful daughter."

"Are you attracted to me, Angel?"

Angelina felt her face warm at his prompting. "Don't call me that."

"Why not? I like giving people pet names. And don't change the subject."

"I guess so. Otherwise, I probably wouldn't be here."

"Now we're getting somewhere."

Before he could pursue the topic further, the waitress arrived with their salads. After saying grace, they busied themselves sprinkling salt and pepper and pouring salad dressings. "How was your day?" Angelina asked, feeling it best not to pursue their previous discussion.

"Creative. That's one of the problems with a one-man operation. Customers must have radar or something. They have a tendency to arrive just about the time I get started with a new piece. I do lots before I open every day and sometimes after I close."

"You need an assistant."

"I'd hoped Mel might help out."

"Wes. . ."

"You don't need to get defensive."

Angelina rested her fork on the plate and focused her attention on him. "I am not defensive," she insisted.

"You are. From the first time we argued about the situation, I've felt you feel I'm attacking you personally when I make a comment about Mel's job."

"I'm feeling caught in the middle," Angelina exclaimed, lowering her voice when she caught the attention of the other patrons. "You feel I control the situation, but I don't. Melody has told me she wants her job, and until she says differently, I don't plan to find a replacement."

"You're right," Wes agreed. "Let me say that I considered Mel might help out before I knew how things really were here. I thought maybe she'd be interested in working in the family business."

"Does she like stained glass?"

"She thinks it's beautiful but isn't really interested in the creative aspect," he admitted. "Back to the apology. Before I got to know you, I thought it was better for you to fill the bad guy role than me. I felt that if you terminated her employment Melody would do what I wanted. I should know my daughter better than that."

"I can understand your feelings to a certain degree, but if she's happy, why can't you accept this is what she wants?"

"You've got me there. Maybe I'm afraid my workaholic tendency will manifest itself in her. I'd hate to see her make the same mistakes I made."

"I think Melody is one blessed young woman to have a father who cares for her as much as you do, even if you do want me to fill the bad guy role," Angelina added with a huge grin.

"I'll try not to say anything else."

"But if you think she's overloaded, you'll let me know, right?"

"Right," he agreed, squeezing her hand in his. The brown gaze held hers. "We make a good team."

"I'm not on the opposing side, Wes. As a parent I know you want the best for your child, but when they're older and capable of making their own decisions, your ideas of what's best will not always match theirs."

"You're so right. We'd better finish these salads."

Later, Wes said good night and let himself out of the house, double-checking the door to assure it was locked. All in all, their first date had been pretty good. Personally, he hoped it was the first of many. Angelina Collier was quite some woman.

Chapter 5

"Angel, you've got to come over here right now."

She sighed. The man was hopeless. Maybe he could walk in and out of his business with the flip of an open/closed sign, but she couldn't. People depended on her being there.

"Ah, come on, Angel. Just for a minute. This you've got to see."

"Wes, I've got customers." Actually, she didn't. There had been a lull in business since the lunch hour had passed.

He didn't seem to hear her words. "You know what they say about everyone having a double?" Wes rushed on, not waiting for an answer. "Yours is in my store right now. You've got to see her."

His determination was a trait she'd come to expect. "I don't suppose I'll get any peace if I don't?"

"I could ask her to go over there."

"No. I'll be right there," she said quickly, not wanting to turn her pharmacy into a sideshow.

After telling her cashiers where she'd be, Angelina walked next door. As always, she was in awe of the showroom in the front of his store. Wes had replaced the large expanses of glass on the front of the unit with paned windows and hung various pieces of glass in the windows that he kept sparkling clean. Inside the store, he had more window units and glass walls featuring the various pieces, all carefully lit to enhance their beauty.

Angelina noticed the woman off to the side. Wes hurried over, grabbing her hand and pulling her toward the stranger. "You're not going to believe this."

"Ms. McDaniel, this is Angelina Collier. The woman I told you about."

She turned, a smile touching her lips as she greeted the newcomer.

"Do you see it?" Wes asked impatiently.

They were around the same height but the similarity stopped there. This woman weighed a bit more, and her shoulder-length hair was a light brown and her eyes hazel—far removed from Angelina's blond, green-eyed appearance.

They looked at each other and then at Wes. Angelina offered a little shrug and apologetic smile. "Not really."

Ms. McDaniel shook her head and said, "Me neither."

Wes looked amazed. "I can't believe you don't see the resemblance. When you smile, you both have that little dimple at the corner of your mouth. Bee has it too, Angel."

They gave each other the once-over again.

"I think you missed the mark on this, Wes," Angelina said.

"I agree. I'm Crista McDaniel," she said, holding out her hand, "a consultant from Phoenix. I'm in town for a seminar, and when I saw the glass in the window, I had to stop and take a look. I'm in love with that piece with the balloons."

Angelina's gaze shot to the wall as the woman's words struck a responsive chord. She adored balloons. Back when they first married and their budget was tight, Robert had often given her helium bouquets instead of flowers. She'd even done the children's nursery in clowns and balloons. She knew exactly which picture the woman referred to. "Don't you just love it?"

"Oh yes."

Angelina glanced at Wes and grinned, teasing, "She has good taste. Perhaps that's where we resemble each other."

"You're blind."

"Don't pay him any attention, Ms. McDaniel. Not all of us have his imagination. Are you enjoying your stay?"

"Very much."

She smiled warmly, this time noticing the little dimple Wes spoke of as Crista McDaniel returned the smile. "I've got to get back. It was a pleasure meeting you."

"You too."

❄

Wes watched Angel leave before turning back to his customer. "You really do resemble each other."

"It happens," Crista said. "I've seen strangers with similar mannerisms. I'm going to have to buy that piece."

"You want to take it with you or have it shipped?"

"Oh, shipping would be perfect." She reached into her purse for her wallet and removed a business card. "Here's the address."

As Wes wrote up the sale, they chatted for a few more minutes before she checked her watch and said good-bye.

Later that afternoon, Wes stopped by the pharmacy.

"I can't believe you couldn't see the likeness with Crista McDaniel."

And I can't believe you did, Angelina thought. The entire situation had been embarrassing. "Must have been some little something that made you think that."

He shrugged. "See you at church tonight?"

She nodded. "I'm helping with the kids' program."

"Care to join me for dinner before we go?"

"There's no time, Wes. By the time I close up here, run home, and change, we'll probably be late. Besides, Melody has plans to feed Robbie and Bee early tonight, like she usually does on Wednesdays."

"Hey, maybe I should rush on over. What are they having?"

"Beans and franks," she said.

"Maybe another time. See you later. By the way, I invited Ms. McDaniel to church."

That caught Angelina's attention. He was certainly friendly with the young woman. Something stirred inside, and she realized she didn't want Wes to be interested in another woman.

"She coming?" she asked, pushing back the thought as she hoped her feelings weren't evident.

"Thanked me but said as much as she'd love to, she's tied up with work. Reminds me of you with that work thing."

Angelina smiled at that. "Give it a rest. You just need to get your eyes examined."

"I'll have you know my vision is twenty-twenty."

"Oh, that's right," Angelina said. "It's your imagination that's out of control."

"I still say you look like that woman."

"Okay, Wes, whatever you say. Except for the hair and eyes, we're almost identical twins."

"I wouldn't go that far."

"Me neither. You're seeing things that aren't there."

Wes didn't say another word as he turned and walked toward the front of the store, holding up one hand in a silent farewell.

"Bye, Wes. If I see your twin around, I'll call," she teased.

"Do that."

Chapter 6

I can't be sick."

Those were the last words Wes had heard from Angelina's mouth as the nurses shooed him out to begin preparations for surgery. Now he waited with her mother in the surgery waiting area. The room was designed to be comfortable, but the feelings being in a hospital evoked made Wes want to be anywhere but there. On the other hand, he needed to be there for Angelina.

Wes thought back over the past few weeks. Every day since Angel had come into his life seemed to get better. He loved her intelligence and wit, her sense of humor, and mostly her ability to accept things as they came.

The only negative was when they butted heads over Melody's job, but when she looked tired or seemed overburdened, his first instinct was to confront Angelina. He had to admit that she generally helped work the situation out. She treated Melody more like a daughter than an employee, and Wes knew it was because she cared about them both.

At times, he recognized she was incapable of totally letting go and trusting God. He had been with her during one particularly painful bout and when he tried to approach the need for her to see a doctor, she told him it wasn't necessary. It had only taken one other episode to convince her she didn't have an option. He wished he could make her understand that relying on her own strength limited her. This sickness required God's power to get her through.

"I'm thankful this is a routine surgery," Ruth said.

"Angel's pretty upset that she requires surgery at all."

Ruth Atkins nodded. "She's been having problems with her gallbladder for awhile now. That last attack was bad enough to convince her she couldn't wait any longer. I think maybe that after Robert she was afraid of what the doctors would find."

"But surely she knows. . ."

"The reality of the situation is that she's sick and feels she can't be. No matter what experience tells her, she's afraid. Her dad and I are here for her. We'll do whatever we need to do until she gets back on her feet."

"Mel and I will be, too. I just hope we can convince her to take it easy and heal before going back to work."

"You can have that task," her mother teased.

"I've heard this surgery has a two-week recovery period. I know she's going to be a challenge."

The two of them idly watched a short news broadcast on the waiting room television. "Who has the kids?"

"Edwin has Bee and the baby. Robbie and Jeremy are at day school. Melody plans to bring Robbie and Bee here after Angelina wakes."

"I know Edwin wishes he could be here. Being foster parents must really be difficult."

"We've always had foster kids. I guess it was hard on Angelina. By the time she got used to a group of kids, they'd go away and we'd get more."

"Angelina was the only child you ever adopted?"

She nodded. "Most of the time they're in foster placement because they can't be adopted, but in this case her parents had died, and there was no one to take all the children."

Wes felt saddened by their separation. "It's awful when a family has to be split up. I hope they were all as blessed as Angel."

The older woman blushed slightly at his compliment. "We were the blessed ones. God sent us our own little angel."

Wes chuckled softly. "You think her actions are going to be at odds with her name while she recuperates?"

"You can take that to the bank. Personally, I think God is telling her to trust Him more completely."

"I've told her that. She seems to feel she can't lose control."

"Given the circumstances, can you blame her?"

He understood. Losing her parents at an early age, then going from foster home to foster home until she came to live with the Atkinses certainly didn't help establish stability. Add to that the early loss of her husband and having to raise two children alone.

"Do you know anything about her family?"

"Their name was Richmond. She was in the system for a few months before she came to us. She was a beautiful child—a lot like Bee now."

"They're very alike."

Ruth nodded. "It took time for her to trust that she wasn't going to be sent away. Deep down, I'm not sure she doesn't still feel insecure."

"She's going to get past that soon," Wes promised. He believed in Angelina and knew she was more than capable. She just needed to place her trust in God—much like he'd done when he got sick and then lost Laura.

While they waited, Wes began the task he'd been putting off. Sending Christmas greetings was his way of thanking his customers and offering a special discount coupon generally increased his business over the holidays.

As Wes applied stickers to the pre-printed cards, he didn't care what etiquette said about hand addressing the envelopes. The labels Mel made saved him a ton of work.

Pulling off the next sticker, he noted the Arizona address. Crista McDaniel. Wes repeated the name in his head before recalling the woman. Angel's look-alike. He still couldn't believe they didn't see the similarities. He affixed the label. She was too far away to take advantage of the discount, but she had been a good customer. She deserved a thank-you.

"Did Angel tell you about the woman who came into the store who looks like her?"

Ruth looked up from the embroidery she was doing. "She didn't see a resemblance."

"I wish you'd been there to back me up. Her name is Crista McDaniel. She looks just like Angel when she smiles. Has that same little dimple."

"Well, they do say everyone has a look-alike."

They sat quietly, each lost in their activity until they were called in the private consulting room to meet with the surgeon. As expected, the surgery had gone well, with no complications. Both breathed a sigh of relief.

"No need to worry. It was a textbook case. She'll be in recovery for awhile before they take her to a room," the doctor said. "They'll let you know when you can see her."

Wes stood and shook the man's hand. "Thanks."

When Ruth dabbed at the tears that sprang to her eyes, Wes pulled her into a hug. "It's okay."

"I love her so much. I'm thankful God took care of her."

"Me, too."

Ruth stepped back and looked into Wes's eyes. "You're in love with Angelina?"

"Yes."

"Oh, I'm so glad," Ruth exclaimed, hugging him again. "She needs a good man."

"I'm glad you approve."

"I do. I've come to love you and Melody a great deal. I don't ever want you to leave our lives."

"Well, I don't want to leave. Let's pray it's God's intent for Angelina to agree."

Chapter 7

Angelina couldn't recall a time when she was more happy to see home. It seemed like she'd been gone for days rather than hours.

Wes hit the remote door opener and backed the SUV into the garage. "You want me to carry you inside?"

She glanced toward the side door. Barely three feet separated the vehicle from the utility room entrance. "You're kidding, right?"

"Well, we don't have a wheelchair."

"I can walk," Angelina insisted, reaching for the door handle.

In one respect, Wes's tender loving care was welcome, but she was afraid to depend on him too much—afraid to let go and need anyone but herself. Right now, she needed to concentrate on getting well and back to work. And that required being strong and doing things for herself. "Only I would require surgery the week before Thanksgiving," she told Wes when he opened the vehicle door.

"Yeah, but think of all those goodies you'll be able to eat now."

"You obviously didn't talk to my doctor. I've got to

restructure my entire diet."

"I know what that's like," he said, taking her arm to assist her.

"I suppose you do," she agreed, grimacing when pain shafted through her midsection. Angelina took a deep breath and said, "It's better if I do it myself."

Wes stepped back, staying within reach. "Take it easy," he said when she stepped onto the bottom step and stopped. "Lean on me."

The short trip took more out of her than she cared to admit, and she was more than a little happy to see the sofa. "Why did you say Mom couldn't come?"

"They think Jeremy might have chicken pox, and she's not sure you ever had them."

Coming to the Atkinses as an older child meant her communicable disease history was sketchy at best.

"She said it's the last thing you need."

"I pray Robbie and Bee don't get them."

"Don't worry. We have a contingency plan if they do," he said, helping her get settled and tucking a pillow underneath her head. He reached for the throw and placed it over her legs.

Wes left the room and returned a few minutes later with her flowers. "Where did you want these?" She indicated the sideboard across the room.

Her gaze fixed on the character balloon her children had picked for her. Angelina thought of how Wes had delighted the children by making it walk. His flower choice had been a dozen peach roses.

"I left your suitcase in the kitchen for now. Is there anything you need?"

She shook her head, and Wes settled in the recliner. "Aren't you opening the store today?"

"I put up a sign that I'd be closed a day or so."

"Oh, Wes, that's not necessary," she insisted. "How can you make a living closing like that?"

"The Lord provides."

In the back of her mind, Angelina suspected Wes's business was more of a hobby—unlike her own which provided for her family's livelihood. Thank God they had been able to get the store established before Robert got sick. Otherwise, she would have been working for someone else. "I hope everything is okay at the pharmacy."

"It's fine. Don't worry so much."

"Don't worry. I've got two holidays to prepare for, children who need their mother, a house to be cleaned and decorated, in addition to earning a living. I won't even mention my Christmas shopping."

"And somehow most of it will get done, and what's not finished won't matter."

She wished she could look at things in the same way. Striving for perfection was the one thing about herself Angelina sometimes wished she could change. Life would certainly be easier if everything didn't have to be done.

"We can do the shopping right from here," Wes said. "And I've got a store full of glass pieces."

"You'd bankrupt me."

He laughed. "I'll give you the family discount. What if I get my laptop and we do some on-line shopping? It's great. You can go to any of the stores you like and cyber shop."

"You've done it?"

"All the time. Never had any problems."

It wasn't a bad idea. If she could do her shopping while she was recovering, it would free her up to do the other things.

"Mel and I are cooking Thanksgiving dinner. We want to invite your parents and the kids."

"I don't know, Wes. That's a lot of work."

"We did plan to use your kitchen."

"Wes. . ."

"Please let us, Angel," he pleaded. "We want to do this for you."

Right now, celebrating was the farthest thing from her mind. "You don't know what you're getting yourself into."

"It'll be fun. We never had a big family gathering. All our family lived pretty far away and it was just the three of us."

"Okay. But you've got to let us help."

"We'll see. I've been seeing signs about the Flotilla this weekend. Do you ever go?"

"It's been awhile."

"Why don't we go? The kids would love it."

"I might be back at work."

Disappointment flared in his eyes. "Why do you do that to yourself, Angel? You know the doctor wants you home for a couple of weeks."

"I can't afford to sit around for two weeks."

"You can't afford not to. If you don't take care of yourself, you could have complications, and it would take you longer to recuperate."

She knew he was right, but Angelina also knew she had people depending on her—her children, her employees, why even his child depended on her for a job. "I have responsibilities, Wes."

"Do you really trust God to provide for you?"

"Of course I do."

"Do you? Have you let go and accepted that perhaps this inconvenient surgery has a greater purpose? I'm not saying you should sit home forever and do nothing, but you should give God some credit. He's not going to let you or the kids go hungry or homeless."

"But He did, once," she pointed out, unable to swallow the knot of emotion that rose in her throat.

Wes moved quickly to her side. "Angel, I'm sorry. But even though the Lord took, He gave in return."

Filled with remorse, she said, "I know. I feel so guilty when I let the past wear me down."

"It's fear making you feel alone."

"I think about my babies, and I get so afraid. What will they do if something happens to me?"

"I care about you, Angel. I'd never let anything happen to you or the children."

He cared for her. Angelina wasn't surprised by his admission. She knew that—had known for quite some time. Wes had slowly worked his way into their lives and hearts, and even though he frustrated her at times, she cared for him as well.

"I try, Wes. I really do."

"But you've never been able to fully let go and let God?"

"My parents died when I was five, and there was nowhere to go. I got shuffled from foster home to foster home until Mom and Dad chose me as their daughter.

Then I married Robert thinking we'd have at least fifty years together, and he died. No one has ever been permanent in my life."

"God has. He's been right there with you through all the difficult times. It took Him awhile, but He sent you the perfect replacement parents. He sent you a handsome, loving husband, and even when He took him, He left you with two wonderful children."

What he said made a lot of sense, but still Angelina struggled with her doubts. "So is that why you do what you do? Close your store at whim? You trust God to provide?"

"I'm not perfect, Angelina. Years ago when my wife was alive and Mel was small, I lived for the rat race. Giving Mel the things I never had and Laura the things I thought she deserved were my only goals in life. It never occurred to me that I was what my wife and child needed. The heart attack started me thinking. I was home with Laura and Mel for several weeks before they adapted to having me there.

"I was a stranger in my own home, strictly of my own making. I vowed right then and there to change. I prayed to God to help me straighten out the mess I'd made of my life, and when the doctor suggested I take up a hobby, I started working with the glass. I liked it so much I decided to try to make a living doing that."

"I wanted to stay home with my babies," Angelina said softly, regret touching her words. "But Robert got sick. It wasn't his fault. Someone had to make a living."

Wes squeezed her hand. "You've had a difficult life, but you're a better person because of it."

Angelina's attempt at a smile disappeared beneath a huge yawn. "I'm sorry."

"Why don't you catch a nap? Mel and the kids will be home soon. We already warned them to be careful with you. Bee knows she can't jump on Mommy."

"Thanks, Wes. I really do appreciate all the things you've done for me. I'll never be able to repay you or Melody."

He kissed her forehead tenderly. "We don't expect anything in return. We just want to help because we love you."

Her eyes filled with tears.

"Don't cry, Angel. Just let me share your burden. You want to go to your room or nap here on the sofa?"

"Here's fine," she whispered. Wes tucked the chenille throw more closely about her and kissed her forehead again. "Sleep in peace, Angel."

❄

Angelina felt better with each passing day. Frequent calls to the store verified everything was going smoothly. The part-time pharmacist was glad of the extra hours, and though it would cut her profit margin, it was a workable situation.

Tomorrow was Thanksgiving. Wes and Melody had worked in the kitchen the past couple of nights, filling the house with the most wonderful aromas.

When she insisted they give her something to do, Wes gave her a bag of pecans and told her to pick them out. Robbie and Bee ate most of the first ones until she shooed them away, claiming there would be none left.

They would attend Thanksgiving service that night, and the next morning they were helping out at church. They planned to take the kids with them to deliver plates to the homebound.

Angelina had taken Wes's suggestion and found shopping on-line much easier than fighting the crowds in the stores. It looked like Robbie and Bee would get what they had requested for Christmas, and she would definitely consider shopping that way more often.

Wes teased the children with the idea of decorating for Christmas. She wasn't sure what he had in mind, but there was lots of giggling as they made plans. The sounds warmed her heart as she considered her children's enjoyment.

All things considered, she was fairly confident the doctor would release her to return to work when she went for her Monday appointment. She was thankful for God's provision in sending Wes to help out.

When Wes invited her parents for Thanksgiving dinner, they readily accepted. Blessedly, they learned that Jeremy's "chicken pox" was an allergic reaction to something he'd eaten.

Wes launched into planning a meal that made Angelina tired just thinking of preparation time. When her mother came to visit earlier in the week, she suggested that Angelina marry the man. He had to ask first, but her mother's recommendation certainly made her think about what life would be like if Wes were her husband.

Because of the morning plans, they'd decided to have their meal in the late afternoon. After getting everyone back home, Angelina waited as Wes unloaded something from his trunk. She followed him to the patio. He began assembling what appeared to be a cooker.

"What is that?"

"A turkey fryer. I've heard there's nothing better so I

figured we'd give it a shot. It only takes a few minutes a pound to cook and is supposed to be more moist."

"Fried? You're going to fry our turkey? We always cook it in the oven."

"So this year will be a new experience," Wes said, picking up the instruction sheet.

Not the only one, Angelina thought. Wes had changed her life. And not all for the bad, she admitted, considering that perhaps moist turkey would be an improvement.

"Can I help?"

"Yes. Go inside and rest for a bit. I think you might have overdone it this morning."

"Don't baby me, Wes. I'm not an invalid."

"I didn't say you were. Please, Angel. Do it for me?" His eyes pleaded with her.

"Oh, okay. Just be careful with that thing."

He winked at her before he went back to reading the instructions.

Chapter 8

The bells he'd hung on the door jangled as the last customers exited the store. It had been a busy morning, the second day following the holiday weekend. Shoppers, intent on getting a jump on their Christmas shopping, came waving the discount coupons and left with a great deal of the displayed stock, not to mention a number of orders to be completed within the next couple of weeks. He was going to be busy.

Too busy to spend much time with Angel, Wes realized sadly. Unless he hired a temporary clerk to free him up so he could work.

He had really enjoyed the holiday. In fact, it had probably been one of the best Thanksgivings of his life. Dinner had been a huge success. The fried turkey had been little more than a carcass by the time everyone ate their fill. Even the kids asked for seconds. Angelina had admitted it was something she'd like to try again.

Friday had been incredible—the shopping day to end all days. Angelina had kept the kids so Mel could help out.

On Saturday night, they sat in his backyard and watched the boats parade down the waterway, all decked

236

out in their Christmas lights. The creative designs on the boats and the fireworks that followed thrilled the children, and not even the rain that started near the end of the display dampened their high spirits.

He'd stayed busy working on his glass on Saturday with Mel handling the walk-in customers. On Sunday, they attended church together and went out for lunch. Afterward, they took the children to the mall to see the decorations.

Angel had gone for her follow-up appointment yesterday, and the doctor had released her to return to work today. He wondered how she was feeling.

Glancing at his watch, Wes decided he was ready for lunch. Might as well break bread with Angel. He called in an order and, after picking up the food, headed for the drugstore. He went to the back and found her hard at work. "Lunchtime."

"Already?"

"Time flies when you're having fun. You wouldn't believe how busy the store's been this morning."

"And you closed for lunch?"

He grinned at her incredulous tone. "You're not sure about my business sense, are you?" She didn't answer, but Wes knew from her expression that she didn't consider closing for lunch when business was good a smart move. "I'll have you know my customer-appreciation coupons are netting me a small fortune. How are you doing on your first day back?"

"A bit tired but otherwise fine."

"I won't say what I'm thinking."

"Which is just as well since I'm not going to listen to you anyway."

Wes pushed a Styrofoam container into her hand. "Here, eat and build up your stamina."

He noted the look of surprise when she flipped the plate open and revealed a large sandwich.

"I can't eat all this."

"Sure you can. One bite at a time."

"Okay, you win. But only because I'm hungry." She peered into the paper bag that accompanied her lunch plate.

"What are you looking for?"

"Utensils. You expect me to eat with my fingers?"

"You could. It's only a sandwich and fries." Wes extracted the package of utensils from his shirt pocket and handed it to her. "Then again, you might need the fork for your pie."

Angelina grimaced. "You are so hard on my diet."

"Why do you need to diet? You look fine to me."

"So will you love me when I gain ten pounds over the holidays?"

"Just means there's even more of you to love," he teased.

"Go back to work, Wes."

"No can do. I don't like eating alone."

Wes launched into a discussion of where he could find a clerk and what to buy everyone for Christmas. Before he realized it, the lunch hour had passed. "I'd better get back to the store. I'm going to be pretty busy the next few days. I've got several orders for pieces."

"Thanks for lunch. I'll see if I can return the favor one night this week." She leaned to kiss his cheek. "Thanks for everything. I can't tell you how much I appreciate the way you take care of me."

"Anytime, Angel."

Back at the store, he used the lull in customers to do a bit of restocking. The phone rang just as he came out of the storeroom with a box of sun catchers. Taking care to place them safely on the countertop, he picked up the phone. "Wes's Glass."

"Hello, is Mr. Robbins available?"

"Speaking."

"This is Crista McDaniel from Arizona. I've enjoyed my balloon piece so much that I've decided to order some pieces as gifts."

"I appreciate you thinking of me."

"Sending that Christmas card with a discount coupon is good advertising."

Wes grabbed an order pad and began writing as she listed the various pieces she'd chosen from his Web site. After totaling, adding tax and shipping, he quoted her a price. She gave him a credit card number. Wes grinned at the blessing. So much for thinking sending a card out of town was a waste. Ms. McDaniel had definitely proven him wrong.

"Thank you very much. By the way, I'm sorry about that episode when you were here before. Angel thought you might have been embarrassed."

She chuckled. "Not at all. In fact, it would have been nice to find another of my long-lost sisters."

"Another?" he asked.

"Yes. I found my oldest sister recently. It was very exciting to learn I had siblings. I was young when my parents died."

"Angel was young, too. Tell me, how did you and your sister find each other? I'd love to help Angel locate her family. From what her mother told me, the family name was Richmond."

"Is Angel her real name?"

Wes caught the surprise in her voice. "Actually it's Angelina."

He jerked the phone back from his ear at the woman's excited scream.

"I can't believe it! Eden will never believe this!"

"Eden?" Wes repeated, wondering whom she referred to. One minute they were having a calm discussion, and then she started shouting.

"My sister. Mr. Robbins, based on what you just told me, I think you might have found our sister for us."

"What?" Wes demanded, finding the situation incredible. "I mean Angelina has no idea where she lived or even her siblings' names. All I know is her name was Angelina Richmond before she was adopted by the Atkinses."

"And my sister was Angelina Richmond!" Crista exclaimed happily. "It's hard to be positive without checking, but her name certainly gives me cause to pursue the matter further," Crista explained. "Then there's this resemblance you see."

Wes heard tapping on a keyboard, and then she spoke again. "Eden has one, too."

"Has what?"

"A dimple. Do you have a pen handy?" She gave him a Web site address. "That's my site for business, but I have a personal link to Eden's page. We posted all the information she could recall about our family and her search there and on the adoption boards. She was eight. This is incredible," she said. "I call to place an order and find a sister."

"You need to verify that," Wes warned, afraid she was getting carried away too soon. He didn't want to raise Angel's hopes only to find out it was a mistake.

"I'm going to call Eden. If she agrees, we'll need Angelina's number so we can call her. She has a birthday coming up on the seventh, doesn't she?"

"Yes. How did you know?"

"Eden remembered the date. It's here on the site."

Things were snowballing, Wes realized as the coincidences continued to pile up. "*If* she's your sister," Wes cautioned once more.

"It does seem too easy. A fluke that I'd come to North Carolina, meet a complete stranger, and later find she's my sister."

"How can we verify this?" he asked.

"I'll start checking here on my end. Perhaps you could see if her adoptive parents have any information that would help."

"I'll ask. What if I call you back with anything I learn?"

"Sounds wonderful."

Wes hung up the phone a couple of minutes later with a substantial order and quite possibly the names of Angel's sisters and their phone numbers. She was going to be mighty surprised if Crista McDaniel really was her sister. He grinned at the thought of being proved correct in his idea that they resembled each other.

Wes reached for the phone. "Hello, Ruth. Wes here. You sitting down? You're probably going to be as surprised as I was."

Chapter 9

There was a festive air about the house as the holiday preparations advanced. Angelina found herself looking forward to going home in the afternoons, eager to see what Wes and the kids had been doing. He closed his shop around five o'clock while she stayed open until six, and that gave them plenty of time to get started on whatever mischief they could manage.

When she mentioned getting her artificial tree out of the attic, Wes insisted she had to have a live tree. Her arguments that they were fire hazards prompted him to find a tree farm. Wes had taken her SUV and gone tree shopping, obtaining not only a freshly cut tree for her but also trees for her parents and himself.

Angelina wasn't certain why he needed a tree. He spent more time at her house than his own, but she really didn't mind. In fact, a day when she didn't see Wes made her feel depressed. She accepted she cared deeply for him, even though she wasn't sure what he intended with their relationship.

He was always a complete gentleman and often indicated that he loved her. It was a comfortable relationship.

Often they just sat and held hands while they talked. A few weeks back, Wes had started kissing her good night, and as much as she looked forward to his kisses, she was beginning to hate telling him good night. Was she ready for their relationship to move forward?

Her thirty-first birthday was in a few days, and Angelina knew she didn't want to grow old alone. When her children grew up and left home, she wanted a companion. She wanted to be in love again. For that matter, she was fairly certain she was in love.

Unlocking the door, Angelina called out. She followed Wes's voice to the family room to find him adjusting the tree in a stand. The room was fragrant with the scent of the magnificent tree.

"Where's everyone?"

"Up in the attic looking for lights."

"They're in the storage chest. Maybe I should—"

"Go change. I'll tell them where to look."

Angelina was anxious to help. "I'll be right back to help get the stuff down. There are boxes and boxes of decorations."

"So you do like Christmas?"

Angelina paused and looked back at him. "Of course. It's my favorite time of year."

Wes grinned broadly. "Mine, too."

"I already knew that," she said, heading for the stairs.

❄

He needed to marry that woman soon, Wes decided as he watched her dash up the stairs. Angel was everything he admired in a woman. When Laura died, he never thought he'd meet someone else, but he had and all thanks to his daughter. Mel had led him to this new family. He just prayed she would be as happy about his decision as he was. His other prayer was that Angel would say yes.

He and Mel were going to visit her grandparents over the weekend since he had plans to spend the holiday with Angel and the kids. Wes envisioned the type of life they would have. He looked forward to having Angelina as his wife, and he wanted to help raise her children. He also had plans to make her upcoming birthday one to be remembered. And when they were married, he could help out with the kids, and Mel would have more free time. Life would be wonderful.

He'd already been to the jeweler's several times in hopes of finding the perfect ring. Thus far he'd been unable to find anything he felt was right for her. He'd look again this weekend. Maybe he'd find something in New York.

"Come along, Mr. Robbins. We have an attic full of decorations to unpack. You're not going to believe what I've got up here."

Wes didn't realize how long he'd stood daydreaming until she spoke. "I can hardly wait."

❄

With Melody out of town, Angelina took Saturday off to be with the children. Ordinarily, she'd be up to her eyeballs in trying to get the house decorated, but thanks to Wes, the task was completed. It felt like a major burden had been lifted from her shoulders, and she was freed to spend time doing her holiday baking.

Bee loved the tree, and they were constantly warning her to be careful and taking ornaments from her inquisitive fingers. Her favorite was a little wooden train that had belonged to her father when he was a boy.

The child also loved the Nativity set. It was one of the things she and Robert had splurged on for their home, deciding that a nice set would last a lifetime. At first, Angelina was fearful that Bee would break the expensive pieces, but she seemed to know just how to handle them, and Angelina resisted putting them out of reach.

Both kids bounced on her bed early, reminding her that they were going to bake cookies. She pulled the pillow over her face, and they tugged it away. "Can I get dressed first?"

"Hurry, Mommy," Bee insisted.

Angelina noted the child had already dressed herself, choosing colors that suited her fancy but didn't match. Her shirt was on backward, the seams on the outside and tag under her chin. She shrugged. No sense in making her change. The clothes would be covered by the time they finished.

They spent a wonderful day baking several different variations of the cookies. Angelina leaned against the counter, sipping cocoa as her children decorated cookies. All the scene required for completion were Wes and Melody. She missed them.

"You guys want to go see Santa this afternoon?" she asked, thinking it best to get out before she allowed the melancholy feelings tugging at her heart to take control. She had some shopping to finish, and she'd promised Wes she'd run by the store and make sure his temp help was doing okay.

"Yeah," Robbie cried.

Bee shook her head. The child hadn't decided she liked the jolly one all that much.

"Let's finish up here and change clothes."

"But we have clothes," Bee said, tugging out the cookie-dough-stained shirt.

"Fereby Collier, you look like a gigantic sugar cookie," she teased, advancing slowly. "In fact, I think I'll eat you up."

"No, Mommy," the child screamed, jumping to her feet and darting about the table.

Angelina grabbed her and squeezed Bee in a hug.

"Do me, Mommy," Robbie insisted.

She hugged her oldest and set him back to his feet, whispering a word of thanks for her two precious gifts. "Let's get going."

❄

Wes called late Sunday night to let her know he was back.

"Melody's grandparents needed her to stay on a day or so. Hope that doesn't cause a problem for you."

Only about what to do with my children, Angelina thought. What were they thinking? Of course, Wes probably encouraged Melody to take the extra time. "I'll have to see if Mom can watch Bee tomorrow. I wish she'd given me some advance notice."

"Mel deserves a break."

"I didn't say she didn't," Angelina snapped, a bit put out by his defensiveness in light of the situation. "But last I heard employees cleared stuff like time off with their bosses."

"She's not your servant."

"I never said she was."

"This is exactly what I meant. Melody hardly has a moment to call her own between classes and this job."

They'd been down this road many times before. Every time she thought it was leveling off, something spurred another argument.

"I'll handle it, Wes."

"You don't have to get so upset."

Angelina was furious. She required people she could depend on in her life. "You wouldn't understand. Good night."

His cavalier attitude irked Angelina to no end. She supposed he'd never been subjected to the aggravation of child care. She didn't think she was being unreasonable to expect Melody to be there to do her job or to make prior arrangements.

Angelina called her mother and thankfully she could take Bee the next morning. Otherwise it would mean she'd have to pay a substitute pharmacist for another day. She went to bed early and fell into a deep, dream-filled sleep. The ringing phone woke her.

"You're right. I'm sorry."

"Wes?" she asked groggily.

"I should have realized that you'd be in a bind. I can take Bee to the store with me in the morning if that would help."

Visions of a bull in a china shop filled her head at the thought of turning her three year old loose around all that glass.

"It's okay. She's staying with my parents."

He released a deep sigh. "I'm really sorry. I was thinking of Mel."

"I know, Wes."

"Next time we'll make prior arrangements."

"It would be appreciated."

"Mel wanted to call. Her grandparents have some estate matters they needed her help with. I told her I'd explain. She's going to be upset with me, too."

"Not if we don't tell her."

His tone perked up considerably. "Now I remember why I love you so much. Did you miss me?"

"Yes." Angelina pulled her pillow up and leaned against the headboard. "We made cookies yesterday."

"I love cookies."

"I'll bring some to work tomorrow. How did your weekend go?"

She listened to him talk about the time with his wife's parents.

"I told them about you. They'd like to meet you and the kids."

He'd told his former in-laws about the new woman in his life. This sounded pretty serious. Still it seemed highly unlikely that she'd ever meet them.

"Melody said to tell you she's sorry and she'll definitely be here for your birthday."

Was he suggesting Melody wouldn't be back until Friday? Angelina kept her thoughts to herself. She'd talk to her mother tomorrow.

"I'll let you get back to sleep. See you tomorrow."

After hanging up, Angelina found herself unable to drift off to sleep again. Obviously Wes was pretty serious if he'd talked to his former in-laws about her. But the creeping doubt arose in her heart as she considered his attitude about the situation with Melody's job. Would he ever stop being so defensive of his daughter?

"What do I do, Lord?" she asked as the turmoil in her spirit grew. "Is this what You intend for me?"

She waited in the silence of the night for an answer and finally drifted to sleep.

Chapter 10

Overwhelming déjà vu struck that night when Angelina paused in the doorway of the family room. Never before did she recall seeing so many balloons in one room, and yet it reminded her of something.

"Happy birthday, Mommy!" Robbie and Bee shouted, running forward to grab her hands and tug her into the room.

"Are you surprised?" Robbie asked.

Angelina nodded.

"More surprise," Bee announced.

"Bee, not yet," Wes said, swinging the little girl up in his arms and leaned to kiss Angelina's cheek.

She looked from children to adults, wondering what else was planned.

"First things first," Wes said. "We're going to your favorite restaurant for dinner. Then we'll come back here for dessert and presents."

"Yeah, presents," Bee said, throwing her arms into the air.

"For Mommy, Bee," Melody said.

"Mommy?" she repeated, looking perplexed. "Me want present, too."

"When you're four," Melody promised.

"Four?" The child worked her fingers, managing to come up with three.

"You can help Mommy open hers," Angelina promised. "We thought about having a big party but decided to limit the celebration to family."

Angelina was glad. She had never cared for big parties. More often than not, because of the number of foster children, the Atkins family celebrated with a cake after dinner.

After giving her a few minutes to freshen up and change, they loaded into the SUV and headed for the restaurant. Like every Friday night, the line of waiting patrons extended along the front of the building.

"Better get our name on the list," Angelina suggested. "Wait here."

Wes disappeared inside and soon returned to guide them to the small room he'd reserved for their celebration. Her parents and the foster kids were already seated, and their cries of "Surprise!" resounded about the room as Wes pulled out the seat of honor for her.

Angelina felt like a queen surveying her domain as she viewed the loved ones gathered around the table to celebrate her birth. Who needed blood relatives when they had love like this? Life couldn't get any better.

After dinner, they took the party back to her house to eat their fill of her favorites, chocolate cake and custard ice cream. Torn between helping unwrap gifts and collecting a balloon bouquet, Bee darted about the room. Soon Robbie and Jeremy joined in her quest to collect all the ribbon streamers their little hands could hold. As the children danced and giggled, Angelina was again struck with a sense of familiarity that refused to go away. All too soon the baby began to whine.

"We'd better be heading home, Ruth. Time to get these children into bed," her dad said.

"It's early," Angelina protested, disappointed that the evening was drawing to a close. "Don't go yet."

Her dad kissed her cheek. "We'll see you Sunday for lunch. Your mom's making all your favorites."

"Don't go to all that trouble."

"No trouble," her mother insisted as she placed the knit cap on the baby's head.

Angelina helped gather their things and thanked her parents for their gift, hugging them good-bye. She stood in the doorway watching them settle the children in the car, stifling a fit of giggles when her dad attempted to fit Jeremy's balloons in the trunk.

"Wish I had a camera," she told Wes as yet another balloon made its escape and danced into the sky. Jeremy's dismayed cries filled the air.

"I'll get Bee and Robbie ready for bed," Melody announced, taking their hands and leading them up the stairs.

Back in the family room, Angelina plopped down on the sofa beside Wes. "I'm exhausted."

He wrapped an arm about her shoulder, giving her a reviving squeeze. "But did you have a good birthday?"

"Wonderful. I couldn't ask for better."

"I'm glad. And thankful to be part of this momentous occasion."

She frowned and tapped him lightly on the arm. "I wouldn't go that far."

"I say the second anniversary of your twenty-ninth birthday deserves to be celebrated."

Angelina grimaced at him.

Wes reached for her hand, holding it tightly in his. From the seriousness of his expression, she knew he had something on his mind.

"I suppose you know me well enough by now to know I'm not the most romantic man in the world," he began slowly. "I wish I knew how to make this more special for you, but I'm just going to come out with it. Angel, we've known each other for almost six months, and I know that's not very long, but sometimes it doesn't take forever to know how you feel about someone. I love you, and I'd like to ask you to do me the honor of becoming my wife." He reached into his pocket for the ring box and flipped it open, showing her the beautiful solitaire he'd picked out.

Angelina didn't know what to say.

"Marry me," Wes implored. "I'll do better than I did with Laura and Mel. I promise. I intend to help with the children. I figure Mel can concentrate on her education if I'm helping out here."

Fear welled up inside Angelina as she considered his words. "Would you marry me to free Melody from her job?"

The moment the words left her mouth, she recognized Wes couldn't have been more shocked if she'd struck him.

"That's ridiculous, Angel."

She pulled away. "I don't think I'm being ridiculous. You told me not so very long ago that you planned to convince Melody to give up this job. This way you still come out the good guy."

"If you don't want to marry me, you don't have to make excuses," he declared impatiently.

What was she doing? She loved Wes and Melody. Why was she jeopardizing their future happiness? She pushed her hair behind her ears. "I just want to be, sure, Wes. I need to know you'll be there for me."

"I'm asking to spend the rest of my life with you. There's no way I can be sure how long that will be, but I can promise no one will ever love you more than I do. Say yes, Angel."

"I don't know. I need to think."

Wes lifted her hands in his. "Don't look back, Angel. Look forward to what we can have. Let go of the fears and doubts. Trust God. He's taken mighty fine care of you over the years."

The phone rang, and she wondered who was calling this time of night. She prayed nothing had happened to her parents.

"Angelina, phone," Melody called.

"Who is it?" she asked, irritated by the interruption.

There was a rumbling of voices. "It's a Ms. McDaniel. She's calling to wish you a happy birthday."

Lines of confusion scored Angelina's forehead as she got to her feet. "I don't know any McDaniels."

Wes shot to his feet. "Angel, wait. We need to talk."

"After I take this call."

"Angel—"

"Not now, Wes," she said. "I'll take it in the kitchen, Melody. Hello, this is Angelina."

"Hi, this is Crista McDaniel. We met at your friend's store. He thought we looked alike."

Angelina recalled the episode. But how had this woman known it was her birthday? She never shared that information with complete strangers.

"I contacted Wes recently, and he told me today was your birthday," Crista explained.

Why on earth would Wes tell her that? Was it her birthday, too, or—and why was she calling Wes?

"Did he tell you I was going to call?"

She glanced around and found him standing nearby, a mixture of emotions, mostly regret, playing across his face. What was going on here? "No."

Crista giggled nervously. "Then I suppose I should explain before you think I've lost my mind. Oh, by the way, happy birthday! I hope it's been a good one?"

"Yes," Angelina responded vaguely, growing more curious by the moment.

Perhaps she was one of the foster kids, Angelina thought, struggling to recall some of their names. Never a McDaniel that she could remember, but then some had stayed only briefly.

"Wes told me you were adopted," Crista began.

Angelina felt stunned by the amount of personal information Wes had taken upon himself to share with this stranger. Nervousness centered in the pit of her stomach.

"I'm adopted, too. It was pretty exciting to learn I have two sisters and a brother."

"I'm sure." Angelina thought of how she'd react to such news. But why was this woman telling her this?

"That's why I'm calling. I think you're my sister."

"Your sister?" Angelina repeated incredulously.

"Our parents were John and Anna Richmond, and we lived in Covington, Kentucky. We're the youngest of their four children. I'm your baby sister."

Angelina had few memories of her childhood prior to the time she arrived at the Atkins's home. The past had been painful—filled with loss. Somewhere along the way her parents had explained she was the child of their heart, and that had been enough for her. "I don't know."

"Your mother verified their names. We also have an older sister named Eden and a brother named Tim."

Angelina sank into a nearby chair and demanded, "Are you sure?"

"I'm fairly confident. When Wes mentioned you were adopted at a young age and said your name was Angelina, I knew that was my sister's name. It's not an ordinary name," Crista pointed out. "I think our mother was a bit of a romantic. Then he said you were a Richmond, and that cinched it for me. You have the same birthday our older sister said you had. Then there's this similarity in our appearance Wes sees."

It was an overwhelming abundance of coincidences, Angelina thought.

"I talked to Eden, and she agrees that it's likely you're the one. Wes and I have been in contact a couple of times. He verified some facts, and when we became more certain, he suggested I surprise you for your birthday."

"But how? Who put you in contact with Wes?"

"It had to be God," Crista explained. "It's too miraculous. I'd hoped to find you one day but never dreamed I'd stumble across you in my travels. Some people might call it luck, but I think it's a blessing from above. I know you need some time to absorb all this, but Eden and I both are anxious to meet and talk with you as soon as you're ready. Wes has a site address where you can look at Eden's research facts. Eden has photos of us there. Be sure to look for the dimple."

"Dimple?" Angelina lifted a finger to her cheek, thinking she must sound like a moron.

"Yes, we all share the dimple."

"This is a shock. Where do you live?"

"I know. It was for me, too. Eden lives in Indiana. I'm in Phoenix."

Overwhelmed, Angelina asked, "Crista, is it possible you can give me a number so I can call you back later?"

"I hope this hasn't upset you?"

"No, not at all. It's just a lot to take in at once." Wes's proposal had already put her mind into overload. And now this stranger was claiming blood ties. "I promise to look into it and get back to you as soon as I have all the facts."

"That would be wonderful. Wes tells me you have two children."

"Yes. A boy and a girl, four and three."

"This is so incredible," Crista said. "I'm a sister and an aunt. I see my Christmas list growing by leaps and bounds."

"Oh no, you don't have—"

"Sure I do. You can tell me more about them next time we talk."

Numbly, Angelina said good-bye and allowed Wes to take the phone from her hand.

He replaced the receiver and dropped to his knees before her. "I'm sorry. I thought you'd be excited to find them."

Angelina's thoughts drifted back to the times as a child when she'd daydreamed about having brothers and sisters who didn't come and go like the foster kids. "I never expected to meet up with one of them in your shop."

Wes's expression softened. "Would you like for me to bring up the site on the computer?"

The future looked vague and shadowy, too confusing for her to grasp. "Just give me the address. I'll find it."

"Angel?"

"You need to go home, Wes."

"But, Angel—"

"No 'buts.' I have to think. I promised Ms. McDaniel I'd look into this and get back to her."

"But what about our discussion?"

Angelina was keenly aware of his scrutiny. Wes didn't understand her withdrawal and she couldn't explain. Not yet. She needed time to consider the ways this would change her life. "I'll be in touch when I'm ready to talk."

"I'm sorry everything went wrong. I love you, Angel. Believe that, please."

His pleas stayed with her long after Wes had gone. The first thing she did was pull up the site. As she read the facts, Angelina found herself hoping it was true. She reached for the phone, "Hello, Mom."

"Angelina, I hope you're calling with good news."

Wes had been busy. "Just questions. Wes says he's talked to you about this woman who claims to be my sister."

"Yes, we've checked what facts we know."

"Do you think it's a scam?"

"No. I honestly feel the woman is your sister."

"This is unbelievable."

"You owe it to yourself to be sure. Meet them. Learn about your family."

Angelina had never loved her mother more. What a wealth of emotions she must be experiencing to encourage her child to form a relationship with her siblings. "In the back of my mind I've always wondered what it would be like. Now I'm afraid."

"No one can ever have too much love, Angelina."

"I suppose."

"Now, what about Wes? Did you say yes?"

"I think Wes should have asked me before telling everyone else."

"You refused? But I thought you really loved him."

"I do. But I'm not sure about his motives."

"Motives? He loves you and wants to share your life. He's a decent, Christian man. What else can you want?"

"I suppose a bit of certainty wouldn't hurt."

"Haven't you heard nothing's certain but death and taxes?"

"And I've had my share of both."

Her mother's sigh reached over the distance through the phone. "I've always given you credit for being a smart girl, but if you let this one get away, I'm going to think I was wrong."

"And you don't think it's smart to be sure?"

"Angelina, I would never suggest you go against your heart. But I do suggest you trust your instincts."

It was all too much. How could she follow her heart

when her doubts were so great? And now her confidence seemed too weak to support a sensible decision. "Why does everyone preach trust to me?"

"Because we can see you fighting God in a battle you can't win. Jeremiah 29:11 says, ' "For I know the plans I have for you," ' declares the Lord, ' "plans to prosper you and not to harm you, plans to give you hope and a future." ' God knows that future, Angelina."

"So God's already made the plan, and I just blindly follow?"

"No. You open your eyes wide and pray mightily that you make the right choice. God gave us freedom of choice, but that doesn't mean the wrong ones don't have consequences."

"But what about Wes's promise to free Melody from her job?" Angelina argued. "He actually suggested he could help with the kids and she could concentrate on her studies."

"Oh, Angelina, you've been a parent long enough to understand how protective parents can be."

"Well, yes," she admitted reluctantly, "but Melody doesn't want him interfering in her life."

"And I'm sure she's adult enough to tell him. Didn't you ever question Robert's motives?"

"Maybe."

"No maybe about it. Every couple does from time to time. The key to the situation is communication. Discuss the matter freely and try to understand what Wes is telling you. Honey, don't reject the opportunity to be happy. Pray about it."

"I will. Night, Mom. And thanks for everything."

"I love you, Angelina. I thank God every day for sending you to us."

"Even when you doubt my intelligence?" she teased.

"Even then."

Chapter 11

Angelina was awake early the following morning, preparing breakfast in hopes of wearing away some of the nervous energy that consumed her. She fed the children and sent them upstairs to finish dressing. When Melody came down, she slid a plate of pancakes on the table in front of her.

"Did you have a good birthday?" she asked as she drizzled syrup over the stack of pancakes.

Considering the jumble of emotions she was feeling right now, Angelina didn't know the answer. She'd tossed and turned until she'd been forced to get up in the middle of the night and remake her bed.

Finally, she'd opened her Bible to the verse her mother had quoted and prayed. She'd long since learned prayers weren't always answered immediately, sometimes never, and often in a way far different than you wanted. Now she only wanted peace.

Angelina set a glass of orange juice on the table. "How much do you know about what happened last night?"

"Dad said he was going to propose."

Angelina nodded. Exactly what she thought. Wes

had been a busy man. No wonder everyone disappeared so quickly last night. "Did he mention his other surprise? Finding my sister?"

Melody's head popped up. "No. I didn't realize you had one."

"Two, actually, and a brother. She called last night. Seems your dad thought it would be a perfect birthday surprise."

Melody's eyes grew wide with amazement. "He's a bit misguided at times, but you have to admire his originality. Not every man can find long-lost relatives for a woman's birthday gift."

Angelina laughed, releasing a flood tide of emotions, and it felt good. "That's true."

"How does it make you feel?"

"Excited. Frightened. Confused. What if they don't like me?"

"They have to like you, Angelina. You're their sister."

She had a point there. They were strangers with a common bond. The relationship with them started now as adults, not with the children of the past.

"That must seem like a blessing from above," Melody commented.

Blessing from above. The words triggered remembrance of the same words Crista had spoken last night. When had she stopped expecting blessings from above? Had she even thanked God for Wes?

"Can I ask you something personal, Melody?"

"Sure."

"How do you deal with your father's determination?"

"I listen to him and respect his viewpoint, but I tell

him what I'm feeling, too."

"So you don't feel railroaded by him?"

"I feel loved," the young woman admitted with a warm smile. "Everything he does is because he cares about me, and even if it irritates me at times, I understand why."

Angelina nervously folded and refolded a napkin. "You know if I marry your dad, he plans to help with the children so you'll have more free time for school? You'd be out of work."

"I wouldn't feel right charging my stepmom, anyway. And having a man around would be good for Robbie and Bee."

"Will it hurt you to see him doing things with them he didn't do with you?"

"I'm sure Dad will do everything in his power to make it up to me," Melody pointed out. "Actually, I'll be glad to get some of the attention focused elsewhere. I'm sure you can distract him until I'm an old married woman giving you both grandchildren."

"You make it sound so simple."

"It is. Just trust God to show you the way." The young woman glanced at her watch. "Look at the time. I'll drop Robbie and Bee off."

Angelina sat at the table long after Melody left, thinking about what she'd said. Just trust God. *Trust me, Angelina.* She looked around the room. No one there but her. And God, she realized. Wes was right. God was with her now and always, providing exactly what she needed.

"I do, dear Father," she whispered. "I know I haven't always given You control of my life, but I'm putting it in

Your hands now. Thank You for these wonderful people You've filled my life with—Mom and Dad, Robert, Robbie and Bee, Melody, Wes, and now my sisters and brother.

"I believe You sent Wes to love me and led me to a trusting relationship with You. I know I've set limitations for myself by trying to be the one in control. Please help me break free of the bondage. Thank You for caring, and please continue to guide and direct my path as You would have me go. I am nothing without Your love."

Peace like she'd never felt radiated throughout Angelina. She'd finally released herself from the bonds she'd imposed over the years. She walked over to the wall phone and dialed Wes's number.

"Wes's Glass."

"Hi, it's Angelina."

"Angel? I didn't expect. . . Are you okay? You said you'd call when you were ready. . . . Does this mean. . . ?"

"Take a breath, Wes. Is it okay if I stop by the store this morning? I need some help planning our future."

"Is that a yes?"

"What do you think?"

"Praise God," he cried jubilantly. "I love you, Angel."

"I love you, too."

For the first time in a long time, Angelina looked forward to the future, knowing that looking back would never hurt as badly when she was loved by such a man.

TERRY FOWLER

Terry makes her home in North Carolina where she works for the city of Wilmington. The second oldest of five children, she shares a home with her best friend who is also her sister. Besides writing, her interests include genealogical research through the Internet and serving her small church in various activities. She is the author of two **Heartsong Presents** titles.

To Keep Me Warm

by Gail Gaymer Martin

Two are better than one. . .
If one falls down, his friend can help him up.
But pity the man who falls and has no one to help him up!
Also, if two lie down together, they will keep warm.
But how can one keep warm alone? . . .
A cord of three strands is not quickly broken.
ECCLESIASTES 4:9–12

Chapter 1

In the church fellowship hall, Tim Richmond leaned against a wall, peering at men and women talking comfortably in friendly clusters while he squirmed. He wished he'd never let his friend convince him to come along. He eyed Jack across the room, looking relaxed and in control. Not Tim. He clung to the wall like ivy. Poison ivy, at that. No one had spoken to him.

"Excuse me," a woman said, brushing past.

He watched her dash across the floor to greet a friend, he assumed.

A singles' group. . .even a church singles' group gave Tim as much pleasure as the thought of poking his eye with a stick. He scanned the red hearts with Cupid's arrows decorating the hall and pushed himself closer to the plaster. Valentine's Day was meant for couples. . .not one, lone, miserable man who still didn't feel at all single. With four years of marriage and a wonderful son, two years widowed seemed like a moment in time.

Refocusing on the crowd, Tim peered at his friend, Jack. A few years older than Tim, Jack had been widowed for four years. Would two more years make that much difference? Tim couldn't imagine it.

Shifting his gaze, he spotted a vaguely familiar face, a woman engaged in conversation with another female. He narrowed his focus, groping through his mind to identify from where he knew her.

She turned toward him, her attention locked with his. A puzzled expression stumbled across her face before switching to recognition and a pleasant smile. After speaking a moment to her companion, she rose and headed straight for Tim.

Pulling his back straight, he heaved his disheartened shoulders upward, hoping to present a semi-pleasant look.

She approached him, hand extended. "Mr. Richmond? You're Timmy's father, right?"

"Yes," he said, embarrassed that he was still in the dark.

"Central Orthopedic," she said. "I'm a nurse at the clinic, Julie Gardner."

The image of her bright smile as she talked with his six-year-old son, Timmy, took shape in his thoughts. "I knew you looked familiar but couldn't place you," he admitted.

"I should have worn my uniform." She flashed an infectious smile.

He sent one back, admiring the wavy ash brown hair brushing against her shoulders. "I suppose that would've helped." Though he tried to joke, he felt tongue-tied.

"What are you doing here?" she asked.

His shoulders drooped for a moment as he asked himself the same question. Nabbing his fading confidence, he straightened his back again. "I was dragged here by a friend for moral support."

A burst of laughter filled the air, and sensing she was laughing at him, he cringed for a fleeting moment until she continued.

"You, too?" she said, amusement bubbling in her words. "I didn't want to do this either." She motioned toward the woman she'd been speaking with earlier. "I'm with a friend." Her gesture faltered. "Was with a friend. I see she's occupied."

When she turned back to face Tim, he had the horrible desire to run out the door. Not that he didn't enjoy Julie's company. . .he did, but he felt awkward, like a man cheating on his wife. He'd never had such feelings—but tonight the emotions bounded through him.

"Care to sit?" she asked, pointing to an unoccupied table.

Angry at his unbidden feelings, Tim found his common sense. "Sure, thanks."

She led the way, and he followed like a sheep, instead of the shepherd. Where was his masculine charm? Buried in memories, he guessed. When they reached the table, he found his manners. "Would you like something to drink?"

"Yes, thanks. A cola, if you don't mind."

He nodded, then escaped, needing time to get himself under control. Why did he feel so inept? This wasn't a date. He was talking to a woman he'd seen numerous times at his son's orthopedic clinic.

Tim's heart twisted thinking of his son bound in braces from Blount's disease. He prayed the supports would help the boy's problem, but the doctor hadn't been hopeful. Surgery, he'd said, would probably be the only permanent solution. Surgery? Tim's heart was weighted with the possibility.

When Timmy was a toddler, Tim recalled his wife and him laughing at Timmy's bowed legs. Yet, concerned, Jan had asked the pediatrician about the problem. He dismissed it as natural. After Jan's death, Timmy's abnormality became more pronounced. Tim pursued the problem and learned about this uncommon deformity.

Tim pulled his thoughts back to his task and ordered two colas, then headed toward Timmy's nurse. If he kept her in perspective, he could handle the evening. She knew his son and the child's disease. They had something in common.

"Here you go," Tim said, sliding the glass onto the table. He settled into the chair across from her, his mind scrambling for something to talk about.

"Thanks." She lifted the glass and took a delicate sip.

Tim's gaze latched onto her full, shapely mouth. Generous mouth. Not large, but eager to smile or articulate with her soothing, mellow voice.

"You're quiet," she said.

Discomfort riffled up his neck. "I'm new at this. I don't have much time for socializing."

She nodded and lifted her glass for another sip, but her eyes searched his as if trying to read his thoughts.

"Your son?" she asked. "I'm sure he takes time."

"Yes, I'm. . .a, uh, widower," he said, finding it difficult to say the word. "My wife died two years ago."

"I'm sorry," she said, a look of sincerity spreading across her face.

"Thanks." He dragged his finger across his glass,

wiping away the condensation. "So I'm, uh, a single parent."

Her face washed with a mixture of responses, and he wondered.

"I'm sure being an only parent is difficult," she said, seeming distracted. "It's often the woman who's left with little ones. . .not men. Divorce and unmarried girls getting pregnant. . . Today's morals are terrible."

"Yes, I guess they are," he said, confused by her comment. "Single or widowed, raising a child alone isn't easy."

She drew her attention back to him. "I'm sorry," she said. "I don't know what got into me. We should talk about something more pleasant."

"It might not be pleasant, but it's real," he said.

Curious, Tim searched her face for understanding. He'd heard an inference in her voice, but it had faded as quickly as it happened.

"I do as much as I can for my son, but he needs more than I can give him sometimes. Then, I don't want to spoil him. It's a tough road to walk."

She gave his arm a reassuring pat. "Timmy's a great kid," she said. "Shame about his problem. . .but surgery will. . ." Her voice trailed off and she flinched. "I don't suppose surgery is what you want, but from my experience, it's proven wonderful in most every case."

"I've heard," Tim said, not eager to discuss the topic.

"There I go again," she said, apparently sensing his discomfort.

He drew his fingers through his hair. "Are you. . .eh, widowed?"

Her head shake answered before she did. "No. Just

plain old single. Never married. I'm too old now."

Surprising himself, a laugh burst from his throat. "You! You're not too old for much of anything."

She grinned. "I feel that way though."

"You shouldn't. You're young."

"Thirty-three," she said.

"I'm thirty-two."

A scowl flashed across her face. "You're a young widower. What happened?"

"Blood clot," he answered. "Jan had surgery. . .a pulmonary embolism took her. . .so fast."

Julie's face paled. "Mr. Richmond. . .I'm sorry. I suggested cheering up our conversation, and now I've pulled it back down again."

"Please. . .I'm Tim," he said, understanding how conversation often tugs at the heart. He despised talking about feelings. "It's not your fault. Happens all the time. I guess that's why I'm not very sociable."

"Sure you are," she said, renewed color brightening her face. "You're always friendly at the office, and sometimes I've watched you with Timmy. I know you're a good father."

"I try." He thought of so many times he'd fallen on his knees begging God to give him strength and patience.

"God is good," she said.

His head jerked upward. Had he mentioned his prayer aloud?

"Are you a religious man, Mr.—Tim? I'm guessing you are."

"Without God, life leaves little to cling to," he said, wishing he hadn't after he saw her expression.

She wanted him to explain, he was sure, but he didn't. Too much background information would be needed. Too much personal pain would be explored. "How long have you been at the clinic?" he asked.

"Two years," she said. "I worked at Beaumont Hospital but decided I'd prefer straight days. I got very tired of the shift changes."

"I can imagine," he said, inwardly breathing a relieved sigh that he'd changed the subject. He knew about shift changes. So often, he'd wished a college degree had been an option. So little money and moral support had led him to take a quick job—not a career like Julie.

Her gaze shifted toward her friend. "Oops, I see Teri's alone over there. I'd better get back." She gestured toward the woman sitting across the room. "Would you like to join us?"

His chest tightened. He would, but he knew it was foolish. "No, but thanks. I was smart enough to drive here myself, and since Jack's pleasantly occupied, I think I'll just slip away. I have a sitter with Timmy."

"Aah," she said, rising. "Well, it was nice to see you. . . Tim. I imagine Timmy has another appointment at the clinic."

"Always," he said, rising. "Thanks for coming over to say 'hi.' "

She extended her hand. "You don't have to thank me. It was fun."

He grasped her small palm against his, giving it a firm shake, and she flashed a smile before she walked away.

Her soft curls bounced as she crossed the floor, leaving

him feeling extra lonely. Though he'd seen her at the clinic often, his attention was always focused on Timmy. He'd never noticed how pretty she was. He was a head taller, he guessed. He liked her figure, not too curvy or thin. Just right. Firm and cozy-looking.

He ran his fingers through his hair, amazed at his wayward thoughts. Single, he was—but not like people who were really alone. He had Timmy and memories. Some mornings he woke, and the empty bed sent shivers of longing through him.

Having a wife to share his life had been a blessing. He'd asked God often what he'd done to deserve the deep ache that he felt from Jan's loss. Then he remembered that the Lord didn't promise a life without sorrow or pain. He only promised forgiveness and salvation.

Tim knew those gifts were his. Still, he wondered if life held anything else in store. A child who walked without pain and braces. That would be a blessing. And a wife? That picture, he'd never envisioned. But today, Julie had rekindled old yearnings.

Perhaps one day God would have another earthly mate for him. Someone like Julie perhaps, but not Julie. She was worthy of far more than Tim could offer. She deserves a man with a career. A man with a suit and white shirt. Not a factory rat like him.

Chapter 2

I can't find Mr. Meier's chart," Julie said, plowing through the stack of manila folders on the office counter.

"Dr. Hubbard took it," her coworker said.

"Thanks, Casey. I thought I'd lost it." She sent her friend a smile, thinking that she'd really "lost it" lately, and pulled the next appointments from the stack. *Timothy Richmond, Jr.* Julie's pulse lurched as she eyed the child's file. But instead of the boy, his father's amiable face rose in her thoughts.

Though she'd given up on men, she'd been riddled with unwanted feelings since meeting Tim Richmond at the singles' group. When she made the invitation, she'd hoped he'd join her and Teri, but he said "no" and vanished shortly after she'd walked away.

It was not his good looks but his gentleness that interested her. He was a good man—a father devoted to his child.

Thinking of them, she inched to the receptionist window and peeked into the waiting room. Her heart skipped when she saw him. Always, he seemed so sophisticated with his distinguished appearance—a large man, not plump, but impressive in size and manner.

Whenever he came into the office, he was softspoken with an air of reserve, almost as if he were larger than life. She'd admired him from Timmy's first office visit.

As she watched through the window, Tim held a story-book while Timmy leaned against his arm, all ears, his tender brown eyes enchanted by the colorful picture book. A lopsided grin turned at the corner of Timmy's mouth. She'd seen that same look on his father's lips, on rare occasions, as if he were hiding a sense of playful mischief.

Before she could duck from the small window, Tim's gaze lifted. A look of recognition washed over his face, and she felt a deep blush shoot up her neck and warm her cheeks. Now she had to go into the waiting room to say hello or he'd think she was unfriendly. . .or disinterested.

Disinterested? Well, yes, she was—at least, she wanted to be. But the truth niggled at her, and she found herself drawn to the man ever since they'd run into each other.

She recalled him saying something that gnawed at her: *Without God, life leaves little to cling to.* Though the thought saddened her, she understood what he meant. Things on earth could be fleeting: success, wealth, friendship, hope, even life—like his wife. The only thing humans could count on was God.

Strong in her faith, Julie wondered about Tim. He spoke of God, but did he really follow God's ways? A bad experience in her past made her leery of men. More than that, she didn't trust men—and that's why being single was how she'd stay. Men's morals seemed different from women's. Women prized their chastity. Men seemed to prize the conquest. She'd had enough of being pursued and then dropped when she didn't give in to a man's demands. And how could she tell from one man to the next? Tim? Did he share her morals? She'd probably never know.

She peered through the window, and Tim's attention lifted from Timmy's book. Catching his gaze, she gave him a nod and headed out of the office area to the waiting room door.

Steeling herself, she headed for the boy. "Hi, Timmy, how are you today?"

"Fine," he said, grinning at her. "Daddy's reading me a story."

"I see that." She allowed her focus to shift to Tim. "And how are you doing?"

"Fine, thanks," he said, his hands fidgeting with the storybook cover.

"I noticed you made a quick escape a few weeks ago." She swallowed, hearing her words. Time had marched along while she wondered when she'd see him again.

"I was miserable that night. I hope I wasn't rude."

She shook her head. "Rude? Not at all. I enjoyed talking with you."

"So did I," he said.

"Thanks." His response caught her unprepared. Had he really enjoyed her company, or was he only being polite? She glanced over her shoulder at the receptionist window. Doctor Brady gazed out at her. "Guess I'd better get back to work." She leaned closer and lowered her voice. "My boss is watching."

She spun on her heel and darted through the doorway. The doctor had vanished, and Julie picked up the stack of folders and tried to focus on her work, but her mind lingered in the waiting room.

By the time she returned to the receptionist's window, Tim and his son were gone. Curious, she wove her way through the examining room corridors. She grinned when she found their room.

From inside, she heard a child's sweet voice singing a Sunday school song. She waited until he finished, then knocked and peeked inside.

"No doctor yet?" she asked.

Tim shifted toward her and shook his head. "We've only been waiting a couple of minutes."

"I'm sure he'll be in soon." She paused, feeling like a ninny, trying to conjure up appropriate conversation. "I heard you singing, Timmy. You have a nice voice."

"Thank you," he said, tucking his head into his father's arm.

"I sing, too," Julie said.

The boy lifted his face, his eyebrows arched high. "You do?"

"Yes, with my church choir. We're having our Easter concert in two weeks. I practice very hard."

"I sing in Sunday school," Timmy said.

"You sing all the time," his dad said with a warm grin before turning to Julie. "So. . .you sing with your choir. That's nice."

"Do you?" she asked.

He chuckled. "No, I'm not much of a singer—but I'm a pretty good audience."

With her pulse gaining speed, Julie garnered courage. "We need all the support we can get. I'd love you to come and be a pretty good audience. It's Sunday at seven P.M."

"I don't know. . . ," he said with a look of discomfort. "Where is your church?"

"First Community on Fifth and Washington in Royal Oak."

He only nodded while she filled with disappointment.

Outside the door, Julie heard the doctor's voice. Saying a quick good-bye, she exited, feeling defeated.

❄

Pulling himself from under the sink, Tim thumped his head against the cabinet. He rubbed the spot a moment, felt a lump forming, and controlled his mouth from uttering a curse. Swearing was something he'd learned to avoid when he'd become a true believer.

His divorced neighbor, Penny, who lived in the adjoining townhouse, often asked him to help with tasks she couldn't handle. . .like plumbing. Tim never refused and did the task without grumbling. Often, she'd pitched in for him by watching Timmy or bringing in his paper and mail when he was traveling.

Conveniently, her son, Buddy, and Timmy were playmates. And the bonus was Sammy, their young spaniel. Timmy adored the dog. Having Sammy nearby saved Tim the need to buy his son a puppy. Before Sammy, his son had begged daily for a dog of his own. Tim prayed his scheme continued to work.

As the thought faded, Sammy bounded into the kitchen and nosed beneath the sink. Tim scooted the dog away, closed the cabinet door, and tried the disposal one more time. "Penny," Tim called through the doorway, "looks like it's working now."

She hurried into the kitchen, a full-figured woman with a flirtatious demeanor. "You always come to my rescue, Tim," she said, giving him a poke. "What can I do in return? I'd be happy to keep Timmy for an evening."

"Thanks, but. . ." Before he finished his refusal, Julie's concert invitation for that evening replayed in his mind. The offer sounded tempting. Tim had done nothing alone in weeks, and Julie would certainly be surprised to see him.

"Maybe you could watch him tonight, if you don't mind," Tim said. "I've been invited to a concert, and if you'll sit with Timmy, I'd like to go."

"Concert? You mean at the Silver Dome? A rock—"

"No," Tim said, grinning, "a church concert. For Easter."

"I should have guessed," she said. "You've never looked like a rocker to me." She let loose a giggle. "I'd be happy to keep Timmy for you."

"I shouldn't be too late, Penny. I'll send him over after dinner."

He gathered his tools, then headed home, wondering why he was tempting himself. Julie was a great woman, but he didn't want to lead her on. . . . He didn't want to lead himself on either. Every time she entered his thoughts—which was more often than he wanted—he knew he was heading for trouble.

Tim slid into the pew near the back of the old church. Surveying the large stained glass windows, he wondered what they might look like with the sun penetrating the colorful glass and washing the room with varied hues.

When the organ silenced, the choir filed in through a side door and formed rows across the front. When Julie stepped into the sanctuary, Tim filled with pleasure at seeing her again. She looked sweet and angelic in her ivory robe and a red stole accented by a gold cross. Her hair fell in soft curls and brushed her shoulders as she moved into place.

The organ struck a chord, and the choir's powerful music filled the vaulted ceiling. Somber, then joyful, the music of Christ's death and resurrection washed over him with waves of emotion. When the concert ended, Tim rose, wrapped in a sense of renewal, and headed into the reception area, sure that Julie hadn't noticed him among the audience.

But before moving too far, a hand grasped his jacket sleeve, and when he turned, Julie's glowing face smiled at him. "Thank you for coming," she said.

"My pleasure. The choir was excellent."

"Really?" Her eyes searched his.

"Really." He tucked his nervous hands into his jacket pockets. "I didn't think you'd noticed me."

"I saw you right away," she chuckled, "but I have to keep my eye on the director."

Tim nodded.

Her arms hung against the front of her choir robe, her fingers woven into a tight knot. "I didn't expect you to be here." Her stifled voice brushed against his ear. "But I'm glad you are."

"Me, too," he said, not wanting to say he hadn't planned to, but providence—or God—moved him to come.

"I have to get out of this robe," she said, a strained look on her face, "but. . .would you like to, uh, drop by the house for some coffee and dessert?"

Tim's shoulders stiffened.

Julie unwound her fingers and lifted one to her neck, playing with the satin collar. "That is, if you have time."

Tim shuffled his feet, eyeing the pretty woman waiting for his answer. He had no reason to say no. . .except his good sense. "I'd like to, but just for a few minutes," he said. "A neighbor lady has Timmy, and I don't want to keep him out too late on a school night."

"Oh, no, I understand." She stepped backward. "Okay, then, I'll get my coat and be with you in a second."

As she darted away, Tim longed to disappear. Why had he agreed to have coffee with Timmy's nurse? Coffee at her house? He felt like a man standing on the edge of a sandy cliff and feeling the ground shift beneath his feet. One wrong move and he'd be lost. No. . .his heart would be lost.

She returned in a moment, and they stepped outside into the brisk air. Julie pulled her coat up around her neck, and Tim walked stiffly beside her. Finding her car, she gave him directions, and he followed.

In a few minutes, Julie turned down a wide street lined with large, well-kept homes—homes he could never afford. Noticing her turn signal, Tim faltered, wanting to drive off.

Julie had pulled into the driveway of a large brick colonial with an attached garage. The door lifted as she edged forward and pulled inside.

A rush of panic filled Tim. He lived in a rented townhouse, one unit joining the next, small rooms, noise seeping through the nicked walls. A classy woman like Julie should be entertaining a man who had. . .

Relief spread through him as he considered a probable error. Looking at the well-kept house with dark shutters and French pane windows, he realized the house glowed with lamplight. Certainly someone was already inside. Could this be her parents' home?

With the thought, he gained confidence and released a fettered sigh of relief. He turned off the motor and stepped into the chilling air.

With a pleasant smile, Julie waited for him at the front walk.

"Your parents have a nice house," he said.

"Yes, they do." She took his arm and steered him up the brick steps. "But they live a few miles away. This house is mine."

Chapter 3

Tim's stomach tumbled to his feet, then slammed into his throat. *Stupid.* A nurse probably made a great salary. She had a career. Why would he con himself into believing this was her parents' home? He should have excused himself at the church and said he had to get home to Timmy.

Too late. When she pushed open the door, he forced himself forward and stepped into a small foyer, featuring an open staircase and a well-shined table holding a vase of flowers—real flowers sending a subtle, sweet aroma into the air.

Swinging open a closet door, Julie extended her arm. "Let me hang up your jacket."

Clinging to it for a fleeting moment, Tim chided his foolishness and unzipped the garment. "I'll just toss it on the stairs," he said, draping it on the steps and sensing that if he left it there, the situation was less permanent.

She shrugged, closed the closet door, and headed through a doorway.

Tim followed and found himself in a cozy kitchen.

"I'll put on the coffee," she said. "Would you be more

comfortable in the living room?"

"No, I'll just watch," he said, afraid if he were alone he'd bolt.

She went about the business of filling the coffeemaker and slicing pieces of orange-colored cake with creamy white frosting. The pungent scent rose from the brew and wrapped Tim in familiar comfort.

Finished, Julie filled his mug with the right amount of coffee and cream. Each carrying their cup and plate, he followed her to the living room.

Sinking into a plush chair, he let his gaze sweep the brick fireplace, the broad mantle adorned with porcelain birds and candlesticks on each side of an antique clock.

"That old clock was my grandfather's," she said, apparently noticing his wandering gaze.

"Your place is attractive, Julie—and homey."

"I like a house to be comfortable."

"You succeeded," he said, pulling his focus to her. He preferred to look anywhere but at Julie. When he did, his pulse galloped inside his veins, leaving him bewildered.

Then, reality smacked him, and his mouth opened, allowing the truth to tumble out. "I'd be embarrassed to show you where I live."

Her head bolted upward. "Why?"

"I rent a townhouse. . .you know, units all connected, each one looks like the next, the size of matchboxes."

She shook her head. "You shouldn't feel uncomfortable about that. You have a son to support as well as yourself. Look at me. I'm single. No one to spend my money on but me."

Her face glowed with sincerity, and Tim felt his stiff

shoulders ease backward into the chair. "Yes, but—"

"No 'buts,' " she said. "You're such a good father. I bet you lavish Timmy with everything you can."

Guilt poked at him, and he lifted a fork of delicious carrot cake and savored the bite rather than respond. She was correct. He did lavish Timmy with what he could. But he wished he didn't. "You see right through me," Tim said finally. "I suppose I try to make up for his loss of a mother. . .and I refuse to allow him to have a childhood like I had."

Her face twisted with concern. "You had a difficult life?"

Sipping the warm brew as a stall, Tim wanted to kick himself. Why had he told her that?

"I was raised by my aunt," he continued, sensing he owed her an explanation, "on a farm in Michigan. Times were hard. My uncle died shortly after I moved in, so I was the only 'man' in the family. At six years old, that was a responsibility. She had only one daughter. No boys to help out. We all pitched in."

"Sounds difficult. . .and sad." She leaned forward on the armrest and gazed at him. "What happened to your parents?"

Tim blew out a stream of pent-up air. Why had he opened his mouth? She didn't want to hear his tale of woe. . .his *vague* tale of woe. God had blessed him with a failed memory. Only indistinct pictures of people from his past poked at his thoughts, and then only on rare occasions. His mother, bound to her bed, was a gentle image. Tim barely recalled his father, a big man, but apparently a defeated one. And sisters. Somewhere in the world he had sisters.

"I shouldn't have asked," Julie said, her face etched with discomfort. "Please forgive me."

Realizing he'd been lost in thought, Tim pushed the hazy memories aside. "No, it's natural to ask. My memories are faint. I was so young when my aunt came to get me, I don't recall much."

Her puzzled expression triggered the need to tell her more. Tim delved into his mind to organize his blurred recollections. "My mother died. I don't really remember it, except the fear and loneliness. I recall the others crying. Sisters. I had three. My aunt didn't want to talk about it much. I mostly think of Eden. She was the oldest."

"Have you ever tried to find them?" Julie asked.

His heart heavy, Tim shook his head. "My memories are so vague, and my aunt was no help. My cousin's as bad. I'm not sure where to look. My father's dead now, but he'd vanished from the picture after my mother died. When my aunt came for me, I was living with a neighbor, I think."

"I can understand why being a good father is extra important to you."

Extra important. That was it. Vital. Necessary. Driving. His son would never know the pain of abandonment and degradation that he'd felt as a child.

Drawing his focus back to Julie, he studied her concerned face. Why didn't she have a husband and children? Her turn, he decided. He took the last bite of delicious cake, then set down the plate.

"Enough about me. Tell me about you, Julie. Why aren't you married with children of your own?"

She grinned as if accepting the inevitable. "I have a career. That's all I figured I could handle. When I worked at the hospital, I was on different shifts, sometimes doubling back. Socializing seemed nearly impossible, and. . .I don't know, I guess I figured all the rituals of dating and courting were more than I could handle."

"You make it sound like a task instead of pleasure. Where's your sense of romance?" Tim squirmed at asking such a personal question. Jan had always called him a romantic. He had loved to surprise her with trinkets and flowers for no reason at all, except that he loved her.

Julie remained silent. Then, she said one word. "Romance?" She paused again. "I've never wanted it."

"What?" Tim said before he could stop himself. "I thought all women reveled in romance. . .candlelight dinners, floral bouquets, sappy cards decorated. . ." His mind flew back to a few weeks earlier at the singles' activity. ". . .with hearts and Cupids."

Julie blushed. "Sure, that kind of romance is fun. I suppose most woman would cherish that."

What kind of romance did she mean? He searched her face. Then, her blush answered his question. Intimacy. Did she think that dating meant being intimate? He'd never be like that with a woman. Not until marriage, naturally. Or did she mean she *never* wanted intimacy? He didn't know her well enough to ask.

"I went with a man for awhile a few years ago," Julie said. "We met at the hospital. Different shifts. Different values. Different—" She stopped. "You know what I mean."

Different *morals*. Is that what she meant? He nodded.

"I suppose sometimes relationships are more work than they're worth." *Like this one,* he thought, though the idea washed an empty sadness over his heart. Julie would make a good wife—for someone.

Tim glanced at his wristwatch. "Listen, I'd better get going. My neighbor will think I'm lost." He stood.

"Timmy needs his sleep for school," she added and rose, following him toward the doorway.

"Thanks for the carrot cake and coffee. The cake tasted homemade."

"It is," she said, giving him a grin. "Really homemade, except I have a secret ingredient."

Playfully, he lifted an eyebrow. "Nothing alcoholic, I hope."

"Heaven forbid, no. I use baby food carrots. No grating."

He grinned at her excitement. "And I didn't even need a bib."

She shifted forward as if she were going to touch his cheek, but she let her hand drop.

"I'll see you around, I suppose," Tim said, wanting to see her but knowing how ridiculous his wish was.

"Well, at the clinic, for sure," she said.

A flash of disappointment shot through him and from her expression, she seemed to have noticed.

"How about the singles' group? They're having a St. Patrick's Day party," she said.

"Do I have to dye my hair green?" he asked, being silly, but unable to answer her question.

"I won't if you won't," she said.

His heart nudged his vocal chords. "Okay, I'll see you then. No green hair."

"It'll be fun," she said.

He sensed she was correct. When he opened the outside door, the chilling air didn't penetrate the warmth that covered him.

❄

Julie took an occasional sip of her foamy, green ice cream punch and eyed the doorway. Tim had said he'd come, but for some reason, she sensed his hesitation. Maybe she'd pushed herself on him. Yet, why would she? He was a nice man with a difficult past, and she longed to help him heal. Her nursing persona, she was sure.

The yearning to aid people in distress, to solve others' problems, to soothe people's hurts seemed part of her nature. It was also what got her in trouble.

She cringed thinking of Jeff, her old steady. He'd pressed her so often to give herself to him fully. She could hear his plaintive voice in her head. "If you love me, you'll trust me not to hurt you. We're getting married someday anyway. What difference will it make?"

She wanted to please him, wanted to make him happy, wanted to meet his need. But she couldn't. And the more he pressed, the more resentment and frustration she felt. She could never trust a man again. What would she do if Tim was like that? If he pleaded with her? Told her how much he needed her? Told her she could make him feel less tense?

Sadness washed over her, and she closed her eyes with a new realization. She'd be better off if Tim didn't come at all. Then she'd never have to face dealing with those issues again. Loneliness prickled at the back of her neck.

Opening her eyes, she saw Tim come through the

doorway. He waved, and her heart lifted with an unexpected joy, then sank to her toes. But watching him smile as he approached her, she set aside her guilty fear and gave him a wave in return.

"Hi," he said, slipping off his jacket and hanging it on the chair back. "My neighbor was late getting home. She's watching Timmy for me."

"I thought you were standing me up," she said, giving her voice a lighthearted lift to cover the real feelings she'd had.

"Me? Never." He gave her a wry smile.

"Neighbor? You must have really great neighbors."

"One, anyway," he said. "It's the same woman who watched Timmy for the concert. She's alone, too, so we help each other out. Besides, Timmy and her son are best friends. . .and Sammy."

Sammy? Concern, as well as curiosity, riffled through her. "Who's Sammy?" But her mind tangled with his single woman comment. What was Tim's relationship with her?

"Sammy's their dog." He chuckled. "Timmy wants a puppy, but I encourage him to play with Sammy and save myself the grief."

"Smart man," she said, longing to ask him more about the neighbor lady.

The conversation drifted to Timmy, the orthopedic clinic, Julie's choir, and finally, food was served. They nibbled on appetizers with green cream cheese and hot dogs with green catsup. Laughing, they lifted their voice with an Irish sing-along. When the others wrapped their arms around each other, shoulder to shoulder, and swayed to the music, Tim drew her to his side, rocking to the lilting tune. Warmth traveled through her.

Too soon, the evening ended, and Julie longed to invite Tim to her house. Still, she'd been the pursuer, and this time she hoped he might suggest an activity together.

In the parking lot, he stood beside her car while she unlocked the door and slid in. "I hate to have you drive alone. I should've been a gentleman and offered you a ride."

"That's okay," she said, knowing in her heart she'd have loved a ride.

Hesitating, he teetered, hands in his pockets, then finally spoke. "If you'd like to follow me home, I can offer you some coffee."

Surprised, Julie stumbled over her thoughts, trying to weigh her decision. Instead, she listened to her heart. "Sure, if it's not too much trouble."

He gave her directions, then closed her door. She sat a moment before backing out of her space. She longed to know more about him—to know where he worked and to see the house that had tugged out an apology. Yet being alone in his house made her nervous. Did he have an ulterior motive for inviting her? Maybe he had a platonic interest only—just a friendship, nothing more.

But if she faced the truth, she liked Tim more than she cared to admit. He needed to know where she stood in terms of her faith and her morals.

Chapter 4

Tim opened the door, snapped on the light, and invited Julie inside. His stomach knotted, and he feared looking at her face, knowing that she'd find his place inadequate compared to hers. Inexpensive furniture, small, and crowded.

"Cozy kitchen," she said as soon as she stepped through the doorway. "Very nice for a small family."

Small. Cozy. The words themselves sounded fine. . . and truthful, but what was she really thinking? As he guided her to the living room, he couldn't help but recall her solid antiques in contrast to his glass and brass tables.

Julie paused in the doorway. "I like it," she said. She stepped into the room and moved to the glass etagere, eyeing the two plants that Tim had managed to keep alive. "Good choice. Big, overstuffed furniture would dominate the room, but you've managed to make it masculine, yet homey." She touched the plant and gestured to a colorful toss pillow that gave life to his plain, brown sofa. "I can't believe you said you'd be embarrassed to show me your home."

Home. He liked the sound of the word as it left her

lips. And no matter how he twisted her sentences, they sounded sincere and positive. "Thanks," Tim said, finally.

She sank into the streamlined sofa, nestling against a pillow, and grinned at him.

"I'll put on the coffee," he said, then turned and hurried from the room to catch his breath. He filled the pot, then picked up the telephone to call Penny. To his relief, she volunteered to run Timmy home.

He rotated his shoulders to relax them before pulling out the mugs and finding some store-bought cookies to serve. He wished he had something more impressive.

A rap sounded on the door, and Timmy entered, sleepy-eyed but curious. "Thanks, Penny," Tim said as she gave a wave and darted back home.

After giving his son a hug, Tim sent him on his way to say hello to Julie while he brought in the coffee. He could hear Timmy's shy, yet curious, tone as he greeted Julie in the living room.

Tim carried in the tray, offering Julie a mug, then led his son up the stairs to bed. When he returned, Julie had slipped out of her shoes and curled her legs beneath her on the sofa with the mug clasped in her fingers.

"Good coffee," she said. "Is it special?"

He grinned. "Hazelnut." He lifted his own cup and slipped into an adjacent chair. "Have a cookie," he said, clamping his teeth together so he wouldn't apologize for the packaged dessert.

"They're my favorite, but I'm too full from all that 'green' food," she said with a smile. "Coffee's great."

She surveyed the room again. "Did your wife decorate, or did you?" she asked.

"We'd moved in just before Jan got ill so most of the choices were mine. What I could afford at the time."

"You've done a nice job, Tim. Never be embarrassed to show your home. It's very attractive." She took another sip of the brew, her gaze riveted to Tim's. "You've never mentioned what you do for a living."

Tim sank deeper into the cushion. Enjoying her company more than he wanted, he'd always feared the day she would ask, figuring she'd be turned off by a factory worker.

Garnering courage, he answered. "I work at Sterling Stamping. In the press room."

"The big three," she said. "Great benefits, I hear. That's important, especially with Timmy."

Studying her face, Tim realized that she didn't bat an eye hearing his confession. "It's not a career, but it pays the bills."

"Nothing wrong with that." Her animated voice touched his ear. "Not everyone has the same opportunities. Have you been there long?"

The question tugged at his old hurts and sorrows. "I joined the army right out of high school. Basic training at Fort Knox, then the Presidio in San Francisco, and finally San Antonio."

"Nice experience," she said. "You had opportunities to see the country."

He laughed. "Right, that and a lot of rain and mud during bivouac."

"I suppose." Her look grew tender. "What made you join the service?" she asked.

"College was out of the question. I'm grateful to Aunt

Selma for raising me, but she didn't have much, especially after my uncle died, so I was a burden."

Julie's expression melted to sadness. Leaning forward, she rested her hand against his forearm. "Never a burden, Tim."

He wanted to say that she didn't know the situation, but he held back his bitterness. His aunt, he supposed, had done the best she could. "It was difficult. I've always wished I could pay her back somehow. . .but now she's dead, too."

Her hand lingered on his arm while they sat in silence as if neither knew what to say.

"Will you be at the April singles'?" she asked, finally. "I heard they're planning some kind of a scavenger hunt or something. It should be fun."

"Sure—that is if Timmy's okay then."

"Right. His surgery's getting close, isn't it?" She looked toward the staircase in thought. "I can imagine you're getting nervous."

"Anxious, but hopeful. I pray a lot and trust that the Lord will bless Timmy."

"Timmy *and* you," Julie said. "God will bless you both."

The warmth from her hand spread up his arm, but a shiver of concern wrapped around his heart despite his faith. He'd never felt totally fulfilled—totally in God's favor—but he asked the Lord to give Timmy a good life. A life with laughter, joy—and health.

❄

Julie stared at the manila file folder with Timmy's name marked on the tab. She knew he was in the waiting room for a checkup following his surgery.

Disappointment had filled her at the April singles' event. Tim hadn't come. Prickled with fear, she'd worried that something had gone wrong with Timmy's surgery. Still, too uncomfortable to call Tim and ask, she'd looked through Timmy's file, feeling like a spy, finding no complications with his osteotomy. The surgeon had used compression plates, she noted, and the procedure had gone well.

Filled with frustration, Julie wondered why Tim hadn't called. He had to know that she cared about Timmy. . .and about him. Her invitation to the singles' group seemed bold enough.

Hit by uncertainty, she ran her finger over Timmy's name on the file tab. Maybe the neighbor woman meant more to Tim than Julie wanted to face. Wisdom told her to back off.

She drew in a calming breath and stepped to the waiting-room door. "Timmy Richmond," she called, giving the boy a smile.

He sent back a shy grin and rose on crutches, his leg in a cast. Tim followed beside him, concentrating on the child, not her.

"Hi," he said, without looking at her as he held the door for Timmy.

"I'm glad to see things went well," she said, motioning him down the hall. "Room five."

He went ahead of her, and at the door, she slipped the file into the holder mounted outside the door. "The doctor will be with you shortly," she said, grasping the knob and stepping into the hallway as she began closing the door.

"Julie?"

She hesitated, hearing Tim call her name.

Drawing in a ragged breath, she pushed the door open. "Yes?"

His gaze caught hers. "I'm sorry I didn't call to tell you about Timmy. Life has been hectic."

"I imagine."

"To confuse things, I've been on overtime. That's so hard with Timmy home now that school's out. . .and the surgery. I've had to depend on my cousin, Nancy. . .and Penny."

But not me, Julie thought, then chastised herself. Why would he depend on her? She worked all day at the clinic. And they were new. . .friends.

"I've been on afternoons at the plant," he continued. "It's a hardship shift change, just temporary while Timmy needs extra care."

"Afternoons?" Understanding filtered into her mind. He left for work before she arrived home.

"On top of that, I've had to work the past two weekends. It's been a challenge."

"I'm sorry, Tim. I was concerned. . . ." She glanced down at Timmy, looking at her with wide eyes. "I hoped everything had gone well." She prayed her comment didn't frighten the child. "How are you doing, Timmy?" she asked, crouching beside him.

"Okay," he said. "Pretty soon, I'll walk good."

"I know. I'm so happy for you."

"But not for my birthday," he said, furrows growing in his smooth brow.

"Birthday? When's that?"

He glanced at his father who held up two fingers. "In two weeks. I'm having a birthday party."

"July twelfth," Tim added.

"You are? What fun. I love parties, don't you?"

He nodded his head. "Will you come? We'll have cake and ice cream."

She rose filled with discomfort and embarrassed that she'd mentioned she liked parties. "I, uh. . ."

"Can she come, Daddy?" Timmy asked, turning to his father.

"Well. . .sure. Why not? That is if she'd like to come."

Struggling to keep her face from announcing her humiliation, she faltered. "I'd love to." She caught Tim's gaze.

He nodded his approval. "It's a week from Saturday. Around six. We'll order pizza."

Timmy slid his tongue over his lips. "Pizza! Yummy!"

Tim grinned, and Julie backed toward the door overwhelmed with confusion. No doubt Timmy wanted her, but did Tim? She asked God for guidance, longing to do the right thing.

❄

"Here we are," Tim said, trepidation inching through him as he turned off the motor and gazed at the singles' crowd gathering for the Fourth of July picnic.

"I'm so pleased you asked me to come with you," Penny said, sliding from the car.

Tim swallowed, wanting to explain that it wasn't a date. He feared he'd made a grave error. Trying to be kind, he'd inadvertently misled her. One thing had led to another. He'd mowed Penny's lawn, she invited him to dinner, and at the end of the meal, he opened his mouth. "How would you like to go to the Fourth of July picnic with the singles' group next weekend? I know it's difficult going places alone."

He'd thought the invitation was clear, but her response nailed him to the spot. "Oh, Tim, I'd love to go with you. My size scares off most men."

Obviously she considered it a date, but that was as far from Tim's mind as mountain climbing. His hesitation wasn't her size at all. She'd been a good friend and neighbor, and an attractive one, but that's all he felt for her. Of late, Julie filled his thoughts.

He'd longed to see her at the picnic, but now with Penny at his side, he feared Julie wouldn't understand. The past week at the orthopedic clinic when she'd called Timmy's name, Tim's pulse had reared on its hind legs like a stallion until he noticed the hurt expression on her face.

Neglecting her. . .not calling had been foolish. Rude was more accurate. She'd shown friendship to both him and Timmy, but things had gotten in the way. He was at work when she was home, and he didn't feel right calling her at the clinic. Weekends he spent running errands, grocery shopping, and trying to spend time with Timmy. Though he missed her smile and easy good humor, too much seemed to be in the way for. . .friendship.

Friendship? No. . .he longed for more than that.

Penny bounded from the car, grabbed a canvas bag, and latched onto his arm. "Let's go," she said with a little nudge to his ribs with her elbow.

"Let me get the cooler," he said, loosening her grip and heading for the trunk. He hoisted the heavy container from the back, grateful that he needed two hands to carry it, and headed toward a picnic table.

Penny scurried along beside him. Reaching the table, she pulled a plastic cloth from the bag and spread it over the surface while Tim plopped the cooler at the base of the table and lifted the lid.

"How about a soda?" he asked.

"Sure," she said, accepting the drink he offered. From the canvas carryall, she brought out a large bag of chips and tore the wrapper.

Groping for courage, Tim scanned the area and held his breath. No Julie. Jack waved to him from two tables over where he sat with a young woman he'd dated a few times. Tim was pleased for him and wished God's blessing on their growing friendship.

Sitting at their table was another man. Tim beckoned to Penny and led the way. "Hi," he said as they neared.

Jack raised a questioning eye, and Tim gave him a "don't ask" look, hoping he could explain his predicament.

"Jack, Cheryl," he said, "this is my neighbor, Penny."

Each greeted her before Jack introduced Ray.

"You're new with the singles?" Ray asked, looking from Penny to Tim as if wondering about their relationship.

Tim took advantage of the situation. "Penny's been such a great neighbor, I invited her to come along and meet all of you."

Penny gave Tim a puzzled look.

Ray focused on Tim. "Then you're not—"

"Oh, no," Tim said, "we're only friends."

He felt Penny stiffen beside him, but Ray's face brightened, and he patted the empty bench. "Why don't you bring your food over here?" Ray asked. "We could all sit together."

Jack nodded in agreement, and with gratitude, Tim turned toward his gear as he overheard Ray invite Penny to be his horseshoe partner after lunch.

Fearing he'd hurt Penny's feelings, Tim felt relieved when Ray showed her attention. God had worked out his predicament. Sorry that he'd bungled, Tim's guilt lightened with Ray's apparent interest in Penny. As Tim neared his cooler, he spotted Julie across the lawn. She looked like sunshine in yellow shorts and a matching top as the light's rays played on her wavy brown hair. He grasped his resolve and headed for her.

❄

Pivoting away, Julie held her breath. She'd seen Tim arrive with a woman, and her heart had dropped to her shoes. He looked so handsome, tall and powerful, his muscles bulging from carrying the heavy cooler. But she'd been right. Apparently Penny meant more to Tim than Julie had hoped. She could handle it though. She had to.

"Julie." Tim's voice sailed on the breeze.

She pushed an amiable smile to her face and turned toward him. "Hi, Tim."

"I hoped you'd be here. I wanted to remind you of the birthday party next week."

Unbidden, her gaze drifted toward the blond woman seated at the distant table. "Oh. . .Tim, I'm, uh, sorry. I don't think that I can—"

"That you can come?" His gaze searched hers. "But Timmy'll be so disappointed. He's talked about nothing else since we invited you."

Guilt filled her. Not one real reason stood in her way of attending the party—except the blond and pure, sinful jealousy. In the span of a breath, she asked God to forgive her foolishness and drew up her shoulders, fortifying her courage. "I don't want to disappoint Timmy." She meant that with all her heart.

"Then I hope you can come. He'll be so disappointed if you don't. To be honest, so will I."

Her heart faltered for a moment. She searched his face, wondering why he would say such a thing. But for Timmy, she reconsidered. "I'll, uh, maybe I can work something out."

"Please do." His eyes searched hers. "Are you. . .with someone?"

She nodded.

"Oh." Surprising her, a forlorn look spread across his face.

She could tell from his expression that he thought she meant a man. "I'm with Amy and Barb. We rode together."

"I thought. . ." He grinned and a flush crept above his collar. "If you're alone, would you like to join us?" He motioned to the table across the way.

"But you're with a date, Tim." Her earlier jealousy spiraled to aggravation. Why was he playing games with her?

"No. No, that's Penny, my neighbor. I invited her to come, hoping she might meet someone."

Panic riddled his face. She stifled a laugh—at his expression *and* her own sense of relief. "I should eat with the ladies, I think. We're sharing a picnic basket."

A look of disappointment crossed his face. "I don't know what's wrong with me, Julie. I should have asked you to the picnic. I'm very backward when it comes to—"

"Don't apologize, Tim. We can visit after lunch."

His expression relaxed. "How about horseshoes?"

"What?"

"They're playing horseshoes after lunch. And don't worry, Penny's playing with Ray." He gestured toward the group at the other table. "I'd like you to be my partner."

His partner? She'd longed to be his partner, but one of a different kind. "Sure. Why not?"

She gave an inward chuckle. When he realized how badly she played horseshoes, he'd know "why not," but for now, it would be her surprise.

Chapter 5

Tim stood in the kitchen, wondering what was keeping Julie. He'd spoken to her on the telephone, and she'd indicated she was coming to Timmy's party.

In the living room, he heard his cousin, Nancy, talking to Jack. She didn't seem pleased when he told her about Julie. Always in her "downing" way, she reminded him that he was a blue-collar worker and Julie was a professional. "That kind of thing only leads to hurt," she'd said. "A woman like that doesn't need you one iota."

Nancy was right. He had nothing to give Julie. Money, home, car, lifestyle—she had him beat in every area. She was worth far more than he could ever dream of giving her. So why did he tempt himself? He shook his head in disapproval. He'd tried to leave it in God's hands, but had he?

Outside, balloons bounced past the window, then a knock sounded on the door. Tim's chest tightened. Penny or Julie? His heart told him that Julie had brought the balloons.

When he opened the door, he found Julie standing on

the porch holding a gift, surrounded by a colorful floating bouquet. Mesmerized by the display, Tim faltered, drawn back in time. So far back, his mind swirled to another place and time, to a scene out of proportion—a vague memory filled with soaring colorful balloons.

"Are you okay?" Julie asked, a frown edging out her smile.

He laughed. "Sure. I was mentally clicking my heels and saying, 'No place like home.'" He pushed the door open, allowing her to manipulate her lavish gift into the room.

She chuckled. "I could have flown to Kansas if the wind had caught me."

"I think you overdid it, but you'll thrill Timmy." He closed the door. "Timmy," he called.

In a heartbeat, Timmy came through the doorway and reeled when he spied the gift.

"Balloons," he said, clapping his hands and scurrying as quickly as he could toward Julie. "Yippee!"

"What do you say?" Tim asked.

"Thanks, Julie." He held the package in his arms and clasped the balloons that bobbed above his head with one hand.

A sense of déjà vu spilled over Tim as Timmy returned to the living room. He heard Jack and his young daughter, Patti, oohing over the bright gift, but Tim remained smothered in undisclosed sensations.

Nancy's voice sailed into the kitchen. "Must be someone with money who could afford that."

Tim caught Julie's glance and motioned her into the living room. Nancy's focus was glued to Julie.

"You've met Jack," he said to Julie. "This is his daughter, Patti."

Patti said hello, her gaze darting from Julie to the balloon bouquet.

"And my cousin, Nancy Johnson," Tim said. "We grew up together."

"My mother raised Tim. . .out of the goodness of her heart," Nancy muttered, interrupting the introductions.

Tim froze at the comment, so inappropriate to the time and place.

"Yes, I've heard," Julie said, her voice calm and gentle. "That was wonderful of your family."

"A hardship for all of us," Nancy added. "We only had a small farm and—"

"I'll order the pizza," Tim said, halting the conversation. "Penny and Buddy should be here any minute."

"And Sammy?" Timmy asked.

Tim stifled a grin. "Sammy wasn't invited, Son, but you can show him your balloons later."

"Okay," Timmy said, his enthusiasm undaunted.

Her hands knotted in irritation, Julie watched Tim leave the room. How dare this woman humiliate him like that! Cousin or not, she had no reason to drag out the past in front of Tim's company.

Deciding to stay as far away as possible from her, Julie headed toward the sofa, but Nancy patted the empty chair beside her.

"Sit here," she commanded. "We can get better acquainted."

That was far from Julie's hope, but not wanting to add

to the uncomfortable moment, she followed the woman's direction. Before Julie could take a deep breath, Nancy began her inquisition.

"You work at the clinic, huh? A nurse, Tim said."

"That's right," Julie responded, turning her focus to the others. "How've you been, Jack?" Julie kept her eyes directed at him and Patti.

Jack grinned. "Great. And you?"

"Why a clinic?" Nancy prodded. "More money?"

Julie swiveled her head. "No. Less, in fact, but I prefer the hours."

"You must be well-off then," Nancy said.

Julie avoided her comment and steered the conversation to Patti and Timmy. From there the talk became safe, until sounds from the kitchen attuned everyone to the new guests who were arriving.

A young boy dashed into the room, ogling the balloons. Then the large blond from the picnic, Penny, stood in the doorway.

"Wow! Those are dandy. Nearly fill up the room," Penny said.

Nancy swung toward Julie. "I'm sure your living room is much larger than this one. You see, Tim and Penny have some things in common that you—"

"Small living rooms are *very* common in townhouses," Tim shot from the kitchen doorway.

Nancy bit her bottom lip.

"What can I do to help?" Julie asked, giving Penny her chair and stepping toward Tim. As she did, the doorbell rang, and the pizza delivery man saved the day.

Doling out pizza and salad kept Julie busy and Nancy's

mouth occupied. By the time they'd disposed of the paper plates, Timmy was eager to open his gifts; then the candles were lit and a round of "Happy Birthday" filled the air.

After dessert, the guests rose and left one by one, but Julie remained behind to help with the cleanup. Rinsing flatware at the sink, she overheard Tim at the door with Nancy.

"Any reason why I should remember a room full of balloons?" he asked.

Nancy sniffed. "Wishful thinking, I'd guess. Don't all kids like balloons?"

"I suppose," Tim said, his voice filled with disappointment.

"You take care," she said, "and I'd keep my eye on Penny. She's a good lady. Suits you well, and she's a woman who really needs you."

Her voice faded, and Tim hesitated a moment before closing the door.

Julie paused, letting the warm water slide over her hands, taking away the chill of the encounter.

"Sorry," Tim said, his voice hushed. "She's like that, and I can't do much about it. But she's the only blood relative I know, and despite her negative attitude, I'd hate to lose her."

Julie wiped her hands and stepped forward, grasping his shoulders. "Look, Tim, you're not responsible for other people's behavior. Nancy's like a mother who hates to lose control of her grown child."

"I know," he said, his eyes looking deeply into hers. "You're a fine woman, Julie. You never balk at anything and always see something nice in the worst situation."

"Don't give me too much credit. I grumble just like anyone." She lowered her hands. "But I sit in a closet so no one hears me."

His face broke into a smile, and a soft chuckle spilled from his chest. "Listen, Timmy wants you to meet Sammy—and show the dog his balloons. Why don't you take him outside and let me finish up here."

He lifted his hand and brushed her cheek, an inscrutable look in his eyes. His touch tingled down her shoulder and reached her heart, sending it skipping for a moment.

"Okay," she said, catching her breath, "if you don't mind."

She called Timmy, and again in a temporary leg brace, he hobbled into the room, tangled in the balloon strings. She laughed and unwound him from the cords, then headed outside with one last lingering look at Tim who watched them from the sink.

Timmy headed across the grass and reached the chain link fence. "Sammy," he called.

A floppy-eared spaniel gave a rousing yip and bounded to the fence. "Isn't he great?" Timmy said, grinning up at Julie.

"He sure is." The dog's shining cinnamon coat glistened in the summer sun, and he darted back and forth along the fence, occasionally scooting back on his front paws to bark at the bevy of color tangled in Timmy's hand.

"I'll give him a balloon," Timmy said, struggling to unwind one of the strings.

Before Julie could dart forward, one escaped, sailing upward on the wind. Timmy shielded his eyes from the sun and watched it. "My balloon's flying away?"

"Sure is," Julie said, watching it lift higher and higher above the houses, moving toward the clouds.

"Is it going to heaven?" Timmy asked. "Like my mom?"

Julie's chest tightened, and she wrapped her arm around the child's shoulders, unable to speak for a moment.

He tilted his earnest face to hers. "Maybe my mom will find it in heaven and know it's from me."

How could she tell him no? How could she say it would fall to earth when the helium escaped? The image of the child's smiling mother finding the balloon filled her mind. "Maybe, Timmy," she said, struggling to keep her voice steady.

Sammy's bark distracted him, and soon they were heading inside minus one balloon, but enriched by a lovely thought and a shared moment.

❄

After tucking Timmy into bed, Tim lumbered down the stairs, caught in a mixture of feelings. Julie had been a positive in his day; Nancy, a negative.

Julie sat curled up on the sofa, sipping a soda, her head leaning against the cushion—like she belonged there. But, Tim feared, she didn't. As much as he disliked Nancy's comments, she'd been right. Unlike Penny, Julie didn't need him. Tim knew he should pry Julie from his thoughts and let God lead him to a woman he could support, a woman who'd be content with his meager living.

Instead of listening to his head, Tim's heart guided him to action. He grasped his soda can and settled beside Julie on the sofa. A sweet, tantalizing fragrance drifted from her—one he'd enjoyed before—reminding him of flowers in the rain.

"Thanks for all your help," he said.

"I enjoyed myself. And so did Timmy." She placed her palm against his arm. "You have a great son. You must be so proud of him. He was well-behaved all evening."

"Unlike my cousin," Tim said, his voice sounding bitter in his ears.

" 'Sticks and stones can break my bones. . . .' Remember that, Tim. Nancy's words can't hurt you one bit, unless you let them. And you shouldn't."

He drew in a deep breath filled with her lovely aroma and slipped his arm across the sofa back, his fingers brushing the silky texture of her blouse.

In silence, she turned to him, their gazes locked as if in understanding.

Yearning swept over Tim. He lowered his gaze to her lovely, soft mouth, her warm breath so near it caressed his neck. Unable to hold himself back, he leaned forward, gently catching her sweet lips beneath his. She didn't resist as he expected, but yielded, leaning into his touch, and released a shuddered sigh that prickled on his arms.

Drawing back, he caught her chin with his thumb and finger, awash in her alluring, heavy-lidded gaze. "You're so good to me, and I give you nothing in return."

"You don't?" she said, her voice a murmur. "I beg to differ."

He didn't understand and accepted her words as kindness. What had he ever done for her? He'd never taken her to dinner or to a concert. If nothing more, he needed to repay her for the joy she'd given him and Timmy. God would lead him. All he had to do was follow.

Chapter 6

Julie stared at the greeting card and shook her head. Tim had outdone himself the past weeks. Telephone calls, dinner dates, greeting cards, and now flowers. Admiring the floral bouquet sitting on the living room gateleg table, she drew in the sweet scent of carnations nestled among lilies and baby's breath.

Letting her gaze drift back to the card, she reread the words, telling her how special she was to him and Timmy—no words of love, but sentiments that touched her heart. The message thrilled her, yet unsettled her.

Tim seemed to run like a faucet—hot and cold. But unlike a spigot, she had no control over which came out. She sensed he was afraid, but of what, she had no idea. In conversation Julie had tried to touch on his past, but since she'd met Nancy, he'd simply shrug and remind her of his cousin's attitude.

If his life had been peppered with words and actions dragging him down, his lack of confidence and feelings of being unworthy were understandable. He'd shown them in so many ways. Now she wondered what she could do to help him understand that he was worthy, both as a man and as a child of God.

The flowers had spurred a dinner invitation, and Tim and his son were due to arrive within the hour for a home-cooked meal. With most of her food preparation complete, Julie walked into the living room and picked up her worn leather Bible, the pages dog-eared from use. What could God's Word tell Tim that he didn't already know?

Her memory guided her to Ecclesiastes, and she studied the verses until her focus faltered in chapter four, verse nine: "Two are better than one, because they have a good return for their work: If one falls down, his friend can help him up. But pity the man who falls and has no one to help him up! Also, if two lie down together, they will keep warm. But how can one keep warm alone? Though one may be overpowered, two can defend themselves. A cord of three strands is not quickly broken."

Sensing God had led her to the verse, Julie bowed her head and prayed that Tim would be guided by the Lord's message. She closed the cover and set the Bible in its familiar spot on the side table. Then she rose and returned to the kitchen. When the doorbell rang, her pulse surged and she hurried to the screen door.

"Hi," Tim said, holding a paper bag in his arms.

Timmy stood beside him, carrying a box of building blocks.

"Come in," she said, trying to monitor her anxiety. "Thanks again for the flowers." She gestured toward the gateleg table. "They're beautiful."

"Are those from us, Daddy?" Timmy asked.

"They sure are," Julie said, giving him a hug. Her focus settled on the package in Tim's arms. "What's in the sack?"

"Homemade bread."

"From where?" she asked.

"From me," Tim answered.

"You?" She saw the pride on his face and believed him. "You bake bread?"

He nodded and handed her the package.

What other wonders didn't she know about this man? She opened the sack and pulled out the large loaf, admiring the golden crust and the yeasty scent. "Looks wonderful. How many more secret talents do you have?"

Tim chuckled. "I hope it goes with dinner."

"Perfectly. I made a couple of salads and thought I'd let you grill steaks. I have hot dogs if Timmy prefers."

"Yummy, hot dogs," Timmy said.

Julie laughed and led them into the kitchen where she set the plate of steaks in Tim's hands and guided them outside to the readied barbecue.

While Tim grilled the steaks, Julie brought out the pasta and lettuce salads, thick slices of the bread, and a pitcher of lemonade, setting them on the umbrella table.

Soon they were forking into the meal and slivering off tender pieces of steak while Timmy chomped on his hot dog, better to him than filet mignon.

"Dessert now or later?" Julie asked.

"Later, if you don't mind," Tim said.

Julie agreed, and after cleaning off the table, they sat on lawn chairs on the small patio surrounded by burnished asters, gold and white mums, and multihued snapdragons. Timmy had made friends with the neighbor child, and the two boys played together on the grass.

"I've been curious," Julie said, hoping she wouldn't

ruin the lovely day, "about the balloons. I heard you ask Nancy the night of Timmy's birthday. What's that all about. . .if you don't mind my asking?"

"I don't mind at all, but I can't answer your question." He shifted in the chair and wound his fingers together, resting his elbows on his knees. "The day you arrived with the balloons, I had a strange sense of déjà vu. I asked Nancy because I thought after I came to the farm—maybe for a birthday or something—they'd given me a ton of balloons like that; but she didn't remember."

"You were six," Julie said. "Was it before. . .before you lived with them?"

She noticed his shoulders tense and was sorry she'd asked.

"I've blocked much of that time from my memory. Fear. Frustration. Anger. I don't know why or what caused it, but a horrible sense of abandonment comes over me when I try to think back. Bad feelings."

Touching his shoulder, Julie massaged his taut muscles. "Maybe you'll know someday, Tim. God can answer those prayers, too. Little miracles."

"Maybe," he said, sending her a tender smile.

The tenseness faded from his shoulder, and he leaned back against the chair and looked into the sky. "Nice to enjoy the end of summer this way, sitting outside."

"It is. Winter comes too soon."

Tim nodded. "Lots of things come too soon."

Frustrated with herself, Julie studied his face, wondering if he was thinking of his wife's death or his mother's. "Life plays tricks on us sometimes, I suppose, but I like to think there's a reason and a season for everything, like God tells us."

"I believe that. But I wish we understood things better." He turned toward her and slid his palm over her hand resting on the chair arm. "Like you and me, Julie— I wish I understood us. You know I care for you. You're the first woman to unsettle my thoughts since I first met Jan. But I'm afraid that I care for you. . .too much."

A twinge of fear spiraled through her. "Too much?" She struggled to keep the concern from settling on her face. "How could that be?"

He wove his hands through hers, then lifted them to his lips and kissed her fingers, his eyes focused across the lawn to where the children played. "As much as I dislike Nancy's negativity, she has a point. I have nothing to offer you, Julie." He shifted his gaze to hers. "You don't need me."

"Need you? Do you mean money? Financial security?"

He lowered his head and nodded.

"You're right, Tim. I don't need your money. I don't need material things. God's blessed me with a good education and a career. I give thanks daily for that." Her body shook with emotion. "But there's so much that I do need."

He sat in heavy silence, a hush so loud she could almost hear the gears in his mind grinding over her words, looking for their meaning.

"But. . .I can't just take from a relationship, Julie," he said finally. "I have to give, too."

Tears filled her eyes, sensing the deep ache so evident on his face and in his voice. She couldn't teach him about love and relationships. Only God could do that. She breathed deeply, letting the cleansing air renew her. "Tim, you spend your life giving to others—doing for others. Don't neglect yourself along the way. God doesn't want that. When you have a quiet moment, read Ecclesiastes, chapter four. Read it and study it. Then you'll understand."

"Ecclesiastes," he repeated, his eyes focused heavenward. "I will."

"Good." She squeezed the large hand wrapped so tightly around hers. "Now, how about some strawberry shortcake with real whipped cream?"

"See, like I told you," he said, "you always know the way to a man's heart."

She smiled as she rose, sending a prayer to heaven that not only she but God's guidance would enter Tim's heart and give him understanding.

❄

The aroma of bacon and fried eggs filled the air as Tim stepped into the diner after the Sunday church service. Timmy followed behind him along with Jack and his daughter, Patti.

"I want pancakes," Timmy said as he slid into the booth.

"Me, too," Patti said, looking up at her father for approval. "And sausage."

Jack chuckled, reached behind the metal napkin holder for the menus, and passed them out.

As they studied the fare, a waitress came by; when their orders were placed and coffee and milk arrived, they leaned back to wait for breakfast.

"So, how are things going?" Jack asked, a teasing edge to his voice.

"Great," Tim said, letting him dangle.

"Seeing Julie?" Jack asked, then lifted his cup and took a swig of the hot brew.

"Now and then," Tim said.

"We see Julie lots," Timmy volunteered. "She likes me."

A lopsided grin tilted on Tim's mouth. "Son, some things are best left private."

Jack burst into laughter while Timmy eyed him curiously.

"Timmy, why don't you and Patti go watch the gold-fish for awhile. I'll call you when the food comes."

"Angelfish, too," Patti said.

"Angels, too," Tim agreed.

The men shifted, letting the children head for the large aquarium filled with colorful species.

Jack leaned on his elbows, pinning Tim with his look. "What are you avoiding, Tim? It's been over two years since Jan's been gone. She'd want you to find someone, and Julie seems perfect."

"She is perfect. She's more than perfect. But I have so little to offer anyone, especially a woman like Julie. And I don't know, Jack, I'm not sure I need anyone. It's hard to explain."

"Doesn't make sense to me," Jack said, falling back against the bench. "She likes you. . .a lot, I'd say."

"And I like her. . .a lot. But I'm not sure I have enough love to spread around. Timmy fills my life, and Jan's mem-ory is still there. What's left for Julie?"

"Be honest, Tim. Your 'like' for Julie has already grown into love. It's obvious."

Tim shook his head, knowing that Jack was right.

"And stop worrying about spreading love," Jack said.

"You don't have to. Love grows like ivy. Ever see how it takes over a building?"

Tim smiled, thinking of the ivy that had crept to the top of Julie's fireplace chimney. In the midst of that thought, the children returned, and he rose. Jack stood, too, while Timmy and Patti settled into the booth.

"You can try to prune ivy back," Jack continued, "but before you know it, it's spread over everything, wrapped around every nook and cranny. Love's just like that."

"I suppose you're right," Tim said. "I loved Jan and seemed to find plenty for Timmy."

Timmy tilted his head. "I love you, Daddy. And I love Sammy."

Tim laughed as a puzzled expression settled on Jack's face. "Who's Sammy?" he asked.

"The neighbor's dog."

"You're in good company, my friend," Jack said.

Before Tim could respond, the waitress appeared carrying their breakfast plates on a large tray. As she set the plates on the table, Tim's mind drifted to more "good company." Julie. Her face rose in his thoughts and, with it, came her suggestion: "Read Ecclesiastes, chapter four. Then you'll understand."

The two families joined hands for the table blessing, and as Jack lifted his voice in prayer, Tim sent up another petition. *Please, Lord, help me find the answer in Your Word.*

Chapter 7

Closing the Bible, Tim placed it in his lap and peered at the black leather cover. He'd never read the book so much as he had in past weeks. The verse from Ecclesiastes had lived in his thoughts since the first day he'd read it. Julie's suggestion had been a good one. The verses held great meaning for him.

He rose and set the Bible on the kitchen table, then wandered to the window and gazed outside. Autumn leaves drifted from the trees, swirled on the brisk wind, and settled into piles along buildings and fences.

Since Jan's death, winter's icy promise had settled on him like a heavy cloud. This year, Tim felt different. No matter how keen the wind or how high the snow, a new warmth radiated through him.

The need to talk with Julie urged him forward. He grasped the wall phone and punched in the numbers. When he heard her voice, a feeling of comfort blanketed his restless thoughts.

"Time to talk?" he asked. "I'd like to see you."

"I'm running out for a few groceries," she said. "I can stop by for awhile."

As always, Julie was there to fill his needs, to wash away his sadness, and to make him smile. A hush drifted over him. Timmy had gone to Buddy's after dinner, Sammy being the special attraction. One day, he'd have to give the boy his dream.

With the sun sitting heavy on the horizon, Julie tapped on the door, and instead of staying inside, Tim suggested they walk. He needed the fresh air to clear his mind and help him say what needed to be said.

"Sounds good," Julie said. "Grab your coat, and I'll run next door and tell Timmy. I saw him in the backyard."

By the time Tim met her on the sidewalk, she'd talked with his son and Penny. He slipped his hand into hers, a feeling he had grown to love, and they set out toward the nearby park.

Julie talked about her day at work, then finally asked, "So, what's up? You said you wanted to talk."

Tim gave her hand a squeeze, pleased that she didn't sound concerned. "I've been reading the Bible."

She tilted her head and smiled. "Was I right?"

He sent her back a reassuring grin. "I think I know what you mean."

"I'm glad. I'd be a fool to say financial security wasn't important, but many things are as important—much more important than luxuries."

He lifted her chilled fingers and nestled them against his cheek. "I know."

They'd reached the park, and Julie broke away and ran toward the swings. She settled on a wooden seat and pushed her legs back, sending herself aloft. Pumping with her whole body, she gained momentum.

Tim pressed into a seat, laughing at the tight fit, then gave up and hurried behind Julie to give her a push. She flew away with his helpful boost, and he jumped to reach the seat as she sailed backward.

"It's too cold up here," she called her voice fading as the swing hurled forward.

He stepped back, letting the swing slow at its own pace. When Julie braced her feet against the ground and came to a full stop, she bounded up from the seat and wrapped her arms around his body.

"Hug me," she said. "I'm freezing."

With joy, Tim wrapped his arms around her, nestling her against his jacket, feeling her body heat permeate the cloth and warm his heart.

"This is what love is," Julie said. "I pick you up when you fall, I hold you when you hurt, I defend you when you're attacked, and I wrap my arms around you to keep you warm."

Tim lifted her chin upward and looked in her eyes. "I thought *I* was keeping *you* warm."

"We're keeping each other warm," she said.

He drew back and slipped an arm around her shoulder, and they headed away from the trees into the brighter sunlight. When they found a bench, Tim drew her down, his arm around her shoulders, and looked into the blue autumn sky.

"What would I have done without you, Julie? I've spent my life feeling I had nothing to give anyone. When I met Jan, she'd just lost her job. I was working and felt on top of the world. She needed me, and I needed to do for her."

He paused, fearing she might not understand. "Don't think that I didn't love Jan. I did. But my love was founded on something different than my feelings for you."

"You don't need to explain, Tim. Love begins in many ways. The result can be the same when God shares in it." She squeezed his arm. "The threefold cord, remember?"

She rested her cheek against his shoulder, the sunlight shining on her upturned face. "Tell me about your parents," she said.

His pulse skipped, then settled. "Most of what I know is what I've been told. My mother was sickly. My dad. . .I don't know. . .I guess he couldn't handle four kids and our mother's death. He lost his job from spending so much time caring for our mother. At least that's what Aunt Selma said."

"That's terrible," Julie said. "How could a company do that?"

"I don't know. We lived in a small town in Kentucky. Supposedly, he went out of town looking for a new job and left us with neighbors. A pastor, I think. He never came back."

With a look of concern, Julie lifted her head, her eyes searching his and a question on her lips that, he guessed, she hesitated asking.

"Cowardice? Maybe. I don't know," Tim said. "He died or. . ." The old memories put a stranglehold on his heart. He swallowed back the emotion that erupted into this throat.

"Sometimes I've hated my father," Tim confessed. "I'm ashamed, but I can't think of anything else. I've prayed so often that one day I'll have the answer. One day

I'll understand and can forgive him."

With misted eyes, Julie leaned up and kissed his cheek. "Telling me this, you've explained so much. I've watched you with Timmy, your love and protection so strong and steadfast—almost as if you're driven. At first I thought it was because of his legs. But it's more than that. I understand now."

"I wanted to be the father for Timmy that I never had. I'll never hurt him. . .God willing. A boy needs a father."

"Children need a father," Julie said, "but you always had a Father, Tim. Your heavenly Father. I know that's different in a way, but Jesus has always been at your side, guarding you and guiding just like an earthly father."

"And God never turned His back and walked away," Tim said, awash in the pure and wonderful reality. He tilted his head toward the sky, expelling air from his lungs and drinking in the rich splash of color washing the horizon in the autumn sunset.

God was as sure as the setting sun. As sure as the love that wrapped around his heart.

❊

With the telephone's ring, Julie rose and grabbed the receiver; she heard Tim's frustrated voice on the other end.

"You're a woman," he said.

"Thanks for noticing."

"That's not exactly what I meant," he said with a chuckle. "Timmy's in the Sunday school program, and he's balking because of his braces."

"What can I do, Tim?"

"There's more," he said.

"More?"

"He needs a costume. I'll get him to be in the play, but I can't sew. The woman in charge gave me a pattern and said I'd have to make the costume."

"You want to borrow my sewing machine?" Julie smiled at the receiver.

"Do you have one?"

"Yes, but I hate to sew."

"Oh," he said, his voice fading with disappointment.

"But I love doing things for you," she added quickly.

"Does the positive negate the negative?" he asked.

His question made her laugh. "I'll be over later."

"I'll cook dinner," he offered.

Julie hung up and reviewed the changes in their relationship since their walk and talk in the park. One of those little miracles she'd mentioned to him.

She found her measuring tape, tossed it into her purse, and headed for her car. *Two are better than one,* she thought, awed by God's wisdom.

In a matter of minutes, she pulled into the townhouse parking lot and walked toward Tim's door. As she passed Penny's, Julie noticed Ray from the singles' group ringing the doorbell. She grinned to herself, hoping God had sent Penny someone special at last.

Julie stepped onto the small porch, and Tim opened the door before she knocked. The scent of food and his smile lured her inside.

"Looks like Penny has a steady," she said.

"Right; I'm relieved. Since the mix-up she's been a little distant with me. Though I have to admit, she's continued to be the best neighbor. I felt bad about it until

Ray started coming by. Now Penny and I talk like nothing happened."

"That's good," Julie said.

He drew her to him, his eyes bright. "Not as good as this," he said, kissing her tenderly before taking her hand and leading her into the living room.

"You're a lifesaver," he said, handing her an envelope detailed with the drawing of a shepherd and an angel on the front.

"Okay, which is he?" she asked

"Which do you think?"

"I think he's an angel," she said, grinning, "but probably a shepherd in the program."

"Right on both counts," Tim said, standing beside her. "So what do you think? Can you make it?"

She arched a brow playfully as she tugged the costume pattern from the package. "Let me look. . .if you don't mind."

While she struggled to unfold the pattern pieces, he pulled her down beside him on the sofa.

"You're not making this easy," she said, but thinking how truly easy it was to love him. They'd never said the words to each other, and she longed to hear them.

Gazing at the simple shepherd's robe, Julie shifted her head and caught a glimpse of Timmy hiding on the stair. "Hey, Mr. Shepherd, come here."

"I'm no shepherd," he said, peeking around the corner.

"Why not?" she asked.

He climbed down the last two steps and stuck out his leg. "Braces."

"So?" She widened her eyes, waiting for an answer.

"Shepherds don't wear them."

"They do if they've had surgery." She beckoned to him. "Anyway, look. The robe goes all the way to the ground. Not even the sheep will notice."

That made him giggle, and he came toward her, allowing her to measure his height and the length of his arms. She jotted down the measurements, then folded up the pattern. "I think you'll be one of the handsomest shepherds in the whole field watching their flocks by night."

"Be happy," Tim said. "They could have made you an angel with wings and a halo."

"Girls are angels," Timmy said, giggling.

"Don't tell Gabriel," Tim whispered in Julie's ear, sending a chill down her arm.

A savory aroma drifted into the room from the kitchen, and Tim hurried away, calling them moments later to a dinner of meat loaf with baked potatoes and a salad.

"By the way," Julie said as the meal ended, "I'd like both of you to come for Thanksgiving dinner. You can meet my family."

"That sounds dangerous," Tim said. "What if they don't approve?"

"They will," she said, remembering a time when his words would've had a sincere ring to them rather than humor.

Timmy asked to be excused, and when he ran off to play, Julie rose and carried the dishes to the sink. When she turned back for the others, Tim captured her in his arms.

"I have something to tell you," he said, his expression serious.

Her heart plummeted to the ground and didn't bounce

back until he drew her closer, his eyes searching hers.

"What?" she asked, her voice breathless.

"I love you, Julie."

The words she longed to hear hung on the air as beautiful and glorious as the sunset they'd shared that day in the park.

"I love you, too," she said, certain that God was smiling down on them.

Chapter 8

"Away in the manger, no crib for a bed." Tim's heart swelled hearing the children's sweet voices filling the church with the words of the familiar carol. With her eyes focused on the shepherds, some kneeling and some standing over the manager scene, Julie sat beside Tim smiling as brightly as he was. The angels—all girls—stood on a platform behind them, their wings and halos glistening with gold foil.

On his other side sat Nancy, who, to his surprise, had called to invite herself to Timmy's Sunday school program. Though she'd not mellowed totally, her recent conversations had been more accepting of Julie and his relationship with her. Tim figured she had to accept the inevitable.

Another treat had occurred when Nancy asked for Timmy to spend the night. She wanted to take him to an animated Christmas display at a mall near her house and let him select his Christmas gift.

After the children recessed from the sanctuary, Tim led the others to the Sunday school classrooms. Timmy waited for them, his face beaming with pride. "I remembered my lines," he said.

"You were great," Julie agreed, kissing his cheek.

Tim's heart warmed at the natural way Julie showed love to his son. After offering his congratulations, Tim located Timmy's coat and they headed outside.

Scattered snowflakes drifted from the sky, and Timmy rushed ahead with Nancy, waving his hand with excitement at the anticipation of seeing the display and selecting his gift.

"He was the best shepherd of the bunch," Julie said.

"He was." Delight shivered through Tim, watching the woman he loved sound like his son's mother. She'd make a wonderful parent for Timmy and. . . His thoughts swelled, imagining marriage and the birth of another child.

Tim opened the car door and Julie slid inside. He joined her, and a cool blast from the heater hit their legs until they pulled into traffic and the heat kicked in, warming their feet.

Enveloped in the Christmas spirit, Tim anticipated their evening, helping Julie put up her tree and hang the ornaments as he'd promised.

With the snow falling heavier, Tim parked in the driveway and, arm in arm, escorted Julie to the front door. Inside, she snapped on a Christmas CD and headed for the kitchen with the promise of hot chocolate.

Tim wrestled the tree from the garage, and he guided it into the stand while Julie directed him. When the last bolt had been tightened and the tree still remained straight, he relaxed his shoulders and sank into the sofa.

"Your turn," he said.

"Oh, no, you don't. I need help with the lights."

Lights, garland, then boxes of bulbs were opened, and

they took turns hanging them on the limbs, then standing back to admire the beauty.

"This bulb's special," Julie said, showing him a pink bulb, decorated with sparkling silver lines and a gauzy angel attached to one side. "My aunt gave me this when I was a teenager. She died a few years ago."

With great tenderness, she lifted the nostalgic piece, placing it in a convenient opening in the branches. "I always think of her at Christmas."

He heard the love in her voice and longed to own that kind of family memory. "I'd guess many of the bulbs have meaning," Tim said, containing the familiar yearning.

"Yes, this one," she pointed toward an ornament, "was a gift from a friend who bought it in Europe. And my mom and dad gave me this one when I had my first Christmas tree." She lifted a golden angel to the tree. "This was a gift from my godmother."

"I envy you, Julie. I know it's a sin, but I wish I had wonderful memories like you."

Her hand drifted from the angel and touched his cheek. "Don't envy me, Tim. Our memories can begin now—ones we'll cherish."

He captured her hand beneath his, then lifted it to his lips and kissed her soft, warm skin. "You've given me a million wonderful moments, times I'll never forget."

She nestled against his chest while his heart pounded wildly against his breastbone. *Cherish.* Not just memories, but Julie herself. He'd cherish her and love her forever.

When she tilted her head back to look into his eyes, he lowered his lips, and she tiptoed to meet him. He'd never known such tenderness.

"Let's sit," she said, drawing him to the sofa. She nestled at his side while carols filled the air and happiness filled his heart.

"I hadn't thought much about my family until I met you," he said. "And since then, I've had the strangest desire to find them—my sisters."

"Why don't you?" she asked, bolting upright. "It's possible now with television and the Internet."

"I wouldn't know where to begin," he said, his mind reeling from his admission.

"At the beginning," she said. "Ask Nancy for help. She's a lot older than you and she's changed. . .a little. Who knows what she might remember if you bug her enough."

He laughed. "And she deserves it. She's bugged me enough for a lifetime."

Like tinkling bells, Julie's laugh rang in his ear. She gave him hope for so many things. He only prayed he could give her as much happiness in return.

❄

Julie watched Tim's anxious face, looking as eager as his son waiting to open his Christmas gifts.

"Ready for your surprise?" Tim asked the child.

Timmy stood beside the tree, studying the packages piled beneath, his face glowing with anticipation. "Which one?"

Julie chuckled. "None of those. Your dad hid it."

"Where?" Timmy said, circling the room, his gaze darting from one place to another.

"At Penny's," Tim said finally. "It's too hard to wrap."

"A bike?" Timmy asked.

"You wait here," Tim said, "and when you hear me coming, close your eyes." He turned to Julie. "Make sure he does." Tim gave her a wink.

"Okay," she said, her heart swelling with the excitement of the surprise. She delighted in watching the boy as he jiggled beside the tree. Though still in braces, his legs grew stronger each day. She'd grown to love him as if he were her own.

"What is it?" Timmy asked, giving her a pleading look.

"Only a minute more," she said, keeping her eye focused on the door. When she saw Tim through the glass, she reminded Timmy of the instructions. "Okay, close your eyes."

The child pinched his eyes shut, his face puckered like fingers too long in water, and Julie motioned to Tim that it was safe to enter. He pushed open the door, his arms weighted by the squirming bundle of canine energy. Beside the tree, he set the puppy at Timmy's feet. "Open your eyes," he said.

Timmy's focus latched onto his father's, but a yip from below drew his attention downward. A mixture of laughter and cheers bubbled from the boy's throat. "A puppy!" Timmy slid into the chair and the floppy, golden-hued terrier jumped into the child's lap.

His face covered with doggy kisses, Timmy giggled and squirmed while his father beamed and Julie brushed tears from her eyes.

"You'll have to think of a name," Julie said.

"Animals tend to name themselves," Tim said, chuckling at the puppy's antics.

Julie bent down and retrieved a colorfully wrapped

present. "Open your gift," Julie said, shoving the box into Tim's hands.

"Why me?" he asked, a childlike grin glowing on his face as he peered at the package.

"You'll see," she said.

He pulled off the paper and uncovered a flash camera. "Perfect timing." He eyed the gadgets and checked the indicator for film.

"It's ready," Julie said, motioning for him to photograph Timmy with the puppy.

When the camera flashed, the puppy bolted from Timmy's lap, darted across the carpet, and squatted. Before they could nab him, the deed was done.

"Puddles," Tim said through his laughter. "I said he'd name himself." He dashed to the kitchen and brought back a stream of paper toweling.

"Puddles," Timmy repeated, running toward the puppy. "No. No. You have to go outside."

Tim knelt and mopped up the mess. "Here's the leash," Tim said as he pulled the leather strap from his pocket. "You can take him out for a minute."

Timmy snapped on the leash, and the dog bounded ahead of him toward the doorway. Tim raced after them with the boy's jacket.

When he closed the door, Tim returned and captured Julie's hand in his. "Now it's your turn."

"Okay," she said, curious about the box that sat beneath the tree.

Tim lifted the package and placed it on her lap.

Too big for what she'd hoped, she studied it, eager to learn what was inside. Peeling back the tissue, she eyed a long gold cord. She picked up the end and studied it, trying not to look disappointed. "What is it?"

Tim sat beside her and slid his arm around her back. "A three-strand cord."

Puzzled, she looked again, plucking at the fibers as if trying to understand. "Three strands?"

"Have you forgotten already? 'Two are better than one; if two lie together, they will keep warm: but how can one keep warm alone? A cord of three strands is not quickly broken.' "

"Ecclesiastes," she said, still bewildered.

"I'm the one God meant to keep you warm," he said drawing the cord from the box. When the end rose from the tissue, a ring glistened at the bottom.

Julie caught the glistening diamond in her trembling hand. The solitaire flashed fire in the soft light.

"I have little to give you, Julie, except my heart, but it's filled with love and gratitude."

"Love is all I need, Tim."

"Will you marry me. . .and soon?" he asked.

Shyness gone, Julie reached up and captured Tim's face in her hands, her lips caressing his. Catching her breath, she drew back and looked into his eyes. "Yes, I'll marry you as soon as you want. You're all I've ever wanted. You and your wonderful son."

"And one day, maybe another son or a daughter," Tim said. "Like the Bible says, 'Two are better than one.' "

Chapter 9

Eleven Months Later

"Sit down, Julie, you're doing too much," Tim said.

"I always bake Christmas cookies after Thanksgiving and freeze them. It's my tradition." She brushed the flour from her hands and leaned her back against the kitchen counter.

"But you've never made cookies while expecting a baby," he said, delighting at the tiny protrusion that protected their unborn child.

"In olden times, women only stopped work long enough to give birth. I'm no more special."

He stepped to her side and clasped her shoulders. "You are to me. I've been thinking these past months how many years I spent yearning for my family, not stopping to think that I already have one." His gaze moved over her belly while his thoughts drifted to his son recently freed from his braces. "The best in the world."

"That's different," she said, swiping his nose with her floured finger. "Now leave me be. I need to finish this so

I can start dinner. Timmy'll be home from school soon."

Tim chuckled and brushed at his face in case she'd left a telltale smudge. "Different, maybe, but I don't have that feeling of being lost. Now I feel whole and complete, and I—"

He halted at the telephone's ring.

"Stir the dough," Julie said, scooting past him, "and I'll get the phone."

Tim picked up the wooden spoon and tugged it through the thick, buttery dough. Hearing Julie's voice lift in excitement, he paused and listened.

"Tim." She beckoned to him. "It's for you."

Her face looked mottled, and fear rose in his heart. His son? Had something happened at school?

"Hello," he said, trying to remain calm.

"Timmy?"

Timmy. No one called him that. . .but a haunting voice rose from the depths of his memory.

"Is this Timmy Richmond?" The woman's voice faltered.

"Yes," he said, struggling with his wavering hope.

"This is Eden. Your sister."

"Eden." His voice was a whisper. "Eden," he repeated more loudly. "Is it really you?"

Soft sobs quivered from the line. "Yes, it's me. You're the last one, Timmy. I've found everyone. You, Crista, and Angelina."

"Crista and Angelina," he repeated, feeling the names on his lips, stunned by her news.

"All of you," she said, her voice tinged with emotion.

"How? Where? What?" Words tumbled from his

mouth. He longed for a lifetime of information.

"Let's wait," she said. "We're getting together at my place in Indiana, the weekend before Christmas. Can you come?"

"You mean my family?" His thoughts tumbled over each other.

"We thought just the four of us for now. Next time, we'll bring our families. It's been twenty-four years. We have so much catching up to do."

"We do," he said, drawing in a calming breath.

"You can come?" she asked.

"Nothing could stop me, Eden. I've waited a lifetime."

Chapter 10

The Reunion

Tim pressed his back against the easy chair and focused once more on his three sisters. The hours had been precious: The greeting, the sharing, the love, and their first meeting were only a beginning. They'd already made plans for a summer reunion—the whole family together, at last.

Eden's husband, Josh, had kindly taken the children on a mini-vacation for the weekend, leaving the four siblings alone to share the two days without distraction.

Studying his sisters, Tim realized Angelina and Crista resembled each other. Their smiles and the dimples. They looked like their mother from what his faded memory allowed him to recall.

He was large and darker, like his father. He recalled his aunt Selma saying the same. The idea triggered a prayer. *Lord, never let me be like our father.* Knowing the love he had for his own son, Tim wondered how a parent could leave his children behind and vanish from their lives.

"Okay," Tim said, "you've told me how you girls got together, but what about me? How did you find me?"

Eden laughed. "Once I was determined, nothing would stop me. I'd tried locating the family we'd stayed with—"

"The pastor?" Tim asked.

"Yes, but they weren't home when we got there."

Angelina chuckled. "What did you expect?"

"Miracles," Crista said. "Like right now. I can't believe we're all sitting here together."

"It *is* a miracle," Eden agreed. "Anyway, I didn't give up. I decided to take a weekend trip and drive to Covington. I figured I'd recognize the house and maybe that would lead to something."

"Did you find it? Did you recognize it right away?" Crista asked, her excitement so evident she appeared ready to catapult from the sofa.

"I have no memories at all of our house," Angelina said.

"Maybe it's for the best." Tim remembered his own feelings of loneliness and abandonment.

Eden arched an eyebrow. "But we have a few memories, Tim. Angelina and Crista have nothing."

Shame washed over him. "You're right, Eden."

Crista reached over and touched his arm. "It's okay, Tim. When you can't remember, you don't have the good times or the *bad* times."

"I just felt something was missing in my life, and I never knew what it was," Angelina said.

Tim wished he'd kept his mouth closed. "I felt the same way. Like I was cheated." He pushed away the negative feelings that had seeped from his old hurt. "Go ahead, Eden, tell us what happened."

"I found the pastor's house," she continued, "but as I said, they weren't there."

"And?" burst from the three siblings. They laughed at their simultaneous reaction.

"So what did you do?" Angelina asked.

"I'd about given up when a woman walked by with her dog; she told us the pastor was out of town. Something about her was so familiar."

A lengthy pause filled the room.

"Well?" three impatient voices said in unison. Another burst of laughter bubbled through the air.

"She'd been a playmate of mine when we stayed with Pastor Brittan's family. She lived across the street and invited us in; it turns out Molly had written to Aunt Selma Johnson, Daddy's sister, in Michigan asking about me. She still had a letter from Aunt Selma and her address! Except when I went there, an elderly woman named Gabby Summers lived there."

"But how did that help?" Angelina asked.

"She was a longtime friend of Aunt Selma's. Apparently she'd bought the house when our aunt and uncle moved to a nearby farm in Remus, Michigan. I thought all along that Aunt Selma was a spinster. Obviously I was wrong. Memories came to Mrs. Summers in bits and pieces. Months passed before she called me. Once I had the right information, that's all I needed to know. I was able to check your school records in Remus, learned you joined the military and settled in the Detroit area."

Tim fell back against the chair. "Are you sure you're not a detective?"

Crista chuckled. "I think my Brad is the detective.

He's the one who found Eden." She pressed her hands together. "I can't wait for you all to meet him. He's perfect for me, although I didn't know that at first. And he loves hot air balloons like I do."

"Remember the stained glass balloon you bought from Wes, Crista?" Angelina asked. "I like them, too. I always feel a little nostalgic when I see any kind of balloon, but I have no idea—"

"What?" Tim and Eden blurted at the same time.

"Balloons," Angelina repeated, her eyes wide, studying them.

The four sat in silence looking at each other.

Tim was awed by the information. So many years he'd felt a strange twinge when he saw a bunch of balloons, like the day Julie brought them to Timmy's party.

"Awhile back, I asked my cousin—" Tim gave a soft chuckle. "I should say *our* cousin, Nancy, if balloons would have some special meaning for me. They always give me a feeling of déjà vu. Nancy said it was natural for kids to love them." He shrugged. "So I let it drop."

"Balloons," Eden said, closing her eyes. "A room full of balloons."

"Yes," Tim said, "all the way to the ceiling."

"Mother's birthday." Eden's voice was a whisper. "I remember." She opened her eyes, her face glowing. "It was Mother's birthday."

"I sort of remember something. . .vaguely," Tim said. "It was in a bedroom."

"Her bedroom," Eden said. "She'd been so ill and. . .I remember it clearly now, looking at all of you. All these years, I've had something in my distant memory nudge at me, and you've all helped to bring it out."

"Tell us," Crista said, sitting on the edge of her seat. "I can't wait another minute."

"We wanted to celebrate Mom's birthday, and she was so sick. Dad suggested we have a cake, but Mom was too sick to eat. . . . We wanted something special."

"Who suggested balloons?" Angelina asked.

"It was my idea, I think. But Dad was willing. I can almost see him going through his pocket pulling out dollar bills and counting them."

"We didn't have much. I remember that," Tim said.

"We were poor. Dad had been let go because he missed so much work caring for Mom. I think that's it."

"You're right, Eden," Tim said. "I faintly remember Aunt Selma muttering about how terrible the company was to fire Dad under the circumstances. I don't think I knew what 'fired' meant back then."

"So our father brought home some balloons?" Crista asked.

"A roomful, Crista. I remember he let us help fill them from a tank." Eden's voice had become a whisper.

"Helium," Tim said as the story settled into his awareness. "Then you mean. . ." His throat tightened, the reality so unbelievable. "You mean that he rented a tank and did all this to give Mom. . ." His voice choked with emotion, and he stopped to gain control.

"To give her a birthday surprise," Angelina said, tears rolling down her cheeks.

Tim swallowed. "I've been angry at him all these years. Angry because he didn't love us enough to keep us together, and now—"

"And now, we learn how much he really loved all of us," Angelina said. "When he didn't have a job, he sacrificed to give Mom a special birthday." Her eyes were rimmed with tears.

"Her last birthday," Eden said.

Tim lowered his head to hide the moisture in his eyes, but when he looked up again, he needn't have been embarrassed. His sisters were wiping away their tears.

"Dad was looking for work, I think," Eden said. "The family I lived with told me when I was older that they'd heard he had slipped on ice crossing a street and was hit by a car."

"I thought maybe he committed. . ." Tim's voice faded, feeling ashamed that he'd thought his father would take his own life.

"Don't blame yourself for wondering," Eden said. "We were only little kids. How would we know?"

Angelina shook her head. "We didn't understand things when they happened. All we knew was that we'd lost the security that we'd known."

"Cheer up," Crista said. "God brought us together now so we could learn the truth and find forgiveness."

"Forgiveness," Tim repeated, his mind boggled with the past and present—pieces of the puzzle telling the true story.

"And love," Angelina added. "God has given me so much love. He's been there for me every step of the way, putting special people in my life, and now. . .He's sent the three of you."

"God's given us all so much," Eden said. She rose and stretched her hands out at her sides. "How about joining in a prayer of thanksgiving."

"For finding each other," Crista said.

"And for forgiveness," Tim said, grasping Eden's hand and reaching for Angelina's.

"And love," Angelina said.

Standing in a circle, Tim gazed at his three sisters, hearing them sniffle and seeing tears of joy in their eyes. He didn't care if his own droplets rolled down his cheeks and dripped from his chin. He was in good company.

He listened to Eden's strong, confident voice and knew that someday he would travel heavenward like one of the helium balloons. One day he'd stand at Jesus' feet with his whole family—including his mother, father, and three precious sisters: Eden, Angelina, and Crista.

He felt Eden squeeze his hand and knew, without a doubt, that God was smiling down on them.

GAIL GAYMER MARTIN

Gail loves nothing more than to write, talk, and sing—
especially if it's about her Lord. Beginning her career as a
freelance writer, she has hundreds of articles and stories in
religious periodicals, many anthology devotionals, and
numerous church resource books, but since 1998, she has
been blessed as a multi-published romance author with
nearly ten contracted novels. "If God blessed me with a
'bestseller,' I'd continue writing worship materials. It's a
direct way I can share my faith with worshiping Christians."
Gail has two **Heartsong Presents** novels and two novellas
published with Barbour fiction. She is also a contributing
editor and columnist for *The Christian Communicator*.

Besides being active in her home church, Gail is an
adjunct English instructor for Davenport University,
Warren campus, and maintains her professional counselor
license in the state of Michigan. She is involved in a number of professional organizations and especially enjoys
public speaking and presenting workshops to help new
writers. Gail loves traveling, as well as singing with the
Detroit Lutheran Singers. She lives in Lathrup Village
with her husband Bob Martin who proofreads all her
work. "I praise God for Bob and my gift of writing."

A Letter to Our Readers

Dear Readers:

In order that we might better contribute to your reading enjoyment, we would appreciate you taking a few minutes to respond to the following questions. When completed, please return to: Fiction Editor, Barbour Publishing, Inc., P.O. Box 719, Uhrichsville, OH 44683.

1. Did you enjoy reading *Home for Christmas?*
   □ Very much. I would like to see more books like this.
   □ Moderately. I would have enjoyed it more if _____
   _____
   _____

2. What influenced your decision to purchase this book?
   (Check those that apply.)
   □ Cover   □ Back cover copy   □ Title   □ Price
   □ Friends   □ Publicity   □ Other

3. Which story was your favorite?
   □ *Heart Full of Love*   □ *Don't Look Back*
   □ *Ride the Clouds*   □ *To Keep Me Warm*

4. Please check your age range:
   □ Under 18   □ 18–24   □ 25–34
   □ 35–45   □ 46–55   □ Over 55

5. How many hours per week do you read? _____

Name _____

Occupation _____

Address _____

City _____ State _____ ZIP _____

E-mail _____

$\mathcal{H}$EARTSONG ❤ PRESENTS

Love Stories
Are Rated G!

That's for godly, gratifying, and of course, great! If you love a thrilling love story, but don't appreciate the sordidness of some popular paperback romances, **Heartsong Presents** is for you. In fact, **Heartsong Presents** is the only inspirational romance book club, the only one featuring love stories where Christian faith is the primary ingredient in a marriage relationship.

Sign up today to receive your first set of four never-before-published Christian romances. Send no money now; you will receive a bill with the first shipment. You may cancel at any time without obligation, and if you aren't completely satisfied with any selection, you may return the books for an immediate refund!

Imagine. . .four new romances every four weeks—two historical, two contemporary—with men and women like you who long to meet the one God has chosen as the love of their lives. . .all for the low price of $9.97 postpaid.

To join, simply complete the coupon below and mail to the address provided. **Heartsong Presents** romances are rated G for another reason: They'll arrive Godspeed!

YES! Sign me up for Hearts❤ng!

NEW MEMBERSHIPS WILL BE SHIPPED IMMEDIATELY!
Send no money now. We'll bill you only $9.97 postpaid with your first shipment of four books. Or for faster action, call toll free 1-800-847-8270.

NAME _____

ADDRESS _____

CITY _____ STATE _____ ZIP _____

MAIL TO: HEARTSONG PRESENTS, PO Box 721, Uhrichsville, Ohio 44683